LUCY

By

CHRIS COPPEL

Pumpkin Pie Publishing
105 Old Bath Road
Charvil
RG10 9QN
UK

Lucy

ISBN:
Paperback: 978-1-80227-017-4
eBook: 978-1-80227-018-1

Coppel, Chris

Lucy

This is a modernised and re-edited version of the novel Far From Burden Dell by Chris Coppel (ISBN: 0-974648167)

I've seen the look in a dogs' eyes, a
quickly vanishing look of amazed
contempt, and I am convinced that
basically dogs think humans are nuts.
–*John Steinbeck*

Dogs have given us their absolute all.
We are the centre of their universe,
we are the focus of their love and faith
and trust. They serve us in return for
scraps. It is without doubt the best deal
man has ever made.
–*Roger Caras*

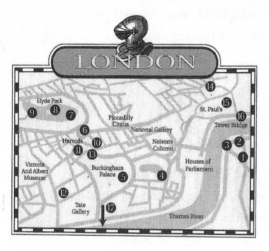

LONDON

1. Bad Kennel
2. Anchor and First View of the Thames River
3. Westminster Bridge
4. St. James Park
5. Buckingham Palace
6. Rear Exit of Palace Grounds, Hyde Park Corner and Underpass
7. Hidden Cave and Restaurant
8. Shelter Island
9. Bridge Across Serpentine (Lake)
10. Harrods
11. Fast Food Restaurant
12. Police Station Behind Walton Street
13. Kinghtsbridge Tube Station
14. St. Paul's Station and Underground Parking Structure
15. Sewer Tunnel
16. Tower Bridge
17. Battersea Dog Home (Good Kennel)

CHAPTER 1

L ucy couldn't have been happier.

She opened her eyes from her early afternoon nap and blinked at the brightness of the spring sun. As she looked about herself, she felt her chest swell with the sheer pleasure and contentment of life.

She watched as a mallard led her four young ducklings to the circular pond at the end of the garden. Lucy smiled as she observed the mindful mother duck watch as each duckling garnered sufficient courage to jump into the still waters. Once in, they immediately regrouped into a single line and moved off with a great sense of purpose and direction.

Lucy couldn't help recalling her own youth and the strict disciplines her mother had imposed on any such trips into the wilds.

Beyond the pond, Lucy could see the fields of the Granger's farm. Two large chestnut mares were peacefully strolling up a gentle grassy slope. Their heads were close together as they walked, probably discussing their strategies for their next horse show. Their strides were fluid and supremely confident as can only come from decades of impeccable breeding. Lucy had no doubt that one, if not both, of Granger's fine horses would return with a trophy. She could almost hear the buzz that was sure to come as the entire village relived every second of every event - from the easiest two-foot cross pole to the fearsome and impossible heights of the wall.

Lucy rolled over and stretched, sending a warm rush through her muscles and limbs. She then stood and looked down in fascination as the lush lawn slowly gave up her body's imprint and blade by blade straightened, returning to its previous uniform plane. Lucy slowly wandered to the top of her hill and looked out over the sprawling vistas of the West Sussex Downs. She could see hill upon hill, undulating endlessly to ... she really wasn't certain where they stretched to, but that didn't matter. She wondered how some of her friends who remained permanently in the city could cope with their limited and artificial view of the world. And the smells! In the city, Lucy could distinguish little over the constant reek of burning vapours coming from the thousands of manmade travelling machines. Here however, Lucy could, on a winter's breeze, detect the succulent waft of a particular thistle that she knew to dwell some three fields away.

She turned and looked at her home. It was incredibly old, even Lucy knew that. She had heard the term Elizabethan used, and though not understanding its meaning fully, she knew that it meant, well.....old. The whiteness of the heavy walls was almost dazzling to her eyes as the sun reflected back at her. The heavy thatch of the roofing was so perfectly set and cropped that it was hard to imagine it as being made up of little more than the hay on which she'd spent many an afternoon napping contentedly.

Lucy walked out of the sun's warmth and into the cool interior of the cottage. She never ceased to marvel at the smell of her home. The mixture of old stone, polished woods, exquisite kitchen odours, and her favourite, the tangy scent of the half-burned logs in the hearth that somehow permeated everything. She could feel the timeless cold that rose from the worn smooth stone beneath her feet. Then as she stepped onto the heavy rug, she would sigh at the difference in feel. It wasn't that she minded the cold sensation, after all, walking the grounds during a January freeze was one of her great pleasures, but still, the warmth offered by a really fine rug was almost indescribable.

Lucy made her way into the kitchen to see what Cook was up to. She realised it was too soon after lunch for her to begin the extensive toiling that preceded each meal in the cottage. She wasn't surprised to find the room empty.

She wandered casually over to her indoor bowl and checked just in case one of those unexpected, yet always appreciated, titbits had materialised. None had. She checked to see that no morsel had been left in any of the accessible reaches, also without success. She wasn't hungry; in fact, she often wondered what it was that compelled her to look for food even on occasions when she wasn't the least bit peckish. After checking a few more potential food spots, she forgot what she was even searching for.

No matter.

Her sensitive ears suddenly picked up the gentle sounds of Cook humming somewhere in the distance. Lucy moved to the bay window of the breakfast nook, and placing her front paws on the sill, lifted herself in order to look out the window. This was not her favourite viewing window as the glass was set in tiny triangular sections with lead frames. Each piece of glass was uneven and gave the world a distorted almost watery look. On a sunny day, each pane was able to catch and refract light into a burst of multi-coloured specks which would dance and dart about the kitchen walls. Lucy vaguely remembered a time when she used to try and catch the luminous droplets with a frustrating lack of success. Now of course, she knew better. But she would; after all, she was almost three!

She squinted through the glass and could make out Cook's matronly form as she knelt at her small but cherished herb and vegetable garden. Oh, the vegetable garden! Now that was a lesson well learnt! Lucy could almost feel the surprising pain that had been dealt out that fateful day by Cook. Lucy didn't hold a grudge, in fact, Cook had quite understandably used the 'bad voice' quite a few times in warning before having to resort to causing the hurt to Lucy's nose. Despite her limited ability to accurately recall many events in her life, that day was still vividly memorable.

Lucy had been only eight months old and was in the garden having a well-deserved post lunch nap. During such naps, she would occasionally open one eye and watch as the clouds formed and re-formed high above her. She would imagine seeing a face then almost immediately it would change to some other shape. One second a rabbit, next a huge oak tree.

Lucy had been watching Cook for weeks as she dug up the smooth green blanket of lawn. As if that hadn't been odd enough, Cook then proceeded to remove a large quantity of soil, only to replace it with completely different soil a few days later. The new soil had a musty, earthy scent that you could almost taste on your tongue. Lucy had tried to join Cook in the soil-filled square to offer support or even help, but Cook had turned her away and pushed her off the plot on each occasion. Lucy had been surprised as she had seen nothing of any great interest in Cook's little project, but she had accepted her banishment with calm indifference.

But the day of the hurt was quite different.

Lucy was awakened from her nap by the sound of Cook tapping little lengths of wood into the soil, along the perimeter of the earthy patch. As Lucy looked on, Cook finished with the tapping then proceeded to string heavy twine between the wood posts. Lucy found this very perplexing. She moved closer and tried to step over the twine, but immediately heard Cook using the unmistakable 'bad voice'. She stepped back and looked on as Cook began burying things in the earth. Different things. Some from thin little

5

envelopes, others from paper bags. It was simply too unusual and tickled every curiosity nerve in Lucy's being.

She had to find out what was going on. She knew why she buried items, but couldn't remember ever having seen a human doing the same. She attempted to cross the barrier again, but once more was barraged with the 'bad voice' from Cook. Well, that was too much for her. Lucy walked away and eased herself down onto the green lawn and pretended to doze, all the while keeping her eyes on Cook and the mystery plot of land.

Cook eventually finished what she was doing, then stepped over her string perimeter and headed back to the house. She hesitated then approached Lucy. She wagged a finger at her then pointed to the plot. Her voice didn't contain the 'bad' edge, but it was firm and definitely not the 'good' voice that always preceded a hug or a tasty tidbit.

Lucy understood the message very clearly, and for a few seconds decided to abide by its meaning. But there was a far stronger force at work inside her. No sooner had she set her mind on giving Cook's land a wide berth, when she found herself on her feet, slowly approaching that very same piece of land. She knew that she should stop but somehow just couldn't. She had to know what was buried in there. She just had to.

Lucy tried to make her approach seem casual, and only occasionally glanced fleetingly back at the cottage. Suddenly she had arrived. She was at the perimeter. She cautiously stepped over the barricade and felt the moist warmth of the turned soil as it spread between her paw pads. She sniffed at the earth to try and get a clue as to the nature of the buried treasure beneath but picked up nothing except the twang of the rich earth itself. There was nothing else for it. She began to dig. It was surprisingly easy to part the soil. It piled up rapidly behind her as she used all her strength in the effort. Suddenly, her nose picked up a new scent. She was close. She was going to solve the mystery. Her entire body was electric with excitement.

That's when she heard Cook.

She'd never imagined that Cook could sound like that. Her voice was so loud, and so shrill it almost hurt her ears.

Lucy turned and spotted the waddling form as Cook stormed towards her. She had one of the funny bundles of paper that her Man liked to sit and stare at every morning.

They were strange things. Each day a young human on two wheels would throw a new bundle at the house before her Man, or even Cook were awake. Whatever they were, they must have been important. Her Man would grab the bundle the moment it arrived, then sit staring at different parts of it for ages. What was truly odd, was that no matter how much attention these bundles were given each day, her Man usually ended up setting fire to them inside the place where the logs were burned.

Humans can be very strange!

Lucy could not imagine what Cook planned to do with the bundle. As Lucy watched, Cook rolled it into a tight tube as she neared the plot of land. Lucy cocked her head to make sure that Cook understood her curiosity. Lucy offered Cook a smile, but to her amazement, and then horror, saw Cook bring the paper tube down onto her nose; extremely hard.

Oh, the pain!

It was as if for a moment, her body became pain itself. For a fraction of a second Lucy's world exploded in bright light. She shook her head to clear her vision and immediately saw that Cook was about to repeat the procedure. Lucy responded by pure instinct and ran. She didn't even know that she was running until she hit the twine fence. She didn't have time to think about jumping, she just went right through it—well, almost through it. Somehow the string got tangled up in her legs, and before she knew it, she was halfway across the garden towing the entire length of Cook's perimeter fence, posts and all. She could clearly hear Cook calling after her in a voice such as she had never heard emitted from a human before. She remembered hiding under the stairs for what felt like an eternity until her Man had, after exhaustive attempts, coaxed her out of her hiding place and back into the kitchen. He had attempted to arrange a reconciliation between her and Cook, but Lucy could sense Cook's hostility, not only for that night but for weeks hence. There were no pats, no titbits, no sweet talk, nothing. The little plot of land was barricaded again, strenuously guarded, and before long produced an array of vegetable foods that Lucy was certain she remembered having seen be produced from shopping bags before all the fuss had begun. Eventually Cook had forgiven her, and things had returned to normal but the memory of the pain!

Lucy stretched herself to her full length, sauntered out of the kitchen, then moved down the narrow hall to her Man's day room. As usual, the heavy door was shut as he worked away inside. She tried pushing it open with her nose, but it was well and truly shut. She considered a good bark to let him know that she was ready for a walk, should he be interested, but decided instead to wait. The rug in front of his door was one of Lucy's favourites, so she settled herself down for a brief nap. She tried to remember a thought she'd had only moments earlier then fell asleep.

Almost immediately, she started to dream.

She was chasing a rabbit through impossibly high grass under a summer's sky. She was only just managing to keep its fluffy tail in view when suddenly, the grass and the rabbit just vanished. Lucy had the most unusual sensation of feeling extremely uncomfortable. She didn't know where she was, only that the sky had turned slate grey and she felt frightened and alone. She was on a narrow path leading down a steep and rocky mountainside. She was limping and saw that her normally golden coat was matted with mud and . . . Lucy shuddered as she realised it was blood. Her blood. The stony trail under her feet was dark and slippery. She felt that something was approaching, something bad. She began to run even though it hurt her leg. She rounded a corner and saw that the path ended abruptly. It simply stopped, leaving a terrifying drop into a seemingly bottomless void. Lucy could see that the path resumed some twenty or so paws across the abyss. She circled where she stood, trying to decide what to do, then felt the nearness of whatever was approaching. A watery chill ran the length of her spine, and she knew she had no choice. She stepped back as far as she thought safe, then ran towards the gap.

She reached the end of the path, then with a mighty surge of strength, launched herself to the other side. She knew she was going to make it and could see the other path as she neared it, but suddenly it wasn't as close. As she flew towards other side, it appeared to move farther away. She realised that she was not going make it after all. Lucy felt herself falling. Down she fell into a swirling, dark mist. She just kept on falling, then felt something on her coat. Something was working its way along her stomach. She heard laughter, then felt something else against her head.

She opened her eyes, and saw her Man kneeling next to her. He was stroking her between the ears and speaking gently to her. She could hear her Man's words very clearly; she just couldn't fully understand them.

"Come on girl, it's all right," her Man gently mouthed. "What a dream you were having."

He patted her golden coat affectionately and eased himself to his feet.

"How about a walk?"

If there was one word that Lucy always recognised, it was that one. Walk! That magical word that always preceded special times alone with her Man. She untangled her legs and jumped to her feet giving him two eager barks. Two barks was the exact and appropriate response needed to convey total interest without any appearance of desperation. Lucy's mother had been extremely strict and specific when teaching the subtleties of bark usage when interacting with bipeds.

One bark was just to let people know that you were around. Two was... well, we covered two. Three was the first stage of a more serious need or concern. The quantity of barks was then to progress in direct proportion to the given urgency of the situation. Her mother had been specific that the bark was never to be abused, as was so often the case with some of the smaller breeds. For some reason, maybe it was a size thing, but smaller dogs didn't appear capable of any self-control when it came to barking.

Her Man opened the front door for her and waited as she politely passed out into the late afternoon sun. What a gentleman he was. Lucy, knowing the routine well, stopped and eased herself onto her haunches. Her Man slipped a leather ring over her head, then turned it so that its shiny metal disk was under her chin. Lucy had no idea what this little ritual achieved, but it was religiously carried out before each walk. When her Man had first started making her wear a... what was their word... ah yes, collar, she'd tried everything imaginable to get it off her. She'd rolled on it. She once got her paw under it, and after some strenuous contortions, managed to get it stuck in her mouth and couldn't free it. Eventually however, she realised that it didn't bother her all that much, and with it being very important to her Man, she decided to allow it to stay in place.

They walked out the front gate and Lucy held her breath in anticipation, hoping that her Man would choose the Taddlesham path. This was by far her most favourite walk.

Her Man hesitated. Lucy knew that it wasn't her place to suggest or even hint, but what a glorious day for a good, hearty walk towards Taddlesham. She let out the briefest of whines and took a single step to the right hoping that he would pick up the extreme subtlety of her move. His face brightened into a warm smile as he looked down at her.

"I suppose you'd like the Taddlesham walk, wouldn't you?"

Lucy pretended to not understand him and cocked her head to one side.

"You can't fool me with that look," he said in mock seriousness. "Come on then."

Yes! He turned to the right, and they walked alongside the ancient roman wall until they reached a break and the tiny white sign that though illegible to Lucy, she knew stated that they were at the beginning of the West Taddlesham path.

As always, she remained at her Man's side until they were off the road and on one of the many trails and paths that webbed out from their cottage. They had taken no more than a few steps when he gave the joyous command.

"Go on then," he said in a breathy and exuberant voice.

That was all Lucy needed to hear. With her ears pinned back and her golden tail outstretched, she broke into a full-speed charge down the narrow, grassy path.

On either side of her, the farm animals turned, and with mild interest, watched her tear by. The herd of Jerseys even moved to the fence to get a better look, but then, the mere fact that the sun rose everyday was an astonishment to cows.

They were kind, and sweet but not terribly bright. Lucy would always give them the single bark as she passed, just to ensure that they didn't miss the moment.

As she rounded the corner down by Blakely's farm, she slowed down. This was her favourite part, and she had learned to savour the anticipation of what was to come. She stopped altogether and waited for her Man to reach her side, then, together, they continued on their way. They passed the Blakely's farm and followed the path as it again turned. They were suddenly surrounded by greenery. The path descended gently beneath a canopy of foliage. The ancient trees which bordered the path chose this location to have, long ago, grown together overhead giving the impression that one was walking inside a long, green tunnel. Lucy loved this part of the walk. It was quiet and surprisingly dark. The ground was softer and smelled of damp. The sides of the trees and stones were all heavily coated with a bright, almost fluorescent layer of moss. After a short while, she came to a very narrow pathway that broke off to the right. She followed this into a dense, but startlingly beautiful patch of greenery and within moments came to her favourite place in the whole world—Burden Dell.

It was little more than a small, grassy clearing within the trees and bramble. The grass was almost ten paws high, densely-packed, and of a colour that words could hardly convey. An emerald green with highlights of pure gold was close, but still not quite it.

Lucy was about to move into the dell but saw to her astonishment that it was already occupied. A single doe stood only a few feet away, looking back at her as she calmly chewed a mouthful of the succulent grass.

Her Man came up alongside her and whispered, "easy girl," which was unnecessary, as Lucy fully understood what was required of her when faced with an inter-species relationship.

She carefully and calmly walked over to the doe, and with slow and cautious moves, stepped to within inches of her. She was a beautiful animal. Her moist, brown eyes were huge and framed with the longest lashes that Lucy ever remembered seeing. Her tan coat looked smooth and soft, touched in a few places by almost perfect white, circular spots. The doe stopped her chewing and looked down at Lucy without any fear. Lucy took a step closer and raised her head. With great tenderness, their noses touched for just the briefest of moments. The doe then playfully stepped back and taunted Lucy into a game of tag. Lucy looked over at her Man to make sure this was acceptable and saw that he was smiling while wiping something from his eyes. Lucy took this for approval, and so proceeded to play a truly fabulous game of tag with her new friend. Lucy didn't have too much experience with the deer family and was pleasantly surprised at this one's skill and agility at the game. The doe appeared to be able to balance perfectly, both the subtlety of the stalk with the tenacity of the chase. Her final cornering leaps were truly spectacular. They played on for some time then, without warning, and with only the briefest nod, the doe turned and ran off. Lucy was surprised until she heard an incessant stream of barks coming towards the dell. Not even the slightest attempt at proper usage was being made. Just a random flow of attention-seeking yips. There was little doubt to whom it belonged.

Jimmy, the Scottie, came charging out of the tree line and into the tall grass. He leapt, he danced, he rolled, he barked. He had, it seemed, no self-control whatsoever. True he wasn't a pure bred, but still—decorum, decorum!

The little dog was truly on form. He wouldn't stay still for a second. Lucy tried to calm him down long enough to set up some ground rules for a game of tag, but the other dog just couldn't concentrate. Lucy politely attempted to play with him for a while, but soon tired of her small friend's frantic and uncoordinated motions. She moved over to her Man and remained on her feet looking back toward the path. Her Man understood her meaning, and the two left Jimmy to his antics within the sanctity of Burden Dell.

As they regained the path, they spotted Jimmy's Man trotting along with a look of deep concern on his face. "Have you seen . . . ?"

Lucy's Man didn't wait for him to finish. "He's in the dell."

The other man shook his head and strode off to locate Jimmy. Lucy and her Man shared a smile, then sedately resumed their dignified progress back to the cottage.

CHAPTER 2

Lucy had a truly magnificent night's sleep, replete with happy dreams. There were no rocky paths or drops into swirling fogs, only joyful frolicking in fields of golden, spring wheat. She encountered many animals in her dreams, all of them full of joyful effervescence as they played. The night's dreaming even included the pretty young doe she had encountered earlier in Burden Dell.

Lucy's sense of smell was her own inner alarm clock, and on that morning, it rang extra loudly. Before she even opened her eyes, she knew that Cook was baking fresh bread. The smell had all but taken over the house. As it happened, freshly-baked wheat loaf was the one treat that Lucy truly adored, although it was also probably the most frustrating. The oven door would open; the yeasty explosion of odoriferous euphoria would then consume her as she watched the perfectly-formed, brown loaves be set on the counter. Then with every gastronomic juice on full rampage—she had to wait! Not a second or a minute, but a full hour! It was a true test of willpower to not pounce on, and bite into one of the steaming golden-brown mounds. Well not really a test, as Lucy had in fact learnt from the experience when she had on one occasion not waited until she was given a piece by Cook. She'd instead bitten off a piece of a loaf without permission and learnt about hot food. It wasn't just that it was hot, it was that once in her mouth she couldn't get the burning morsel out again. Lucy couldn't chew it, she couldn't swallow it, and worst of all she couldn't settle it in one spot long enough to spit it out. She had learnt that day to wait when it came to oven-fresh bread.

Lucy rose from her warm rug that was tucked under the stairs and strolled down the hallway to the kitchen. She stuck her head around the door so that Cook would know that she was awake and available, should any piece of cooled wheat bread be in the offering. Cook looked over at her and smiled in that way that always gave Lucy a warm, almost tingling feeling inside. When Cook smiled it was as if her entire face lit up. Every wrinkle, and there were quite a few, all appeared to tilt upwards giving her feature a joyously happy lilt.

"You'll be wanting a piece of new bread, I should wager," Cook said in her Welsh, sing-song manner. "Well, you'll have t'wait, you know that."

Lucy, of course did know and showed her understanding by not lingering too long in the doorway. She turned and moved through the cottage to the mudroom and stepped out through, what Lucy always assumed, was her personal door.

A strange square thing in the middle of the wood door, it was. An odd contraption made from some material that still had Lucy puzzled. It was clearly not made from anything she had ever encountered during her walks. It smelled a little like a mix between the black goop she'd seen being laid on the road to fill cracks, and the smelly liquid that her Man poured into the side of his driving machine.

Now there was another bizarre thing. Why anyone would want to sit in a metal enclosure that did nothing but make a din and belch smelly smoke from its rear was beyond Lucy. She had been in her Man's vehicle only a few times and was perfectly content to leave it at that. Oh, she'd seen other less intelligent breeds deliriously hanging their heads out the side windows, allowing the force of the wind to distort their features and whip their coats into a most undignified mess. Nope. Not for Lucy. She was entirely happy to find her thrills with all four feet solidly planted on terra firma.

Then there was the rather odd relationship that her Man had with his vehicle. After all, it wasn't as if the blessed thing was alive. Far from it! Yet her Man would pamper the thing endlessly. He would bathe it, dry it, caress it, find it shade in the summer and shelter it in the rains. Lucy had repeatedly attempted to point out her human's error in believing that his vehicle required such treatment, but he seemed quite oblivious to her attempts at enlightening him.

Lucy eased herself through her door contraption and glanced over at her outside bowls. She thought for the briefest second that they were empty! A cold, damp shiver ran through her body. She dashed over to them, and immediately saw that she had, of course, been mistaken. Her food bowl was filled with the usual mix of both dry and moist food - a tasty combination by any account, and her water bowl had clearly just been cleaned and refilled. As Lucy marvelled at the sparkling properties of the refreshingly cool liquid, a tiny moth landed right in it. Typical! It sent out a pattern of concentric waves to the very edge of the bowl. Lucy was fascinated by the uniformity of the water's distortion at the hands, or indeed wings, of the struggling creature. Lucy realised that she had to help before the poor thing wore itself out. With slow and gentle skill, Lucy placed her nose into the bowl, and brought it to within a hair's-breadth of the baby moth. It seemed to know what was needed to save itself and managed to climb onto the lumpy surface of the offered muzzle. Lucy carefully raised her head, and with concentration, focused her eyes down her nose and saw the tiny survivor clinging on for dear life. She moved over to the nearest bush and placed her nose among its leaves. It took a while for the small aviator to dismount as it was totally preoccupied with drying itself off. Lucy was, however, in no rush and allowed her passenger the necessary time to pull itself together. Finally, satisfied that it was in one piece, the little crash survivor stepped onto a nearby leaf and opened its wings to assist in the drying operation. Lucy backed away and thought how she must return later to check on its progress.

Feeling suddenly quite hungry and pleased with a job well done, Lucy returned to her bowls. As she reached her food, and sank her muzzle into the well-deserved breakfast, something caught her eye. She turned to her water bowl and was stunned. It couldn't be! There were now four tiny moths, all desperately paddling for dear life. The water in the bowl was quite choppy as the moths struggled away. Lucy realised that she was going to have a remarkably busy morning.

By midday, Lucy was exhausted. She had rescued the five moths and had a marvellous game of chase with a small rabbit, who'd run from her with such convincing enthusiasm and drama, that it was almost as if he believed the pursuit to have been of a serious nature. She had helped Cook pick some fresh tomatoes from the vegetable garden (Lucy stayed outside the perimeter, of course) and had been rewarded with a piece of indescribably delicious wheat bread (cooled to perfection). Most recently she had enjoyed an exceptionally good roll on the front lawn. All this and it wasn't even time for her Man's midday break.

Lucy was in mid-ponder about what to do next when she heard Old Fergus as he pedalled up the gentle hill towards their cottage. Almost every day, Old Fergus would appear and deposit funny paper things through the funny slot in the front door. Sometimes her Man would seem pleased at what was left, other times a cloud would cross over his normally pleasant features. On one occasion, he even tore up the paper bits that Old Fergus had left him.

Fergus was a good sort. He would always have a word or two to share with Lucy. He never crossed the line and attempted to touch her, instead, he would simply lean over and chat. At first, she had found this behaviour somewhat off-putting, but eventually Lucy came to accept it. Today was no exception. Fergus lent his bike against the wall, ambled to the cottage door and pushed some paper bits into the slot while smiling at Lucy.

"So, me fine girl, how's the world treating you? Are ya being a good girl for Mr. Cotter?"

This was clearly a two-bark situation which Lucy offered up happily.

"I thought so! Well, you take care and make sure to tell Miss Windle that I asked after her," he said with a gleam in his eye.

"You can tell her yourself," Cook said as she surprised them both and appeared waddling up the path. Fergus' hat was off in a second, and his face turned a peculiar beetroot colour that was visible to Lucy even under his substantial beard.

"Oh, it is you yourself, is it?" he stammered, while staring down at his feet.

"And who else would you be expecting then?" She looked directly at him and waited until his head rose and he returned her stare.

"None other than you Beth, none other than you!"

"I should hope not," she replied with a touch of shyness following the directness of his response. "Well off with you now Bert. I've got a house to run here. Maybe I'll see you down at the market tomorrow."

Fergus replaced his cap and gave her a warm smile that even had an effect on Lucy. She emitted a loud sigh before she could help it or even knew it was coming.

Cook and Fergus both looked down and grinned at Lucy's gesture. Lucy was so embarrassed that she wasn't sure where to look. She ultimately chose to drop to her belly and place her head on her outstretched paws.

Fergus gave Cook a brief wave, then remounted his bike and headed back down the hill. Lucy wondered what the sensation was that she'd picked up between the two people, then promptly dozed off.

She didn't nap for long before she was awakened by some very strange sounds coming from the cottage. She eased herself to her feet and allowed her front legs to walk forward while keeping her back ones firmly planted. She had found this to be by far the most expeditious method of getting a really good post-nap stretch. Feeling her muscles loosen, she made her way toward the odd noises that were still emanating from her home.

Suddenly her Man and Cook came dancing out the front door. Dancing! They were at arm's length to each other, spinning around on the front lawn, while her Man laughed almost to the point of crying, such was his state. Cook was trying to act as exuberant as him but was clearly focusing her full concentration on staying upright as he swung her around.

Assuming it was expected of all parties, Lucy stepped between the pair and began to bark joyously (this was one of the few times that random barking was permitted).

Suddenly her Man let go of Cook with near disastrous consequences then ran back into the house. Cook and Lucy stopped what they were doing and gathered their composure as they watched the front door, waiting for him to reappear.

They heard a loud pop and glanced at each other with curious expressions until her Man came charging out of the cottage with a bottle in one hand and three glasses in the other. White foam was pouring out of the dark green bottle and was leaving a trail behind him.

Her Man poured a glass of the bubbling liquid for Cook, who looked aghast at the golden beverage.

"Oh Mr. Cotter, I don't think I should!" she said, shaking her head from side to side.

He held out the glass to her and grinned boyishly.

"Beth," he said." this is probably the happiest moment of my life, and if that isn't cause for celebration, I don't know what is!"

"In that case," Cook responded. "I'll try just a wee sip." She took the glass from him and downed it in one.

He looked at her in sheer amazement. "I was thinking we should toast," he said.

"That one was for thirst," she purred. "This one'll be the one for toasting." She held her glass out to him.

Though surprised, he refilled her glass then looked to Lucy. "This concerns you too."

He poured another glass, this one half the size and much lower to the ground and placed it in front of Lucy. She approached the glass cautiously, circling it once to make sure it was safe.

He finally poured his own glass, then held it high in the air.

"To you, Beth Windle, and to you, Lucy Cotter, I offer a toast," he orated grandly. "Without you this could never have happened. I would like to offer you both my deepest gratitude for all that you've done."

As he was about to drink from his glass, Cook cleared her throat loudly.

"Yes?" He queried.

"I'm sorry to be interrupting your fine toast there Mr. Cotter, but are you aware that we still haven't got the foggiest notion as to what you're prattling on about?" she said, with a slight slur to her voice.

Lucy had finished inspecting her glass and finally decided to risk taking a small taste. She lowered her muzzle into it and was immediately rewarded by the strangest prickling sensation that climbed her tongue and then assaulted her nose. Before she could stop herself, she backed up a step and let out a volley of surprised barks.

Oh, the embarrassment! She realised what she'd done almost as soon as she started and immediately ceased, but it was too late. What a faux pas! And in front of her Man and Cook! She looked up at them with sad, guilty eyes, and to her amazement, saw that they were not at all shocked by her disgraceful display, indeed, they both began laughing joyously at her outburst.

Lucy decided that the least she could do was to give the liquid offering another go. She again approached the glass, this time prepared for the gaseous assault. She closed her eyes and lapped up almost half of the golden liquid. She would have had more but couldn't get her tongue any farther into the glass. That seemed to please her Man and Cook, who proceeded to laugh even harder.

Her Man tried to bring himself under control and looked at them both.

"I'm so sorry," he said between laughs. "Of course, you don't know. Today I received an email from Hollywood."

"Hollywood in America?" Cook asked in disbelief.

"None other," he responded with exuberant pride. "and they have advised me that they plan to make a film from one of my books!"

Cook's jaw dropped open, as she swayed unsteadily. "A film, for the cinema," she stammered. "Of one of your books?"

"Does that surprise you?" he said, feigning hurt.

"No," she replied as tears began to roll down her cheeks. "Not at all. It's just that, that's the best news I've ever heard in my life."

"There's more. I am being paid to go to Hollywood to write the movie myself."

"No?" She screamed with delight. "Hollywood!"

Lucy looked on with fascination. Not at their antics, but at the fact there were now four of them dancing on the front lawn. She felt very warm and incredibly happy. She had no idea what was being said but clearly anything that made them this joyful had to prove to be an exceptionally good thing for her as well. Lucy hiccupped gently, then felt her eyelids closing on their own. Oh well. A nap wouldn't be that bad anyway. Lucy lowered her head to her front paws and was asleep within seconds.

CHAPTER 3

"Six months!" Cook exclaimed. "That's a fair bit of time to be away."

"It is, isn't it," Lucy's Man replied, while pensively looking out the sitting room window.

"I had no idea they'd need me for that long. I thought two to three weeks, maybe a month, but no. 'We'll need you here spittin' out pages right up to and throughout production,' he said with excellent mimicry of an American accent. "You'll simply manage the cottage as you do now," he continued. "Just prepare less food."

Cook tried to smile at his attempt at levity but found it difficult. "I'm not going to pretend that I like the thought of you being out there among those savages for that length of time," Cook said.

"If you're referring to all those gangs and criminals we hear about," he smiled as he spoke. "I wouldn't worry. I'm sure they're kept a suitable distance from the film studios."

"Gangs and criminals, indeed! I'm talking about the savages that work *in* the studios!" she said with conviction. "I read the magazines. I know what goes on out there."

He couldn't help but smile at Cook's concern. "I'll try and keep to myself whenever possible."

Cook nodded her acceptance just as Lucy entered the room. She was still a little dizzy after the earlier goings on outside, but at least her vision had cleared. Though now, she had the strangest pounding sensation in her head and a very unpleasant taste in her mouth. Even after consuming her entire bowl of water, the taste just wouldn't go away.

The moment she entered the room, she felt the tension. Cook and her Man were sitting facing each other in the two huge chairs by the bay window. Lucy didn't think she'd ever seen Cook seated anywhere but in the kitchen before that moment. They both watched Lucy as she approached.

"What about Lucy? She'll pine something terrible for you while you're gone," Cook said with a slight waver to her voice. "Could you not take her with you?"

He looked over at Lucy with great affection, then turned back to Cook. "I can't. I mean I could, but what with the eleven hour flights back and forth, my having to spend most my time at the studio, and there's the fact that she wouldn't have any open space to play in. I just don't think it would be fair on her. She'd spend her time either in a cage, a hotel room or a kennel."

"Oh my!" Cook exclaimed while wringing her hands forcefully. "Well, we can't have that. She'll simply stay here and have to put up with me for a while."

Lucy stood between the two and allowed them both to stroke her.

Her Man smiled across at Cook. "I somehow don't think that would be such a hardship for her. You'll probably end up spoiling her rotten and I'll come home to the only Golden Retriever in England that's too fat to even stand."

"You might at that," she chuckled. "Aye, you might at that."

Lucy could sense that she didn't have either human's full attention, so she wandered into the kitchen and checked for titbits. There were none, so she made her way down to the pond. A cloud passed in front of the sun, momentarily turning the vivid colours of the landscape into muted pastel shades. Lucy looked up and watched as the wispy tendrils of the cloud seemed to reach out and pull themselves bodily across the sky. Once it passed clear of the sun, Lucy had to look away as the fierce brightness of the golden orb was again unleashed upon the countryside.

Once at the pond, Lucy lowered herself to the ground and dipped her tongue into the still waters. It was an entirely different taste from the water in her bowl, or the water she sometimes drank from the raised porcelain chairs in those odd, cramped, rooms inside the cottage. The taste was somehow, not cleaner exactly, it was more...full-bodied. It had an earthy, almost lived-in taste that Lucy found not entirely unpleasant, and on an occasion such as today, when her thirst was rampant, the dark waters couldn't have tasted better.

As she drank, she watched the ripples spread out from her tongue and traverse the entire length of the pond, rocking the small fleet of lily pads as the waves passed through them.

She stopped drinking, and as the water regained its previous mirror like quality, Lucy spent a moment looking down at her own image.

It didn't seem that long ago, when her Man used to have to fish her out of the pond on more than one occasion, trying to chase what had turned out to be her own reflection. It wasn't that she was stupid, just that the concept of reflections was slightly out of her grasp. Her Man had finally, with a wonderful display of patience and caring, lifted Lucy right up into his arms, carried her to the cottage and took her up into his sleeping room. He had opened his closet door and shown Lucy his full length dressing mirror. After exhaustive examination, she came to terms with its reflective properties. Once convinced that Lucy had a good grasp of reflections, her Man again hoisted her into his arms, and transported her back to the water's edge and her reflected image therein. He repeated this arduous undertaking three more times. To be honest, Lucy had grasped the concept after the second trip, but was so enjoying being carried in and out of the house that she didn't let on.

Lucy adored her Man. She couldn't have picked a better one had she tried. He was still a Man, and therefore, a human, but aside from his breed's usual shortcomings, he seemed to have a far greater insight into the thinking of most other creatures. He had never raised a hand to Lucy, even when she was young and seemingly bent on single-handedly laying waste to the entire cottage and surrounding property. When she had misguidedly chewed through his favourite footwear, or shredded sheet after sheet of scribbled-on bits of paper in his private room, he hadn't beaten her. He had, in fact, hardly even raised his voice. Instead, he had sat her down and held in front of her the remains of her bad deeds and had slowly explained why what she had done was wrong. Even without being able to understand his words, she had clearly understood the overall meaning. When he wasn't buried in his work, her Man would take her for long, sometimes magical walks into the small village, and if stopped for conversation by passing acquaintances, would never forget to introduce Lucy. He was indeed an exceptionally good man to be paired with.

Even as she thought of her Man, his image suddenly appeared over hers in the pond's reflection. He was smiling down at her.

"Where's shoe?" he asked. "Come on, find shoe!"

Lucy scrambled to her feet. It was time for an unscheduled game of shoe! Shoe was what remained of one chewing indiscretion that had transpired a long time ago. Her Man had given her the talking to while holding out the severely gnawed remains of one half a pair of penny loafers. The barely recognisable shoe had then, for some reason, grown into and remained one of Lucy's favourite playthings.

Lucy charged across the lawn to the back of the cottage where, in a small recess in one wall, she stored her favourite possessions. A deflated soccer ball, a fuzz-less and permanently spittle-soaked tennis ball, the wooden handle to some gardening implement now long vanished, and of course, Shoe.

She grabbed the slightly damp and almost unrecognisable piece of leather, and dashed back to her Man. He dropped to his knees, patted her affectionately on the head, and reached for shoe. That was when the fun really began. You couldn't simply let him have it. Oh no! Part of the fun was to make him work for it. Lucy took a good strong hold of Shoe, and even as her Man rose to his feet and pulled with all his weight, she held on tightly. He tried to turn it from her mouth, but she clenched her teeth even harder. He tried to lift it, but Lucy simply rose with it. He walked it backwards, but accomplishing little except dragging Lucy along the lawn. There was no question that he had some good moves when it came to Shoe, but then again, so did she, and at just the right moment she suddenly let go, causing her Man to topple over backwards. Once on the ground, he then made his biggest blunder and loosened his grip on the now, very moist strip of leather. Lucy lunged and grabbed Shoe in her mouth before her Man knew what was happening. Lucy kept right on running, all the while hearing him laughing heartily after her. She completed one victory lap around the pond as was the custom, then eased her pace to a gentle trot and approached her Man. She gently deposited Shoe next to him, then waited for his next move. She made sure that she kept her gaze firmly rooted on it, with only the briefest glances at her adversary. Fully expecting him to make a sudden move on Shoe, she was caught entirely off-guard when he instead lunged at her! Before she knew it, he had flipped her over on her back, and was tickling her stomach with unbridled abandon. Then as if that weren't enough, just when she was almost delirious with love and adoration for him, her Man grabbed the shoe and was instantly on his feet.

Brilliant manoeuvre!

Lucy got up and charged after him as the game continued.

Lucy had no idea that this would be the last game of Shoe that she would have with her Man for some time.

They played on until Cook called him inside to speak into another of the bizarre objects, he surrounded himself with. This one was an odd black thing that her Man would hold against his ear after it made a sound like the other thing that woke him up every morning. Sometimes he would speak into it, other times he would just stare at it and tap his finger against it for hours. Lucy could, at times, hear the distorted sound of human voices coming from it, but on other occasions, like when she tipped it over one day to examine it more closely, it lit up and a robotic voice and began speaking to her. Her Man seemed content to use whatever it was on a regular basis, so it must have had some purpose.

After a good dinner, Lucy settled herself by the unlit fireplace (it was summer after all) and gazed up at her Man. She watched as he toiled away in front of a lit screen. On it, were line after line of symbols that looked similar to what was on the paper bundles her Man looked at every morning. Sometimes, he looked over at one of the paper bits he'd scribbled on and appeared to compare it to what was on the screen. Humans seemed to find the strangest ways of passing time.

Lucy dozed and dreamed of Shoe and reflections in the pond. At one point, she opened her eyes and saw that her Man was looking down at her with an expression of great love and concern. Lucy moved over to him and placed her head on his lap while still looking into his eyes.

"What's up girl?" he whispered. "Can't you sleep either?"

She gave him the double tail-floor tap, so he would know that she was fully receptive to whatever he wished to say or do.

"I'm going away for a while," he began explaining in a low and gentle tone. "I'm going to a place called America. Ever heard of it?"

Lucy provided another pair of tail taps.

"It's a huge place," he continued. "Larger than anything you could imagine. It's filled with every race of people you could think of - all living together. I'm going to be gone quite a long time. Do you understand?"

Again, double tail tap.

"I'll be leaving you in charge here, so you will have to promise me that you'll take care of everything, especially Cook. She won't be able to walk as far with you as I can, so have patience with her."

He took hold of her head in his large hands, and in a voice filled with emotion said, "I've never been away from you for more than a few days since you've been here. I will miss you more than you will ever know. Please try and realise that when I'm gone, it's not forever, though to you it may just seem like it is. I can't make you understand, I know, but please don't hurt too badly for me. I will be back."

That was all he said. They slowly readjusted their positions so that he could resume his work on the screen and the paper bits. Lucy fell into a deep, contented sleep at his feet as he continued to toil long into the night.

When she woke the next morning, her Man was gone.

CHAPTER 4

Lucy was quite surprised to find that her Man was out of the house when she awoke. It had happened before on a couple of occasions, and both times his absence had proved highly traumatic. She hoped that it wasn't going to be the case this time. She nosed her way to the dark storage area under the stairs and found, much to her chagrin, that the square thing he filled with belongings when he went away, was indeed, gone.

Even when he was totally preoccupied with his paper bits and didn't play Shoe or even take Lucy for a walk, life was somehow more complete, just knowing he was huddled over his desk up in his private room.

Of course, as with most bad situations, there is always some good to be found, and in the case of her Man going away, it was that Cook seemed to feel that the situation warranted severe over-indulging of Lucy at every turn. Lucy considered pointing out that such behaviour really wasn't necessary, but finally decided not to spoil Cook's fun. So, with a brave face, and rapidly enlarging belly, Lucy would sombrely accept tidbit after titbit from her. Alright, it didn't replace her Man, but it helped a little.

The first few days passed with relative ease. Lucy spent the time catching up on naps and lower garden exploration. On the second day, she even found time to mark out some unclaimed areas at the farthest reaches of the property. When she woke on the third day, she didn't feel quite right. She couldn't put her paw on it, but she felt an unease somewhere deep within her. By the afternoon of that day, the feeling had grown to one of deep concern. Her Man had never been gone this long. Something bad had obviously happened. Lucy began pacing the cottage, checking her Man's favourite spots repeatedly, and with growing frequency.

By early evening, Lucy was a wreck. She didn't know what to do. She kept rushing to Cook but she only offered her something to eat. Lucy was beyond titbits by that point. Finally, in complete despair, she climbed into her Man's chair, and though normally frowned upon, was left unhindered as she fitfully slept on and off. For the next three days she rarely left his chair, and only then because she needed water or a visit to the garden to do her private business.

Cook was at a loss as to what to do. Lucy wouldn't eat, she rarely went outside, and she wouldn't even leave the chair. On the eighth day after his departure, Cook's prayers were answered when another strange object that sat on its own little table in the hallway, began to make a loud ringy noise. Cook lifted part of it and placed it cautiously against her ear then suddenly bubbled over with excitement.

"Oh, Mr. Cotter! You have no idea how glad I am to hear from you. Lucy's pining away somethin' awful fer ya," she said in a rapid torrent. "She won't eat, she misses you so!"

Her Man had only said two or three words in reply when Lucy, hearing his voice coming from downstairs, came charging down the stairs and into the room. She began barking frantically at Cook and the black thing. Manners be damned. She'd heard her Man and was going to bark until she dropped.

Such was the din caused by her orating, that Cook could hardly hear a word her Man was saying. She finally turned to Lucy, and with a rigidly pointed finger gestured to a spot on the floor inches from her.

"Lucy!" she commanded. "You come here this minute and sit!"

Lucy knew when an order needed to be obeyed and did as she was told. Cook then, to her complete amazement, held the black thing to Lucy's ear. Lucy was about to protest when she heard his voice. Slightly distant, and mildly distorted, but there he was (or wasn't). It was very confusing. He obviously couldn't be in the black thing, but then, where was he? Lucy sniffed the air and confirmed that he certainly was not nearby.

"Hello girl!" her Man said from his mystery location. "Sorry I'm not there to give you a big hug. Don't be sad

Lucy. I'll be home before you know it." Lucy felt her legs go weak at the sound of his voice. She let out a small whimper, wanting so much to see, and feel him, to play Shoe again, to—what was the point? He wasn't anywhere close. She knew that. She listened to his voice and at least could tell that he seemed well, and in fact, quite happy.

Cook finally raised the black thing back to her ear, and after a few brief words, put the thing back into its holder on the desk.

"Well, I hope you're feeling a wee bit better now that you've had a chat with him."

Lucy looked up at her and sighed deeply. She felt very empty and suddenly, slightly hungry. Not just slightly—very hungry!

She realised, much to her amazement, that she couldn't remember her last meal.

Cook stroked her head, and asked, "Would you like a wee spot of dins?"

Dins! Cook's pseudonym for food. What timing! Lucy leapt to her feet and wagged her tail rapidly, in a clear display of agreement.

"Well, well. Look who's back with the living then!" she exclaimed.

Lucy was so excited that she bounded towards the kitchen, leaping two dog lengths at a time. She'd not only heard her Man's voice but was about to get some well-deserved dins as well. What a great day.

The days passed slowly by, as Lucy watched summer slip quietly away and morph into the season when the leaves fell to the ground, and the temperature changed from hot to only lukewarm. The sun lost some its fiery ferocity and no longer reached its zenith directly overhead. She thought of her Man every day, but began to realise that, though she was able to frequently hear his voice on the black thing, he was obviously never coming back.

On one particularly dreary day, Lucy had a light lunch then moved out to the garden to have a nap. She found a spot that was free from falling leaves (exceedingly difficult at that time of year) and shut her eyes, listening to Cook's Welsh lilt as she sang away in the kitchen.

Lucy was dreaming of Burden Dell when her nose twitched her awake. She could clearly smell meat. Fresh, raw meat! She opened her eyes and urgently looked about her. She spotted, much to her amazement, two humans leaning over the front garden wall. One was holding a very tempting steak in his hand and was waving it gently from side to side. Behind the men was a grey vehicle similar to her Man's, but longer and windowless. She had noticed it on their street for the past few days but thought nothing of it. The men were unusually attired by Lucy's way of thinking, and though only able to see their top halves over the wall, they seemed somehow rougher than the humans she was used to. Seeing that Lucy was now awake, the men began to coax her over to partake of their meaty offering. She couldn't imagine what they could possibly have to gain, but that steak did look good!

"Oh, why not," Lucy decided as she trotted toward them. When she was within a few dog lengths from the wall, the man tossed the steak onto the lawn next to her. She looked over at them to ensure that there was no misunderstanding, then seeing their eager gesturing, lowered herself to the tasty task at hand. She began chewing with delight, for it was, as suspected, a delicious piece of meat. As she ate, the two men watched her intently. Lucy found this slightly disconcerting, but if that was their only condition for sharing then...

Lucy suddenly felt dizzy. Just for a second, then it cleared. Strange! She lowered her head for another bite, then felt it again. She also felt very sleepy. She decided that maybe a sip of water would help. She tried to get to her feet but couldn't. It was as if her legs could no longer lift her. She then felt most peculiar. Her vision became blurred and distorted. On top of that, she felt a little queasy.

"Oh my," she thought.

She felt herself spinning. She tried closing her eyes but that only made things worse. She looked over at the two men hoping that maybe they could help, and indeed saw that they were climbing over the fence. She couldn't keep her eyes open any longer and was now feeling very warm. She felt hands on her, and realised the men were lifting her. Thank goodness. They would take these nasty feelings away. She was being raised into the air. She managed to open one eye and saw the cottage swimming in a grey haze. Cook was running out the front door screaming at her. Why? She hadn't done anything wrong. Lucy's eyes closed, and as she sensed herself being carried over the wall, she heard Cook's voice reaching higher and higher pitches. Lucy sensed all light suddenly vanish, then heard the sound like her Man's vehicle just before it moved. She could still hear Cook's voice only now it was far away. Very, very far away. Lucy began to dream of Burden Dell again, only now instead of being surrounded by deer and other animal friends, there was no one there but herself, and she began to feel afraid and very alone. She wanted badly to wake from this dream, but she couldn't. It went on and on. Lucy began to cry in her dream, and although unaware of it, in real life as well, as she lay in the back of the grey van as it sped out of West Sussex on its way to London.

CHAPTER 5

L ucy did not want to open her eyes. She was painfully
tired, and still felt the after-effects of the terrible dream
she'd had. She just wanted to keep her eyes closed a little
while longer. She adjusted her position and realised how
hard and cold the floor felt. She must have rolled off her
rug during the night. Yes, that must be it. Her other senses
began relaying very discomforting signals to her foggy, and
slightly achy head. The smells were not right. There was no
scent of fresh food being prepared, or of polished woods
or . . . . there were no smells of home at all, only smells of
dirt, and stone and other odours that Lucy simply refused
to acknowledge. The sounds weren't right either. She could
hear a steady rumbling all about her, almost like the noise
vehicles made on the village high street only a hundred
times stronger. She could also hear other dogs, only they
didn't sound like any she'd ever encountered. These voices
all sounded pained and forlorn. Some were singing songs
of misery, others of imprisonment and ill treatment. Then

there were those who were simply crying. Not about anything in particular, just crying openly and with total abandon. Could she still be dreaming? Lucy hoped against hope that that was indeed the case, as she slowly opened her eyes.

Her mind had trouble accepting what her eyes were seeing. She definitely wasn't at home. She was in an old and very worn brick enclosure, not much wider than herself, and around twice as long. The floor was not stone as she had earlier thought, but a smooth, hard, stone-like substance, which sloped gently to one corner where a small hole was located. Lucy had no idea what it was for, but even from where she lay, she could distinctly smell the vilest of odours emanating from it. The walls that surrounded her on three sides were stained, scarred and so covered with green mildew that were it not for some recent dings and chips, she would never have known them to have been brick at all. The fourth side of the enclosure was made up of a heavy, and very rusted wire mesh gate. A metal latch kept the mesh barrier from opening. Lucy could see across a narrow, dark passageway that there was an identical enclosure across from hers. Lucy tried to focus her eyes to see if it was occupied but found it to be empty.

With great difficulty, Lucy got to her feet. Her legs felt more like bendy flower stems than the firm bones and muscle that she was used to. She shook her head and tried to clear the cobwebs that still lingered. She moved stiffly to the front of the enclosure and by resting her head on the rusty fencing, was able to look down the passageway. She was shocked at what she saw. It seemed to go on forever, one enclosure after another. She could only see one side of the passageway clearly, but she knew that the other side would be the same. She swivelled around and looked down the other way and was greeted by the same vision. Some of the enclosures were clearly occupied as their canine occupants leaned against or stood at their locked gate. Some were barking, others crying, while still others simply stood there with blank, almost helpless expressions on their faces.

Lucy backed away from the gate and used all her willpower to not burst into tears. She was frightened yes, and hungry too, but she knew that she mustn't cry in this place. She didn't know why, just that she had to keep her emotions in check until she found out what was going on. She was obviously not meant to be here. There had been some silly mistake which would most certainly be discovered very shortly, at which point, she would be returned post-haste to her cottage, Cook, and hopefully, breakfast.

She distinctly felt a sudden tension run the length of the passageway, then heard a door opening. She moved to the gate, and saw that almost every enclosure or cell, as she was beginning to think of them, was occupied. There must have been close to a hundred dogs in the place, all of which began to howl, and bark, and some even threw themselves at the wire mesh.

At first, Lucy didn't understand what was going on. After some deep concentration she began to pick up a word here and a word there. The mix of breeds, plus their diverse accents, made them difficult to understand, but she soon realised that this was feeding time. Thank goodness. Maybe after a nice breakfast, Lucy could better focus on what to do about her situation. She wondered if there would be any fresh bread, though even the wet and dry mix would go down quite well this morning.

She continued to look down the passageway and could hear a strange high-pitched squeaking that almost hurt her ears. She continued looking and finally saw the source of the din. A fat and very shabbily dressed man was pushing a cart of some sort along the passageway. The intrusive noise seemed to be coming from one of the vehicle's wheels. As Lucy watched, she saw the man open one cell after another and toss a dented metal bowl into each one. She found it odd that as he reached each cell and opened the gate, the occupant backed far inside, not even attempting to offer their benefactor even the most perfunctory of good mornings.

After what seemed like an eternity, the man reached Lucy's cell and opened the gate. Lucy stepped forward to introduce herself and was about to raise a paw, when the man, without any warning whatsoever, raised what to Lucy looked like a long cylindrical piece of wood. He brought it down with amazing speed and force, hitting her savagely on her rump. Her back legs gave out and she collapsed to the cold floor. She looked up at the man with true pain in her eyes, as well as complete bewilderment. She'd never been hurt like that before. This was not like Cook and the rolled-up paper bits. This was different. This man had clearly intended to cause her pain; but why? She didn't recall ever having seen him before, and certainly didn't remember having done him wrong in any way. As she looked up at him, he glared down at her, then raised the piece of wood. He didn't swing it. He just held it up as a warning. Lucy slid her sore backside away from the gate and moved as far back into the cell as possible. The man lowered the wood thing, then, with a sneer, tossed a metal bowl onto the floor. He slammed the gate shut and moved on to the next cell. Lucy tried to stand but found it too painful. Her eyes were brimming over with tears, but she still managed to hold them back, bravely determined to not show any emotion.

She moved herself carefully across the cell towards the bowl. She knew she had better eat something, if only to keep up her strength. She approached the food and saw immediately that this was most certainly not her usual dry and wet mix. In fact, it was like no food that she had ever seen. It was light grey! The only parts that weren't that shade were the areas where it had started to congeal and harden. Those were dark grey. And the smell! There was nothing meaty anywhere to be found in its scent. It smelled of metal and . . . and mould. Lucy had never smelled anything quite like it, especially something that was intended for her consumption. She took a small bite, hoping that it would at least taste of something recognisable. It did not. In fact, it tasted of surprisingly little, which after the smell was a bonus.

Lucy realised that she wasn't that hungry anymore. Her backside was throbbing, and the look of breakfast had somehow diminished what appetite remained after the unexpected beating. She was, however, very thirsty, and suddenly noticed that she had no water bowl. She thought about approaching the gate and advising Fat Man as to the missing water, then decided to leave him be. He might, after all, still be angry with her for whatever had set him off in the first place.

Lucy lowered her head to her front paws and tried to recall the events leading up to this - her unjust and totally unforeseen imprisonment.

Her thoughts were interrupted by a loud, "Psst!" She looked to the gate and saw, much to her amazement, a small Yorkshire Terrier standing in the passageway, anxiously checking both directions.

"Psst!" the tiny animal repeated.

"Are you pssting me?" Lucy asked in amazement.

"Shh! Don't say a word." The dog had a strong but pleasant Yorkshire accent. "I've only got a second. I heard you got the bat earlier. Don't get near the gate when they open it. Got that?"

"Well I..." Lucy began.

"Quiet. I told you not to speak! Just move to the back of the cage when they open it. I'll tell you more in the courtyard later. Oh, by the way, you'd better eat that slop. I know it's vile but it's all you'll get all day." The terrier scanned the passageway nervously. "I'll fill you in later." He then vanished out of sight.

"But who are you?" Lucy called out.

The small dog instantly reappeared. "Rodney, and for the sake of us all... shh!" And again, he was gone.

Perplexed and yet, somehow relieved to know that there were some friendly breeds incarcerated with her, she lowered her head again to the ground, and much to her amazement, fell asleep.

She dreamt of Cook and of a huge loaf of fresh bread that was just out of her reach. As she turned to Cook and asked in her best, and most well-mannered way, if it had cooled sufficiently for a piece to be given to her, Cook's face took on a distorted and vicious leer. She removed her hands from behind her back, and in one hand was holding a dented metal bowl filled with grey food, and in the other hand, a long piece of wood. Lucy woke up with a start only to find her gate, wide open. She only had the briefest instant to ponder this before Fat Man appeared and stepped right into her cell. He stepped around her, and to the back of the enclosure. He raised the 'club' and began shouting unintelligibly at her. She had no idea what he wanted. She suddenly realised that perhaps she had offended him by not eating her food. She rose painfully to her feet and took a step towards the bowl. The man yelled even louder and raised the piece of wood still higher.

"Get out!" snapped a powerful-looking Boxer dog who was standing in the passageway.

Lucy hesitated.

"Now!" the dog barked.

Lucy looked up at the man, and while involuntarily cringing, she obeyed the Boxer's orders. The moment she moved towards the gate; the club was indeed lowered. She stepped into the passageway and saw that all the cells were open and that their occupants were all heading to the far end of the hallway, towards an open door.

Lucy tried to ask a few of her fellow prisoners what was going on but was told to shut up on each attempt. So, still unenlightened, she followed the group as it neared the exit. For one brief moment, she thought that it was the end of the nightmare, and that the door would in fact lead back to her cottage and gardens. As she neared it however, she immediately saw that nightmare was nowhere near ending. The doorway led to a dark, dreary, stone courtyard. As Lucy stepped into the cold, damp air, she saw that the square concrete yard was flanked on all four sides by very high, and incredibly old, brick walls. To ensure that no beast could escape over them, strands of vicious-looking barbed wire had been coiled atop all four ensuring that no animal would be stupid enough to try and escape. It dawned on Lucy that she had been spot on in thinking of her enclosure as a cell. The more she saw, the more she realised that she truly was imprisoned.

As she stepped into the yard, she noticed how the dogs immediately seemed to form into groups and began talking in whispers amongst themselves. There were a few loners such as herself, but they appeared either very sullen, or as in the case of one, incredibly sad and pathetic-looking Spaniel, completely deranged with despondency.

Lucy approached the spaniel, hoping to console the miserable creature, but with each attempt at getting a word in between the breed's violent sobbing, she would scream even louder, and wail with unrelenting determination. Lucy soon gave up, and with a gentle nod, backed away from the pitiful creature.

She slowly walked around the perimeter of the yard, feeling very self-conscious and out of place. As she passed each new group of dogs, she felt their eyes on her as they evaluated the new prisoner.

Suddenly, she saw Rodney holding court before a group of much larger breeds, all of whom appeared to be hanging on his every word. Lucy stepped into the group and smiled over at the small terrier. Rodney stopped talking. The others all turned and glared menacingly towards her.

"Hello," Lucy stuttered. "Sorry to intrude, I thought I'd just introduce myself. I'm…"

The group instantly disbanded, leaving Lucy with her mouth wide open as she looked down at Rodney.

"Lesson number two," Rodney said in a patient, and calm voice." In this place, never step into a group uninvited, especially until the dogs get to know you."

"But why?" Lucy began.

"Just listen for now," Rodney said, interrupting her. "We don't have long outside. You probably haven't the vaguest idea where you are, have you?"

Lucy shook her head in acknowledgment.

"That's usually the case," Rodney said. "You were, to put it in simple terms, dog napped!"

"What! But that's ridicul..." Lucy began to exclaim.

"Hush! Let me finish." Rodney voiced sternly. "I don't know where they took you from, south I'd wager from the colour of your coat; but you're now in London. The docklands to be exact. And I'm relatively certain that these breeds are not the sort you are used to dealing with. I've only been here a few weeks myself, but from what I gather, these bipeds are part of a much larger ring involved with smuggling, and possibly even worse.

"But what's a biped, and what do they want us for?" Lucy asked, incredulously.

"Bipeds are what we call humans, and they use dogs to smuggle things when the load is small enough. There's a couple that you'll see... Anyway so I told them it's steak or nothing for me." Rodney's voice completely changed as he spoke the last sentence.

Lucy looked at him with confusion and was about to say something when Rodney gestured with a brief flick of his head. She couldn't at first gather what he was referring to, then realised that it had something to do with the Boxer dog that was just passing them. He nodded politely to Lucy and

Rodney, then continued on his way. Once out of earshot, Rodney stepped close to Lucy.

"That was Champ," he began. "And don't let his demeanour fool you for a second. He'll turn you in to the bipeds as soon as look at you. He's a bad'un that one. He's sold a few of us out already for no more than a few scraps of beef trimmings. Anyway, so where was I..., oh yeah, I remember... there's this couple you'll see occasionally. Very posh and toffee-nosed bipeds, both of them. Apparently, they put on this charade of travelling to some place with their dearly loved family pet in tow. Of course, the pet is one of us and we're dearly loved because we have something valuable and illegal hidden in, or on ourselves."

"In?" Lucy asked with a look of revulsion on her face.

"We'll cover that later," he continued. "Once whatever it is, has been delivered, they have no use for us anymore, and besides, they're then out of the country and they don't bother bringing any of us back through customs. That's why they pick the sort they do. Good breeding, fine health and with a gentle disposition."

"What's customs and what could possibly be so valuable for them to need to steal dogs? And what happens to the dogs after they are used?" Lucy asked in a rush of words.

"Customs is the law over here. They say what comes into the country. If you leave the country for even 5 minutes, they have the right to give you a full going over. As for the valuables, who knows! I hear sometimes it's these little shiny stones, and other times some kind of powder. Whatever the stuff is, it's important to the bipeds."

"And after the dogs are used?" Lucy asked hesitantly.

"We don't know. We just know that they never come back. I suppose the best we can hope is that they're let go free wherever the journey ends."

"And the worst?" Lucy asked with wide, horrified eyes.

"Let's not think about the worst, that's not going to happen to us," he said encouragingly.

"But how..." her words were cut off by the piercing sound of a whistle being blown. They both looked over at the doorway and saw Fat Man as he raised the whistle again to his mouth.

"Just don't worry, Goldie," he said in a whisper, his voice carrying a slight edge of urgency as they began to move towards the door. "Just take my word for it. Things will only get better."

They were in a crowd of breeds as they funnelled back into the building. Lucy was caught in a veritable sea of dogs and was soon separated from Rodney. She tried to see his tiny frame among the teaming mass of dog hair but couldn't. She realised suddenly how much better she'd felt talking to the tiny terrier, and now he was gone as well. Lucy kept up with the flow and found herself in front of her cell. She wasn't certain how she knew it was hers, but she did. She also found out why the dogs were given the break outside. All the cells, hers included, had apparently been very thoroughly hosed down. The entire enclosure was sopping wet from the ceiling to the floor. A diminished, but still sizeable stream of water ran along one wall, and down the black hole in the corner. Lucy suddenly felt incredibly tired, and desperately wanted to sleep, but she couldn't even contemplate lying on the floor until the cell was a least partially dry.

"Psst!" Rodney signalled.

Lucy turned and saw her new friend just outside her cell, trying to not be swept away by the continuing flow of dogs returning to their enclosures.

"I was trying to tell you before we were separated," he said in an excited whisper. "Don't get too depressed about this place. You won't be here that long."

Lucy's entire frame sagged. "You mean they're going to use me to smuggle?" she began tearfully, "And then leave me in some foreign country or even… even something worse. How can I…"

"Will you pipe down, you silly girl!" he snapped. "There'll be no more smuggling, or anything else out of this place." He smiled smugly as he let his words sink in. Lucy looked over at Rodney, and tried to read something, anything from his expression.

"Get in your cages, ya bloody mutts!" Fat Man yelled from the far end of the passageway, sending dogs slipping and sliding chaotically down the hallway as they tried to carry out his order. Rodney, however, remained very calm as he leant against her cell.

"Tomorrow, my golden beauty," he whispered. "We're going to put an end to all this nonsense."

Lucy tilted her head in curiosity.

The Yorkie gave her wink. "Tomorrow, we break out!"

CHAPTER 6

A s Rodney spoke and Lucy realised what he was saying, she desperately tried to stop him. Just behind Rodney, moving with deliberate slowness, was Champ, the Boxer. He didn't acknowledge having heard the terrier's words, but after Rodney's earlier warning, Lucy felt very uncomfortable indeed. By the time Rodney had picked up on her display of facial contortions, it was clearly too late. They both watched in silence as the other dog continued down the passageway, and without a backward glance, entered his enclosure.

"Whoops," Rodney whispered.

"Do you think he heard?"

"Hard to say. Fact is, he was going to be taken care of prior to the big event anyway, so don't worry about it. I'm not going to." With that, Rodney gathered up all eleven mighty inches of himself, and with a brief wink for Lucy's benefit, sauntered back to his cell.

Lucy spent the rest of the day, as did the other inmates, shut in her enclosure attempting to grab fitful naps. Lucy had made a few rather dissatisfying attempts at conversation with an Afghan hound in the cell adjacent to hers but found the other animal to be almost staggeringly vain, and not terribly intelligent. The Afghan was far more concerned about the condition of her coat, than of her own skin. She considered the entire ordeal troublesome, but only because she had not kept her weekly appointment at the pet groomers. Lucy had tried to guide the conversation to other subjects, yet each topic somehow found its way back to her appearance. Eventually Lucy gave up and left her neighbour bitterly complaining that the least her abductors could have done was provide her with a mirror.

"Different needs for different breeds." As Lucy's mother used to say.

The one constant during the day was the endless crying from the spaniel she had seen earlier in the yard. Lucy now knew her to be called Angel, which pretty much gave one the entire picture of her previously pampered existence. Apparently, her entrapment had been totally unpremeditated. The dog-nappers had their eye on her housemate, a fine and even-tempered Labrador. As in Lucy's case, the piece of steak laced with a sleeping powder had been used (Lucy had learned that this was the napper's usual M.O.). Only as the gentle Labrador made his way with slow dignity towards the offered piece of meat, Angel had appeared out of nowhere and before the men could dissuade her, had grabbed the steak and devoured almost half of it. She keeled over right in the middle of the front lawn just as her owner was pulling into the drive. The men, not wishing to leave any trace of their misdeeds, had waited until the owner was out of sight in the garage, and then grabbed Angel. Amazingly, she still had the remains of the meat clenched in her jaws. Apparently, the whole cell-block had heard the row when the dog-nappers were refused any payment for Angel's capture.

Now the poor creature simply cried non-stop, such was her fear and homesickness. Lucy had at first felt great sympathy for the animal, but by mid-afternoon the sound of her bawling had become like toenails on polished stone. Occasionally, other dogs would yell threats down the passageway, but these seemed to have no effect on the distraught creature. Fat Man had even given her a dose of 'the bat' but this seemed to only change the pitch of her crying, not stop it. Lucy knew that if she didn't shut up, it was only a matter of time before some great harm befell her. She also knew that there was little she could do. Besides, despite her wish to help the other dog, she had her own future to worry about.

By late afternoon, Lucy was very hungry. She hadn't touched any of the grey slop they'd given her for breakfast, and after returning from the yard had found the metal bowl to have been removed. Earlier in the afternoon, each dog had been given a small bowl of water, then shortly after, this too had been taken away. It had been explained to Lucy that their captors didn't want to deal with too much mess in the cells, so their food and liquids were heavily restricted.

CHRIS COPPEL

Sometime in the evening, Lucy heard the passageway door open and a group of human voices heading towards her cell. There were three of them. A female biped that was, Lucy felt, exceptionally unattractive, even for humans. She was short and dumpy, with features that seemed to have been squashed, as if by some enormous pressure from above. She was holding a white cylindrical tube in her hand and occasionally placed it in her mouth and sucked on it. Lucy could see that it appeared to be burning, and that after sucking on it, the woman would breathe out a large cloud of smoke. The second human was equally as frightening. It was a male. A very tall, very thin one, with what appeared to Lucy, to be not enough skin on his face. What there was, was pulled far too tightly over his bones, giving his head a skull-like appearance. His black hair was exceptionally long, greasy, and was pulled into a ponytail at the back. He was wearing all black and was also sucking on a burning tube - only his was brown and longer. The third person was Fat Man. The three stopped at each cell, as skull face and squat lady gave the occupant a long look, before giving Fat Man an instruction that he would note on a paper bit that he was carrying.

After what seemed an eternity, the group arrived at Lucy's enclosure. As was her well-mannered way, she got to her feet and acknowledged their presence. This seemed for some reason to please Skull Face. His lips pulled back across his long, and very yellow teeth, in what Lucy had to assume was some horrific parody of a smile.

60

"This is a fine bitch," the ghoul stated. "Put her down for the Geneva run."

Fat Man nodded and made some squiggles on the paper bits. The males moved on, but the squat female stayed back for a moment, and lowered her already low frame close to Lucy's gate. Lucy decided to risk it and moved over to her. The woman stared back at Lucy through the wire mesh, then suddenly expelled a plume of pungent smoke directly in her face. Lucy recoiled, almost tripping over her own feet, as the woman shrieked with a high, horse-like laughter, before rising to her full height and re-joining the others.

Lucy felt a new emotion inside her. Something vastly different. It was a tightness, and a raging heat that she'd never felt before. As she lowered herself to the cold floor, she could only think of the ugly woman and her sour, smoky breath. She couldn't seem to take her eyes off the mesh gate, or let her body relax in any way.

Though she didn't realise it, Lucy was, for the first time in her life, feeling real anger.

When much later, Lucy finally fell asleep, she didn't dream of Burden Dell or of warm kitchens and fresh bread. She dreamt of stalking something through a dark, and dismal countryside. She didn't know what she was hunting, only that she was driven, body and soul, to seek it out, and, by her own paw and tooth, destroy it.

CHAPTER 7

Lucy woke the following morning an felt a distinct electricity in the air. She could almost see the tension it was so thick.

When Fat Man appeared with the grey slop, Lucy was certain that the big moment had arrived; but as she listened to him toss each bowl into a cell, then retrace his steps along the passageway with the squeaky cart in tow, she realised that the breakout was obviously not at hand after all.

She decided that she should try to eat something as she was bound to need her strength for whatever lay ahead. She wanted to ensure that she was both mentally and physically ready for whatever was needed of her. She took a mouthful of the slop and almost gagged. Even with her great hunger, it was near impossible to swallow. It tasted not only of mould and metal, but also had a strong after-taste of the liquid her Man used to put into his vehicle. On top of that, it had a very slimy feel as she tried to chew the almost un-chewable lumps that she encountered under the grey sheen.

She finally managed to eat half the bowl, but instead of the expected rush of energy she had hoped for after nourishing her body, she simply felt heavy and a little bit queasy.

She tried to settle down and relax until the morning exercise in the yard but couldn't seem to stop herself from pacing within the narrow confines of her cell. Finally, after what seemed to her to be two eternities, Fat Man reappeared and opened their enclosures. The inmates were all anxious to get into the open air on this special day. Lucy could feel the excitement as she stepped into the throng of other dogs, as they almost tripped over each other to reach the door.

Lucy was one of the last to step into the yard and could immediately tell that something was wrong. The sense of excitement that she had felt only moments before had vanished. She looked into the crowd for Rodney so she could find out what was going on but couldn't see him. He was a rather small animal, so this didn't particularly phase her. She began a more thorough search, and soon realised that he wasn't there. Rodney had vanished.

Lucy was so shocked that she didn't know what to do. She stood for the longest time rooted in place, as her mind swam with a veritable potpourri of possibilities. He was sick. He had left without them. He'd... He'd... She couldn't stand not knowing where her new, but very trusted, little friend had gone. She was suddenly nudged quite roughly, causing her to almost yelp in surprise. She turned and came face to face with three exceptionally large, and very tough-looking, alpha dogs; two Dobermans and a Rottweiler. One of the Dobermans stepped forward and looked her coldly in the eye.

"Rod said you was alright," he said with a surprisingly rich Eat End accent. "We noticed you were looking for something."

"Yes, yes I was," Lucy said, trying to keep the trepidation out of her voice. "Where is Rodney? I thought today was..."

"Shh," the Doberman whispered forcefully. "It was, but something unexpected happened. They came for him during the night. They've only taken him on a bloomin' run, haven't they!"

Lucy couldn't believe what she was hearing. "You mean he's gone? Just like that?"

The Doberman tried to look somewhat understanding. "That's how it works around here, love."

"Oh my." Lucy tried not to let her emotions get the better of her. "Does that mean the... well you know... is off?"

"Has to be," he said in a voice laden with disappointment. "He was the only one who could pull off the plan," offered the Doberman.

The Rottweiler suddenly cleared his throat loudly. They followed his glance and saw that the Boxer was approaching.

"Filthy snitch," the Doberman growled.

Champ looked their way, and with a distinct lack of concern, walked right up to, and through their little group. The Doberman at first blocked his path, but then, with a brief growl, let him go.

"I was looking forward to dealing with him," the Doberman stated in a frighteningly cold voice.

"Is he really that bad?" Lucy asked.

"Ha! There have been two attempts to get out since I've been here, and on both occasions, guess who alerted the bipeds?"

"Oh," Lucy murmured.

"And what's more," the Doberman continued, "on both nights following his snitching, and after the escapees were dealt with, very brutally by the way, who do you think got a nice big steak for dinner, while the rest of us bloody starved?"

Lucy simply shook her head, as she watched the Boxer as he paraded around the yard. "So, what happens now?" she asked.

"Not much. Rodney was the key to the whole plan."

"Can't I help," she offered. "I'm certain I could do something to…"

"You're too bloody big," the Rottweiler interrupted.

Clearly offended, Lucy stepped up to the dog. "That's hardly called for! I'll have you know that I take good care of myself. I eat sensibly and…"

"Not your figure," he said, with thinly veiled exasperation. "You. You're simply too big. We all are. Look, without drawing any attention, have a gander over at the wall on your right. You'll see a very small hatch."

Lucy nodded.

"Well, we've been working at that for weeks, and it's now to the point that with one really good shove it'll give way, but only one of us could ever fit through."

"Rodney," Lucy said, finally understanding the Doberman's point.

"Right," the Rottweiler continued. "At which point Rodders was gonna do a bunk through the hatch, then nip round to the other wall on the left in which you will see a door. A door without a latch on this side. Well, according to our little missing friend, his human had the same type of door at the bottom of their garden. Rodders had, so he claimed, become quite the little expert at jumping up, and smacking the handle down as he dropped. He guaranteed he could do the same with that one."

"Isn't there anyone else who could get through the hatch?" Lucy asked, hopefully.

"There's no one here close to Rod's size. The only other small-ish breed in the whole place is … well forget it."

"What do you mean, forget it?" she said urgently. "Who is it? Come on. If there's any chance at all, we must take it. Now tell me, who is it?"

All three males turned their heads and together looked over to a far corner where a lone dog sat in the shadows. Even from a distance, Lucy could see that the animal was in a terrible state, as it whined pathetically to no one in particular.

"Angel!?" She exclaimed.

"You asked," retorted the Doberman.

"Has anyone spoken to her?" Lucy enquired.

"What's the point in that?" the Rottweiler said, stepping closer to the group. "Look at her, she's a mess. You can't even get a word in between her sniffling and whining. Typical female!"

The Doberman cleared his throat loudly.

"Present company excepted, of course, Miss," the Rottweiler hastened to add, nodding at Lucy.

"Do you mind if I give it a try? After all, maybe, female to female...?" Lucy asked hesitantly.

The three males looked to each other, then shrugged their shoulders. "Why not?" the first Doberman said, speaking for them all.

Lucy gave them an encouraging smile, then, with a casual stride, moved across the yard to the shadowed corner and the sad and pathetic outline of Angel.

"Hello," Lucy began. "I couldn't help but notice how upset you seem to be. I thought that perhaps a nice chat would help."

Lucy was stunned when the Spaniel, instead of calming under her gentle words, broke into an even louder and more intense outbreak of tears.

"Now, there's no need for that," Lucy chided gently. "I only want to help."

Angel was clearly nearing a state of hysteria. Her sobbing and wailing were beginning to attract the attention of others in the yard. Including, much to Lucy's horror, that of Champ, who was now facing them.

"Please lower your voice, we don't want to attract any attention," Lucy whispered urgently. It had no effect on the other animal whatsoever. Lucy turned to the yard, and gave the onlookers a calm and unconcerned smile, then while pretending to sniff at the base of the wall, gave Angel a brief, but very sharp nip at her backside. The Spaniel leapt to her paws, and with a yelp of surprise, looked at Lucy's face for the first time.

"What was that for?" Angel asked in a weak, and sob-riddled voice. "Why'd you bite me?"

"I'll bite you again, only much harder if you don't stop carrying on," Lucy retorted.

"Leave me alone, I don't want to talk to anyone."

"That's just too bad," Lucy responded with a sharp edge to her voice. "I happen to wish to speak with you, which I most certainly can't do with you making enough noise for six dogs."

"Well, I'm miserable," Angel said, pathetically.

"We all are, you silly girl. Look around you. Do you think any of us wants to be here? Do you think we wouldn't all prefer to be home with our humans right this very minute?"

"I guess," Angel said.

"Then stop behaving like a spoiled puppy," Lucy continued. "and maybe, just maybe we can all work together and find a way out of here."

"How?" she said with a definite edge to her voice.

"That's better," Lucy whispered reassuringly. "You see the little latch over on your right. Well..."

"You mean the one Rodney and his bullies have been working on for the past two weeks?"

"Keep your voice down," Lucy hissed. "What do you know about that?"

"I know they've been wasting their time," Angel said with some certainty. "This yard is below street level, and that hatch is the bottom of an old coal drop."

"A what?" Lucy asked, as she felt an uncomfortable icy knot develop in her stomach.

"A coal drop. This yard was the storage area for some sort of factory, and that hatch is the lower end of a chute that leads to the street."

"That sounds promising," Lucy tried hopefully.

"No, it doesn't," Angel corrected. "It's probably a four-foot drop to the hatch and at street level there will be a set of double doors, which will almost certainly be locked even if we could climb up the chute which, by the way, we most certainly could not. Oh, and another thing, the door that Rod thought he could simply open with a quick leap and a tap..."

"Yes?" Lucy asked suspiciously.

"Check out the hinges." Angel gestured with her head.

"They are rusted solid. That door hasn't been opened in years, and certainly couldn't be made to open by anyone from this group."

"What makes you so knowledgeable?" Lucy asked in a troubled voice, dreading the thought of having to pass on Angel's 'tips' to the others.

"Just am that's all," she said.

"But this escape is particularly important to them. Were you just going to stand back and watch them fail?" Lucy asked, as she stared into the spaniel's face waiting for some show of remorse.

Angel didn't speak for a long moment, then in a very quiet and calm voice said, "No. I was in fact going to take full advantage of the situation."

"How's that?" Lucy queried.

"Look, I may as well confess now, as what was supposed to be my diversion has been scuppered," she said, scanning the yard for anyone listening in. "You've heard my crying and carrying on, haven't you?"

"Who hasn't?"

"Exactly," Angel said. "But that's all you've heard isn't it? You haven't for instance heard the work I've been doing in my cell, have you?"

Lucy shook her head, confused at what the small dog was saying.

"Because I'm the pathetic, harmless one, they thought nothing of leaving me in a cell with a window."

"What?" Lucy exclaimed.

"Shh," Angel snapped. "Keep your voice down."

"Sorry," Lucy whispered.

"It's high up, and at first I didn't know how to reach it, but after a while, I found that with a good run up, I could push off the side wall, and get up onto the ledge."

"But surely, it must be closed."

"Of course, it is," she said smiling. "Which is why I've been chewing off the window putty for the past two weeks. That's why I've been making such a din with the crying, and such. It's to cover my work."

"Haven't they noticed the bits of putty in your cell when they hose it out?" Lucy asked, incredulously.

"Why do you think I'm over here every day?" Angel asked, as she subtly touched Lucy with her front paw, and then pointed to a small drain tucked in the corner of the yard. It was well concealed from view by the deep shadows cast by the height of the wall.

Lucy glanced down at the drain without moving her head and saw to her astonishment that a sizeable wad of putty was jammed down into it. Lucy tried to stop the joy she felt inside from registering on her face.

"How much longer do you need?" she asked as her mind swam with this new possibility for freedom.

"I could probably force that glass out in a couple of days, but I was hoping for a good diversion to cover the noise."

A thought suddenly hit Lucy. "You were going to break out alone, weren't you?"

"Absolutely! It's safer that way," Angel replied, with surprising calm.

Lucy studied the other animal, then said, "You realise I'll now have to tell the others?"

"I guessed as much. Only do me one favour," Angel asked. "Let me finish up first. I don't want someone to tip the humans off before I'm ready."

"But weren't you going to give it a go today, if Rodney had been here and had gone through with his plan?" Lucy asked.

"Yes, but I really need two more days. Please give me that," she practically pleaded.

"You won't go off without us?" Lucy asked suspiciously.

"Not likely, now that you know," Angel replied.

Lucy shrugged.

"Just two days, then you can tell everyone," Angel assured her.

"Alright, you've got your two days."

"Thanks," she said with conviction. "Now if you don't mind, I feel a cry coming on."

Lucy nodded her head as the other dog began almost instantly to howl miserably with amazing conviction. Lucy couldn't help but grin as she walked back towards the others.

She most certainly wouldn't have felt anything like as pleased, if she'd had any idea of the chaos and drama that was about to unfold.

CHAPTER 8

Lucy slept surprisingly well and woke feeling, not contentment exactly, but some strange underlying sensation that things would turn out all right. She even ate a good quantity of her grey slop, without hardly gagging at all.

Her sense of well-being continued right up until mid-morning, when an elegantly dressed male and female biped appeared at her cell with Skull Face, and the squat lady. The four stood chattering for a moment, then Squat Lady opened the gate and stepped into the enclosure. She was using a friendly tone of encouragement in her voice, but after the smoke incident, Lucy didn't trust her one bit.

The woman placed a surprisingly heavy collar over Lucy's head, causing her to have sudden flashes of memories. She thought of her Man and of their wonderful walks. She could almost smell the scent of the emerald-green grass, but the memories only lasted until Squat Lady attached a lead to the collar, then pulled her roughly out into the passageway.

Lucy saw that all the inmates seemed to be gathered at the front of their cells as she was led by. A few gave her a nod of encouragement, but most simply looked sadly back at her.

They passed by Angel's cell and Lucy was surprised to find that she too was at her gate, trying to force a smile for Lucy's sake. They arrived at the door at the far end of the passageway, and as Skull Face reached for the handle, the door flew open, and Fat Man almost ran into him.

"Oh, there you are," he said breathlessly. "I thought you might have left."

"Well, clearly we haven't, have we?" said Skull Face.

"Yes... I see that," Fat Man stammered on. "I just checked with the coast and apparently there's a gale blowing in the channel. All ferry crossings have been cancelled."

The other bipeds looked distraught at his words, though of course Lucy had no idea why.

"How long did they think the storm will go on for?" Squat Lady asked, while setting fire to a white tube in her mouth.

"Couple of days apparently," he replied.

"What about the tunnel?" She asked, as she blew out a plume of smoke.

"Totally booked for today. Want me to see about tomorrow?"

"You do that," she croaked.

"Blast it!" the elegant man swore. "Well, let's put the dog back."

Much to Lucy's surprise, Fat Man reached down and roughly removed the collar. "I'll put this back in the safe." He turned and headed into the main building.

Lucy, misunderstanding what was expected of her, started to follow. Squat Lady suddenly grabbed her by the neck, and literally threw her back into the passageway. She landed hard but froze in place so as not to upset the human any further. Squat Lady moved towards her with a menacing expression on her squishy face. Lucy got shakily to her feet and backed away from the woman. She was not particularly good at walking backwards and kept stumbling. Finally, she realised that she had reached her own enclosure and practically dived into her cell. The woman appeared at the gate, and with a truly nasty sneer, slammed it shut. She glared at Lucy for a long moment, then strode off.

Lucy couldn't seem to stop trembling. Even after Squat Lady left, she just couldn't relax. Finally, with the help of some deep breathing (recommended by the Afghan), she began to calm down. By the time Fat Man appeared to release them for the yard, she felt almost canine again. She was surprised at the warmth of the greeting she received.

"That was close," The Doberman said.

"What was?" Lucy asked.

The second Doberman who, to date, had never said a word, stepped up to her, and in a voice laced with a mild Welsh accent, said, "Young lady, do you not know how close you came to being taken away this morning?"

"No," she replied with surprise. "You don't mean...?"

75

"Yes, I do. That couple was here to escort you out of the country, and just possibly out of your life too."

Lucy sat back heavily on her haunches. She suddenly felt dizzy.

"Now there, young lady," said the Welsh Doberman. "They didn't take you away, did they? We will simply have to find a way to ensure that they don't, that's all."

Lucy pondered for a second, then said hopefully, "I have a feeling that Angel might just have something up her collar."

"Looks to me as if she's about to end up in a very sticky situation," the Rottweiler exclaimed, gesturing to Angel's corner.

The rain was pouring down in a steady and unrelenting stream. As Lucy and the others looked on, they saw that the water wasn't draining on Angel's side of the yard.

"The putty!" Lucy exclaimed. "It's blocked the drain."

Sure enough, Angel was frantically trying to dig out the mound of putty but with little success. They couldn't run over to help, as the Boxer would be curious as to their concern. Lucy and the Rottweiler casually strolled across the yard, and through the rising waters. It was over an inch high at Angel's end.

As soon as they reached the corner, they could see that there was nothing to be done. Angel had jammed the grey material very tightly down into the narrow drain, and her attempts to dislodge it may have had the opposite effect than intended. The drain was completely blocked.

They looked into Angel's face and were utterly surprised at the calm they read in her eyes. The water was now above their paws, and it was only a matter of time before someone noticed. Lucy glanced into the yard to check the whereabouts of the Boxer but couldn't spot him anywhere.

Angel got to her feet slowly and said, "I don't know about you, but I can't think of a good reason why we shouldn't make a break for it today."

"You may have a point," Lucy replied with feigned calm.

The Rottweiler nodded his agreement, then in an almost military voice said. "I'll prepare the others. Can you two finish off the window?"

"We'll manage," Angel replied.

Angel and Lucy moved over to the passageway door and confirmed that it was ajar. They then slipped inside, and eased the door shut behind them. Once out of the rain, and with all the other animals being in the yard, the passageway was strangely silent. The two dogs moved past the empty enclosures, making as little sound as was possible on the hard flooring. They were highly relieved to not encounter the Fat Man hosing down the cells. They didn't know where he was, and quite frankly didn't care so long as he wasn't near them.

They reached the enclosure before Angel's, and with a great surge of relief stepped passed it, and into Angel's cell.

They both froze in their tracks as they instantly spotted Fat Man, as he stood on his toes examining the loosened glass in the window frame. At his feet was Champ, contentedly chewing a slab of meat.

The man and the dog sensed the other two and swung their heads around. Lucy just had time to notice how similar the two heads looked as they glared across the cell at her before Angel shouted, "out!"

Lucy didn't have to be told twice. As she spun out of the cell, Angel turned the other way and with a hard flick of her muzzle managed to swing the gate closed. As the handle was on the outside, she had in fact managed to shut Fat Man and the Boxer in her own cell.

The two dogs wasted no time in self-congratulation and charged back down the passage and into the yard only to run smack into a veritable sea of dogs. They were being led by the Doberman and the Rottweiler toward the planned escape route.

"Sorry," Angel yelled to be heard over the rain. "Spot of bother back there. Escape's off!"

There was a distinct murmur of disappointment from the crowd.

"What do you mean, off?" the lead Doberman asked.

"I mean that our friend, Champ, has done it again!" Lucy replied, while fighting to hold back tears of pure anger.

"And uh... we may have also upset the Fat Man," Angel added casually.

"Oh great," said the Rottweiler. "Now we're all in for it. If only there was some other way out,"

"Well, unless you believe in miracles," Angel said forcibly. "I suggest we all... what is that god awful noise?"

Sure enough, the air was filled with a terrible squealing sound that was piercing even over the din of the downpour.

They all looked around but couldn't locate the source.

"Anyway, as I was saying we'd better just," Angel continued, "set our minds to the fact..."

"When the blazes did you stop crying," asked a voice from the crowd.

The masses parted to reveal a very wet and thus, seemingly even smaller, Rodney. "I hate to break up your little prayer meeting, but I've been pushing at that bloomin' door for hours and now that it's open, I think the least you could all do is have the courtesy of using it to escape."

Because of the rising water in the yard, only the top half of the Yorkie was visible above it. There was a moment of stunned silence from everyone, then one by one they began to move towards the door, slowly at first, then progressing to a mad dash.

Lucy, Angel, Rodney, and the three males were suddenly alone in the yard. They all looked to Angel with expressions of contempt.

"So much for the rusted hinge theory," the Rottweiler said sarcastically.

"Well excuse me!" Angel retorted, "I only thought that..."

"May I suggest," Rodney said interrupting. "that you continue this fascinating little discussion once we're on the other side of these walls?"

Angel and the Rottweiler gave each other a brief look, then both began to laugh.

"Come on then, let's check out the city, shall we?" the lead Doberman said, excitedly.

"On the double, if you don't mind," the Rottweiler said as they could now quite clearly hear the yelling and barking of Fat Man and Champ coming from inside what, only moments before, was their prison.

"Right!" said Rodney. "Follow me!"

With that, the six dogs marched across the sodden yard, out the partially open door and into the unknown city, and what they hoped, was freedom.

CHAPTER 9

Lucy's first thought as she climbed the short flight of stone steps and walked out onto the cracked and filthy pavement, was that they were still inside the prison. They seemed to be surrounded by tall, scarred, brick walls. It was dark, gloomy and smelled of age and disuse. She was feeling an anxious gnawing in her stomach when Rodney nudged her with his tiny, sodden head.

"So, what do you think of the big city, so far?" he asked in a serious voice.

Lucy glanced down at him with a look of great concern on her face.

"Don't worry, Goldie," he said, suddenly grinning. "It's not all like this."

"He's not wrong," added the Rottweiler. "Some of it's even worse!"

The others all laughed at the expression of horror that crossed Lucy's face.

"They're just having you on," Angel said, as she glared with reproach at the others. "It's not that bad a place really. We're currently in what's called The Docklands. It's a bit smelly and run down, I'll grant you, but some parts have been done up and are actually quite lovely."

"How do you always seem to know so much about everything?" Lucy asked.

"I think it has something to do with the size of my ears in comparison to the rest of me. I just hear more, that's all."

The others all laughed until Rodney, in a serious tone, pointed out that perhaps it would be advantageous to put some distance between themselves and their recent place of incarceration. They all nodded their agreement and decided to make Rodney their provisional leader. Angel was clearly far more book smart than the terrier, but Rodney had very recently, not only escaped from his captors, but had also, single-handedly made his way across the city and freed the entire canine population of the prison. He had certainly earned the leadership role.

Rodney suggested that their priority was to get out of the Docklands then, when safe, decide on a more formal plan of action.

The other inmates had formed into their own groups and were nowhere in sight. Lucy imagined they were probably all still running, and quite possibly were even out of the city by now. She had little idea of the actual size of London and thought that around just a few corners, there would be the rolling hills and sheltering woods of 'her' countryside.

She was soon to learn otherwise.

Rodney arranged the six in single file under the belief that they would be less conspicuous that way. They proceeded to walk along one brick wall, then stopped at the first corner. Rodney stepped out, and then almost instantly jumped back.

"Blast it!" he whispered.

The others all carefully edged up to the corner and peered around it. Skull Face and Squat Lady were roughly manhandling a pair of dogs back into what was apparently the front entrance to the prison. Fat Man and the Boxer were standing by the door, smiling as the escapees were forced back inside.

"They're simply going to restock the place and carry on as before," the lead Doberman said, sadly.

"And probably pup-nap more animals to replace those they can't recapture," the Rottweiler said.

"They've got to be stopped," Rodney hissed, through clenched teeth.

"Maybe," Angel interjected. "But not now and not by us. We just got out, and speaking for myself, I don't wish to go back in just yet."

The others all murmured their agreement. Even Rodney begrudgingly had to concur.

"Oh no!" Lucy exclaimed, "Look!"

She gestured across the street from their concealed corner to a run-down entryway of what once had been the entrance to a factory office building. In the doorway, sheltered from the rain and totally preoccupied with her reflection in a piece of glass, was her cell neighbour, the Afghan.

"Brilliant!" Angel snapped, sarcastically. "There stands probably the vainest, and clearly most stupid animal I have ever met!"

"Psst," Rodney hissed at the Afghan. It was pointless as the rain was drowning out most sounds.

Lucy glanced over at the prison entrance and watched in horror as Skull Face and Squat Woman stepped back outside and began to scan the street for more escapees. The Afghan was until then, out of their view because of her position in the recessed entry, but as they all looked on in astonishment, the animal began backing into the street to afford herself a better reflection from a larger piece of glass.

"Stay here!" Rodney snapped. He suddenly broke into a fast sprint heading back along the wall and away from the group.

"Now what is he...?" Angel began.

"Hold on a sec," the Rottweiler said, grinning broadly.

They all stood rigid, and waited as the humans continued to search, and the Afghan neared her backside closer and closer into their line of sight. Suddenly a loud yapping could be heard from the other end of the street. The two bipeds stopped and turned the other way. Even through the torrential rain, they could still make out the tiny shape of Rodney, as he hollered furiously at them.

Skull Face and Squat Lady broke into a run of sorts, and headed towards the drenched Yorkie. Rodney waited just long enough to make sure that the bait was fully taken, then dashed around the far corner and out of sight.

"Now! Quick!" the Doberman barked.

The three males dashed across the street and to the total surprise of the Afghan, surrounded her on all sides, and marched her double time back across the street. They regained their corner just as Rodney reached them breathless, but clearly exhilarated.

"I've left a good distance between us," he panted. "but I think we should get a move on anyway."

There was no need for a vote on that and the group, now numbering seven, moved off as their newest member bemoaned her now drenched coat and soaking-wet paws. She was clueless as to just how close she'd come to being recaptured.

Rodney led them along some dark and very oppressive alleyways and back streets until they came upon a most peculiar sight. They rounded a corner and entered a square. There were no gardens as would have been normal. Instead, in the centre of the square was a huge black, metal... actually, Lucy wasn't sure what it was. She turned to Angel who veritably radiated importance as the others all turned to her for information.

"That is an anchor," Angel began. "Actually, it is only a sculpture of an anchor, as it's clearly too large to have ever been used. This monument was dedicated in..."

"Used for what?" Lucy asked innocently.

"... was dedicated in 1873 after the..."

"Used for what?" Lucy asked again, this time with determination.

Angel simply stared angrily back at her.

"I just wanted to know, that's all," Lucy said gently. "You said it was too large to have ever been used. I just wondered for what?"

Angel seemed to visibly melt before their eyes. A haunted look appeared on her face, and tears began to form and roll down her cheeks.

"Angel, what is it?" Lucy asked stepping over to her. "What did I say?"

"Nothing," Angel replied sadly. "Nothing at all." Angel turned her back on the group and moved over to a leaf-covered bench. She crawled under it and put her head down on her paws.

Lucy turned to Rodney with a look of concern and confusion on her face.

"I think perhaps that all these facts that she knows are just that. She's memorised a great deal of information but doesn't seem to really understand a lot of it." Rodney suggested.

"Is that bad?" Lucy asked.

"It's not exactly bad," Rodney replied. "Just a shame, that's all. If she went to the trouble of studying, it's a pity she didn't spend a couple of extra moments to comprehend it, as well as just memorizing it."

"I don't see why she would...," Lucy began.

"She didn't learn what she knows for the knowledge it would bring to her, but for the prestige and popularity she thought would go with having it," Rodney said. "She's too young yet to realise that, whereas the knowledge would have lasted forever, the friendships founded solely on her ability to impress, would be very transient and short lived."

"Yorkie!" Lucy exclaimed, "That was beautifully put."

"She's right Rod," said the lead Doberman.

The other Dobie and the Rottweiler nodded their heads in total agreement.

"Very beautiful indeed," said the Afghan almost dreamily. The others all turned to her in amazement to find that she was standing in front of a parked vehicle and was examining herself in the reflection of a metal disc in the centre of one of its circular rubber legs.

The others all burst out laughing. Lucy then realised that their joy was not being shared by Angel, who was still lying dejectedly under the bench. She walked over to the Spaniel and eased herself down next to her.

"You know, I think you're very clever. Just because you don't know everything, that doesn't mean we like you any less," Lucy explained.

"I'm useless. How could anyone ever like me?" she replied.

"Useless!" Lucy exclaimed. "How could you possibly think you were useless?"

"I've always been useless. When I was a pup I was always getting into trouble, and my human used to... well... I just know I am that's all."

"What did your human do to you?" Lucy asked, gently.

"Nothing," Angel replied with sad defiance.

"Angel, tell me?" Lucy asked softly, watching as the other dog's eyes began to brim with tears.

"He used to beat me!" she sniffled. "All the time. It didn't seem to matter if I was bad or not. He would just suddenly hit me, and yell, and sometimes even... even... sometimes he kicked me... hard. He hurt me Lucy. He hurt me very badly. Finally, one day he got really mad, and threw me outside. He never let me back in again. I had to run away to find food. Then humans in a big vehicle picked me up. They took me to a place that was filled with other dogs, who also didn't have homes. I was in that place for a long time until this family came by and before I knew it, they took me to their home. It was wonderful and they really seemed to love me. But then—well, they must have changed their mind because... well, look where I ended up."

Angel began to cry almost uncontrollably.

"It's okay, Angel, you're with friends now," Lucy said nuzzling her neck.

"If I believe that, you'll just shut me out one day just like my family did. I trusted them and thought they loved me, then I ended up here."

"Your humans didn't put you here," Lucy explained gently. "You were stolen from them. I bet that right now they're going mad trying to find you."

"You really think so?" Angel asked, between sniffles.

"I know so," Lucy said, giving the other dog a gentle lick behind the ears.

They were interrupted by the sound of Rodney, noisily clearing his throat as he stood patiently with the others.

"We'd better keep moving," he said as he watched Angel trying to compose herself.

"I feel so embarrassed," Angel sighed. "What must you think of me?"

"I think of you as a very sweet friend, who's had a rough time of it, but whose life is only going to get better from now on," Lucy replied. "In fact, look, the rain has even stopped."

"Thank you, Goldie," Angel said with a brave smile.

"Come on then, let's keep moving."

They re-joined the others and set off again past the huge anchor thing, and the dark and abandoned warehouses.

They soon heard a new sound. It was hard to place. Lucy sensed that it was a mix of sounds she knew yet couldn't put the pieces together. There was a dash of the noise her pond made when the wind whipped the water into a frenzy and tossed it against the banks. Then there was a hint of the run-off, as the rainwater rushed down their narrow street, and vanished out of sight around the corner at the base of their hill. Whatever this new sound was it was getting closer, and louder. She glanced to the others but saw little concern on their five excited faces. Five!?

"Where's the Afghan!?" Lucy cried.

They all stopped suddenly and looked about themselves, frantically searching for the other dog.

"Great!" exclaimed Rodney. "If she can't stay with us, we'll have..."

He didn't finish his sentence, as the missing hound suddenly reappeared round a corner, a good distance behind them. She was humming contentedly to herself as she stared up at the patches of blue sky that were starting to peak out from behind the dark rain clouds.

"Yo there Miss," the Rottweiler called. "Would you mind staying with the group!"

"Hmmm?" she replied distantly. "Have you ever noticed how blue the sky can be after a good rain? I often wondered how I'd look with blue eyes. What do you think?"

"I think you're a few puppies short of a litter," Rodney mumbled under his breath.

"Shh," Lucy said, trying to keep a straight face. "Why don't you walk with Angel and I for a bit so we can have a nice chat."

Lucy could feel the incredulous glare she was receiving from Angel, without even looking at her.

"Alright," the Afghan said. "That would be nice."

The hound walked right past the group, and clearly expected Lucy and Angel to catch up. They gave each other a look of mild dismay, then shrugged and trotted after her. They could hear her as she chatted away, oblivious to the fact that no one was in fact walking with her. "... at the Suffolk County fair, I took a second place," the Afghan rattled on. "which was quite unfair as the winning animal, I felt, was of questionable lineage at best. I mean really...

an English sheepdog with a French accent? I don't think so. Sometimes the humans seem quite unaware of what they're judging. I remember last winter at Crufts when I was up against a really, quite impressive Irish Wolf Hound, and as I..."

Lucy couldn't keep focused on the words of the other animal, as she droned on and on, telling of one beauty show after another. Lucy found that she could allow her thoughts to drift away, while the Afghan's words played on in the background.

She was back at the cottage lying in a patch of warm sun as it streamed in through the kitchen windows. Her Man was kneeling next to her, scratching her ears as they both watched Cook removing a fresh loaf from the oven. She could hear someone calling her name and wondered who it could be, then suddenly felt a sharp pain in her rump. She opened her eyes and spun round. Rodney was looking anxiously at her, and by his proximity, it was clear that he had just bitten her.

"Ouch!" Lucy exclaimed. "What was that for?"

"Step towards me very carefully," Rodney said, in a forced, calm tone.

"What are you...?"

"Now, Goldie! Don't ask any questions. Just do it," Rodney urged.

"Oh, very well," Lucy said as she stepped towards Rodney and the others. They all looked very relieved. "What's wrong with you?"

Suddenly, Lucy was deafened by a deep horn sound from almost directly behind her. She spun around and felt her knees go weak.

She was mere inches from where the pavement they had been on, simply vanished. Lucy looked over the edge and saw a sight like nothing she had ever seen before. There was water. More water than she'd ever thought possible. It was a huge band of water that seemed to be moving slowly, carrying on it, strange vehicles with humans seated contentedly in and on them. There were little ones dashing in all directions, honking horns at each other, and there were big ones like the ones directly under Lucy's nose at the base of the drop. It was massive and longer than many cottages put together. In its centre was a tall cylinder out of which trickled a thin plume of smoke. As Lucy watched, a sudden jet of steam appeared out of it, accompanied by the loud horn that had startled her before. She realised that had Rodney not alerted her, she would most certainly have fallen into the vehicle or into the moving waters of the ... the ...

"Never seen the Thames before, I take it?" Angel asked, with a mix of relief and exasperation.

"The what?" Lucy stammered.

"The Thames River. The big, wet thing you almost fell into," Angel stated with sarcasm.

"Oh that," Lucy replied, nodding her head knowingly.

"You've never heard of it have you?" Rodney asked in a gentle tone.

"Actually," Lucy said, while still nodding. "No!"

"Well, neither had I until yesterday," Rodney reassured her. "How about you?" he asked, turning to the others.

The three males shook their heads in unison, then looked to the Afghan who was again staring up at the sky.

"How about you, Miss?" Rodney asked, in a somewhat louder voice.

"Hmm?" She sighed back at him.

"Never mind," Rodney mumbled, as he turned back to face Lucy again.

"You must have been daydreaming or something. We turned a corner, and then lucky for you, Angel here noticed you'd strayed off."

Lucy looked to Angel and gave her a nod of thanks.

"Well, if that little scare is done with, can we keep going?" Rodney snapped.

"Sorry," Lucy offered shyly.

Rodney was clearly embarrassed by her apology. He stretched his tiny frame before forming the group back into a single line and marching them away from the river's edge towards Central London.

CHAPTER 10

They marched on for hours until they eventually came to a road that seemed to span the entire river. Angel recognised the oddity to be the Westminster Bridge. On the other side of the water was a spectacular structure larger than anything Lucy recalled ever having seen. The entire building appeared to be made of gold, and on one end was a very tall tower with huge circles cut into it. On these, there were long pointed arrow like things. As Lucy watched, one of the arrow things moved, and pointed straight upward. The air was suddenly filled with the sound of bells, followed by a louder, and far deeper-toned gong that rang four times.

"That's Big...?" Angel began. "Big... Bill. No! Bob, Burt... oh dash it! It's Big somebody or other."

"Well, I'll grant you," said the Rottweiler. "it is big!"

They all nodded in agreement as they looked across the Thames to Big Burt, or Bill, or whoever.

They moved on, and still in single file, crossed the bridge. They tried to ignore the pointing and laughing from the many humans who were either walking by, or sitting in their noisy, smelly vehicles.

Halfway across, Rodney stopped and looked back from where they had come. He seemed pleased with their progress. Even the Afghan had kept up.

During the long morning's march, Lucy had struck up a conversation with her and learned that her name was Prunella, or Pru, as she preferred to be called.

Pru was, it turned out, a city dog. She had been on a two-week holiday with her mistress when she had been dognapped. She was surprisingly bright if one could get her to talk about something other than herself. She was four years old, a show champion many times over, and a devoted fan of the 'telly', as she called it. That was that odd contraption that Lucy's Man also occasionally sat in front of and stared into. A large, thin box, which put out a bright light on which images danced and moved, almost like real life. Pru told of how she would sit with her Woman and stare at the thing, sometimes for days on end. She would become quite entranced with the screen and find herself unable to break away from it. Her Woman would, on occasion, do the same, only according to Pru, would also use the opportunity to consume amazing amounts of salty, little snack things. She would then take in a lot of liquid, then follow that with a lot of sweet foods.

During the weekdays, Pru would be left alone in the home she shared with her Woman. On the weekends however, she would be powdered and brushed, and the two of them would get into their vehicle and seek out the next beauty show. Pru had been doing this for so long that she was surprised when Lucy explained that she had not only never been to such a had never even heard of such a thing.

Lucy had, at one point, asked Pru what she would do when she was too old to compete in the shows, and was amazed at the look of bewilderment that appeared on her face. This eventuality had clearly never been considered. Pru became noticeably quiet after that, and at one point, Lucy was certain Pru was actually crying, but thought it best not to mention it.

Rodney got the group in motion again, but after a couple of steps, froze in place. At first the others weren't sure why, then they spotted what he had seen. Walking towards them were Fat Man and Champ. Rodney turned the other way and immediately spotted Skull Face and Squat Lady, also making their way along the bridge.

Rodney's reaction was astounding. He seemed to act by pure instinct and without any thought whatsoever.

"Follow me," he yelled, and then dashed into the line of vehicles that had thankfully slowed for a group of bipeds who were on foot further along the bridge.

The seven of them weaved between the smelly things, causing raised voices and angry horns. They crossed the centre of the road, and if the second Doberman hadn't stopped Pru from moving any further, a speeding van that tore by them in the opposite direction, would most certainly have struck her.

"Thank you," she said in a startled voice, and gave him a warm smile. Their eyes locked for a brief second, and something magical passed fleetingly between them.

Rodney gave the all-clear and they dashed the rest of the way across. They glanced back and saw that their pursuers were waiting for a gap in traffic so they too could cross. Rodney led them to a set of old stone steps that dropped down one side of the bridge. They followed him and found themselves on the north bank of the Thames. Lucy was startled by the majesty of the great river and would have liked to have stayed where she was, and truly take in the enormity of what she was seeing. Rodney however, had other ideas.

"Come on, don't slow down," he commanded.

They followed him under the stone arch of the bridge, then, much to everyone's surprise, ran them up another set of steps. As they neared the top, Rodney signalled for the others to stay behind him as he poked his nose around the corner of a wall. He gave them an all clear and they trotted up onto the top of the bridge again.

"Where are they?" Angel asked in amazement.

"Hopefully, if it worked, they should be...," he said confidently. "right about... there!"

He gestured for the others to look through the stone pillars that spanned the side of the bridge. Far below, and rushing away from them, were all four of their pursuers. Champ was sniffing urgently along the riverbank, trying to pick up a scent. Suddenly to their utter amazement, the Rottweiler let out a single, but very audible bark. The Boxer stopped and looked right up at them. He was about to alert the bipeds, when Fat Man viciously yanked at his lead, dragging him after them. The Rottweiler apologised profusely for his outburst, explaining that the excitement had simply got the better of him.

The seven then all broke into a joyous fit of laughter as they sauntered the rest of the way across the bridge.

Pru came into her own as they reached a busy street that simply had to be crossed. She seemed to understand the odd red light, green light contraption, and knew how one was to use it to gauge when it was safe to cross the road. At first, the other six were highly sceptical of Pru's knowledge in that area, until, using the odd light system, she crossed the street three times without incident. Finally, the others followed her, and much to their astonishment, made it across unscathed. Rodney was especially pleased, as he'd had to battle the same streets recently without any knowledge of the crossing 'trick'.

Food became the next issue as they'd only really toyed with their grey slop that morning. None of them had eaten properly. Rodney, in fact, hadn't eaten a thing since the previous day.

The three males told the others to hold on for a moment, and they would remedy this situation. As they huddled and strategized a plan to get some food, Lucy took a moment to relax and reflect on what they had just been through. Despite the harrowing adventure of having to crisscross the streets to avoid capture, Lucy had been able to use the time to learn the names of the other dogs.

The second Doberman was called Lester, and he was from the picturesque (so he said) village of Denham, not far outside London. He had been grabbed as he'd been strolling down the village high street. His Man knew he had good sense and maturity, so allowed him free reign to walk by himself. He loved to stop outside a wonderful Italian restaurant on the high street, where the owner's whippet was teaching him the Italian language. He'd in fact, just had a lesson and was heading back to his home when the dog-nappers had grabbed him.

The Rottweiler's name was Hans. He had never stepped foot in Germany, couldn't speak a word of the language, in fact he had no contact with anyone or thing Germany, yet his man called him Hans!

He came from a horse farm, just outside Cambridge, where he apparently had the task of keeping an eye, not only on the bipeds and their home, but also on the horses themselves. According to him, his life was as near perfect as could be. He loved his bipeds, and they him. Yes, the work was hard at times, especially in the winter months, but to watch and help turn stumbling foals into the cream of the horse racing circuits, made it all worthwhile. He told of times when his humans had let him travel with them to a race meet and watch as one of his charges nosed across the finish ahead of the pack, destined to become a champion.

The lead Doberman was Rex. Unlike the others, he did not regale the group with tales of a contented home life or of special humans left behind. Rex was in fact a guard dog who, at a young age, had been taken from his home, and trained to attack, restrain, and generally distrust any biped, other than those who knew the special command words. His life was spent going from one assignment to another. He usually had to guard dark and terrifying yards where he was made to stand vigil alone, through long lonely nights. He had demonstrated to the others his frightening ability to suddenly bare his teeth in a ferocious snarl, while producing a deep guttural growl that literally caused the hair on Lucy's back to stand on end.

When Lucy had asked him where he would go once they were free of the city, he had thought long and hard, then turned to her, and in a voice laden with sadness, told her that he truly had no idea. Seeing the look of concern on Lucy's face, he had given her a huge smile and told her that she wasn't to feel sad for him. She and the others all had to go back to the same predictable lives they'd had before. Lucy would have Cook and the cottage, Lester his Italian lessons, Hans his horses, Pru her beauty shows, Angel her constant rivalry with her Labrador housemate; even Rodney, who had surprised them all when he had owned up to having a very swishy, male human whose job it was to cut people's hair into all sorts of funny shapes. He had even confessed to being forced to sometimes wear bright ribbons on his head, as his man flitted around the heavily perfumed establishment where he worked. Rex explained that while they would all go back to the same lives they had left, Rex would not. He saw his freedom as a second chance. An opportunity to live his life in some, as yet uncertain pursuit that would allow him to finally trust others and permit him to roam free when and where he wished. No, he explained, he was the lucky one.

With the plan in place, Rex, Hans, and Lester strolled casually down the street and stopped outside a store where slab after slab of every type of meat imaginable, hung behind a large display window. There was meat from cows and sheep, deer and pig. Even some from rabbit, which Hans vowed to not even consider touching. The three paused at the entrance, and as the others watched in fascination, they put their scheme in motion. First they walked the group a few blocks away, where they would be safe.

The three then dashed back, and led by Rex, charged into the shop. There was yelling, and screaming, and the sound of items being thrown. There was even the sound of one human laughing in a deep baritone of a voice.

Finally, after what seemed like an eternity to the other dogs, the three reappeared with their booty. Rex, still leading the group, had an entire leg of lamb in his mouth. He was closely followed by Hans who had, what appeared to be, a standing rib roast clenched in his jaw. Lester, bringing up the rear, was indeed a sight. He had grabbed a string of delicious looking sausages and was clearly unaware that he was trailing a substantial length of links behind him. Hans told how, as they came barrelling out the shop door, a large and terribly upset man in a bloody apron, chased after them with a very sharp looking cleaver held high over his head. A pair of elderly human females began to scream at the sight of him. This din attracted the attention of a patrolling policeman who, thinking the elderly matrons to be in some dire peril, tackled the butcher to the ground. Through almost crippled by fits of adrenaline-spurned laughter, the three dogs all dashed round the nearest corner, and kept right on going as the trail of sausage links whipped on after them.

Rodney led them to a small, enclosed garden, which Angel explained was called a square. Here they concealed themselves under some heavy shrubbery and tucked into their fine feast.

As they ate, Pru told them of a huge park with a giant pond in its centre, that was less than a day's walk from where they were currently situated. Rodney felt he had a good idea where it was, and they all voted to try to find it the next morning. According to Pru, it was large enough for them to stay in, undetected, while they came up with a more formal plan.

After dinner, Angel tried to get each animal to in turn, tell a bedtime story, but everyone else seemed too sleepy. As she began to tell one of her own, she too was overtaken by sleep before her story was even finished. It was the first night spent in the open air for many of the group, but any anxiety they might have felt was soon dispelled by the realization that they were free from their captors and among friends.

CHAPTER 11

Lucy woke before the others when a small, but surprisingly inquisitive, grey squirrel began making angry noises in her direction. She opened one eye and saw that the little creature was only inches away from her nose as it glared at her, while chattering away in what was clearly a display of pique. Lucy lifted her head and cocked it to one side so the squirrel would know that she wasn't at all clear as to the reasons for the reprimand. Once her muzzle was off the ground, the squirrel darted under Lucy's chin and began digging in the soft dark earth. Within moments, it had uncovered a small cache of acorns, which it gathered in its cheeks. Once loaded, the squirrel gave Lucy one last, livid glance before dashing out of the shelter afforded by the bushes, to seek out a new and safer hiding place, far from sleeping dogs.

Lucy sat where she was for a moment, listening to the morning sounds of the big city. Some were familiar like the bird song and the slight breeze as it rustled the leaves overhead. For the most part however, the aural sensations were quite different. In the country, there were spaces in between sounds when, even with Lucy's keen ears, there was nothing to be heard. At those moments, when wind hesitated, birds sat silent, cows pondered and even the humans put down their tools, Lucy could recall the memory of the total peace that seemed to blanket the world.

Not so in the city, where there was a steady rumble that Lucy knew to be an omnipresent backdrop of sound. There could never be true peace as long as so many people lived so close together, doing noisy things. She thought how sad that must be to live amidst such a din. Upon hearing Pru stirring close to her, Lucy looked over and watched as the Afghan raised her head and listened.

"What a beautiful morning," Pru said joyously. "And listen. Isn't it peaceful?"

Lucy had to smile, knowing that she had just learnt a valuable lesson. How one dog perceives a situation is not necessarily how the whole kennel will see it.

"Yes," Lucy responded. "It is a fine day. You look stunning this morning, if I may say so."

"Do you think so?" Pru replied. "So often when one sleeps heavily, one can't do a thing with one's coat in the morning."

"Well, I think your coat looks smashing today, Pru," Lester said, as he slowly rose and stretched out his long lean body. "I really do."

Pru looked over at the Doberman and again their eyes met, this time staying locked for a longer period.

"Thank you, Lester," Pru mouthed, breathlessly.

Rodney rolled onto his side and looked over at the pair. "Will you two please give it a rest, until I've at least had breakfast?"

Everyone turned and smiled over at the terrier, who at first seemed serious then suddenly winked. They all laughed.

After some brief route planning, the seven eased their way out of the bushes and down a quiet back alley. Pru gave Rodney some general direction tips as to the park's location, but for all of them, it was going to depend very much on keen instinct, and even keener luck to find it.

By mid-morning, they still couldn't detect any sign of the park, so decided they should stop for food. They had all begun to feel stabbing pangs of hunger with each additional step. The bigger animals like Rex, and Hans, and even Lucy, seemed to be able to cope with the problem, but Rodney and Angel were clearly starting to drag.

Rex had suggested they check out the contents of rubbish bins as he'd heard that they could be a good source of leftovers. The others were shocked at the idea and not remotely eager to lower their standards and do something that desperate. They did however agree to keep such an option open, but only as a last resort.

Rodney then demonstrated a wonderful trick. He located a suitable residence, then made a monstrous din outside until the front door was opened. He then proceeded to swoon pathetically, finally allowing his tiny body to drop in a sad heap at the feet of the human. Their reaction, Rodney had explained, was always the same, and as the others watched from hidden locations, he seemed to be correct. A frantic, female biped scooped up the small terrier, and with great care, transported him into the house. Less than ten minutes later, Rodney came flying out an open window, sending freshly laundered net curtaining billowing out after him. In his mouth was a very tasty looking chicken leg. Rodney offered to share his prize with the others, but they all agreed that he had earned it, and besides, there was only enough for one anyway. With a display of truly superior tact, Rodney took his breakfast a decent distance from the others so as not to offend anyone as he ate.

The others were so impressed by Rodney's display that, after he consumed the chicken, they inundated him with questions as to the finer points of his method. The most important part, he stressed, was to ensure that a good exit was available before ever attempting the ruse. Look for an open window or door. If none exist, go to plan B. This is where you continue your dying-swan routine on the doorstep, but flatly refuse to go into the house. This can have two effects. The human will still take pity and bring the food out to you, or, and this should be noted, sometimes take offence at your distrust of their home, and shut the door in your face. Rodney then went on to explain plan C.

"If you can't see any exits," he began. "and you don't want to risk plan B, then this one usually does the trick. First you get their attention, as with the other plans, but then, and this is where you'll need to bone up on your acting skills, you act in pain when they try and pick you up. This will keep you on the ground and under your own power. Then, as you make to enter the house, you cringe and back away as if there is something truly terrifying inside. Now when I say cringe, I mean cringe! You've got to make the biped believe that you desperately want to go into their home but are simply too nervous to do so. They rarely take offence at that. If you're not getting your point across satisfactorily, go for the side-glance up at them and the mid-air paw wave. If you wish to try a light whine at this point, go ahead, but don't overdo it. You mustn't let it appear over rehearsed. If all goes well, they will leave the door open, even once you're inside in an attempt to make you feel comfortable."

The others listened to Rodney's lecture with awe.

"How do you know so much about this line of work?" Rex asked suspiciously.

Rodney stared back at the other dog with a slightly defensive look. "I get around," he replied. "That's all."

Rex nodded his head but was clearly not satisfied with the answer.

Angel stepped forward from the group and asked if Rodney thought she could give the scam a try?

"I don't see why not," he responded. "You've certainly got the looks for it."

Angel hung her head in mild embarrassment then gave Rodney a brief lick on the forehead. Rodney pretended to ignore this; however he couldn't hide the almost ridiculous grin that covered his muzzle.

"Come on then," he said in a commanding tone. "Let's find you a good house to try it out on."

The group walked along the street and saw what most of them considered being perfect sites for the trick, but Rodney simply shook his head and found something wrong with each one. Front windows shuttered, too big a drop from the windows, house not well kept, even one where the brass letter slot and door handle were tarnished. He explained that though seemingly minor, such traits showed a home without pride and, therefore, a human that was probably lacking in a true devotion to animals.

Finally, after a good half hour, he led the group down a narrow cobblestone lane with a dead-end, a mere hundred yards further on. On each side were adorable, terraced homes, all with bay windows and window boxes, exploding with colourful displays of flowers.

Angel explained that these were called mews cottages, and that although they looked quaint and exceedingly comfortable, they used to be the homes for the carriage horses. The upstairs quarters were for the drivers and grooms. The luxurious residences used to be little more than stables annexed to the very much larger, and far grander, homes at the front.

Rodney chose one particular house halfway down the mews. It was painted a cheerful yellow with immaculate white wood trim. The bay windows were open, faced onto the mews, and only had a drop of a mere few paws or so to the cobblestones.

"This'll do nicely!" he exclaimed. "You know what to do? If you're not ready, I could go over it again or even give another demonstration. I don't want to rush you. I..."

"Rodney, stop," Lucy chided gently. "Let the poor girl speak."

"It's okay Rodney," Angel said grinning. "I'll be perfectly fine."

Rodney looked uncertain.

"I promise," she added softly, and with that, stepped toward the front door.

The others all scattered to various hiding places to watch her performance. It was spectacular. She could easily have turned professional had she wished.

She began with the merest whimper accented with an occasional yelp of discomfort. She progressed effortlessly into an outstanding act of howling, while still maintaining an overall sense of hurt and anguish. The others were most impressed by the oration.

Before long, the door opened, and an elderly woman poked her head outside. She looked to the left then to the right before she realised that the pitiful sounds were coming from under her very nose. She grabbed her heavily blue-rinsed hair in shock, then immediately reached down and stroked Angel's back. Angel let out a slight moan and looked up into the old woman's face with wide, wet eyes that clearly captivated the poor, unsuspecting human. The biped, without warning, suddenly scooped the poor dog into her frail arms and vanished into the house, shutting the door behind her.

Rodney looked over to the others with an expression of great pride as a teacher would for an excellent student. He was still grinning as he heard the distant sound of windows being closed behind him.

He spun around and saw that the woman had already closed one half of the bay window and was reaching for the other.

"We don't want you sitting in a draft now do we, you poor little thing," she said as she shut, and latched the other window.

Rodney ran to the house and verified what he already dreaded to be the case. There was no way for Angel to get out!

He turned and faced the others, who had moved from their places of concealment, and were now looking to him with anxious expressions.

"Anything like this ever happened before?" Rex asked, in a concerned yet military tone.

"To be honest, no. It's always been a straightforward get in and get out proposition."

"Well, she's certainly in," Pru said.

Rodney studied each face in the group, knowing that they needed his leadership more than ever at a time like this. "Ladies if you'll excuse us for a second," he said looking toward Lucy and Pru. "The boys and I need a moment to come up with a plan."

Lucy looked to Pru with utter disbelief at the terrier's inference that planning was the male's domain. She was about to speak up when Pru caught her eye and gestured her over to the side.

"Don't even think about it. They're as stubborn as humans," Pru warned her. "Let them have their little boy talk. It makes them feel superior."

"Superior to what?" Lucy snapped.

"Don't take it so personally. It's nothing against you or me. Males simply believe they're better, that's all."

Pru could tell by the look of total astonishment on Lucy's face that all this was new to her.

"Trust me Goldie, this is how it is in the real world and it's far easier to let them believe that they are right."

"Not for me it isn't!" Lucy walked defiantly across the mews and up to the brightly painted door. Only Pru was watching her as the others were in deep conversation. Pru wanted to say something to stop her but gauged that Lucy was clearly upset, and therefore best left to do what she felt needed to be done.

Lucy reached the door and began scratching it roughly with her front paws. She saw that she was gouging the paintwork with her nails, and though knowing that such vandalism was normally a mindless, and abhorrent act, she continued anyway, such was her anger and determination.

After a few moments, and a good deal of scratched paint, the door opened. The kindly woman spotted Lucy, and again raised her hands to her blue hair.

"Oh my! Will you look at this! Another one! Well, I never. And I suppose you're also a hungry puppy? Well, I'm just going to…"

Lucy did not let her finish. She was not in the mood for human cuddle talk. She did something then she had never done before, yet considering the situation, felt no remorse, only a great fury that was still churning in the pit of her stomach. She growled. Not only that, but she also barked! Not a single or a double bark, but repeatedly in a rough and completely uncultured manner!

The effect was highly rewarding. The colour drained from the woman's face causing her skin to turn a shade closer to that of her hair. She backed away from Lucy, leaving the door wide open. Without a moment's hesitation, Lucy stepped into the hallway and immediately spotted Angel. The Spaniel was lounging on a bed of fluffed up pillows while nibbling on a plate of chopped meat right next to her.

"Lucy!" she said in a calm almost sleepy voice, "Come in, come in. Have some lunch. It's quite tasty."

"Come on Angel, we're leaving!"

"No, I don't think so; this is simply perfect for me. It's cosy; it's warm and old blue top over there can't seem to do enough for me."

Lucy walked over to the Spaniel, then without warning, grabbed hold of the pillows in her teeth and pulled them forcibly out from under the other dog. Angel and the plate of meat went flying.

"What was that for?" Angel asked as she righted herself on the floor.

"That was for being a spoiled and selfish little... little... mongrel! Now come with me immediately, or I'll really get cross!"

"I'm not a mongrel!" Angel whined, as she stumbled to the door. "I'm not! I'm a pure bred. I am! Really I am!"

Lucy followed the subdued little creature out the door, then felt a strong pang of guilt, and turned back to the house. The blue-haired woman was still trembling as she leant her fragile frame against the wall, halfway along the hallway.

Lucy walked over to her, and with great courtesy and gentleness, took her frail hand in her mouth and led her to the sitting room and a large, overstuffed, flowery chair.

The woman sat down as instructed but still looked at Lucy with fear and distrust. Lucy did not want to leave her with a bad memory of dogs. She placed her front paws on the arms of the chair and raised herself up, putting her golden head only inches from the woman's face.

The woman was scared, that was clear. There was only one thing for it. Lucy leant over and licked her face three times with a slow and gentle stroke. That always worked. Some smaller breeds believed that quantity was the ticket, and usually only succeeded in half drowning their victims in saliva. No - three gentle passes was the way Lucy had been taught, and by the woman's reaction, it was obviously exactly the right approach.

The woman instantly began to get colour back into her face and even reformed her wrinkled features into a smile. She reached out and, though still nervous, patted Lucy tenderly on the head. Lucy gave her hand a lick of thanks (standard protocol), then dropped to the floor and calmly walked out of the mews cottage, trying to ignore the powder from the woman's face which still clung to her tongue.

She strode over to the group of males, who were still standing around trying to come up with a plan. Lucy nudged Angel in between the plotting dogs, then sat herself defiantly onto her haunches.

"So, you boys come up with a plan yet?"

CHAPTER 12

Once they had left the mews behind, the problem of food again dominated their thinking. Except of course for Angel, who was not only far from being hungry after her gluttony at the hands of 'Old Blue Top', but also seemed unable to refrain from belching quietly to herself as they made their way down a quiet, side street. Lucy had given her a couple of severe glances, which had no effect except to make Angel cringe and keep as far from her as possible. Their salvation came in the form of a supermarket delivery van and its romantically inclined driver.

Rodney spotted it first. It was parked and the side panels were open revealing the tiers of bins in which individual customer orders were kept chilled. The driver of the vehicle was about half a block further down the street, chatting to a female biped as she stood on the top of some basement steps. Much to the dogs' delight, the female must have said something intriguing and funny, as the delivery driver laughed very boisterously, then, after a quick glance up and down the road, followed her down into the basement.

Rodney wasted no time and covered the distance to the van. He sprang up onto the side of the vehicle, then gingerly made his way between the tiers seeking out the best bins.

He began handing down packages of mince beef, sausages, cheese and in a delightful coup, snagged a two-kilo bag of dry dog food. They opened all the sealed packages except for the dry food, and wolfishly gobbled down the contents of each one. The dog food would be taken away for later.

Just as Rodney was about to devour a block of cheddar, there was a loud screeching of brakes inches away from them. As they turned to face the source of the din, they immediately spotted Skull Face as he jumped out of the passenger side of a grey van. The rear door flew open and Fat Man, followed by the Boxer, emerged. The dogs all gathered, cowering behind the delivery van. Nobody moved until the Squat Lady stepped out from behind the wheel, holding an evil looking gadget in her hand.

"A dart gun!" Angel shrieked, "She's got a dart gun!"

Lucy had no idea what this meant, only that it was obviously not a tool associated with happy goings on.

No one will ever know if Rodney was truly brilliant that day or just exceedingly lucky. He began to back away from the humans as he crouched in the delivery van. He managed to accidently (though he later insisted that it was completely intentional) tip a bin that was filled with wine bottles onto the road. As the bin struck the hard surface, bottles flew everywhere. Some broke, sending plumes of red liquid into the air, while others remained intact, rolling in every direction. The terrier started to tip all the crates off the van, then screamed for the others to make a dash for it.

Even as he was giving them these instructions, he himself was in mid-air, having leapt off the van just as Skull Face was about to reach for him.

The seven broke into a furious gallop, not even daring to look back as they ran. Finally, Lucy cast a brief glance behind, and had to stop as laugher overtook her.

Their pursuers had not, in fact, gotten very far. As Lucy and the others looked on, they giggled openly. Between the sea of Burgundy, and the rolling bottles, the humans were finding it near impossible to stay upright. Even Champ was having trouble, and he had four legs! The final coup de gras, certainly from a comic sense, was when Squat Lady got shakily to her feet, and aimed the dart gun towards the dogs, then lost her footing. As she fell backwards, the gun went off. The Boxer suddenly yelped in pain, then began to stumble around with a drowsy expression on his face, right up until he toppled over, fast asleep. It was at this moment that the delivery driver came dashing up the stairs with his shirt untucked, yelling hysterically at the wine-covered bipeds by his van.

The seven decided that although this was highly amusing, they had better keep moving and trotted off around the corner, hoping that their ex-captors were unlikely to disentangle themselves for quite some time.

They headed down a wide, tree-lined boulevard until, as they rounded a bend, they all stopped to stare at the amazing sight in front of them.

"The park!" Angel cried. "Look, the park!"

"A park," Pru responded. "Not *the* park. The one we're after is still a little way further."

"What's wrong with this one?" Hans asked excitedly. "I mean it's big, it's green, it's full of trees and bushes. Look there! I just saw a squirrel. What's wrong with this one?"

"It's not that big, and it has policemen in it all the time," Pru replied.

The others all felt that perhaps Pru was being just a little picky and was, for some reason, obligating them to seek out one specific park, when here was one that seemed to fit the bill perfectly.

"Trust me," she pleaded, "This is nothing! Where we're going is a real park. If I'm wrong, I'll get food for all of you for a week."

"How do you know this other park so well?" Rex queried, with mild suspicion.

"It's where my biped took me every day for my walk when she got home. Even if it were dark, she'd walk me as far as the lake then back to the flat."

The others all felt the sense of loss and homesickness that was emanating from the Afghan, and silently decided to let her at least show them 'her' park.

They carried on until they came upon the most incredible sight that most of them had ever seen. It was a truly magnificent, human building surrounded by tall, black and gold railings. Dotted around the perimeter were numerous immaculately dressed male bipeds, all in red and black uniforms.

Angel explained that they were looking at Buckingham Palace, and that it was the home of the Monarch. When asked to explain exactly what that meant, Angel hung her head and began to withdraw, as she had the previous day when confronted with her lack of knowledge.

"Hey," Lucy said, nudging her. "Just say I don't know. Nobody is going to think badly of you for that."

Angel raised her head and in a very weak voice, said, "I'm sorry. I don't know."

True to Lucy's words, the others did not seem to care one way or the other. In fact, they were so riveted at the sight of the grand structure beyond the railings, that they didn't react at all.

Though they weren't aware of it, they were only seeing a very small section of the palace, as they were in fact, looking at it side-on. As they moved further towards the front, the full splendour of the palace began to unfold before them.

"Oh, oh!" Rex shouted as he pointed his long muzzle off to the side.

The grey van was emerging from around a corner, driving slowly as its occupants stared out looking for them.

"Come on!" Rodney cried. "Follow me."

"No! You can't do that." Pru uttered in astonishment, as Rodney walked through the palace railings and onto the forecourt.

She watched as the others followed the Terrier's lead, and with a feeling of great trepidation, eased herself between the ornate fencing and followed them.

They could hear peals of laughter coming from the crowd of human onlookers, standing on the other side of the front gates of the palace. Lucy glanced over and saw a sea of wide-eyed, amazed expressions as she ran by. She also saw small, rectangular things being pointed at them by almost every biped. As they ran past the onlookers, she heard an odd, beeping coming from some of them and bright flashes from others.

It looked as though they were going to make it across the palace forecourt and through the railings on the other side when a line of uniformed humans appeared from within the building and cut off their line of escape.

The seven dogs came to an abrupt halt, as they looked for another route. They turned back the way they had come and saw that more uniformed humans had blocked off that route as well. They began to panic. It could not end now! Not because of a silly shortcut.

"Psst," a voice said, "You lot. Over here!"

They turned and faced the palace. There, under an elaborate portico, were two Corgis, frantically signalling to them.

"Through here, quickly," one of them commanded, in a fine well-bred voice.

The seven didn't give it a second thought, as the humans were closing in fast. They dashed towards the two sturdy little animals, and at their direction, followed them through a side door and into the palace itself.

"I'm William," said one of their benefactors, "and she's Mary."

Mary nodded back at the others as they ran. They charged through a small hall then into a far grander, marble-floored entrance. The highly polished floor caused them all to slip and slide as they tried to follow the corgis down another passageway. That one was covered in a deep red material and contained dozens of images of very serious looking bipeds, all hung one after the other along the walls.

Just before they reached the end of the hallway, the Corgis gestured for the others to slow down.

"We have to walk here," Mary stated.

"Rules of the house you know," William added.

They led the seven down a couple of steps and into an extremely attractive room, decorated in rich blues and floral prints. As they passed through the space, they saw a familiar looking female biped seated in a large, comfortable, wing chair drinking a cup of what Mary announced was tea. The woman looked over the top of the two circular glass things that she wore on the bridge of her nose, and though clearly surprised, smiled at the passing canine troop.

The two Corgis gave her a slight bow then proceeded on. The others all followed, except for Angel, who stood stock still staring at the woman.

"Angel," Rodney snapped." Yo! Angel, come on."

Angel turned and looked to the others with a dazed expression.

"But that's... that's..."

"Now Angel!" Rex commanded.

Angel turned back to the woman and dropped her head to the floor in a truly grand bow, then backed the entire way out of the room.

The Corgis led them out of the Queen's sitting room and into what was doubtless, the most beautiful garden any of them had ever imagined.

"Do you know who that was?" Angel asked in a whisper, as she nudged Lucy.

"No, and we haven't got time for your trivia just now Angel," Rex stated, flatly.

"But that was the Queen!" Angel said in an awed tone.

"What's a queen?" Lucy asked.

The entire troop came to an abrupt halt, as William and Mary turned and stared at Lucy in complete and utter astonishment. "Did I hear you correctly?" William asked, incredulously.

"What's a queen?" Mary also sounded shocked.

Even Rodney seemed amazed. "Lucy!"

"Sorry," she said, with a slight edge to her voice. "Alright, so tell me. What is a queen and what's all the fuss?"

"The Queen, or Her Majesty, is the sole ruler of Great Britain, the Commonwealth, and all her kingdoms and subjects around the world," William stated proudly.

"She's the crowned Monarch," Mary added, also with great pride.

"She looked a little familiar," Lucy said, trying to recall just where she'd seen the face.

"I would think so," William tried to keep the exasperation from his voice. "Her Royal Highness is . . ."

"I know," Lucy said excitedly. "It was on those funny, little, sticky things that my Man would put on paper bits, before giving them to Fergus at the gate."

"What!?" William exclaimed.

"I think she's referring to stamps," Angel volunteered. "I think Lucy's referring to the picture of the Queen on postage stamps."

"Ah," said William.

"I see," said Mary.

There was a slight pause, at which point both William and Mary turned to Angel and asked, "What's a postage stamp?"

"I hate to break up this delightful and highly entertaining conversation," Rodney said sarcastically, "but can we get a move on."

He gestured back to the Palace, and to the scores of uniformed humans that were flowing out of it.

"You may have a point," William offered. "Come on then, let's make for the wall."

Mary and William broke into a fast run, which surprised the others considering the Corgis exceptionally short legs.

They dashed through hedges, under thickets, over a stream, and finally, out of breath, came to a halt at the base of an enormous wall. It was so high that Lucy wasn't even certain where it ended.

"You're not expecting us to get over that, are you?" Rodney asked, nervously.

"Hardly, old boy," William responded. "Actually, I'm going to show you a little trick of ours, if you will permit my indulgence."

"Please," Rodney replied. "Be our guest."

"Good! You see that door just behind those bushes?"

They all looked and did see a very secure-looking metal doorway, set into the formidable wall.

"Yes," Rodney replied.

"Mary and I have been working on a little something that we've been dying to try out. What we hope will happen is that the guards, that's what those uniformed bipeds call themselves, will open the door for us, allowing you lot to make a dash for it while we keep their attention.

"Why would they do that?" Rex asked.

"Watch and see. Here they come," William whispered.

Sure enough, the guards were approaching the wall with long, purposeful strides.

"Stay hidden until we give the word," Mary's voice was full of almost childlike enthusiasm.

William and Mary edged along the wall, and made their way to a small, open drain located under a particularly thick bush. As the others looked on, William to their surprise, stuck his muzzle down the drain and began barking. Mary moved to the metal door and started whining and scratching at it in both a believable, and quite pitiful, way.

The seven were impressed. William was giving the impression that he had somehow become shut out of the palace gardens. His voice, directed into the drain, did indeed sound muffled and distant. Mary's antics at the door completed the ruse perfectly, giving the bipeds good reason to believe that her brother was somehow stuck on the other side of the wall.

"Oh, blimey!" one of the guards exclaimed. "One of Her Majesty's Corgis has got out! Quick, open the gate!"

Another guard stepped forward and located the appropriate key from a large ring. He inserted it into the metal door and opened it wide. The guards stepped out onto the pavement. William chose that moment to dash out from under the bush, and together with Mary, sprinted through the doorway, and dashed between the legs of the puzzled guards.

"Good luck!" William cried to the others, as he and Mary charged down the road, followed closely by the breathless humans.

Rodney led the group through the wall and in the opposite direction from the Corgis, who seemed to be doing an excellent job of keeping ahead of their pursuers. He kept the others running at a fast pace because, as he pointed out, the grey van was probably not that far behind.

They came to a large road that seemed to run into an even larger circular one. There were only a few red and green lights to control the vehicles, and for a moment, there was great concern as to how they could circumnavigate this obstacle. Pru rolled her eyes then suggested that they all relax and simply follow her.

She led them to a flight of steps that seemed to descend into a good-sized tunnel. Though slightly apprehensive, Pru insisted that she had travelled within these passages hundreds of times; and other than them smelling a bit rank, they were perfectly safe.

They followed the Afghan down the steps and proceeded along the lengthy tunnel, all the while, garnering amazed glances from passing humans.

As they neared the halfway mark and could clearly see the steps on the far end, they suddenly spotted two unmistakable shapes, descending into the same tunnel. Skull Face and Squat Lady. Both grinned menacingly as they approached the dogs. Lucy looked over her shoulder and was not in the least surprised to see Fat Man with a club at the ready, as he too descended the steps while eyeing the group.

"Quick! They haven't got us yet," Pru cried, and suddenly turned down an adjoining tunnel that the others hadn't even noticed.

They were instantly surrounded by hordes of bipeds, all oblivious to their presence, as they dashed every which way in a crazed, manic manner.

"We're in a tube station," Pru yelled, trying to be heard over the noisy crowd. "Keep going!"

They passed through the human obstacle course, with more than one abrasive tone being directed at them. They came to another set of steps that seemed to delight Pru enormously.

"You ready?" she asked, excitedly.

"For what?" Rodney snapped.

"For heaven," Pru cried over her shoulder, as she bounded up towards a square of light..

The others all followed, as her excitement began to infect their own senses. They reached the top of the steps expecting to see an extremely different world, but instead only saw a busy street filled with an astonishing quantity of very loud, and very smelly, vehicles. They could taste the odour of the street on their tongues and turned to Pru in anger for tricking them into believing that some form of utopia had been near to paw.

Pru ignored their fierce glances and signalled them to keep moving. They were about to refuse when they heard a commotion at the base of the steps. They saw Skull Face and the others break free of the tube station crowd and start up towards them.

They followed Pru, who after only a few yards, turned sharp left then waited for the others to catch up.

As they reached her side, they each in turn showed complete and utter astonishment at what they were seeing before them.

Only one, traffic free road separated them from the biggest park in London. All they could see were trees and grass for miles in almost every direction.

"It's beautiful!" Angel cried.

"It is that," Rex agreed.

"And it's all ours," Pru cheered. "Let's go get it!"

As they started across the street, they looked back and saw that their pursuers weren't even attempting to follow them into the park. It was simply too big a challenge to catch them in there.

"We'll get ya, you little beasts!" the Squat Lady yelled after them.

The seven kept right on running until their paws were solidly planted on the soft, sweet-smelling grass of Pru's favourite park.

"We should be able to stay hidden in here for weeks," Rodney stated confidently.

"That must be how they named it," Pru said, smugly.

"Named what?" Rodney asked, as he lowered his muzzle to a little bunch of wildflowers at his feet.

"The park! It is the perfect place to hide. That's why they named it...Hyde Park."

"Nice going Pru," Rex said, with sincerity. "Very nice going indeed."

CHAPTER 13

The park was as wondrous as Pru has promised. Even for a country animal like Lucy, who was used to almost limitless expanses of green, Hyde park had a great deal to offer. True, one could turn and face the looming structure of brick and stone that surrounded it, but there was certainly no need to do so.

As the seven moved along one of the seemingly endless selections of pathways, Lucy was astounded to observe just how beautifully maintained the place appeared to be. Off to the side, were little fenced-in enclosures that looked like Cook's vegetable garden, only far better tended. Each contained different varieties of plants and blooms that fascinated Lucy, not only because they were so different from what she was used to, but by the extent of the varieties themselves. As she looked from one type to another, then saw still more ahead of her, she began to realise just how narrow her own view of life had been prior to her leaving the cottage. She had become comfortably content believing that her surroundings at her home were all that existed. It never dawned on her that the world continued on far beyond her line of sight. That was an entirely new concept for her. Lucy began to realise, even in her limited way, that there was clearly so much more to life than she could possibly ever see. At least on that day. Maybe tomorrow she would see it all.

The thing that utterly amazed her once they were in the park, was the behaviour of the males. Prior to entering the green oasis, they had been responsible, even if somewhat pig-headed animals, whose general goal was to do little more than seek out shelter and food. Lucy considered those to be good, sensible challenges, and was therefore caught completely unaware by their startling actions once in the park.

Rodney was the first, and his downfall was a lone pigeon that was attempting to sun itself on a small patch of dense lawn, well off the pathway. One moment Lucy had been having a thoughtful conversation with him, and the next, he was charging at a near breakneck speed toward the poor bird. Added to that, was the fact that Rodney began barking. Not in an adult manner, but in a rapid-fire, almost maniacal way. He began to drool, to pant, to yell, and to chase his flying adversary every which way imaginable. Needless to say, he never came close to his prey, and only served to bring the group to the attention of any human within a two-mile radius.

The pigeon finally gave up any hope of a restful moment in the sun and flew off towards the city for some peace.

Rodney returned to Lucy's side, breathless, wet, and by that point, embarrassed by his slip in decorum. Lucy was about to ask him what had made him go from a serious and mature leader to a ranting, dribbling beast in a matter of seconds, when Rex suddenly yelled at the top of his lungs, "Squirrel!"

Well, that was it. The four males practically tripped over each other to pursue one tiny, grey creature, whose only great sin was to have descended from his tree to recover a dropped acorn. Lucy could hear, even from where she stood, the poor animal's yelp of surprise as the four crazed lunatics charged towards it.

The squirrel made it to the next tree and scaled its barky side in mere seconds, leaving the dogs barking like crazy animals at its base.

Unfortunately, this was just the beginning. The males chased every pigeon, every squirrel, and even other male dogs for most of the remainder of the day. At one point, Pru, Lucy, and Angel walked the other way, praying that no one would think them associated with the four idiots that were clearly suffering from some sort of lunacy.

The final straw came when they first saw the lake in the centre of the park. Lucy was just thinking how truly serene and picturesque it was, when her four disgraced friends came charging by her, yapping away like puppies, and proceeded to chase a family of geese into the water. As if that were not bad enough, they followed the poor waterfowl, and paddling as best they could with their non-aquatic bodies, tried to keep up with the geese.

When the males eventually wore themselves out to the point of exhaustion, they stumbled back to the peeved faces of the three females. Rodney shook his soaking coat over them all, sneezed, then asked in an almost childlike tone, "So what's to eat round here?"

Lucy looked at the sopping wet Yorkie then at the other three equally soaked and exhausted males. She had to smile. Her annoyance ebbed, and though realising that she could not allow herself to let go to the extent they had done, there was something strangely liberating about their actions. The four dogs looked young and alive, as they stood panting and dripping before her. Their eyes held a new sparkle that had not been there that morning. There was a distinct glow emanating from them that Lucy tried to accept as being the result of a day in the sun and fresh air; though deep down, she knew different. This was not simply a sheen on their coats. This aura was coming from inside. Their mad, carefree, cavorting had somehow released from these simple hounds, the spirits of their wild and unrestrained ancestors. Much to her amazement, Lucy felt a pang of jealousy. She wanted to experience the same total release of energy as they had done. She wanted, for just a moment, to relinquish all shackles of her heritage and breeding and behave like a wanton beast of prey. She didn't have a clue how this could be achieved. She just knew that she wanted it.

Somehow, Lester must have read her mind because he suddenly stepped forward and spoke gently into her ear.

"No one will think badly of you Goldie," he said in a peaceful, almost dreamlike voice. "Go on, give it a try."

Lucy stepped back in shock, realising that Lester had somehow picked up her thoughts. She tried to compose herself and ignore both him and her own inner urge. As she tried to fight down the intrusions that had seeped into her usually sensible and correct thinking, she spotted a flock of pigeons land less than twenty dog lengths from them.

Even though exhausted, Rodney and Rex looked about ready to charge this latest target when Lester stopped them, and calmly told them to just hold on. They'd had their fun. It was time for someone else to try it.

Pru and Angel looked around, wondering to whom Lester could be referring. Then, with the beginnings of a smile rising on her muzzle, Lucy moved away from the group and took a step towards the birds. She took another and felt no different inside at all. She looked back to Lester who simply gave her an encouraging nod while the others looked at her with puzzled expressions.

Lucy realised that if she was going to do it, she was simply going to have to let go. She took a deep breath, closed her eyes, then charged!

For the first few moments, she felt nothing special, but then something happened. Maybe it was the wind blowing her coat out behind her. Maybe it was the fresh air washing over her exposed tongue. Whatever it was, Lucy felt a rush of energy surge through her body. A sense of joy and euphoria cascaded over her every nerve and cell. She ran faster, and without any conscious willing, began to bark. Openly and with total abandon, Lucy barked like she had never barked before.

The pigeons could now see and hear her, as she lunged towards them. They began to lift off into the safety of their own air space, but this didn't faze Lucy in the least. She was no longer simply chasing after a couple of birds in a park. There was something older and more primeval swirling through her. She could almost sense the urgency and instinctual need to chase and consume that was rising within her muscle memories and reflexes that had been lying genetically dormant in her senses for thousands - maybe even millions of years. Surprisingly, these emotions did not evoke any real blood-lust in Lucy, probably because of the irrepressible docility of her breed. She simply felt more alive as she charged through the rising cloud of birds, than she'd ever felt in her life. Her body tingled. Her senses were ready to explode with delight. As a grand finale to her new sense of freedom, she gave up on the birds, and rolled over, and over, and over on the soft and slightly damp carpet of sweet-smelling grass.

She glanced over at the others and saw that the males were all beaming at her, fully understanding her experience. Pru and Angel, however, were looking over at her with expressions of utter distaste. Suddenly feeling self-conscious, Lucy felt that she'd somehow let down their side. So, what! Maybe for once she had, but she would savour this experience for the rest of her life; of that she was certain.

She gave them a joyous bark, which the boys immediately acknowledged and returned. Pru and Angel however, turned away, clearly embarrassed, and pretended to be in deep conversation.

"It's wonderful to be alive!" she suddenly cried out, much to the delight of the males, and even greater embarrassment of the females.

She smiled to herself knowing that on that day, she was definitely one up on life.

CHAPTER 14

Food. That was still the big issue. By early evening, they were all feeling the exhaustion that comes from an exceptionally long, and arduous, day. Most of all though, they felt hunger. They knew they'd eaten at some point in the day. They could even vaguely recall snippets of images involving exploding wine bottles and the dog food bag breaking open in the tube station, but that was about all. The point was, when were they going to eat next?

They located a very secluded and cosy spot at one end of the small lake. Just off a biped path, and within earshot of a modern glass structure in which humans had been dining all through the day; they stumbled upon a fenced-in area that encircled a picturesque pond with water cascading into it from a pool above. Behind this waterfall was a cave. Not a real cave mind you, it was more like a carved-out area for storage of some kind. Anyway, it was perfect for the seven of them. They could look out, but no one it seemed, could see in.

Once settle in their new lair, Rodney crept out so that he could scout local food prospects. As they waited for him to return, they began discussing what they would do next. One thing became very evident, and that was that they all wanted to go home. All except Rex, who of course didn't have one. The strange thing was that as he'd never had a proper home, the very concept of a cosy family life was utterly foreign to him.

It became a challenge to see who could think up the best examples of what home life meant, so they could get the point across to the Doberman.

Pru felt that home was where almost constant grooming took place. It was where one was brushed, teased, powdered, clipped and bathed on an almost continual basis.

"If you were not in the process of making yourself look beautiful, you were planning how next to tackle the challenge," she explained.

Hans felt that home was the feeling of warmth when he was let in after a hard day with the horses and was allowed to stretch out among the family in front of a roaring fire.

Angel felt that home was the constant struggle of wills between herself and the family's other dog, the black lab. After some prompting from her, she did admit that there was a certain feeling of security to her life, especially when she took her place at the foot of her mistress's bed and moulded herself to the warm contours of the young human as she slept beneath the covers.

Lucy started to relay that, to her, home was where she was allowed into her Man's room upstairs. There she would lay at his feet as he worked, feeling his gentle hand stoke her coat. Lucy stopped talking when she noticed Rex turn away and bow his head. She stepped over to him and tried to speak so as to offer some kind words, but he simply pushed her aside and ran out into the fresh air, now slightly chilled since the sun's departure sometime earlier. Lucy followed, and as she approached him, marvelled at the transformation the world undertook as soon as the golden orb descended from view each day. Colours that had been so vibrant and varied, now seemed somehow muted and of a singular hue. Where, during the day, Lucy could clearly see and define each and every blade of grass beneath her feet, they now looked more like part of a dark blanket that stretched out before her.

Rex was standing alone under the grey silhouette of a large chestnut tree, staring up at a single cloud as it passed across the night sky. Lucy moved to his side and gave his neck a gentle nuzzle of greeting.

"I'm sorry Goldie. I don't know what came over me. Those stories you were telling, they hurt me somehow. I felt an ache in my chest and...," he shook his head as if trying to shake of a bug. "Never mind. I shouldn't complain. I've not had such a bad life really. I've been fed well and given shelter and... and..."

"Rex, it's me. Let it out. Maybe I can help."

"There's nothing to let out," he said, while consciously trying to bury his emotions. "I just got a little sad for a moment back there, but I'm fine now. Honest."

"You're sure?" she asked.

"Absolutely," he replied.

"Then you won't mind my finishing the story."

Rex simply stared back at her in silence. Lucy couldn't clearly make out his expression in the darkness, but she knew she had to get through to him while his emotions were near the surface. She had no idea what made her feel a sudden need to help this dog that she'd only known for a matter of days. She only knew that it was essential for her to try.

"Late at night," Lucy continued. "when my people were in bed, I'd walk slowly through the house and make certain that all was well. I would check that the doors were securely shut; that the embers in the fireplace were dying out safely within the hearth, and that Cook and my Man were sleeping soundly in their beds. There's a feeling at such moments, when they are entirely in your care, of pride at the responsibility with which you've been entrusted. Maybe it's similar to how you feel when you stand guard on one of your assignments."

Lucy's timing was obviously spot on. Rex looked up into her eyes, and she could clearly see the tears as they welled up and held the reflection of the starlight from overhead.

"Oh Goldie, you have no idea what my life has been like. I've never felt comfortable anywhere. I don't feel pride at guarding an empty factory building or a fenced-in yard, filled with junk. There's no emotion there. I was taught to attack people, not love them. I always assumed that was normal, and that all dogs were taught the same, until I met you lot. Now I don't know what to think. I thought I was perfectly content to live alone and to do my job every day and simply... simply..."

"Exist?" Lucy offered.

"Yes, that's it! Exist. But now I feel this aching inside. I want to know what it's like to have a human brush me or hold me out of affection rather than just leading me by my collar to the next assignment." Rex sighed. "Goldie?"

"Yes Rex?"

"What's it really like? You know...being stroked and petted?"

She looked into his inquisitive face and couldn't help but smile. "It's wonderful Rex. It truly is."

"I don't know why, but I thought it must be," Rex whispered, dreamily.

"I'll tell you one thing that's for certain," Lucy said, with conviction.

"What's that?"

"You will know what it's like before long. I promise you."

"How?" he asked. "How's that ever going to happen to me?

"I just feel it, that's all. I think that any dog that's ready to love, as you are now, will find a way to make it happen."

"Do you really believe that?"

"Dog's honour!"

Rex, now deep in thought, looked up at the night sky as Lucy smiled to herself.

"Yo!" Rodney shouted from the direction of the cave. "They told me you were out here. So, tell me, just how hungry are you?"

Lucy and Rex glanced apprehensively at each other as Rodney trotted over to them.

"Why?" Lucy asked suspiciously.

"Well, it's like this," he began timidly. "I've located food, lots of it, but there's a slight drawback."

"Such as?" Rex inquired, as he looked down upon their fidgety leader.

"Such as," he swallowed deeply. "It's in the rubbish bins."

"No! I won't even listen." Pru, who had come out to join them, turned away and pretended to sniff at the base of the tree.

"It's not like it sounds. It's the bins out back of that restaurant place by the lake. For some reason, they dump masses of perfectly good food before going home. I had a good sniff, and it wasn't half bad."

"But Rodney!" Lucy said turning to face him. "Bins?"

"Look, I know it's not proper and all that, but I think we've all got to bend a little. Hopefully, this little ordeal will be over soon, but in the meantime, I think we'd better settle for just about any food and shelter we find."

"He has a point, Goldie," Rex added.

She looked at the two shadowy silhouettes, imagining the hopeful expressions that were hidden from her in the darkness.

"I suppose you're right," she said with resignation. "Let's go and have a look at what you've found."

"I think you'll be pleased," Rodney's voice was filled with pride.

"We'll see," Lucy said, pretending to be coldly critical of the entire event. In fact, even talking about food had made her even more hungry.

As it turned out, the meal wasn't bad at all. The seven crept up to the deserted restaurant, then made their way to the back where the bins were kept, well out of sight from the occasional passing human.

The one initial problem was that the upper part of the bins were filled with quite an astonishing amount of paper bits and cardboard, making scavenging for edibles, overly complicated.

Rex had the solution. He placed his front paws onto the metal lip of one of them, then backed up. The bin tipped, then fell over, sending its contents cascading onto the hard ground. Rodney then demonstrated his ability to wade right into the pile and separate out the worthwhile parts with astonishing grace and agility. He could locate a sausage, dig it out, and then toss it onto the nearby grass without hardly even bruising it.

After Rex had tipped a few more bins, and Rodney had scouted out and retrieved the good bits, the seven retired to the grass for dinner.

The meal consisted of numerous whole or partially eaten sausages. Two intact meat pies, four rashers of bacon, two chicken legs, one entire chicken breast, and an unlimited supply of bread rolls. Alright it wasn't exactly home cooking, but it certainly beat the alternative of a long, hungry night.

Satisfied, and suddenly very sleepy, the seven strolled back towards their cave, marvelling at their own shadows that were cast by the tall lamps that bordered the path.

As they reached the waterfall, Angel stepped behind it and out of sight. Just as Pru was about to follow her, there was a loud hiss, followed by a volley of furious 'fowl' language. Angel came out yelping as she ran through the water and into the pond.

"Back!" Rex commanded authoritatively. "Get back all of you."

He waited until they were all a safe distance from the cave, then stormed in. Again, there was a moment's silence before another hiss, and even greater torrent of livid, avian expletives. Then another noise filled the air. It was deep and guttural. A sound that made the hair on Lucy's back rise in fear. She knew exactly what it was but could not believe the intense ferocity that it contained.

Rex was growling. The bird abuse suddenly stopped, and moments later, a very disgruntled goose waddled out of the cave. It gave the group a filthy glare, and an angry honk, then rose into the night sky and was gone.

Rex stuck his head out and grinned at the others. "We talked. He gave me his opinion. I gave him mine, and we reached an agreement. It's ours for as long as we need it."

Angel stormed passed him, mumbling to herself about how wild birds shouldn't be allowed out at night, then gave her coat a good shake prior to entering the cave. The others tried to suppress their grins as they followed her inside.

It turned out to be a very cosy sleeping place. The steady sound of the waterfall became almost hypnotic. Coupled with their recent feeding, plus a very full day's activities, all seven were fast asleep within moments of lowering themselves to the ground.

Lucy awoke to a bright shaft of sunlight that seemed to cut through the waterfall and blanket the sleeping forms of her friends. She watched as the light refracted off the water, creating the illusion of thousands of diamonds suspended in the air, dancing excitedly before her sleep-filled eyes.

She lowered her head back onto her front leg and tried to recall the events of the past few days. She felt that on one paw, she had been away from the cottage for a very long time, but also knew that it had, in fact, only been a matter of days. It was extremely hard for Lucy to keep time in any logical order. Humans always think that dog thoughts closely mirror their own. They do not. Humans become too involved in agonising over little things, while dogs usually only concern themselves with the bigger issues, like food and warmth. There is simply not enough room to keep bad thoughts in their head. It's hard enough to recall what took place the previous day without lingering on specifics, especially negative ones.

Lucy could vaguely remember Cook screaming and the sensation of movement as the paper thing was raised in anger. She had a hazy recollection of her cell and the yard. She did, however, have a vivid memory of the Fat Man hitting her, and of the Squat Lady taunting her, but even those recollections had begun to fray like some aged piece of fabric.

One thing that Lucy found very surprising, was that she no longer felt the fear that had consumed her only days earlier. It was not an emotion she'd been used to or enjoyed in the least.

She looked around the cave at the others and realised just how important they had become to her. Through their company and camaraderie, she had learned the importance of friendship and how, even when faced with fear or doubt, the burden could be greatly lessened when shared with others. The concept was still foreign to Lucy, as she had been raised relying solely on her own devices to still any internal disquiet. Certainly, her Man or Cook were there to play with her, or cuddle at times that she felt the need, but they could never help her with the deeper sensations, the ones that were capable of creating stronger, more consuming anxieties. She'd learned that, on those occasions when Cook and her Man tried to help with a rare bout of troubled emotions, they somehow didn't have what it took to fix her wounded spirit. She would try to explain what it was that was bothering her, but found at those moments, the canine-human gap, mysteriously widened into an insurmountable abyss.

As she looked to her sleeping friends, she realised for the first time how much she'd been craving the company of others of her kind. There were the neighbourhood dogs of course, but these were mainly local breeds or farm dogs, whose idea of a stimulating afternoon, was to challenge each other to see how many trees they could mark on only one bowl of water.

Her thoughts were interrupted by a loud, honking sound coming from outside the cave. She attempted to ignore its persistent and intrusive tone, but it was then joined by another honking noise, then another. Lucy thought this very odd and eased her sleepy limbs to an upright position, so she could poke her head outside the cave.

She stared at the sight that greeted her with total disbelief. There, on the grassy knoll at the base of the falls, were well over thirty geese - all honking angrily up at Lucy. At the front of the ranks was the goose that Rex had ousted the previous evening and was clearly the one in charge of the assembled gaggle.

Lucy didn't speak much goose at all. Her mallard wasn't bad, but goose—well, she had simply never had the opportunity to learn. She could only make out every other word or so.

"...come... you... my home... friends to help. You... now... or we... come... get you," the goose voiced, threateningly. The goose's anger conveyed the meaning quite clearly even with the missing words.

Rodney appeared by her side, and after a brief glance outside, started leaping in place excitedly.

"Rumble! We're going to have a rumble!"

"A what?" Lucy enquired as the tiny Terrier dashed back into the cave and began waking the others.

Rex sleepily moved to Lucy's side, and with exceptionally bleary eyes, stuck his head right through the waterfall. After a moment, he withdrew it and faced Lucy.

"Well, it looks like the Yorkie's right. Those geese are asking for a rumble."

"What in heaven's name is a rumble?" she asked in a near exasperated tone.

"It's a fight, Goldie," he replied. "They've challenged us to a fight for this cave."

CHAPTER 15

And so, the rumble began. At first the geese stood back and simply honked abuse towards the dogs, who as tradition dictated, returned the same via barks. The lead goose, who they learnt was named, Vol, was by far the most demonstrative, urging the others on to greater and greater heights of ire. Vol, of course, had the best reasons for being so livid, having been the one forced to vacate his shelter.

The barking and honking lessened as each side began circling the other, all the while evaluating their opponents. By some almost mutual instinct, battle adversaries were chosen, and the dogs and geese focused specifically on those they knew they were going to fight. Lucy was amazed at her own calm assessing of three wildfowl that were, in turn, eyeing her with the same intense curiosity and apprehension. She was not in the least bit scared, which also surprised her. In fact, she felt highly exhilarated and was finding it increasingly difficult to hold back from charging the birds. She had no idea what she was supposed to do once the attack was sounded. She only knew that she wanted to get on with it.

Finally, Vol gave the signal and the geese lunged forward, all seeking out their assigned canine targets. It was like nothing Lucy had ever imagined. She had assumed it would be relatively well-organised and, like all games of its sort, be halted prior to any great pain or damage being caused.

Lucy found out almost immediately that a rumble was not that sort of game. In fact, it was not a game at all. Vol was the first to attack and with one goose on either side of him, went straight for Rex. Lucy couldn't believe the ferocity of their attack and was totally transfixed by it, right up until her designated opponents began their assault.

"Keep them away from your back," Rodney yelled to her, as he himself battled a bird.

The first goose began nipping at her front leg, causing surprising pain when its strong beak clamped down against her bone. She tried to shake it off, but a second bird came in from the other side and began to assault her other front leg. Just as she thought things couldn't get worse, a third goose landed on her back and started in on her neck.

It was at this point that instinct took over. Lucy spun herself in the air, shaking off the one goose. She then dropped to the ground and rolled to the side, releasing her limbs from the beaks of the other two. Without thinking, she lunged out with her back legs and connected with one surprised bird who was thrown backward, right into the pond.

"Nice one," Rex shouted, from his own battle area.

Lucy didn't have time to revel in her success, as the other two geese leapt into the air and descended on her exposed stomach. Lucy twisted herself away from them, and with a ferocity that surprised her, she brought her jaws together on the rear of one bird who was trying to grab hold of her tail. It honked loudly in pain and pulled itself free, leaving Lucy with a mouthful of feathers.

The battle raged on and on, with neither side giving in. There wasn't one animal that didn't sustain an injury of some sort, and in some cases, quite serious ones. Pru had a painful looking bump over her right eye, while Angel was bleeding from a nasty looking wound on her hindquarters. The geese however, had fared the worst. There was an assortment of bitten wings, bleeding legs, even one dislocated tail feather.

Finally, Vol gave the signal to cease the fight. He walked up to Rex, who amazingly appeared completely unscathed, and looked him straight in the eye.

"You fought well," Vol began, formally. "I wish I could claim a draw, but I fear that you lot definitely took the match."

"I can't agree," Rex responded with perfect decorum. "It's way too close to call. You and your flock fought bravely, and I would like to say on behalf of all of us that it was an honour rumbling with you."

Vol bowed proudly, then turned to the other geese and raised his wings high into the air.

"The rumble is finished," he announced majestically. "the result is a draw."

The geese were surprisingly happy at his announcement, and began honking, and flapping their wings. Those that could, that is.

Vol turned back to Rex and with a gracious smile nodded his head. "A good rumble! An exceptionally good rumble!"

"Thank you," Rex replied.

"I would like to invite you and your friends to a small, post-battle supper tonight, if you'll grant us the honour?" Vol offered.

"I would need to ask our leader and the others."

"Of course, I understand."

Rex turned and looked to Rodney, who simply smiled back at him. Rex tilted his head, puzzled by the Terrier's expression.

"Rodney?" Rex asked. "What's going on?"

"I agreed to be your leader while we searched for the park." The terrier spoke in a calm, controlled tone. "But now that we're here, I think it's time this group had a real leader. Someone who can not only think, but also show real power when needed."

"But..." Rex tried to say.

"No buts! I'm more of a rear-guard kind of dog anyway."

"What are you two rattling on about?" Lucy asked, as she approached the pair.

"I would like to announce that we have a new leader," Rodney said. "Rex, we are in your paws now."

Rex glanced over at the others and smiled at each nodding, agreeing face. He stopped when he came to Lucy's and searched deeply into her eyes.

"What do you think, Goldie?"

"Do you have to ask?" she replied.

With a nod of thanks, Rex turned back to Vol and proudly accepted the invitation on behalf of all the dogs.

The supper was to take place on Bird Sanctuary Island just across from the lake's old, and dilapidated boathouse. Vol explained that it was only a few yards offshore, and though requiring a small paddle to get there; they would be undisturbed and able to enjoy what he described as, the victory feast.

The geese gathered themselves up, collecting some of their more vital lost feathers, and waddled off towards the lake. After tending to their wounds, the dogs decided to return to their cave and sleep for a while so they could recover some of their strength after the morning's exhausting activities.

After their nap, the group spent the balance of the day recounting tales of battle that, with each new telling, seemed to take on greater and greater dramatic intensity. Details were added, specifics embellished, soon the rumble that was being described bore hardly any resemblance to the one that actually took place.

Even Lucy found herself drawn into the emotional story-enhancing and heard herself describing one attack with such terrifying and vivid depictions, that she began to almost believe her own recounting of the events. The only one who seemed to remain calm and distant from the frenzy of exaggeration was Rex, who simply nodded and smiled at each new addition to the ever-expanding saga.

Finally, having embellished to the point of utter silliness, the entire group got a case of the giggles, which lasted right up to the time they were scheduled to leave for their special supper.

Some hasty grooming took place, then, in as dignified a manner as possible, the seven warriors left their cave and made their way to Bird Sanctuary Island.

It wasn't far. They passed the restaurant whose rubbish they had raided the previous night, then walked along the side of the lake passing a couple of small vending huts that were securely locked up for the night. They came upon the ancient boathouse as instructed and saw the tiny island only a few yards offshore.

Vol spotted the dogs and signalled for them to paddle across. There was a moment's hesitation, then Rodney, for no reason other than impatience for dinner, dived in, and paddled fiercely across the narrow stretch of water. At his lead, the others followed him. Even Pru, who had spent the entire day ridding her coat of any signs of battle, slipped into the lake and gracefully swam across.

As they reached the island shore, the geese stood politely back as the seven soaked dogs went through their drying process, sending sprays of water in every direction. The birds tried to keep a straight face, but the sight of the seven canines, all shaking themselves in unison, was just too amazing.

Once groomed, the dogs were led to a clearing in the centre of the island, out of sight of the shore. Lucy was stunned at the turn-out. She, like the other dogs, had expected the geese that they had battled that morning and maybe even a few family members, but nothing like the number and variety of birds that she saw before her.

There were geese, swans, ducks, herons, and some variations that Lucy didn't recognise. They were greeted with great aplomb and honest hospitality. Those who, only hours earlier, had been their mortal foes, were intent on making sure that their guests had plenty to eat and drink, and a comfortable piece of dry ground on which to sit.

The food was superb. The geese had arranged with a team of pelicans that specialised in catering, to deliver fresh fish from the lake continuously throughout the night. The ducks had brought very tasty pastries made from breadcrumbs, lake flowers, and sunflower seeds which they had mixed and then baked in the sun.

The swans had brought decorative baskets constructed from water reeds, which they had filled with wild mushrooms and fennel stalks.

The herons brought nothing, claiming they were unaware that it was a *bring something* sort of party. Vol whispered to Lucy that they always said that, and if there was a more tight-taloned flock of birds anywhere, he would like to meet them.

The greatest surprise of the evening was the special drink that was being served in their honour. It was made from dandelion stems, cherry tree bark and orange rind. This latter ingredient was thoughtfully, though unconsciously, provided by the humans who left a seemingly endless supply of it behind in the park almost every day after picnics and bagged lunches. The geese had used a hollowed-out log to hold the ingredients, which had been mixed with fountain water (transported by the pelicans). The dogs learned that the beverage had been ready for over two weeks, and that the birds were delighted to have finally found a suitable excuse to dip into it. It tasted delicious, and after a couple of good gulps, Lucy also found that it made her feel quite jolly.

After the supper had been served and cleared, Vol honked loudly for everyone to be silent. He hopped onto a raised mound of earth and looked down at the assembled multitude.

"My friends," he began. "Those old and those new; I welcome you all to our little gathering. Today my gaggle and I went in search of vengeance for what I'd felt was an injustice carried out against me and mine. I felt that by being forced out of my waterfall habitat, these animals were questioning my position within the community. I have been your leader for some time now, and I have always tried to make the right decisions for us all. When I called for a rumble this morning, I was wrong. These canines meant no harm to the community or me. They were simply seeking shelter for the night. I allowed my own pride to influence my thoughts and as I stand here before you, I ask the forgiveness not only of my peers, but also of our newfound friends in whose honour we give this dinner. Canines, waterfowl, and other guests... please join me in a toast to our continued well-being within the safe boundaries of our park, as well as to our new friends Rex, Pru, Lester, Angel, Rodney, Hans and Lucy. You are fine warriors and true friends. Welcome!"

The other birds all rose to their feet and began flapping their wings together joyously. The pelicans performed a dazzling fly-by overhead, which brought tears to Lucy's eyes, as she watched them gracefully pass before the muted illumination of the mist-covered moon.

After the speech, the party switched to high gear, and as more victory drink was consumed, the revellers began to dance and frolic long into the night.

Intoxicated by the special beverage and the events of the evening, Lucy sat at the island shore and looked out at the lights of the city. Rex walked up and gently sat next to her.

"Quite an evening, isn't it?" he said.

"I feel so... so content at this moment," Lucy said as she turned to face him. "It's as if the last few days have opened my mind to a whole new world, filled with nothing but happiness and adventure."

"Sounds like the victory beverage talking."

"I don't think so," she replied, laughing. "Well, maybe a little, but I definitely feel like a different dog from the one I was a few days ago."

"Are you saying that you don't want to go home, Goldie?" Rex asked, with mild concern.

"Not at all. I love my home, and my Man, and Cook. It's just I feel there's more to me now and I like it."

"Good for you," Rex said. "You deserve good things Goldie. You're a special dog."

Lucy looked into his eyes and could see the warmth of his soul shining out from them. "What about you Rex? You can't go back to your life the way it was."

"We'll see. We need to sit and decide, all of us, exactly what our plans are going to be. We can't just hang out in this park for the rest of our lives."

"What a pity," Lucy whispered into the night. They sat in silence for a while, looking out across the lake as fish rippled the surface of the water, catching the moon's reflection, and sending it dancing out across the dark, mirror-like surface.

"Hey, look at me!" Rodney shouted from the clearing.

They turned and saw the very inebriated terrier dancing on his hind legs, while hopping into the air.

"My biped taught me this," he exclaimed, excitedly.

"I'm sure she did," Rex whispered to Lucy. "I really am."

Lucy tried not to laugh, as they continued watching Rodney dance with total, carefree abandon, the moon spotlighted him within the clearing. His tiny eyes seemed more like luminous jewels as they twinkled beneath a wild bang of dog hair.

A silence descended over the party as everyone watched Rodney, while letting their thoughts drift into the night towards their own personal dreams and fantasies.

CHAPTER 16

When Lucy woke the next morning, she had no recollection of how she'd got back to the cave. Her mind felt extremely fuzzy and as she opened her eyes, she found that she had a fierce, pounding sensation in her head. She looked over at the others and saw that they looked to be in just as poor shape as she was. Poor Rodney was trying to stand, but after each attempt, his little body would teeter, then collapse back to the ground followed by a pained moan.

"What happened to us?" Lucy croaked, somewhat surprised by the raspy quality of her voice.

"It was that damn drink they made," Rodney said weakly.

"We may have had a drop too much," croaked Lucy.

"A drop?" Lester exclaimed, from deeper in the cave. "We drank the poor birds out of nest and shelter."

"We did, didn't we," Lucy sighed, remembering vague images from the previous night. "It was a fabulous evening though, wasn't it?"

They all growled or moaned their agreement as they continued trying to pull themselves together.

"There's only one good cure for feeling like this," Rex stated with authority.

"Oh, oh," Angel moaned. "I don't like the sound of this."

"A good run, that's what we need. A brisk sprint in the morning air will clear out the cobwebs and cool down our noses."

They all looked at him with expressions of mild loathing and disbelief. Despite their feeble and fragile condition, they all followed Rex out into the exaggeratedly bright sunlight.

Once they were out in the open air, they did indeed begin to feel somewhat better. Rex led them at a good pace once around the lake. It was still relatively early, and there were few people to be seen. The park took on an entirely different mood in the early morning. A light mist hung over the lake, giving the waters a still, grey sheen. The only sounds, other than their own panting, were coming from the boats moored in the centre of the lake, as their fibreglass hulls gently bumped and scraped against each other.

Though the route took them past many squirrels and pigeons, no dog was remotely tempted to give chase or even bark in their direction.

After a few minutes, they came upon a large bridge that traversed the lake, dissecting it roughly in its centre. They watched from below as bipeds sped across above them, some in smelly four wheeled vehicles, some on two wheeled ones that though smaller, made even more noise than the four-wheeled machines. There were even some bipeds on two wheeled things that they themselves had to peddle. Humans seemed to go out of their way to devise any means possible to not use their limbs for walking. They were a strange lot.

They continued their run under the bridge by means of an old, and somewhat smelly tunnel. As they entered it, they found that any sounds they made were somehow amplified as they echoed back at them off the curved stone walls. A few dogs barked to test out the effects, and though fascinated, they soon found it too painful for their fragile heads.

They emerged on the other side of the bridge and saw the other half of the lake spread out before them. The shoreline vegetation was far wilder at this end, and the paths were a good distance from the water's edge. Huge willow trees hung their branches into the glass-like surface of the water, creating natural sheltered hideaways, which the waterfowl had clearly claimed as their own.

They continued the run, passing through an odd, stone-terraced area on which were dotted a series of rectangular ponds, some with fountains in their centre, some simply filled with still water. Though man made, the structure was very serene and pleasing to the eye, especially situated amongst the natural beauty of the park. A few geese were sitting next to one such pond, and though they didn't recognise them, it was quite obvious by their ragged state that they had been present at the previous night's party. One of the birds tried to raise a wing in greeting, but the effort was clearly too much for it, so it settled for a weak honk instead. Lucy nodded back, fully understanding the poor creature's woes.

They trotted down a few stone steps and began the return leg of their jaunt around the opposite side of the lake. They came to the bridge again, and to their surprise, another tunnel almost identical to the one on the other side. This one at least smelled better. None of them were tempted to try out its acoustic qualities.

The run began to take its toll, and as they made their way towards a small wooden structure on the water's edge; the noise level from their panting reached a new high. Poor Rodney began having difficulty keeping up and as Lucy offered him words of encouragement, she realised that the little terrier had, by reason of his short legs, actually run almost double the distance of any of them.

"Will you look where we are," Lester voiced with surprise, as he gestured beyond the wooden structure.

They all looked in amazement at the tiny island just off the shore and realised that they were standing next to the old boat house.

"Looks pretty quiet over there," Hans said smiling, knowingly.

They slowed their pace to a sedate walk and reached the nearest point of land to the island. They stopped and listened. They all began smiling as their sensitive ears picked up the distinct sound of a large flock of birds snoring deeply away within the safety of their sanctuary.

Suddenly, Pru drew in her breath. As Lucy turned to see what had caused this reaction, she saw the look of shock on her friend's face.

"Pru? You alright?"

Pru continued to stare at something further along the shore without saying a word.

Lucy tried to see what it was that was causing her to act in such a strange manner, but aside from a small flock of pigeons and a lone human sitting on a bench, there was nothing out of the ordinary.

Pru began to walk down the shore as if in a trance. The others turned from the island and watched her, wondering what she was up to.

The flock of pigeons rose into the air and Pru kept going, seemingly oblivious to their flight.

The lone human turned at the sound of the birds' departure and Lucy could see that it was a female, and that she had recently been crying. She spotted Pru as she looked back towards the lake then suddenly stiffened. Her expression turned to one of stunned amazement, similar to Pru's.

The biped slowly got to her feet and faced Pru, who'd stopped in her tracks some distance from her. They stared at each other for the longest time. The female's face began to light up in a blaze of joy.

"Pru?" She called out with slight hesitation. "Baby, is that you?"

Pru moved towards her, slowly at first, then as the biped took a step forward, she broke into a mad, hair-whipped run. Suddenly, they were wrapped in each other, and even from where she stood Lucy could see that both were crying openly.

"Think they know each other?" Rex asked, trying to cover his own emotions with a little humour.

As she continued to watch the pair hug and reacquaint themselves, Lucy felt a sharp stab of longing to feel her own Man's embrace. She was suddenly very homesick and turned herself away from the others, as she too shed a quiet tear.

After a moment, Pru broke away from her mistress' hug and ran over to the others.

"I'm going home now," she said between tearful gasps. "Thank you. Thank you all for everything. Maybe I'll see you in the park one day when we go for our walk."

With that, she trotted back to her mistress, and as the other dogs looked on, the two walked off the path. With their blonde hair billowing out behind them, the pair traversed the park and vanished into the impersonal vastness of the city.

Seeing the two of them together, Lucy understood that their relationship was not one of dog and mistress, but of best friends, as they chatted and laughed comfortably with each other.

Once they were out of sight, the remaining six looked at each other with expressions of mild confusion, until Rex stretched himself then turned to face the group.

"I hope you lot don't think that gets you out of finishing our little run?"

They all laughed as Rex again set a pace, and the six dogs resumed their morning jog - though now with slightly heavier hearts at the loss of one of their own.

CHAPTER 17

The rest of the day was spent close to the cave as each animal tried to rid him, or herself of the previous night's aftereffects.

During one nap period, Lucy dreamed that she was back in Burden Dell. At first it appeared as it always had to her - a gentle clearing of long, sweet grass nestled between the aged and sheltering trees of the woods. In her dream though, something was different. She turned and looked in every direction, unable to sense what exactly was wrong. Finally, she realised that where normally there would have been gentle, background sounds of birdsong and wind, now there was a steady hum of city noise. Lucy looked at the line of trees to try and locate the origin of the unwelcome sound and saw that the trees themselves were not what they appeared to be. They were in fact buildings. Man-made structures that looked like trees. She spun around to check the other side of the dell, only to find the same thing, except now the trees, or whatever they were, had moved closer than they'd been only moments before. She looked about her, and realised that the strange structures were slowly, but very deliberately, hemming her in.

She awoke with a start, causing Angel who was dozing next to her, to jump as well.

"Sorry," Lucy whispered, embarrassed.

"Bad dream?" The Spaniel inquired.

Lucy nodded, then shook her head with enough force to hopefully rid her mind of the dream's remnants.

"Oh my," Lucy said, as a smile began to form on her sleepy features. "That was most unpleasant."

Angel grinned at her with a mix of affection and mild peeve for having been woken up by her. "I was dreaming about a huge steak all to myself. I had just started to eat it when you woke me."

"Well," Lucy said. "Serves you right for not sharing doesn't it."

This brought laughter from everyone in the cave. Lucy smiled proudly at her audience then noticed a missing face.

"Where's Rodney?"

"He went out to check on dinner prospects," Lester replied as he stretched out his little frame in typical, post-nap style.

"You know," Rex said with a look of concern on his muzzle. "The little chap's been gone quite a while. We may have to send out a search party if he's not back..."

"If who's not back?" Rodney said cheekily as he stepped into the cave.

"About time!" Rex smiled at his tiny friend.

"Well, I've got good news and I've got bad news," the terrier began. "First of all, the bins at the restaurant are out. For some silly reason, they've put up a fence around them. There's no way in, I checked. I did a quick scout of the park and I've got to tell you that, unless you're ready for a diet of nuts and berries, there's no food here."

"But that's terrible," Angel interrupted. "What will we do? We must eat. I mean how will we ..."

"Will you please let me finish?" he chided gently.

"Sorry," Angel said, as she lowered her head back onto her front paws.

"If you don't mind a slight risk and are ready for a small adventure, I may have the solution." Rodney's eyes sparkled as he spoke.

"We're listening," Rex said, cautiously.

"Okay, I'll need volunteers," he began. "What we'll do is ..."

He laid out the plan in surprisingly, well thought-out detail. It was definitely risky, but Rodney was convinced that what he had in mind could be carried out successfully as long as they were careful.

Fully briefed, Rodney, Rex, Lester, and Lucy left the safety of their lair, and under cover of darkness, made their way diagonally across the park towards the lights of the city.

For security reasons, Hans stayed behind to guard the cave. Angel had desperately wanted to join the group, but was, as Rex had explained as gently as he could, too small to be effective in the operation, and lacking in the necessary speed and manoeuvrability should a rapid escape be needed. She had clearly been disappointed, but had taken it surprisingly well, and had simply stretched herself out on the floor of the cave and wished the team God's speed.

The team reached a road which seemed devoid of traffic. They crossed it with caution anyway, as one could never trust people once they got into one of their noisy vehicles. It was as if even the mildest and most passive of individuals could be instantly transformed into raving lunatics, forcing their smelly machines down peaceful roads as if possessed by some crazy force.

Once across the quiet street, they came to a truly terrifying intersection of roads. They saw vehicles of every conceivable shape and size converge from five different directions, all avoiding certain destruction only by means of observing red and green lights on posts, strategically placed before them.

"Don't worry," Rodney shouted above the din. "We don't have to deal with that."

The others looked very relieved as Rodney led them off to the right and to a tunnel that passed under one of the streets. They all stared at him uncertainly.

"Come on, you've done it before," he coaxed. "It's just like the one that got us to the park the other day."

"Yes, and the bad bipeds were waiting for us, weren't they?" Lucy said with conviction.

"They won't be down here, I promise Goldie. I already checked earlier. We're safe."

After taking a moment to summon their courage, they cautiously descended the concrete stairs. Once at the bottom, they were relieved to find the tunnel empty of people. They took a few hesitant steps, then burst into a mad gallop, reaching the far end of the tunnel and the rising stairway at the end in record time. They laughed at their own nervousness as they climbed up and out onto another section of road. Rodney led them at a brisk pace around a corner and saw a huge building that was decorated with, what to Lucy, looked like millions of little stars that seemed to cover every surface of the structure.

"Wow!" Lucy heard herself exclaim.

"Not bad is it?" Rodney said as he continued pushing the team along the front of the immense edifice. They passed window after window of merchandise as well as not very realistic copies of humans, all standing in odd, unnatural poses.

"What is this place?" Rex asked in a voice filled with awe.

"I haven't the faintest, but it's quite something isn't it?" Rodney replied.

"Ha… Har… Harro… Harrods… that's it, Harrods," Lester announced with pride.

The others came to a stunned halt. Lester had stopped long enough to read the name of the store from the gilded lettering on a set of brass-framed doors.

"You can read?" Lucy asked in an astonished tone.

"Don't be ridiculous," Rex said. "Dogs can't read."

"I can, actually," Lester replied meekly. "Not very well, but I can usually put the words together."

"You're not suggesting that you understand biped talk, are you?" Rex demanded.

"No, of course not... well actually, that's not true. I can sometimes pick out a word here and there."

"Come off it," Angel exclaimed. "No non-human understands biped talk."

"Sure, they do. I bet you understand when they say your name, right?"

"Well..." she responded, hesitantly.

"Of course, you do," Lester said. "We all do. That's the start, then you just concentrate on what they're saying and eventually, you begin to pick out patterns. The trick is to look them right in the eye when they're speaking. It's amazing what you can tell from the words that way."

"Can we talk about this later?" Rodney said impatiently. "We have a mission to complete."

The others all nodded their agreement and followed him past even more of the store's beautifully arranged windows. No more was said about Lester's boastings as their focus returned to the task at paw. They reached the end of the block and waited as Rodney checked their route.

"Okay. We're almost there," he whispered. "You know what to do?"

They all nodded. Rodney gave his tiny frame a good stretch then signalled for the others to stay close. They moved along the next block, carefully staying tight against the building, seeking out the shadows with every step.

"There it is." Rodney pointed with his muzzle past the next building, to a brightly lit doorway. "Can you smell it?"

The others all raised their noses, and after a brief moment spent filtering out the other city odours, locked onto a very tasty scent indeed.

"You ready?" Rodney asked, excitedly.

They nodded their heads enthusiastically as their noses twitched in joyous anticipation of the delicious goodies to come.

"Right then, let's do it!" Rodney yelled, as he dashed towards the light.

He reached the entrance and took his position by the open doors as the team lookout. The other three followed him in, and as prearranged, split up to carry out their specific assignments.

The place was a small biped feeding shop specializing, if the huge displays were to be believed, in hamburgers, fried potatoes and other odd-shaped items that were breaded and forced between two tasty-looking buns. There were around ten customers milling about, whom Lester immediately herded into a corner by baring his teeth and growling menacingly. The startled staff watched in horror as Rex and Lucy vaulted the counter, and with the aid of a couple of fierce barks, forced them against one wall.

Their luck was definitely in. The staff had obviously been in the process of packing a couple of large orders before being interrupted. Lucy checked and could see that there were two plastic carrier bags loaded with square, plastic looking containers all filled with food. She gestured for Rex to grab one as she grabbed the other. They were heavy but just manageable. They dragged them off the counter and across the white, tiled floor.

As they neared the door, one of the patrons, a large and discontented looking male, bravely barred the two doors by closing them from the outside then leaning on them.

They were trapped. Lester tried push the doors, but biped's weight was simply too much.

As Lucy looked back into the restaurant, she saw that the patrons were beginning to lose their earlier fear and were slowly edging towards the trapped animals. She turned and looked frantically towards Rodney, who was leaping in place yelping to no avail whatsoever.

Suddenly, the man at the door let out a blood-curdling scream. Dogs and humans focused their attention beyond the doors and saw an immensely proud-looking Spaniel with a large piece of trouser leg dangling from its mouth. The human ran off, limping and cursing as he went.

Lester held the door open for the others as they charged out into the night.

As they ran towards the tunnels and the park beyond, each one praised Angel from the bottom of their still anxiously, beating hearts.

All she could say, was, "Too small, too slow? Really?"

They made it back to the park, and despite one of bags rupturing and losing a good number of plastic boxes, their haul was substantial. Once they reached the cave, they divided up the containers prior to opening them to make it fair. Nobody knew what they were getting until each container was opened.

They were startled to find that, tucked inside the buns and under the breaded batter, was real food! Lucy found chicken, and Rex managed to locate some fish. Most of the containers, however, contained thin circles of cooked ground beef that weren't that bad once you'd shaken off the rather strange pink goo that was centred on each one.

They ate to their heart's content. They finished off the meat, the buns, the fried potatoes, even the strange pastry-like tubes filled with something akin to fruit. As they ate, they regaled Hans with stories of their expedition. With each new telling the details became more elastic as they expanded to quite astonishing dimensions, while somehow still allowing the story to stay intact.

The team became warriors, while the bipeds were depicted as the feared and undefeatable foe, and as for the captured food - well, it may as well have been the Holy Grail itself, such were the embellishments!

Finally, sated and exhausted from their recounting and feasting, the six dogs didn't even have the strength to clear away the debris from the meal, and simply collapsed on top of the mass of wrappers and containers.

They slept the sleep of the victorious.

CHAPTER 18

Even in her sleep, Lucy heard the sound of human voices. There were a few of them, all speaking in gentle coaxing tones. She opened one eye and saw Rodney and Rex standing at the cave entrance, staring nervously outside.

"What is it?" Lucy asked in a sleepy voice.

"We're not sure," Rex answered. "It doesn't look good."

Lucy got to her feet and joined them at the entrance. Through the wall of water, they could make out a large number of bipeds encircling the cave. Suddenly, the water stopped flowing, and in almost miraculous fashion, the fall simply ceased to exist. The three dogs were now standing in the unsheltered entry to the cave, clearly visible to the humans. Without the liquid shield, Lucy could clearly see that there were at least a dozen humans, all male, and all attired in almost identical, dark-blue uniforms. Each one wore a tall, domed hat with decorative silver work on the front.

Lucy vaguely recalled seeing bipeds like that before. One had come to the cottage to talk to her man after another human had been trying to climb through the kitchen window one night. As far as she could remember, the uniformed biped had been very pleasant, even taking the time to have a brief chat and a tummy rub with her.

The group outside didn't look particularly menacing. In fact, a few of them seemed to be quite enjoying the goings-on, whatever the goings-on were!

Lucy was still trying to fathom the biped's presence when something caught her eye. In front of the uniformed males was a pile of wrappers and containers, identical to the ones strewn about the cave. How could that be? She gestured to the others, who upon seeing the colourful pile of debris, turned to each other with expressions of deep distress.

"Those are from the bag that broke last night," Rex stated, flatly.

"Oh blast," Rodney sighed. "We must have left a trail the entire way.

"You think?" Rex said, rolling his eyes.

"So, what do we do?" Lucy asked, trying to keep the nervous edge from her voice.

"I do believe," Rex began. "that that's going to be up to our visitors out there."

Lucy turned and looked towards the humans who, though not appearing particularly menacing, were staring with amused determination right back at them. As they wondered what to do, Lucy woke up the others and explained their predicament. She was just getting to the part about the wrapper trail when Rex called for her to return to the entrance.

She saw immediately that the uniformed bipeds had been joined by six new, grey-clad humans, who were not only dressed differently, but seemed to be taking the situation far more seriously than the others. There were no smiles from the newcomers. They gave the cave and the three visible animals a cold evaluation as they stood in front of a pair of vans. One of the newcomers broke away from the others and climbed into the rear of a vehicle. He reappeared moments later with a strange canister clutched in one hand. He said something to the other bipeds then walked towards the cave. Once he was about halfway between the dogs and the humans, he pulled something from the canister, then deftly tossed it over the heads of the three canines standing at the cave entrance.

Rex, Rodney, and Lucy watched as the thing bounced into their shelter then rolled into a corner. The others frantically danced out of its way, then all stared at it nervously. Almost immediately the thing began emitting white smoke which started to irritate all the dog's eyes.

"What's going on?" Lucy gasped, as tears rolled down her cheeks.

"I don't know," Rodney replied coughing. "But we can't stay here."

"He's right," Rex stated between his own bouts of tear-filled coughs. "Everybody out, now!"

They didn't have to be told twice. Whatever the humans were after, couldn't be worse than the pain they were now feeling in their eyes and noses.

They dashed out of the cave and saw that the humans had moved close to the entrance and were holding a cordon of netting between them, cutting off any escape routes for the dogs.

The six animals were by now scared and having trouble seeing clearly out of their tear-filled eyes. They tried to locate ways around the humans, but there were none. Angel was the first to be taken. She charged the centre of the line, hoping to startle the humans, but they simply dropped the net before she even reached them. She was swiftly grabbed and carried to one of the vans. Rex and Lester were next. They stood their ground and growled with full-on fury only to find themselves netted, then bundled off to the other vehicle. Hans made a brave attempt at climbing up the dry waterfall gully but lost his footing near the top and fell into the pond where, with a great deal of barking and splashing, he was captured and taken.

Rodney gave Lucy a brave smile and encouraging head nod then made his move. He almost managed it too. He pretended to charge one particular human focusing on the man's ankles, then at the last moment leapt high into the air and made it over the net, only to be caught in one of the uniformed biped's hands.

That left Lucy. She could see that she was well and truly trapped. The line of net-toting humans was closing in fast.

She backed herself against the waterfall rocks, and out of pure fear and hopelessness, closed her eyes as she waited to be grabbed.

At first, she only heard one honk. She thought she recognised the voice but was too scared to open her eyes. Then she heard others and had to look. She opened her eyes just as at least fifty low-flying geese began dive-bombing the human net line.

The grey-clad humans were taken by complete surprise and realising that they were greatly outnumbered, dived to the ground covering their heads as the huge birds flew at them with great precision. The uniformed bipeds, though having to protect themselves like the others, seemed to find humour in the attack. They were lying flat on the ground with their hands over their heads laughing themselves silly. Finally, one human shouted a command, and the others made a break for their vehicles. This made the uniformed ones laugh even harder as they rolled across the grass trying to keep their domed hats in place.

Lucy would have laughed herself if Vol hadn't landed in front of her at that moment.

"Sorry we didn't get here sooner," the goose said, breathlessly. "You'd better follow me!"

"What about the others?" Lucy asked anxiously.

"It's too late, Goldie. They've been taken."

"But I can't just…" Lucy began.

"Yes, you can, unless you want to just wait until they come back for you. Now move it girl!"

With that, the goose took to the air and with Lucy running along beneath him, earth-bound, led her up past the restaurant, along the bank of the lake and to the dilapidated boat house. Vol landed on the roof and scanned the area.

"Okay Goldie it's all clear. Ready for a swim?"

"Swim?" she replied, confused.

"Yes, swim! You can't stay over here can you? We'll just have to put you up on the island for a while until we work out what to do next."

"It won't be too much of an imposition?" Lucy inquired politely.

Vol had to laugh at the dog's sense of propriety even at such a critical time.

"I think we'll manage," he responded with amusement. "Now, get in the water."

Lucy did as she was told and dived into the lake. She paddled across the narrow stretch and was met by a couple of anxious ganders that led her through the bushes and out of sight of the shore.

"You poor thing," one of them cried.

"What an awful situation," the other added.

Lucy gave them both a brave smile and was about to shake off her coat when she stopped and asked them to step back. Once they had moved a respectful distance from her, she gave herself a good shake then she moved into the clearing just as Vol landed next to her.

"Why don't you have a rest for a while?" Vol suggested. "You're safe here,"

"Oh, I couldn't," Lucy exclaimed. "My friends have been captured. I have to..."

"You have to what?" Vol interrupted. "There's nothing you can do. They're gone, Goldie. What you need is to rest so that when you wake up, you'll be thinking clearly.

"Do you really think so?" she asked, sadly.

"I promise. In fact, I think I'll join you."

With that, he tucked his head under a wing and without any further ado, was fast asleep. Lucy looked to the other birds and found that they'd all done the same. She decided she might as well join in and stretched herself out on the warm earth of the island clearing.

With one deep sigh, she closed her sad eyes and went instantly to sleep.

Lucy woke in the early afternoon and found that she was alone in the clearing. She stared out through a gap in the greenery and watched as various humans lapped up the tranquil atmosphere afforded by the park. They rowed on the lake, they rode horses, they fished. Some hardy individuals even swam on the far side in a sheltered area reserved, Lucy presumed, for just that purpose.

Lucy could clearly see, even from her place of seclusion, the looks of sheer enjoyment on the faces of the humans. They seemed to revel in the natural surroundings. She wondered why, if they loved the park environment so much, they built the city in the first place. Before they'd constructed the concrete jungle, had not the land on

which it now lay, been just as countrified as the park?
Lucy suddenly missed the cottage and Cook, and her Man.
She felt both thankful for living in such a setting and pained
by not being there. It was a very frightening feeling to know
exactly where she wanted to be, but not have the slightest
idea of how to get there.

Lucy spent most of the afternoon in deep reflection of
her present situation. By evening, she had managed to make
herself quite morose, and even as Vol and the other geese
returned from their day's efforts, and she pretended to feel
otherwise, the sensation of loneliness and homesickness ate
away at her very soul.

Vol could tell that she was troubled and tried to ease her
sorrow with some light-hearted small talk, but to no avail.
He whispered to one of his flock then took to the air with
a determined expression on his bill.

Lucy tried to join in with the flock as they recounted
amusing tales of human encounters. She even told of her set-
to with Cook over the vegetable garden, but it only seemed
to make her more miserable. Finally, feeling completely sorry
for herself, she moved off to a spot of ground away from
the others, and with her head facing away, had a quiet cry.

After a few moments, she heard a loud flapping of wings
and turned just in time to see Vol as he landed with great
precision while holding a huge slab of beef in his beak. He
waddled over to Lucy and gently placed the meat at her side.

"I thought that perhaps a nice dinner would cheer you
up," he said, as he turned to go.

"Wait," Lucy said as she tried to wipe the tears from her eyes with both paws. "Where'd you get this?"

"It's amazing what people try to cook on those funny little outdoor fires of theirs."

"This was being cooked?" She asked in amazement.

"Not yet it wasn't," Vol responded. "The poor biped had just brought it outside and made the mistake of putting it down for a moment, and then turned his back."

"And you grabbed it?" Lucy found the concept quite remarkable.

"We do that a lot. In the summer we can fly about overhead and check out what's for dinner. People will try to cook just about anything outdoors as long as it's not raining. We wait until they go inside for something and Voila! We're not mad about meat, but it's amazing how much fish bipeds are starting to eat. Or at least trying to," he added with amusement. "Bol over there grabbed an entire salmon earlier this season."

Sensing his name being used, Bol, a fine specimen of goose, turned and waved a wing in their direction.

"I'll leave you to feed. You look like you need the time alone. Enjoy your meal."

"Vol," Lucy said gently. "Thank you. You're very sweet."

"Don't be silly! We're all in this world together. If we can't help one another when the need arises, then what's the point?" Vol gave her a nod of encouragement, then waddled off to join the rest of his flock.

"What a nice goose," Lucy thought to herself as she bit into her dinner.

CHAPTER 19

The next morning, Lucy was awakened early as the geese prepared themselves for their usual dawn patrols. They would send out teams to scour the park and to make sure that all was well within their kingdom. It was a tradition handed down from generation to generation.

The birds would take off in groups of six with one bird in the lead. Each group would cover one particular quadrant, then return and report their findings, while also picking up their next assignment. Lucy watched in fascination from her corner of the clearing. After a short period one of the groups, with Bol as the lead, returned from a sortie. Instead of reporting to the command group, he waddled with urgency over to Lucy.

"Wasn't one of your group an Afghan?" he asked.

"Yes," Lucy responded with curiosity. "But why..."

"Name of Pru?" he continued.

"Why, yes!" she exclaimed. "Where is she?"

"Walking with her mistress by the cave and waterfall. I picked up her bark from the air. She's calling for you and the others. I didn't want to alarm the human, so I came right back to tell you. Want me to show you where they are?"

"No, thank you Bol. You've done enough already."

"It's been a pleasure, ma'am," he replied.

She watched as he returned to his flight group and immediately took to the air to complete their mission. Lucy rose to her feet, and after a good stretch and perfunctory scratch of her hindquarters, made her way to the island's shore. She checked that all was clear then dived into the water. She reached other side, and after a thorough shake, trotted off towards the waterfall. She wanted desperately to run, but at the same time knew that she mustn't attract any attention to herself.

Lucy passed the restaurant and saw a long line of people waiting to select their meal from a brightly-lit display case. What with the harsh neon lights and the bright metallic packaging of the food itself, Lucy was surprised that anyone would be tempted to consume any of it.

She passed by the heavily fenced-in bins and smiled at the brief memory that struck her. She reached the sloping path that led to the cave that had sheltered them so very recently. Lucy looked anxiously for Pru but couldn't see her anywhere. She hoped that she hadn't missed her chance to speak with her friend. She had to find her and tell her what happened, then the two of them could start a search for the others. She checked all around the enclosure but found no trace of the Afghan. She began to panic. She ran along an adjoining path and still couldn't spot her friend. She should have let Bol lead her from the air as he had offered.

Lucy turned another corner and found herself next to the soft earth of the park's horse trail. A well-groomed Arab mix was cantering by, trying to train his nervous rider, when he spotted Lucy he came to a sudden halt, almost dismounting his charge.

"Is your name Lucy, by chance?" he neighed.

"Yes, it is!" she cried.

"Thought you might be. Her description was spot on."

"Whose description?" Lucy asked excitedly. "Have you seen Pru?"

"If you're referring to a fine looking, blonde canine, then yes, I have," he replied calmly, while trying to ignore his rider's futile attempts at moving him on. "She's about a hundred yards down the path just over that rise. I passed her only a few minutes ago. She's very anxious to speak with you."

"Thank you. Thank you very much," Lucy shouted over her shoulder as she began to run toward the last sighting of her friend.

"Good luck!" the Arab mix called after her. "Now let's deal with you shall we." he stated, as he turned his head to glance up at his irate rider.

Lucy covered the distance in mere seconds, but again saw no sign of Pru. She scanned the park from her excellent position atop the rise but couldn't spot her.

Finally, out of breath, exhausted and with a heavy heart, she made her way back to the boat house and the island beyond. She passed the waterfall and pond, climbed the sloping path to the restaurant, then walked despondently along the shore of the lake.

"So, there you are!" Pru screamed with delight.

Lucy looked up and saw her friend as she sat obediently next to her mistress by the same park bench where the two of them had been reunited just the other day.

"I've been looking for you everywhere," Lucy cried out, dashing over to greet her friend. "I've got to speak with you. Can you break away for a bit?"

"I suppose so," she replied hesitantly, glancing up at her mistress who seemed completely engrossed in a bound bunch of paper in her hands. "Let's pretend to chase birds. She'll allow that."

"Good idea," Lucy nodded. "I'll lead."

With that, Lucy suddenly dashed by the bench at full speed, barking frantically as she headed for a flock of pigeons lunching on the grass. Pru tugged urgently at her lead, and with great understanding from her mistress, was released to join in the fun.

The two dogs tore after the startled birds who greatly resented having to take to the air, especially after having found an exceptionally rich amount of newly-laid grass seed.

Once away from her mistress, Pru turned to Lucy with a worried look on her fine, exotic features.

"Where are the others?" she inquired in a tone that she hoped masked her concern.

"They're gone Pru. They've been taken!"

Lucy could see the colour pale under the Afghan's fine coat. She suggested that they sit so she could explain what happened. She was worried that Pru suddenly looked very unsteady on her feet and was afraid the other animal might fall over.

Once seated, Lucy told of the events leading up to the capture of their friends. Pru sat and listened intently, occasionally shaking her head in amazement at the antics of the others. As Lucy recounted the details of the capture and her subsequent lonely night spent on Sanctuary Island, Pru's eyes welled up with tears.

" . . . .and then . . . well there you were!" Lucy said, finishing the story. She looked into the Afghan's misty eyes and could see, not just the sadness that rested there, but also the constrictive shackles of guilt that were beginning to grow within her mind.

"Pru, there were too many of them," Lucy reassured her. "If you'd been there you would have taken like the others. At least this way you're free, and between us we can go into the city and track them down!"

"Oh Goldie, I wish I could," Pru said in a sad and troubled voice, "But I really can't, don't you see?"

"Don't I see what?" Lucy tried to conceal her irritation.

"I can't leave home again. It was too much for my mistress. You saw how she looked the other day. Alone, hurt, sad . . ."

"And what about Rodney and Rex, and the others?" she snapped. "Don't you think they're feeling just a bit alone and sad right now?"

"Please don't be angry with me, Goldie. I am what I am. I'm a show dog. All I have are my looks. I'm not brave or smart like you. I'm not fast like Rodney, or fierce like Rex or Hans. I'm certainly not cunning like Angel. I'm just a pretty hound, who likes to look her best and be groomed by her mistress. I'm no good for anything else. I never have been.

Lucy studied the other animal, and though angry at her weakness, also felt a stab of pity for the pain that Pru obviously carried around inside her.

"I'm sorry Pru," Lucy said, soothingly. "I didn't mean to suggest that you give up your home again. That was very unfair of me. I'm just at a loss as to what to do. I don't have a clue as to where to even begin looking for the others. Pru? Pru?"

Pru was staring up at the sky with a very pensive look on her muzzle.

"Pru?"

"Oh, sorry. I was just thinking. You know, I really am a silly dog sometimes. I swear if I weren't on a leash half the time, I think I'd..."

"Pru!" Lucy interrupted impatiently. "What did you think of?"

"Oh, yes... sorry," she said, blushing. "I do go on, don't I? Well, you said that they were taken by humans, some in grey uniforms, and others in blue ones with tall, funny hats."

"So?"

"The ones in blue, sound like policemen. Those are good humans. They're here to help and protect."

"Help and protect who?" Lucy asked.

"Other humans."

"Protect other humans from what?" Lucy was beginning to lose her patience at Pru's confused ramblings.

"From bad humans," Pru stated, frankly.

"Let me see if I've got this straight," Lucy began. "The blue uniformed bipeds protect other bipeds from still other bipeds?"

"Precisely!" Pru exclaimed with delight.

"That's ridiculous Pru. Why would one biped need protecting from another biped?"

"That's right, you're a country dog, aren't you?" Pru stated, as she nodded her fine head.

"What's that got to do with anything?"

"Where you come from, things are different," Pru explained. "In the city, bipeds don't always get along with others of their breed. They steal from each other, cheat, sometimes even kill."

"Oh, come on!" Lucy said, shaking her head. "You're having me on."

"No, I'm not," Pru insisted. "In fact, canines do the same thing in the cities. They fight and steal, and sometimes even harm each other.

"I'm not sure I like the city anymore, Pru. It doesn't seem to bring out the best in creatures."

"Why would it! I mean look around. It's not exactly a natural place to live, is it?"

Lucy nodded her agreement to her friend's words. The two of them then sat and looked across the park to the city beyond.

"Weren't we discussing something important before?" Lucy asked.

"Were we?" Pru tried to recall.

"Of course. The others. You started to tell me about policemen and..."

"Oh yes," Pru interrupted, suddenly remembering her earlier train of thought. "I think I know where they are."

"What!" Lucy exclaimed in frustration. "And you didn't say anything!?"

"I'm saying it now," Pru responded calmly. "You know Goldie, you need to relax. You seem very touchy today."

"I'm sorry Pru, please... go on."

"On our daily walk route to the park, we pass a police station."

"A what?" Lucy asked, in an attempt at a calm tone.

"That's where policemen live! Anyway, there's a kennel behind the main building and I think that's where stray dogs are kept after capture, before being sent to the pound."

"What's a stray and a pound? Really Pru can't you talk canine? I don't know half these words."

"A stray is a dog that doesn't have a home," Pru began.

"But we do have homes," Lucy stated, matter-of-factly.

"Yes, but the policemen don't know that do they? And the pound is... well the pound is the ultimate bad place."

"Okay... okay... we'll get back to that," Lucy said, impatiently. "So, you think there's this kennel where... how bad a place?"

"You don't want to know. I've heard that if you end up in the pound, you're never seen again."

"Oh my!" Lucy exclaimed.

Pru gave her a grave nod. "So anyway, there's this kennel which I'm certain is used to hold the strays that are picked up in the park. It takes them a couple of days before the animals are moved to the... the other place." Pru had to swallow hard just at the thought of the other place. "I'll bet you the others are still there."

"Well, let's go. You can show me where it is!" Lucy cried with delight.

"I'm not going to leave my mistress, but I'll tell you what. I'll let her know that I've had enough of the park for today, and I'll lead her down the road with the police station. You just follow us, and I'll signal when we're there."

"What if she takes you a different route?" Lucy asked, worriedly.

"I can usually get her to go my way, but if I can't, you need to find Walton Street."

"How do I do that?" Lucy inquired.

"Just ask directions and read the signs."

"You can read too? I give up." Lucy replied, burying her muzzle beneath her front paws.

"I'll go over to my mistress now and let her know that I want to go home. You stay behind us and follow. Not too close. I don't want her upset."

"Thanks, Pru!"

"I wish I could do more, but I simply can't. I hope you understand."

"I do... really!"

After a brief nose touch, Pru ran off towards the lake and her waiting mistress. As promised, Pru let her biped know that she was ready to leave. Normally, with humans not being as bright as canines, it takes repeated attempts before they caught on to a request. Not in Pru's case. She walked up to her mistress, picked her lead up in her mouth, then turned to face the pathway that led back to the city, and their home. The female caught on instantly and rose to her feet. She attached the leash and allowed Pru to lead the way.

Lucy followed at what she felt was a sensible distance behind them. Not too close to be seen by casual glance, and not so far back that she'd miss any key direction adjustments. As they walked past the waterfall, Lucy noticed Pru give their old shelter a brief look, then as if being driven by the memory of her recently captured friends, she picked up the pace.

After crossing the horse path, they reached the end of the park and the beginning of the city. Lucy watched as Pru and her biped crossed the first of what she knew would be many streets, and felt a shiver run through her body. She took a moment to look back at the park with its gentle hillocks and sheltering trees and knew somehow that she would not be coming back. She took one last deep breath of the sweet-scented park air, then turned and faced the harshness of the looming city. She swallowed hard, then stepped off the grass and onto the cold hardness of the paved walkway.

CHAPTER 20

Lucy soon found that the biggest problem was not them seeing her, but of her making certain she could see them. Pru was maintaining a good pace, and though in the park it had been puppy's play to keep up with them, it was a different thing altogether on the crowded streets. There was a definite method to city walking that Lucy hadn't realised before. When the group had been together and they'd moved through the city, they'd kept mainly to residential streets. This was an entirely different game of fetch!

There were bipeds everywhere. Moving in every direction at once, with what seemed to be little or no order whatsoever. She was amazed to see that on occasion, the humans would actually bang into each other. Sometimes a rapid verbal exchange took place, but for the most part, they would simply collide, readjust their heading, and speed off without any indication that something so silly had occurred at all.

What astonished Lucy the most were the expressions on the faces of the bipeds. They were clearly all in a mad rush to get somewhere, that was a given, and yet they all looked so intensely unhappy to be doing what they were doing. Lucy couldn't understand why, if this maniacal rushing and colliding ritual were so distasteful to them all, they didn't just stop or at least slow down. She felt that if they would all just take the time to perhaps visit the park, and who knows, chase a squirrel or a pigeon, they would feel a whole lot better.

She had to dismiss her ponderings as she was having an exceedingly hard time keeping Pru's hindquarters in her view.

Pru was astonishingly good at city walking and seemed able to dodge and weave with amazing skill and success. Even her mistress had the moves down, and rarely seemed to collide with anything.

Lucy on the other hand was having an extremely hard time of it. She had been tripped over, stepped on, kicked and once almost fallen upon. Luckily, she'd seen the shadow and side-stepped the large, heavily-perfumed female before the toppling biped landed on her.

As she strode to keep up with Pru, something caught her eye and she glanced over to her left. Her jaw dropped open as she looked into the beautifully arranged windows of what she had only recently learnt was a place called Harrods. She realised in horror that if she was next to Harrods, then just up ahead had to be—before she could even finish the thought, she saw it. She was about to pass right in front of the biped feeding place that they had attacked the previous night. She felt her mouth go dry, knowing that they were certain to still be looking for the perpetrators of the heinous crime. There was, however, no choice.

Pru and her mistress passed right in front of the feeding place without so much as a glance. Lucy readied herself, and with every nerve end screaming within her tense frame, she ran past the glass-paned entrance. She waited for the screams and shouting that she knew were imminent, but nothing happened. Nothing at all. She risked a glance over her shoulder and verified that no one even seemed to have noticed her. She returned her eyes to the task of following Pru and saw to her utter disbelief that Pru was gone!

Lucy's sense of panic lasted only as long as it took her to reach the next corner. Pru and her mistress had turned left off the main street, and somehow sensing that Lucy might have missed the move, the Afghan had feigned sudden intense interest in a large, tabby cat that was seated on a nearby window ledge. Pru's mistress tried to urge her away from the startled feline but Pru stood firm, barking at the other animal just long enough for Lucy to reach the corner and spot her.

Lucy was a good distance away from Pru, yet couldn't miss the admonishing expression being thrown at her. It was as if to say, 'Pay attention, silly dog!'

The tracking became much easier once they'd left the main street. There were far fewer bipeds to avoid and plenty of stairways on which she could raise herself to get a better view of her two targets. The street they were on was narrow and crammed on either side with one feeding place after another, many of them located, not on ground level but down stone stairs in converted basements.

Lucy couldn't believe the smells. She had been around food prepared in lots of different ways. Cook herself was always trying something new to please their Man, and Lucy tried to make herself available whenever possible for a taste just to give Cook her verdict. But those dishes with their mildly altered scents were nothing compared to the full-frontal nose assault that she was being subjected to on the narrow city street.

In one place, she could see candles burning atop dark green bottles. They were hardly recognisable because of the layers upon layers of multi-coloured candle wax that had been allowed to dry haphazardly, forming grotesque, waxy sculptures.

The bottles sat on tables covered with bright, red and white checked cloths that were huddled so close together that Lucy presumed it had to be for warmth. She couldn't fathom any other reason for people to sit so close to others as they ate. She raised her muzzle as she passed the basement entry, and felt her senses being transported away on a velvety carpet of garlic and oregano.

Lucy passed another feeding place that was filled with humans who had eyes of a different shape to any she had ever seen, other than perhaps on a cat. As she inhaled the pungent aromas of ginger and garlic, she watched how the almond-eyed bipeds ate their food with sticks instead of metal utensils.

She could tell, even from her position outside the eatery, that the bipeds did not simply eat for the sake of nourishment, but rather ate in an intense manner that showed the deep appreciation they held for the meal's creator.

It was exceedingly difficult to keep her attention focused on Pru and her biped with so many distractions so close at hand. She tried to close her senses but found that to be nearly impossible.

Even as she kept her eyes locked ahead of her, she smelled another establishment. This one was giving off aromas of hot oils, coriander and other spices that she had never encountered before. She couldn't resist a quick glance and saw a tall human with dark skin standing rigidly at the front door. His head was covered with what looked to Lucy to be a piece of cloth, and in the very centre of his forehead, there was a round dot painted right onto his skin.

"Goldie! Will you keep up!" Pru barked from the end of the street, startling her mistress.

Lucy refocused herself to the task at hand and followed Pru at the prescribed distance. Though still being veritably assaulted by the sights, sounds and smells of the place, she kept her head forward and simply inhaled the spiced air without letting it distract her.

Pru made a right turn at an intersection, then glanced back to ensure that Lucy had seen the turn. She had, and the threesome continued their journey for a short distance further. Pru then stopped at a particular lamppost and made a great show of examining it. Her mistress stood patiently by as the Afghan went through the motions of claiming the post as her own. Unbeknown to her biped, Pru was signalling to Lucy that they had arrived.

Lucy looked over at her friend, then at the building next to her and other than spotting a blue lamp hanging in its entrance, saw little difference between it and the many other buildings she had seen in the city. As she watched, three blue uniformed humans stepped out of the front door and climbed into a bright blue and white vehicle with a funny-looking coloured bar on its top.

Lucy decided that this must be what Pru had referred to as the police station. She glanced over at the Afghan and saw that she was staring back at Lucy with large, sad eyes.

Lucy couldn't just let her walk away, so with a show of complete indifference, trotted over to Pru and gave her a sniff as if meeting for the first time.

"Are you sure you don't want to stay with me and free the others?" Lucy asked in a whisper.

"Stop it Goldie! You know how I feel. Please don't make it harder than it already is."

Lucy nodded her understanding as she looked upon the features of her friend.

There was no more to be said, and with a final parting lick on the cheek, Pru turned and led her woman to the end of the block, then turned and walked out of sight, and out of Lucy's life.

Lucy stayed standing where she was for a moment, until she realised that a couple of policemen were pointing at her from the front door of the building. Lucy could see the irony of being grabbed at that point and thrown in a cell.

Pru had told her that the kennels were located at the rear of the building so her priority was to find a way to get there. This, it turned out, wasn't that simple. The Police station was just one building in a row of nearly identical structures, all built together without any space between them. Logic told Lucy that if there was a front, there certainly had to be a back, and that she was just going to have to search until she found it!

It proved to be quite an undertaking. She walked the entire length of the street and found no alley or even a gap between the buildings. She rounded the corner and found to her amazement that the structures on that street were also built tightly together with no access whatsoever to their rear.

Lucy sat for a moment and gave the matter some very deep pondering. She had walked one length and found no breaks. She had turned right and done the same. Having no concept of geometry, and thus the basic knowledge of a square, the puzzle was so intangible to her that her brain began to actually hurt as she tried to focus on its complexities. Every time she came close to even the most basic framework of the problem, the pieces of the puzzle would simply disappear like wood smoke dispersed by a summer's breeze.

Such was her determination that she retraced her steps just to be certain of the paradox. It was, as it turned out, the best thing she could have done. Lucy retraced her steps right back to the front of the police station where she again sat herself down in complete frustration. As she tried again to piece the puzzle together, she heard the distinct sound of another dog's growl. She turned and spotted Champ leading Fat Man out of the police station. The Boxer tried to charge Lucy, but only succeeded in nearly choking himself because of the Fat Man's slow reflexes in releasing the leash.

Lucy used the extra seconds she had been afforded to run at full speed away from the police station and towards the street with the wonderful restaurant smells. After only a few yards, she noticed on her left, one of those cobblestone lanes that Angel had referred to as a mews. Something instinctual told her to make the turn even though she had no idea where the mews led. She managed a quick glance over her shoulder and was relieved to see that Fat Man and Champ had somehow got themselves tangled around a streetlamp, with the lead encircling the metal column at least five times, and Fat Man's legs at least twice. The Boxer was straining to be released to give chase to Lucy, but Fat Man was far more interested in his release from the leather restraint.

Lucy dashed down the mews and found to her utter delight that it was in fact dissected about halfway down by another mews that led to, and opened onto, the back of the police station. Attached to it was a long single-story building with high set windows.

She edged round to the back of the structure and saw that it was made up of small, meshed-in enclosures; each one housing a canine. Some were out in their respective 'pen' areas. Others were lounging in the interior part of their cages.

It all seemed frightfully cosy. Lucy approached the first enclosure and caught the eye of its occupant, a large, fluffy old English sheep dog.

"Excuse Me," Lucy said. "Would you have perhaps seen my friends? It's a group of five dogs. A Yorkie, A Rottweiler..."

"A what? "the old dog asked. "Porky and a bottle of wine?" I say old girl. I'm not certain that I can be of much help."

Lucy stared back at the other animal utterly lost for words.

"Psst," came a voice from an adjoining pen. "You'll have to excuse him. He's deaf as a post."

Lucy smiled at the animal and with a weak grin, slipped away from the old English's confused glance and came face to face with the oddest-looking hound she had ever seen.

He was slightly smaller than herself, had short, brown hair and was made up, or so it appeared, of nothing but wrinkles. Not the thin narrow lines that appeared on the faces of bipeds when they laughed, cried, or simply got older, but huge furrows of flesh that Lucy couldn't remember ever having seen before on any living thing.

The strange breed smiled broadly at her, sending a couple of facial folds in an entirely different location. Lucy tried not to stare at the fleshy migration and instead focused on the animal's eyes, which she found to be quite beautiful.

"You'll have to excuse Godfrey," the wrinkled hound said in a surprisingly well-bred voice as he nodded towards the old English's enclosure. "He's quite deaf, poor chap. Did I hear you asking about a group of five?"

"Yes, you did," Lucy responded, excitedly. "Have you seen them?"

"Not personally no, but I've had a lengthy bark chat with a couple of members of the group. They're isolated inside the barracks, but that's never stopped a canine from having a tongue wag has it?"

"No, I suppose not," Lucy said, warming to the odd-looking dog.

"I spoke with a Yorkie and a Doberman. Fine fellows, both of them," he said as he tried to recall something from the back of his mind." Goldie! You must be Goldie!"

"Lucy actually, but they call me Goldie . . . yes, that's me. So, they really are here, and they're safe," she cried, near to tears. "Oh please, tell me where they are. I must see them."

"Not a chance. They're shut up in the big holding cell inside the building. No windows to the outside and only a skylight on the roof. That's how I've managed to talk with them. Bit of a strain on the old voice box, but you can do it if you really try. It's simply a case of . . ."

"No!" she interrupted." I've come here to see my friends and I won't settle for long distance barks. There must be some way to get inside the place. Please think. I need your help.

The other animal looked at Lucy with great pity, understanding her plight. He closed his eyes and repositioned a few more wrinkles as he gave the matter some deep thought.

"There's one way," he said proudly as a thought struck him. "I've only been here a couple of days, but throughout the day, bipeds show up to look for their lost animals. They're always accompanied by policemen and usually don't stay long, but while they're here, the outer door is left open. You could, if you were truly daft enough, slip in after them and see your friends."

"Really! Do you honestly think I could?" she asked excitedly.

"Yes, I'm certain you could... it's whether you should." His face took on a serious expression, requiring the gathering and resorting of a full battalion of wrinkles. "But! Once you're inside, the humans will see you. There's nowhere to hide. You'll have to dash in, say hello then dash out and keep your paws crossed that someone doesn't close the door."

Lucy looked back at the other dog with an expression of concern mixed with excitement. "I'll just have to be careful, won't I!"

"That you will. Are you certain I can't tempt you with a simple bark chat with them? I'm sure they'd be delighted with that."

"No, but thank you for the suggestion. Those canines and I have been through quite a bit together. I don't think any of them would do any less to see me."

"Well, it's your pelt," he replied with an encouraging grin. "The door's just down on the side wall. I wish you all the best."

"Thank you. Thank you very much. Do you realise I don't even know your name?"

"How rude of me," he uttered, clearly embarrassed by his own bad manners. "My name is Rumple."

Lucy had to use every ounce of will power in her soul to not laugh at the sheer perfection of the animal's synonymic moniker. "Rumple... thank you."

She gave him a brief nose touch through the wire mesh then moved off to locate the fabled door. It was exactly where Rumple had said it would be, and to Lucy's relief, directly across from a row of bins that made an excellent hiding place.

As it turned out, she didn't have long to wait. She heard the bipeds before seeing them, as was often the case with her fine hearing. She could tell that there was a young boy and his mother, who was attempting to console the child. They were being led by a female policeman, who was trying to act official, but was having trouble remaining cold and professional when faced with a small, distressed child.

They reached the door, and as Rumple had promised, once they entered they did indeed leave the door open. Lucy took a hard swallow then dashed across the yard and through the door. The bipeds had only progressed a few paws into the building and were astonished at the sight of the speeding mass of golden hair that streaked by them.

Lucy didn't even look at the humans as she sped by. She tore down the narrow corridor, passing one cell after another as each occupant began barking encouragements for her brave manoeuvre. At the far end of the building was a large holding pen with a huge cloth that had been hung to ward off prying eyes. Lucy covered the distance in milliseconds, and without even so much as a thought, grabbed the cloth in her teeth and pulled it down.

Inside the enclosure, a startled looking Labrador looked up at Lucy from her recumbent position as a group of hungry little pups nursed themselves hungrily on her exposed teats.

'Oh my!' Lucy exclaimed, "I'm so sorry I thought..."

"Nice one, Goldie!" Rodney said.

She spun around and saw the entire gang locked up in an identical cell next to the one with the new mother and her pups.

"I can't stay. I just wanted you to know that I'm here and I'll think of some way to get you out," she said as fast as she could, for even as her words poured out, she could hear the sound of biped feet running towards her. She turned and saw the female policeman coming right for her.

"I'll stay close," she cried. "I love you all, but I have to go!"

She charged right at the oncoming human, which was clearly not what the startled female expected.

As she ran off Rex called after her. "Be careful Goldie. Fat Man and the Boxer were just here."

"I know!" she shouted back, just as she dived under the legs of the female policeman. The young boy and his mother stared in open-mouthed amusement as Lucy dashed by them for a second time.

Just as she was about to reach the door, Lucy clearly heard the young boy scream with delight and yell, "Rumple! You're here. Mummy - look we've found him! Rumple! Oh, Rumple!"

Lucy couldn't help but smile, knowing that the strange looking animal's recent good deed was being almost immediately rewarded.

CHAPTER 21

Lucy made her escape cleanly. As she crept along the mews, she was relieved to see no trace of Fat Man and Champ. She kept in the shadows as much as possible until she reached the intersection with Walton Street.

She'd seen the others, if only for a fleeting moment. Lucy knew they were safe, yet something was troubling her. Some seed of discontent was trying to take root within her thoughts, but she just couldn't seem to grasp what it was. She did however realise that she was starting to feel quite peckish.

She wandered down Walton Street until it curved sharply to the right then came upon an astonishing vision. A restaurant was taking delivery of their fresh provisions. It must have been their big delivery time, as three vans were parked up on the pavement. One carried the fruits and vegetables, another fish and poultry, and the last and by far the most interesting one, meat!

What was truly astounding was that the biped drivers of the vehicles were all gathered in the restaurant doorway, laughing with exaggerated gusto seemingly for the benefit of a female biped. She seemed quite pretty for a human but something unforeseen had happened to her clothing. The damaged garment that she was wearing on top seemed to be so loose fitting, the mounds that female bipeds were so careful to keep concealed appeared to be about to break free of their protective covering. Lucy couldn't help but think how sweet those young male bipeds were to feel enough charity in their hearts to keep company with the female.

As Lucy began to creep towards the meat van, the thought that had eluded her earlier suddenly came into clear focus.

Fat Man and the Boxer! What were they doing at that police station?

Lucy gave the question some deep thought, but as she couldn't even come close to finding a suitable answer, she allowed it to drift away as she turned her attention back to the meat. She glanced over at the drivers and saw that they were still being kind to the female, who seemed to be almost enjoying their charitable attention.

"Poor thing," Lucy thought to herself as she watched her toss her lengthy red hair from one side to the other, as she laughed toothily at the three males.

Lucy reached the meat van unseen, and carefully stepped up into its open storage area. Lucy had never seen anything like it. There was so much food! If only she could take it all, she could feed herself and the others forever! She even had a moment's fantasy about how, if she could only drive the vehicle like she had seen her Man do, she really could abscond with the whole lot! She could not drive however and had to therefore settle on a choice leg of lamb, which though heavy, she was able to half drag, half carry onto the street.

"Hey, you little thief!" the driver of the van screamed from the restaurant entrance.

Lucy froze in her tracks and turned her trembling head to face him. The man was about to step towards her when the deformed female, who was laughing joyously at Lucy's antics, grabbed his arm and gently calmed him down.

Lucy heard the words. "Oh, let the poor animal have it, Bert. Look how hungry she looks."

Whatever the words meant the male seemed to almost melt under her touch and voice.

"Oh, what the 'eck," he said, in a gruff, but resigned tone. "Get off with ya and enjoy it."

Lucy suddenly realised that for some unknown reason, she was being allowed to make off with the pilfered meat. She slowly edged her way back around the corner of Walton Street, eying the humans every inch of the way, expecting them to change their minds at any instant.

They did not, and she made it around the corner and out of sight. Still terrified, but also somehow elated, Lucy hoisted the leg of lamb into a better carrying position between her teeth and ran off in search of a secure environment in which to partake of her booty.

She located the perfect spot at the bottom of a flight of basement stairs belonging to a residence that appeared to have been vacant for a long time. Lucy slid herself and her feast into a small nook under the stone steps, and though the hiding place was a bit damp and smelly, she was able to relax and enjoy her meal.

As she ate, she listened intently to the sounds of the city as they reached her ears, amplified slightly by the stone steps that surrounded her. The sound never let up for even a second. It was as if layer upon layer upon layer of noise coexisted to ensure that, should one level of sound stop for a rest, another would instantly fill its place to guarantee a constant and seamless aural level.

Lucy found one thing very puzzling. She knew that the city was built by humans for humans, and that the place was teeming with bipeds, yet she could hear hundreds of different varieties of sounds as they cascaded down towards her alert ears, but not one of them was the sound of a human. Vehicles, tools, machines, but not even a trace of laughter or conversation from the very people who had created the environment. It was almost as if they didn't want to hear themselves.

Lucy felt her eyes slowly shut as the recent feeding worked to soothe her nerves and warm her belly. She knew that she needed to stay close to the police station and the others, but she had to nap for just a few moments.

Lucy slept soundly.

CHAPTER 22

E ven in her sleep she heard the sound. Even over the cacophony of city sounds, she couldn't miss it. Even tucked at the bottom of a basement stairwell with her head buried under her paws, she could hear her friends.

They were calling for help.

Lucy's head shot up and she listened. She at first thought that it must have been a dream, but then her senses again separated the ambient decibels into appropriate groupings, and she clearly heard them. Something was wrong at the police station.

She roused her sleep-filled limbs and climbed the stone steps up to street level. She had a clear view down Walton Street to the station entrance but could see nothing out of the ordinary. Carried along on the molecules of air however, she heard the pleading cries from her imprisoned friends. Lucy broke into a run and passed in front of the station then rounded the corner and turned down the mews. She reached the intersection of the two lanes and heard an engine. A familiar engine. Then she saw the vehicle to which the sound belonged. The grey van was leaving the kennel area and Lucy could hear the metallic, echoing, cries from within. The afternoon sun was reflecting off the vehicle's windscreen, making it impossible for Lucy to see who was inside operating it, but she had a pretty good idea.

What she didn't have was the slightest clue how to stop the van. It was heading straight for her and she was all that stood, all be it trembling, between her friend's freedom and the villainous hands of Squat Lady and the others.

Lucy felt herself go calm. A coldness ran through her body and she knew that she had to stop the vehicle. She eyed the approaching van then sat herself defiantly in its path. As it closed in on her, the sun passed behind a cloud and she could see clearly through the windscreen. Fat Man was at the wheel. Next to him, tightly wedged together, were Skull Face and Squat Lady. Lucy heard the engine grow louder and suddenly higher in pitch. They had speeded up.

Lucy then realised that a dead retriever was not going to be of much help to anyone. She dived off to the side of the mews as the van sped by. She turned just in time to see Squat Lady as her pudgy features glared out through the side window. For the briefest second, Lucy's eyes locked with the monstrous female's, and Lucy suddenly understood that she wasn't looking into the eyes of a normal human at all. Those eyes were dark and lifeless, almost like those of a fish that she had seen Cook de-head just prior to preparing it for her human's supper.

The van reached the end of the mews and turned off towards Walton Street. Lucy broke into a run and chased after it. She could hear her friends calling for her from behind the grey metal panels of the van.

Lucy reached the street and saw that the vehicle had picked up speed and was already crossing the intersection of Walton Street, and the funny road with all the restaurants. She continued running after it, but she already knew that her speed was no match for the power of a human-built engine.

Lucy watched as the van rounded a series of bends, then as the road straightened out, the vehicle began to accelerate pulling even further away from her. As she used every last ounce of strength in her system and ran faster than she had ever thought possible, she saw something very odd happen. First there was a loud squealing of rubber, then Lucy saw the van swerve violently off to one side. To her utter astonishment, the grey vehicle then brushed against a lamp post, bounced off it, and flipped onto its side. With a deafening sound of grinding metal, it skidded along the pavement until it finally came to rest against another lamp post belonging to an adjoining street.

Lucy couldn't fathom what had caused the vehicle to act is such an odd manner until she looked back to where the incident began. There, standing on a biped crosswalk, was Pru and her mistress. The Afghan had somehow managed to pull her female onto the crossing in the path of the speeding van, forcing it to avoid hitting the human by whatever means possible.

Pru's mistress was deathly pale, wide eyed with fright and shaking like a leaf. Pru also looked somewhat anxious but was clearly proud of her brave and seemingly successful ploy.

Lucy gave the Afghan a big smile and a nod of thanks but didn't have time to say more. Her immediate concern was for her friends within the now battered vehicle. Pru tried to force her woman to move over to the wrecked van, but the female had clearly had quite enough, and dragged the straining hound off in the direction of the police station, presumably to report the incident.

Lucy approached the smashed vehicle which, though mechanically silent, was now leaking a variety of unpleasantly odoriferous fluids out onto the pavement and street. Steam was also escaping from the thing. It rose in a blue-white plume from the front end of the overturned beast and made a sound not dissimilar to when Lucy had once bitten down a little too forcibly on her Man's favourite kicking ball.

Lucy saw that the rear doors of the van had sprung open during the accident leaving a sizeable gap between them. She climbed over a pool of black liquid and raised her paws to the opening. With only the slightest weight needing to be applied, the left door, or rather the bottom one, as the van was on its left side, flew open slamming itself onto the pavement.

She immediately saw that the occupants of the vehicle had all been dumped unceremoniously to one side of the van's interior, and in the case of the canines, into a large pile of hair, heads, and paws. At least that's what it looked like.

As she stepped into the van, she saw with relief that the furry mass was moving. Hans was the first to extricate himself from the pile, then one by one the others untangled themselves and stepped shakily out of the wreck. Lucy urged them to hurry as the humans were busy disentangling themselves at the same time. Champ was also trying to sort himself out but was stuck on his back with the vehicle's spare tyre pinning him to the floor. He was struggling madly and was clearly about to hurt himself.

Lucy stepped further into the van and raised one side of the tyre with her head, allowing the other animal to crawl out from under it. The Boxer got to his feet and shook himself vigorously, then faced Lucy with a cold and angry stare.

"What did you do that for?" he asked, in a low growl.

"You were stuck and about to hurt yourself."

The Boxer looked over at his humans and saw that they were near to freeing themselves. "You know this doesn't change anything?"

"I didn't help you for that reason," Lucy responded matter-of-factly. "Go help your bipeds, while I help my friends."

"Lucy!" Rex called out urgently. "Over here, quick!"

Lucy turned away from Champ and looked over at Rex who was kneeling next to the very still form of Rodney. She moved over to them and anxiously nosed her little friend.

His eyes were closed and at first her heart went cold at the thought that he'd left them, but then realised that he was, in fact, breathing.

Rex turned to Lucy with worried eyes, "He's hurt, Goldie. What are we going to do?"

As if in answer to the question, the humans began moving towards them. Squat Lady had a nasty cut over one eye, which gave her already unpleasant features an even greater boost towards true ugliness. She slid her squat shape along the side of the vehicle, as an evil smile began to form on the thin, blue surface of her lips.

Skull Face also began edging towards them, following Squat Lady so closely that her posterior was only inches from his face.

He didn't seem to mind.

Fat Man was also on the move as he tried to heave his sizeable bulk up and through the driver's side window. His heavy footsteps echoed with metallic, cracking, sounds as he walked along the top side of the overturned van.

The dogs all looked anxiously at each other, desperately seeking a solution to their predicament.

"Go!" shouted the Boxer.

"We can't leave our friend," Lucy responded gesturing to the small, still terrier at her feet.

"You don't have a choice - now get moving before they get all of you!"

"He's right, Goldie," Angel said, as she gently nudged Lucy towards the exit.

Lucy looked over at the Boxer, then at the humans, then at the others. She took a deep swallow then glanced down at Rodney. "I'm sorry, little friend."

She gave the injured terrier a final lick then dived out of the van just as Squat Lady was about to grab her. She joined the others as they broke into a fast run but felt no elation at all, only the stinging of her tears and the weight of the heavy band that encircled her heart.

She managed one quick look back at the wrecked vehicle and saw that Fat Man was attaching a lead to the Boxer, presumably so he could follow their trail. Her final view, however, was one that almost froze her soul. Squat Lady had picked up Rodney in her hands and was holding the stricken animal out for Lucy to see. The message was clear.

Very, very clear.

CHAPTER 23

The five dogs charged across the street and started down a narrow road off to their left until they saw a pair of policemen walking towards them. They turned and saw that Fat Man and Champ, who was straining angrily against the leash, were effectively blocking their other escape route.

The five dogs came to a nail-screeching halt, turning every which way, searching for a way past the biped obstacles.

"Harrods!" yelled Lester.

"What?" Lucy shouted back.

"Harrods! They'll never find us in there," Lester insisted.

"We're nowhere near Harrods," Rex said, urgently.

"I beg to differ," Lester said. He gestured to a pair of brass-framed doors right next to them. The gilded lettering on the door was becoming familiar to Lucy, and she began to smile.

"This place must be huge. It's everywhere," she exclaimed.

Fat Man and Champ were rapidly closing in on them, all the while, the policemen was approached from the other direction. Five pairs of nervous canine eyes exchanged looks of desperation as the bipeds approached.

"Well?" Lester asked urgently, as he again gestured to the double doors.

As if in answer to his urging, the doors suddenly opened as an exceptionally large, and heavily perfumed female tried to exit the building. She seemed determined to get, not only her own bulk, but also an armful of dark green parcels out of the portal at the same time.

Thinking almost as one, the five dogs dashed for the door at the same time.

They all dived between her fleshy legs and managed, with great protestation from the hefty human to all squeeze through and enter the store. In their wake, they could clearly hear the angry voices of the policemen as well as the high-pitched squealing of the large biped who was by then, firmly wedged in the doorway.

Lucy risked a quick look back and saw with great amusement that the police and the Fat Man were trying desperately to coax the female into releasing her parcels just long enough to free her from her entrapment. She did not seem to understand them as she continued screaming and wiggling, which only resulted in her wedging herself still tighter within the door frame.

The dogs dashed through a huge room which was filled with items of male biped clothing. Lucy had never seen so many varieties of apparel. She wondered why bipeds made it so difficult for themselves by insisting that such a wide choice be available. It must surely, she thought, be a constant struggle to decide what piece of clothing to wear each day. As the purpose could only have been for warmth, why such a range of colours and fabrics. Very odd.

Bipeds were literally leaping aside as the dogs ran through the store. As they reached the centre of the male's clothing area, they were all suddenly struck by an all-consuming scent. All five animals came to a halt as their noses began twitching uncontrollably. Their minds were not capable of coming even close to analysing the information that their noses were picking up. It was an odour that went far beyond any normal scent. It had power. It had body and soul. It had weight as it hung on every molecule of air around the dogs. This was not a scent like the ones that arrive on wafts of air, pass over you, then dissipate into nothingness. This scent was powerful and held both history and depth. It had something to do with food, that they knew, but it wasn't simply one food or even the smell found say, in a butcher's where many odours were compounded into one odoriferous melody. This scent had layer upon layer of subtleties and varieties that simply baffled the senses of the canines. It was almost too much to bear as their salivary glands began to involuntarily lubricate their mouths. Lucy felt herself begin to drool and, though incredibly embarrassed by the act, she seemed completely incapable of stopping it.

The animals all looked to each other and began to laugh as the vision of their friends standing there drooling, struck home.

"Well, I don't know what it is," Angel stated. "but I sure am going to find out."

With that, the Spaniel turned toward a marbled corridor that led towards the source of the smell. The others glanced at each other then, without a word needing to be said, followed Angel towards the heart of the huge store.

They didn't have far to go. They passed a row of very odd, heavy brass doors that kept opening and disgorging a new and different selection of bipeds every few seconds. They had to stop and observe this ritual for a moment, because it really was terribly baffling.

The doors would slide open, and a few humans would step out, leaving the small room beyond, totally empty, then, other bipeds would walk in and the doors would shut. A short while later, a light would illuminate above the doors as a gentle chime sounded and they would again slide open. The strange thing was that the little room was again full of people, but they weren't the same ones that the dogs had seen walk in only a short time earlier. There were six of the strange little rooms and they just kept magically changing one set of bipeds for another.

The dogs would have liked to stay longer, watching this odd ritual, but they were beginning to attract way too much attention. Humans, looking both alarmed and even scared, were pointing at them as they scurried as far from them as possible. Lucy thought this very odd until she looked at her friends with a different eye, seeing them and herself as the bipeds would. They had been through quite a lot, and were, for the most part, rather ragged looking. Lucy decided that they had best keep moving, besides, the source of the mystery scent was getting very close.

They left the hallway with the funny doors and stepped into a cavernous chamber, filled with food. It wasn't the type of food that would normally be of interest to the dogs, it was more the type that the humans seemed to prefer. Cooked, seasoned, decorated and packaged, but still, what a selection. They moved through the hall, astounded at just how many varieties of food there really were.

"Hey!" Angel cried excitedly. "Over here, quickly!" The Spaniel looked stunned and clearly unstable on her four legs as she gestured through a large archway into another massive chamber. The others caught up with her and then felt the same sense of awe that had overcome their friend.

"Oh my," Rex stammered.

"I've never seen anything like it," Lester whispered in shock.

"It's... it's..." Hans tried to find words but couldn't.

"Have we died?" Angel asked in a quiet and serious tone. "Is this Heaven?"

Lucy didn't know how to answer, or indeed even what to say as she stared open-mouthed into the giant hall spread out before her. The chamber was truly massive and seemed to contain every imaginable form of meat, poultry, and fish, that the dogs had ever imagined, and many that they had not.

Against one wall was meat. It was in display cases, on counters and hung in massive slabs from the tiled ceilings.

Against another wall was poultry. Everything from the tinniest quail to massive turkeys were hanging neatly in a row with heads down and eyes closed.

Then there were fish. Not that the meats and poultry weren't the dog's favourites, but seeing the fish laid out on a massive bed of ice that sloped up into one corner of the room was enough to impress anybody. Lucy decided that there must have been more fish here than existed in well, wherever it was that fish lived.

They all felt decidedly weak, both from their recent escapades, and from the awe and wonderment that filled their minds as they looked on at the splendours within the hall.

Just as they began focusing on which section to choose from first, their attentions were rudely distracted as a team of uniformed bipeds came charging into the chamber. It was immediately apparent that the humans were there specifically to deal with them, and that judging from their expressions, they had no plans to be gentle about it.

With one last, soul-wrenching glance into the chamber, the dogs bolted the other way as they tried to ignore the still awe-inspiring odours that followed them out. They dashed back through the room with the human food, then into another hall, this one filled with strong scents of perfumes, oils and creams that female humans seemed to adore splashing all over themselves to hide their own, individual, odours.

They made it through that hall, even though more of the uniformed bipeds had joined in the chase. Ahead of them they saw doors. A row of them that seemed to lead back outside. The bipeds were getting awfully close, and the canines' options were few. They made for the doors!

As they approached the them, they saw that still more bipeds were moving in on them from the sides, and from stairways that emptied right next to them. It was going to be close.

An exceedingly kind-looking human in a green uniform and top hat stepped forward and ceremoniously opened one of the doors for them, even as the other bipeds screamed at him to bar their way.

They ran past him and out into the street, missing a speeding taxi by only a paw. They made it across and as they looked back, they saw that the bipeds were not following them. They relaxed slightly until they saw that Fat Man and Champ were running straight for them. The dogs sprinted as fast as they could, knowing that if they were this close, then Skull Face and Squat Lady were certain to be near as well.

They saw up ahead, a busy street that they'd almost certainly have trouble crossing and decided to simply turn and brave the pedestrian traffic instead. They hoped that maybe, if they were extremely lucky, they might even find their way back to the park.

Those thoughts vanished as Squat Lady appeared directly in front of them, in effect blocking their progress.

"Down here!" Lester shouted, as he dived down a flight of steps off to his right.

The others had, like Lester, no clue where the steps led, but they had no choice. They ran after the Doberman, down a couple of flights of stairs until they reached a large concourse that seemed to lead to yet another set of steps that descended still further into the earth. They had no time to even consider their options as Fat Man and the Boxer were right on their heels.

They ran for the stairway, diving under and through strange, metallic devices, whose only purpose seemed to be to stop any human from reaching the stairs. This struck Lucy as exceedingly odd as presumably the steps had to have been built for bipeds to use, so why stop them? She couldn't dwell on this for long as every conscious thought in her mind suddenly evaporated as an icy wave of pure fear swept over her.

They had reached another set of steps and looked down the ludicrously steep flight that seemed to go on forever. That wasn't the worst part. The steps were moving! All by themselves, they moved in a constant motion, seemingly materialising out of the very ground they were standing on. They then formed into stairs and simply carried whatever was upon them down to the bottom where they again flattened and vanished into the ground.

None of them had ever seen anything like it before, and though they tried to conceal it, each animal's defence system had taken over. Each dog's ears were laid flat against their heads as their hackles rose to a thin raised line that ended at their tails. Lucy thought of how comical it would have looked if she were not herself, scared beyond belief.

Rex didn't even glance at the others. He knew that one of them had to make a move and he had, after all, been appointed to be their leader.

He stepped onto the next stair as it formed in front of him and looked back at the others with a brave smile as he began being transported down the moving stairway.

"No way am I getting on that," Angel announced to no one in particular.

With that she moved away from the others in search of other means of descent.

Lucy looked at the tense faces of Hans and Lester, then with her eyes firmly shut, stepped onto the metal stairway. It was a very peculiar sensation; especially with her eyes closed. There was a definite feeling of motion, both horizontal and vertical. What made the effect still stranger was a strong draft that seemed to rise from somewhere below. It was a warm wind that smelled of, well basically it smelled of age. She opened her eyes and saw Rex sitting rigidly on the conveyance below her as he neared the end of the ride. She looked up and saw that Lester and Hans were on board as well, though clearly not enjoying the experience.

She couldn't see Angel anywhere. She barked her name and was rewarded with her own voice being both amplified and echoed as it reverberated off the tiled walls of the stairwell. Her bark was immediately returned by Angel who, though invisible to her, sounded very close.

"Where are you?" Lucy asked.

"Right next to you," came the breathless reply.

"Where? I don't see you."

"You will," Angel said, with clear cockiness in her tone.

Rex had made it to the bottom and was standing at the end of the moving stairs grinning encouragingly at the others, as they descended towards him.

"Careful of the last bit," he called up to them. "the steps just disappear. I jumped off a little early. It might be a good idea to do the same."

Suddenly Angel appeared, out of breath but laughing madly! "Looks like I beat you lot doesn't it," she managed to cry between gasps and laughs, "There's a regular stairway right next to this one. You should have followed me!

"Why?" Lucy asked in a calm and superior voice as she hopped off the steps and moved clear to allow room for the others. "I believe I quite enjoyed the experience, and if I may point out, I didn't have to lift a paw... unlike yourself."

Angel simply glared playfully back at Lucy as she tried to control her panting. The others made it to bottom, and by their expressions, were obviously relieved to be clear of the strange metal-stepped contraption.

"Oh no!" Rex shouted suddenly, as he pointed his muzzle up the moving steps. Fat Man and Champ were just getting on the top stair. Unlike the others, they didn't simply stand still allowing the stairs to do all the work. They began walking as well, giving them extra speed in their descent.

"I have an idea," Lester stated calmly.

The others all turned to him with urgent expressions.

"These buttons," he said, pointing to a pair of large, and important looking knobs located at the base of the stairs.

"What are they?" Rex asked anxiously.

"I don't know but it says 'start' on one and 'stop' on the other," Lester responded. "and something about a fine, though I have no idea what that is."

"Stop . . .? It says stop. I think we all know what that means," Hans said. "Humans are always saying that word to us."

"It's about time we used it back then, isn't it," Lester grinned mischievously, as he reached up with his front paws and hit the red button marked 'stop'.

The result was far better than they could have hoped for. The moving stairway immediately stopped moving with a jolt. Their two adversaries were about halfway down the flight when Lester hit the button, and without advanced warning, they were taken completely unawares. Both man and dog sailed forward and began tumbling down the metal steps in a confusion of limbs and curses.

Though wishing they could stay and observe the results of their deed, the dogs realised that the opportunity was far better used for their own escape rather than for simple amusement. They turned and dashed down a narrow-tiled corridor that loudly echoed their every sound as they galloped along at full speed.

They had gone only a short distance when they came to a split in the tunnel. It branched off in two separate directions. On a wall in front of them were two odd tree-like drawings, each different, and each with an arrow pointing down their respective branch of the corridor.

They all turned to Lester.

"Well?" asked Angel in a somewhat nervous voice. "What do they say?"

"It looks like names of places," he responded as he tried to read the strange signs. "This way says Gre... Green... Pa... Par... Park... then... Pic... Picca... Picca... Piccadilly something.

"Oh, for heaven's sake!" Angel snapped impatiently. "What does all that nonsense mean? What about the other way? Where does that go?"

"South Ke...Ken...Kensing... ton and Glo... Glouc... Glouces..."

"This is ridiculous; we don't know what any of these places mean. They could be..."

"Angel, let him read. He's trying to help," Lucy said in a stern voice, trying to calm the anxious Spaniel. "Lester go on. Do you see anything that might help us?"

The Doberman kept on reading, but the others could now hear the unmistakable sounds of Fat Man and Champ as they neared. They were moaning loudly somewhere down the corridor and were moving towards them.

"As quick as you can," Rex added, with feigned calmness.

"Sai... Saint... Paul! We can get to a Saint from here!" Lester announced excitedly.

"Is that good?" Hans asked, innocently.

"Saints are always good," he stated, assuredly. "They are the best of bipeds that even the humans look up to."

"And this ... St. Paul, he can help us?" Rex asked, urgently.

"Who said anything about it being a he?" Angel interjected.

"Whatever ... he or she," Lucy interrupted, trying to calm the others. "Do you really think this St. Paul could help?"

"I think it's worth a try," Lester replied.

"Good enough for me," announced Rex. "Let's go!"

He began to lead the others, then stopped suddenly.

"Lester!" he called. "Which way?"

"To the right! The sign says to the right," Lester replied as he pointed his muzzle down the appropriate corridor.

"Right," Rex commanded. "Follow me." he began leading the group down the correct passageway and to yet another flight of steps. This time they were unmoving, and the dogs descended with ease. They turned and exited into a large, rounded chamber on which were posted huge pictures depicting humans performing various actions. In one, they drank liquid. In another, spoke into the hand-held plastic things. They rode horses, drove vehicles ... they were strange illustrations! In each one the bipeds looked beyond ecstatic even while carrying out the most basic of chores.

What struck Lucy as most odd within the chamber, was the fact that the stone floor only covered half of the ground. The other half was far lower, filthy dirty, and contained three strips of oily metal that ran the entire length of the room then vanished at either end into dark tunnels.

"Stop! You mangy mutts," Fat Man screamed from behind them.

The dogs burst into a frenzied charge along the slippery floor of the chamber as Fat Man, now limping slightly, and Champ, raced after them.

They covered the distance quickly as they headed for another exit at the far end. As they neared it, they saw with heart-stopping realisation that it was shut off with a heavy metal gate. They turned and looked back down the room.

Fat Man and the Boxer stopped running. They knew they had them cornered. Both man and dog shared an evil smile, as the pair stepped towards the cowering group.

"I can take them!" shouted Hans.

"He's right, between us we can stop them!" Lester said in agreement.

Fat Man reached into his dirty leather jacket and removed a nasty looking knife of sizeable proportion.

"It's too risky," Rex stated with resignation. "We've got to find some other way..."

"There is only one other way," Lucy interrupted as she leaned over the edge of the upper concrete level and stared down at the filth between the metal strips. She gave the others a resigned nod then jumped off the edge.

CHAPTER 24

"Lucy!" Rex cried in horror.

"Yes," she responded, calmly.

Rex moved to the edge and saw that she was standing between the metal strips smiling back up at him.

"I can't believe you did that," he began to scold. "Do you realise..."

"Do you realise that if you don't shut up and get down here with me, I'm going to have to rescue all of you; again?" Lucy grinned up at the others.

Rex turned and saw that Fat Man, and Champ were closing in fast. "I'll hold them off while you lot get down there with Lucy," he instructed.

"Excuse me," Angel said, as she looked over the precipice with an expression of great disdain. "You're not thinking that I'm going to go down there, are you?"

"It's your choice, Angel, but I think that Fat Man plans to make you into a coat," Lucy replied.

Rex moved towards the approaching pair and began to growl viciously as he lowered his body close to the ground, ready to pounce should the need arise. He turned back briefly to the others and in a booming voice filled with authority, yelled, "Jump!"

Hans and Lester got on either side of Angel and coaxed her over the edge. Because of her size, the drop was far more substantial for her. She had to ease herself over, keeping her backside on the upper level for as long as gravity would allow. Complaining all the way, she finally released her hind legs and dropped to the lower ground.

"Yuck!" She exclaimed. "It's filthy down here."

"I told you," Lucy said, smiling at her friend's attempt to not let her dainty feet make contact with the dirty surface.

Hans and Lester leapt and landed next to Lucy with loud grunts, as their breath was literally bounced out of their bodies. They all then turned to face up to the ledge, waiting for Rex to make his move.

They saw his rear first. He was backing away from his two adversaries - keeping them in his sight at all times. His posterior reached the edge and seemed to hang over it for a moment.

"Jump, come on Rex," Hans called up to him.

The others all joined in the chorus of encouragements until finally, feeling the time was right, Rex spun around and leapt just as Fat Man dived at him. The biped missed by only a few paws and found himself lying flat on his sizeable stomach with his head leaning out over the precipice. His fleshy features were drawn into any angry mask as he stared down at the five dogs. Not wishing to be left out, the Boxer lowered himself next to the human as he too leant over the edge and glared at the escapees.

"We'd love to stay," Lucy said coyly. "But we have another commitment. I am sorry!"

She gave the pair of angry faces a happy grin and tongue-pant then, with tail raised high, proceeded to move towards the nearest tunnel.

The others joined her, and keeping close together, entered the dark confines of the tunnel's mouth.

"Do you know where you're going?" Rex whispered in her ear.

"Not a clue!" she whispered back. "My feeling is that St. Paul's is either somewhere down this tunnel or the other one. That gives us an even chance of being right."

Rex nodded his agreement but clearly wasn't that happy with the odds.

"I don't believe it," Lester said, incredulously. "Look!"

They turned to see what he was referring to and saw to their utter amazement that back along their path, in the brightly lit chamber, Fat Man was edging his large rump over the ledge and onto the lower ground. As they watched, the Boxer leapt down to join him as the two resumed their pursuit of the dogs.

"I'll give him this," Rex said. "He may be a biped, but he sure acts like a bloodhound!"

The others nodded then began to move faster along the dark interior of the tunnel.

Lucy was not happy with the current circumstances. Here they were, deep underground, running inside a pitch-black tunnel stepping on, well she had no idea what they were stepping on, but thought it best that it remain a mystery. Meanwhile, they were being chased by a pair of truly despicable characters, who appeared intent on causing them great harm. Lucy had been taught both by her mother, and then by her Man, that life gave you back almost exactly what you put into it. She'd never quite understood the part about proportions, but she understood and believed fully in the principle.

She knew that if she assisted, say a young bird who'd fallen from its nest, it was almost certain that some good occurrence would befall her soon afterwards. The reverse also applied. If she'd say, been greedy and buried her favourite toy so that her man couldn't find it, odds were that when she attempted to retrieve it, it would either be impossible to find, or so grimy and misshapen that she'd no longer even be interested in it.

The basic rule was very simple; do good to get good. Which was why she couldn't for the life of her understand why she was being forced to flee from a fellow canine and an overfed biped to whom, far from doing harm, she'd only met a few days earlier. She tried to think of what possible infraction of the moral code she could possibly have broken but could see none. She'd been minding her own business, lying in front of the cottage, napping contentedly, when the bipeds had given her the drugged meat.

"The meat!" Lucy cried out loud.

"What meat?" Angel asked anxiously.

"Nothing. Sorry! I was just thinking."

"Sounds like nice thoughts," Rex added with amusement.

The meat; of course. That day at the cottage, she'd had a proper meal only hours earlier. She hadn't really been hungry at all. But the moment she saw that steak, she'd been drawn solely by greed. That was it. This whole thing was a punishment for being greedy!

No! That wasn't it. She argued back with herself. That simply didn't work. Firstly, say she had been mildly greedy. It had happened before, the appropriate bad reaction would have been a scolding from Cook, a sour stomach, or even having to bring up her food in an embarrassing display of overindulgence. Secondly, if she had been bad, then the reaction would be focused on her alone, not on all these other animals. No this was something else entirely.

She started to form just the haziest outline of a thought about how maybe bad things could sometimes happen to you even if you didn't deserve them, when her thinking process was interrupted by the sudden halting of the others.

"What is it?" she whispered.

The others stood stock still, hardly moving even their tails. She was about to ask the question again when she sensed it. They were not alone. This had nothing to do with their pursuers. This was a sense of being surrounded by something very foreign and very unpleasant.

Suddenly a pair of small, yellow eyes lit up only a couple of paws from them. They were off to the side, halfway up the tunnel wall.

As the nervous dogs edged further along the dark tunnel to get away from the following eyes, another pair lit up, then another, then, almost instantly, the tunnel was filled with hundreds of pairs of small, piercing, yellow eyes all staring right back at them.

The dogs moved closer together as they tried to focus their own eyes on their observers.

"What are they?" Angel whispered in a small and very frightened voice.

"Rats," Rex stated. "Nasty things. I had many a run in with them on night security."

"What are they?" Lucy asked, trying to keep the cold fear from her voice.

"You've seen mice, right?" Rex said, with a controlled and level tone. "Well imagine a mouse the size of a cat, with the temperament of a rabid dog and you've got a rat."

"Oh my," Angel said, snuggling close to Hans and Lester.

"Stop talking nonsense," said a whining, high-pitched voice from the gloom. "We're not that bad."

"Yes, you are," Rex said back to the tunnel wall.

"Are not," replied a chorus of whining, high-pitched voices that surrounded the entire group, causing the hair on their backs to rise involuntarily.

"Excuse me," Lucy tried to sound as casual as she could. "If I may interject here, if you're not bad..."

"We're not!" The lead rat announced. "We're simply misunderstood."

"Really!" She continued, "Then why do you hide yourselves down here in this filth and darkness waiting to sneak up on unsuspecting individuals, frightening them half to death?"

"Who's sneaking? We haven't moved an inch. You lot walked up to us, and as for the filth and darkness remark, how would you like it if I turned up at your home unannounced, then criticised your housekeeping?"

Lucy tried to think of a good answer but couldn't. The lead rat had a point.

"I apologise for my comment, it was uncalled for," Lucy said as she tried to make out even the slightest shape within the sheer blackness of the tunnel wall. "You know it's very difficult to carry on a conversation with someone you can't see."

"So?" replied the rat.

"So, I was wondering if we couldn't have some light of some sort," Lucy requested.

"We will," the rat said smugly. "Very soon in fact."

Even as the rodent spoke, the dogs felt the beginnings of a warm draft of air move over them as they stood squinting in the darkness. They listened carefully for a moment, thinking that they'd heard an unusual sound in the distance. All they could hear however, was the loud panting of the fat man as he and the Boxer moved towards them, still some distance sway.

"Are they with you?" the lead rat asked.

"Not really," Lucy said to the wall. "They happen to be trying to catch... look it's bad enough that I can't see you, but I don't even know your name!"

"My what?" the whiney voice snapped back.

"Your name... you know... what they call you!"

"What does who call me?" he asked, clearly confused by her line of questioning.

"The other rats!" Lucy tried to remain patient. "When they talk to you, they must call you something."

"Why?"

"Because they must! Everybody does!"

"I'm terribly sorry," the rat said, actually sounding quite apologetic. "But I'm not following you at all. When a rat speaks to me, they look at me and speak. That's it! What more is there?"

"Names! That's what's more. You have to have names otherwise you can't identify yourselves," Lucy insisted.

"What nonsense!" he said, with a nasty, little whining laugh. "We always know who we're talking to or about. Why would we want to confuse everything with... what was it you said... names?"

"Look," Lucy said with great patience. "I don't think you're..."

"It's quite simple, "Rex interrupted, with a definite edge to his voice. "My name is Rex, hers is Lucy, though we call her Goldie, that's Angel, Hans, and the darker shadow at the end is Lester... That's odd! Why am I able to see more clearly? I'm certain it was darker a moment ago."

"It's expected. Don't worry." The rat answered calmly. "You may want to lie down though."

"I beg your pardon?" Rex asked, in astonishment.

"You don't have to," the rat continued. "I mean it's up to you, but I really do suggest you lie down."

As the dogs stared at the tunnel wall, they noticed that the bright eyes of the rats seemed to be fading, as the furry outline of their bodies became more distinct.

"It's getting brighter," Hans exclaimed.

"And windier," Angel added, as she tried to control the flapping of her long, droopy ears.

"We know," said the rat. "It's expected!"

"What's expected?" Lucy asked, sensing great unease.

"What's about to happen!" the rat replied. "But it's expected, so there's no problem."

The tunnel was brightening rapidly now. Lucy looked back down the way they'd come and saw Fat Man and Champ silhouetted in the grey light. The biped looked totally petrified and was trying to drag the Boxer backwards out of the tunnel.

"This is preposterous," Hans snapped. "Something is definitely wrong. The wind is stronger. The light is brighter and... listen to that sound. Will you lot please tell us what's going on?" He had to raise his voice slightly to be heard above the grinding, squeaking, metallic and groaning sounds that were filling the tunnel.

The dogs could now see the rats clearly in the growing light. There were hundreds of them, perched on wooden supports and cables that ran along the tunnel walls. They were large, just as Rex had said. Maybe not cat size, but certainly as big as rabbits. They each had long, thin, tails which hung down behind them making it near impossible to judge which belonged to which rat. As the rats stared down at the anxious dogs, Lucy noticed that they were all smiling, with their yellow teeth exposed.

The lead rat was a slightly lighter shade from the rest, who all seemed to be a uniform dark grey. He stared at the five dogs with expressionless eyes, then in a voice that sounded almost bored, said. "I can't begin to tell you how crucial it is that you lie down."

"Why?" Rex shouted back at him above the increasing din.

Suddenly all the rats, every single one of them stood up and glared down the tunnel towards the source of the light and sound.

"You know," Lucy said nervously, shouting at the others. "Maybe they're right. Perhaps we should lie down."

"In this mess?" Angel exclaimed in a shrill voice.

"Yes!" Lucy yelled back. "And quickly!"

"Why?" Rex looked at her uncertainly.

"I don't know," she said.

Begrudgingly, the five dogs stretched out on the dirty ground below the level of the three metal strips. The rats nodded their approval of the canine's new position as the tunnel suddenly grew much brighter, and the noise level doubled. Lucy raised her head to see what was going on and saw that they were, in fact, awfully close to a bend in the tunnel and that something was approaching. Even before she could alert the others, a brilliant, blinding light appeared at the curve.

"Oh, my heavens!" she exclaimed, as she flattened herself to the floor.

Angel gave her a puzzled look just as the world directly above their heads erupted in a thunderous explosion of sparks and grinding metal. The air was literally sucked from their bodies as the dark entity above them tore by at astonishing speed. The dogs kept their heads pinned to the ground as the thing sent showers of soot over their already soiled coats.

Lucy had never been so scared in her life. She wished that whatever it was would go away and leave them alone. Then, as she tried to cover her ears with her paws to shut out the deafening noise, it ended.

She just had time to raise her head and watch as a glowing red light on the thing's rear, grew smaller as it speeded away. Whatever it was, it rounded a corner and vanished from sight. The tunnel was again thrown into total darkness.

As the dogs lay there in shock, trying to recover from their recent ordeal, they could hear their own frightened panting.

"Is it gone?" Angel was the first to speak. Her voice was little more than a squeak.

"Oh, yes," the lead rat announced. "As expected."

Rex got to his feet, and with a look of severe annoyance on his face, approached the tunnel wall. He placed his muzzle only inches from the lead rat's glowing eyes and slowly revealed his savage looking teeth as he spoke.

"Is there anything else ... expected that we should know about?" His sarcasm and anger were very clear.

"Hard to say really. What's interesting for us might not be for you," the rat replied.

"Let's just pretend that everything interests us. That way we won't be disappointed."

"Alright ... let me think ... oh yes ... well ... It's time for us to eat," The lead rat announced casually.

"That's hardly of interest!" Rex stated.

"Oh, I don't know." the whiney voice responded. "You may be mildly interested in learning just exactly what we plan to eat."

"Why should we be?" Rex asked with growing impatience.

"Rex!" Lucy whispered in the darkness somewhere behind him.

"What!" his voice had an angry edge to it.

"Move away from the wall," she insisted.

"Why would I want to do that?"

"Just do it!"

"But..."

"Now!" she commanded.

Rex moved back to the group and was about to speak when the dogs heard some movement on the tunnel walls. Suddenly thousands of yellow eyes snapped open, all staring at the five dogs.

"I think you'd be very interested in knowing what we're planning to eat!" The lead rat stated in an excited squeal that sent shivers up the canines' spines.

"Perhaps we should be going," Lucy said with feigned calmness.

"No, I don't think so," the rat replied. "Do you?"

The entire tunnel filled with rat voices all replying in unison. "No!"

"Run!" Lucy screamed.

The others didn't need any other prompting and broke into a mad dash back along the tunnel. They weren't in the least bit concerned about Fat Man or Champ. Anything those two could dole out was insignificant compared to becoming lunch for a thousand rodents.

As they ran at full speed away from the infested walls, they heard the spine-chilling sound of rat laughter as it echoed after them. They finally rounded a long curve and could see the end of the tunnel before them. They felt a huge relief as the first particles of light began infiltrating the darkness.

They charged by the spot where they last saw Fat Man and the Boxer but could see no sign of either of them.

"Do you think that horrible thing got them?" Angel asked with a mixture of horror and disgust.

"Yes," Lester said with complete certainty.

The others turned to face him, curious as to his conviction that their two foes had been taken by the giant metal beast. As they looked at Lester he bent over and picked up something between his teeth. The others all felt a chill pass through them as they stared at the leash & collar that had, until very recently, belonged to Champ.

"It's odd," Angel said. "But I actually feel slightly sad."

They all quietly nodded their understanding of the Spaniel's emotion.

Lucy was the first to speak. "May I suggest that we do our mourning once we're out of this place? I'd prefer to have a little more distance between myself and those rats."

She didn't have to push very hard. The mere mention of the yellow-eyed rodents was enough to get the others instantly back on their feet as they resumed their mad dash towards the tunnel's end.

They covered the distance quickly and had to blink their eyes repeatedly as they burst out into the brightly lit chamber from which they'd escaped only a short time earlier.

The descent from the ledge to the lower ground turned out to have been far easier than the reverse. After a few very unsuccessful, and ungainly attempts to reach the higher level, they found a system.

Basically, they used Hans as a step. Due to his bulkier body size, he proved perfect for the job. He leant himself against the side of the wall below the ledge and allowed each animal to leap on his back, one at a time, then step up onto the higher ground.

Various bipeds stood staring at, what to them, must have been a peculiar sight as the dogs scaled the formidable wall. Even Angel made it, though Lucy had to nose her rump up onto Hans' back as the Spaniel kept slipping off.

Lucy was the last to go and tried extremely hard to put as little weight on her friend's back as possible. Once up, the dogs looked down to Hans for him to make his move. He stepped back and jumped at the wall. His front paws just touched the rim of the platform then he tumbled back to the ground. He made the attempt a couple more times but with similar results.

He was becoming visibly frustrated, but somehow kept smiling through it all.

They all felt the strange wind at the same moment. Coming from somewhere within the tunnel, it sent shivers through the five animals. Hans tried the jump again, this time without the smile. His front paws brushed the lip of the platforms edge but got no further. The dogs then heard the sound. It was the same as before; metallic and powerful. Lucy looked to the mouth of the tunnel and saw that the blackness had been replaced with a grey glow as the beast approached them.

"Hans you've got to get out of there!" she urged her friend. "You've got to jump like you've never jumped before!"

Hans nodded up at her then took a few careful steps backwards as his eyes darted back to the tunnel and the approaching creature. With a deep swallow, he charged the wall.

It was a great jump, and he got his paws a good distance up and onto the platform but again, he began to slide backwards.

Lucy looked into her friend's panicked eyes as they darted back and forth between the tunnel with its approaching terrors and the faces of the dogs already safe on the ledge above.

Suddenly a pair of human arms reached down and grabbed Hans by his front legs and hoisted him up and out of danger. As he was lowered to the safety of the platform, all the animals looked towards the saviour of their friend.

The squat and angry features of the woman stared menacingly back at them as she reached down and took a firm hold of Hans by the scruff of his neck. With her other hand, Squat Lady produced the dart gun she he'd aimed at them only a few days earlier.

At that moment, the beast exploded from the tunnel with a squeal of metal and a loud exhale of its foul and evil breath.

Lucy turned to face the emerging creature and was utterly astonished to see before her, a harmless looking, shiny metal conveyance that was partially filled with a variety of bipeds who all appeared completely relaxed within its interior. All along the length of the thing, doorways seemed to suddenly appear, allowing humans to both enter and exit the thing.

She never knew what came over her that day, but Lucy suddenly felt possessed by an anger such as she had never thought possible.

She'd finally just had enough.

Squat Lady was levelling her pistol at Rex, who was to her the most obvious target due to his size and ferocity. Lucy used the moment to lunge at the female biped. She drew back her lips to reveal her full arsenal of sharp teeth that she'd been trained to never use on any human, and with a sense of devout pleasure, sank them into the pistol-wielding arm.

The female screamed as Lucy kept her jaws firmly closed around the pudgy flesh. She had to balance herself on her hind legs as the human tried to spin away from her attacker.

Hans used the distraction to twist his heavy bulk out of her grasp and leap out of her way. Rex then stepped forward and sank his teeth into the spinning biped's ankle.

The reaction was spectacular. The human shrieked and howled as she tried to free her arm and leg from the two, firm sets of canine teeth.

Just as the other dogs made a move to join in the fun, a loud whistle pierced the air. From the far end of the chamber, a dozen or so policemen had appeared. As one of them continued blowing urgently into his whistle, the others ran towards the melee.

With deep reluctance, the dogs released their hold on Squat Lady as they tried to find some avenue of escape from the charging, uniformed bipeds.

"Follow me!" Lucy shouted as she leapt through one of the openings of the metallic conveyance. The others followed instantly, seeing no other choice at hand.

As the last of them leapt into the silver beast, its doors, as if by magic, slid shut behind them. The Squat Lady lunged after them. She managed to poke the end of the dart gun between the closing portals and tried to pry them open. The dogs cowered on the opposite side of the brightly lit interior, as the female began to succeed in forcing the doors open.

That's when the strangest thing happened. A male biped dressed immaculately in a dark suit, rose from his seat and went to the doorway. The dogs assumed that he was about to help the woman and began edging away from the activity.

To their utter astonishment, the human grabbed the end of the weapon and pulled it out of the Squat Lady's grasp. Then as if that were not enough, he used the weapon to tap on the female's clutching fingers until they released the sliding doors. As soon as the doors closed, the dogs felt themselves moving and watched in rapt fascination as the irate face of Squat Lady, and the concerned expressions of the policemen, all seemed to slide by them with ever increasing speed. Within seconds, they were gone from sight as the conveyance entered a tunnel.

That's when the lights went out.

CHAPTER 25

In fact, the lights were only out for less than a second, but it was long enough to truly terrify the already anxious canines.

Once the lights stopped their flickering and settled back to their harsh, but stable brightness, Lucy had a good opportunity to examine the biped that had saved them. The human stepped over to the dogs without even the slightest sense of fear. He dropped to his knees without any thought for his clean and neatly pressed clothing. He reached out a hand and held it politely under Lucy's nose so that she could evaluate his scent.

Her mother had been a fine instructor when it came to the sometimes tricky challenge of categorising a human's scent. It wasn't easy, especially as most humans seemed to go out of their way to conceal their personal odour whenever possible. Between the soaps, oils and perfumes, it was indeed quite a challenge to trace a human's original smell beneath the camouflage.

In this instance however, Lucy was able to locate the true scent very easily, as the biped used little to conceal his odour other than a mild, natural-smelling soap. Beneath that was him. Gentle, patient, calm and without any fear that she could detect.

She lowered her head and allowed the human to stroke her. It felt wonderful, and for a moment, catapulted Lucy's memory back to the safe and gentle sensations of the cottage and her man's affectionate touch. She looked into the human's eyes and saw the same type of caring and intelligence within them.

"So, what's your story, you lot?" The human spoke in a gentle tone. "On the run, are you? Well, I have no idea what you've done, but looking at you, I can't somehow believe it's that bad." As he spoke, he continued to stroke her head.

The entire group, biped, and all, suddenly lurched forward as the transport applied its brakes and began to slow down. The dogs became instantly wary and even Lucy pulled away from the gentle touch of the kind man.

The biped seemed very understanding, as he rose back to his feet grabbing a metal pole for support. He smiled down at the dogs, but especially at Lucy.

"I have to get off here," he said, apologetically. "Take care of yourselves."

The conveyance suddenly burst out of the tunnel and back into, what to the dogs, looked like the same chamber they'd started from. They could see the same lights and posters. It was very confusing until Angel pointed out that though similar, it was in fact different in subtle ways.

As the transport came to a complete stop and the doors slid open, the dogs stared nervously out, looking for Squat Lady or indeed anyone who meant to do them harm. The kind biped gave each animal a brief, but friendly pat then walked through the doors and onto the platform. The dogs decided that they preferred to stay where they were, having no wish to encounter Squat Lady again so soon.

As they anxiously waited for the doors to slide shut, Lucy watched the nice human male as he turned from the platform and produced the dart gun from his jacket pocket. Almost ceremoniously, he deposited it into a waste bin then, with a brief wave, turned away and vanished from their sight up a flight of stairs. The doors then slid shut.

They felt the ground under them jolt as the vehicle began to move again and immediately pick up speed.

Lester was the first to notice that, posted above them, were drawings and names just like the ones they'd seen back at the initial underground chamber. Lester soon managed to read the names that were printed above each stop and then locate the same on the drawings. He was able to work out where they were and amazingly, where they were going. It was very impressive to the others.

He located St. Paul's name and calculated how many more stops they had to go before actually reaching it. The others found such a theory a little far-fetched. As the doors slid open at what Lester insisted would be the correct stop, they were stunned as the lettering before them did indeed seem to back up the Doberman's claim. They stepped out into the tiled chamber, and with every nerve-ending in their bodies ringing with energy, they waited to be pounced upon at any moment. Nothing happened. Other than a few startled glances from passing bipeds, they were able to continue on, unhindered.

Rex gathered the group together, and with a voice filled with leadership and strength, spoke to the others. "I think the most important thing at this point is to get back above ground. We need to find a way out."

"How about over there?" Lester voiced smugly as he gestured to a large, illuminated sign on which was clearly printed... WAY OUT.

"That should do," Rex stated, trying to ignore Lester's smirking grin.

The five animals edged their way along the platform until they reached the sign which hung above a break in the wall. Rex took a deep breath and stepped through the opening first.

"It's safe," he whispered back to the group. "Come on, follow me."

He led them up a stairway, then down a long and twisting, white-tiled corridor. They continued on until it finally emptied into an open area at the base of a row of moving stairs, just like the ones they'd battled earlier.

"Not again," Angel pleaded.

"It should hopefully be a bit easier going up," Lucy said, encouragingly.

"Why?" Angel pouted.

"I don't know exactly, it just seems that it would that's all," Lucy gave the Spaniel a gentle nuzzle to show her understanding of the other dog's trepidation.

"Come on then," Rex said. "Let's do it." He marched over to one of the flights of stairs and leapt onto it. To his amazement and the other's amusement, the steps simply lowered him right back to the bottom again. Puzzled, but clearly determined, the Doberman turned and again lunged at the steps, this time continuing to run up them as soon as he landed. All he managed to do was stay in almost the same place. As fast as he ran up the stairs, they moved back down. Finally flustered, embarrassed, and somewhat exhausted, Rex allowed the steps to return him to his starting place once more.

"I don't understand it," he gasped. "I can't seem to make any headway at all!"

"Oi, you lot!" Angel's voice rang out through the sloping chamber.

The others spun around but couldn't see her.

"Up here, silly dogs," she said.

Lucy spotted the grinning Spaniel on another of the stairways, only this one was moving upwards. Angel was almost at the top as she smiled down at the others.

With the others watching, Angel's cheery face vanished from view as the stairs carried her to the top of their run and then flattened out.

Suddenly they all heard a squeal of pain from up above. The dogs mobilised instantly and charged up the moving steps that Angel had used.

Lucy was the first to reach the top and found the Spaniel sitting against a wall nursing the top of one of her ears.

"What happened?" Lucy asked gently.

"My ear... it... it... got caught," Angel cried, between teary intakes of breath, "I got... to the top... and was... was... laughing so hard... when... when... suddenly the steps... suddenly my ear got caught... caught in the steps!"

"Let me see," Lucy moved close to the frightened and very miserable Spaniel.

The others arrived and stood in a circle around her as Lucy examined the damage.

"It's just a little nick, Angel," she announced, finding the wounded area.

"Are you sure? It hurts!"

"I'm sure it does, but it's not serious. Let me just wash it out for you. Alright?"

"Alright," Angel replied weakly.

Lucy gave the wounded area a good cleaning with her tongue. She even gave the flesh around the wound a gentle soft-chew to get it good and damp.

"There we go," Lucy said as she gave the ear one final lick. "Good as new."

"Thank you," Angel tried to force a smile.

"I hope you learned a lesson today." Lucy's voice became serious.

"A lesson?" The Spaniel sounded utterly mystified.

"Yes, a lesson. You were showing off, weren't you?"

Angel hung her head and tried to look away, but in every direction another dog was watching her.

"This is what can happen when you show off. You're lucky it was only a nick. Next time it could be far worse?" Lucy advised.

"You sound like my mother," Angel said, as a smile began to form on her tear-stained face.

"Maybe that's because you were behaving like a naughty puppy," Lucy answered, trying to suppress her own smile.

The two dogs looked tenderly into each other's eyes then stepped forward and licked muzzles.

Rex cleared his throat to get everyone's attention. "I think we should keep moving, don't you?"

The others nodded and regrouped themselves into a line as they set off in their pursuit of St. Paul.

Rex led them down two more corridors and up one more flight of stairs. Then, after turning one final corner and with no warning whatsoever, they found themselves on the street level, breathing the slightly damp, slightly dirty evening air that hung over the huge city.

"I never thought I'd say this," Hans said, as he took a deep breath of the city air. "But doesn't the city look beautiful!"

The others all nodded their complete agreement, vowing silently to themselves to never venture belowground again. It was simply too fraught with danger. Maybe it was alright for bipeds, but for canines. No! Even battling city streets was preferable to the subterranean alternative.

"Which way do we go?" Lucy asked to no one in particular.

They all glanced in various directions, clearly not having the slightest clue.

"In that case, may I suggest that we find a place to hole up for the night," Lucy suggested as she studied her friend's anxious faces.

"What about St. Paul?" Angel asked with her large, blinking, Spaniel eyes trained on Lucy.

"It's getting dark, we don't know where he…or she is, and besides, it wouldn't be very polite to turn up this late unannounced, would it?" Lucy looked to each face for some acknowledgment. "Also, I don't know about you lot, but I'm famished. I think we should start thinking about dinner."

At the mention of the word 'dinner' every tongue appeared as if by magic, as their owners began to pant at the mere thought of food.

"I'll take that as a sign of agreement," Lucy stated with amusement as she felt her own tongue begin to moisten at the very thought of food.

The weary dogs began a search for sustenance. They stayed close to the shop fronts and office buildings as they sniffed at each doorway. They noticed almost immediately that the area they were in was different from the others they'd encountered. At first, they couldn't quite put a paw on what it was they found unusual, but after covering a few more blocks, Lucy stopped the group as a thought formed.

"Humans don't live here," she stated flatly.

"What do you mean?" Rex asked, not certain that he understood her meaning.

"That's what's so different around here. There are plenty of bipeds, but have you noticed how none of them look comfortable. The ones we've seen through the windows… did they look relaxed? No! This area seems to be where they come to… I don't know… not relax!"

As they talked, the dogs continued moving down the street, which was growing less inhabited with bipeds by the minute.

"Why would they want to do that?" Angel asked, clearly very sceptical about Lucy's theory.

"I don't know, but even back at the cottage, I remember when my Man would shut himself up in his room, he sometimes looked just like these bipeds. He'd be very serious and would become completely focused on paper bits and an illuminated box and the black rectangle they like to talk into. He'd also tap his fingers on a funny black tray thingy for hours on end. When he'd reappear much later his eyes would be dull, and his scent would be a little sour."

"Did he stay like that?" Lester inquired, with concern.

"Oh, no! Usually, I was able to get him back to normal with a couple of back rolls and a good lick or two. Sometimes, if he was really in a bad way, he'd pour himself some foul-smelling brown liquid. I never knew how he could, but he'd drink the stuff and become quite merry and playful."

"I've seen that happen to my humans too!" Hans said, smiling at the memory. "Only they'd drink a lot of this odd, fizzy liquid that smelled a little like bread, then, as you said, they'd get very playful and clumsy. They'd sometimes even fall down."

As Lucy laughed trying to imagine her Man ever falling, she noticed that Rex was facing away from the group, looking up at the darkening sky. She stepped in front of him, but he turned his head away from her.

"Rex, what's the matter?" she asked gently.

"Nothing, Nothing at all. Just go back to the others and enjoy your memories." his voice had a definite edge of pain to it.

"Rex, look at me," Lucy commanded.

The Doberman slowly turned and faced her. She could see immediately that his eyes were moist, and his expression, strained and sad.

"What is it? Tell me and maybe I can help."

"Thanks, Goldie, but you can't help me. No one can," he spoke in a whisper so the others wouldn't hear.

"You're sad. I can see that." She nuzzled his neck trying to help relieve his despondency. "Maybe if you talked about it, it would help."

"I can't Goldie. I don't even think you'd understand. That's part of the sadness."

"Why don't you at least try?" she coaxed.

Rex again looked up at the sky, as he tried to hold down his rising emotions. Suddenly without any warning, he let out a long and soul-wrenching howl that made Lucy shiver at the strength of its emotion.

The others all turned and made a move to approach the pair, but Lucy signalled for them to stay put while she talked with Rex. For a long time, Lucy sat patiently next to him, waiting for him to begin speaking. Rex's eyes were closed as he kept his head high and his muzzle pointed upwards.

Angel nuzzled Hans and Lester away from Lucy's vigil, then coaxed them to join her in a food hunt while their friends had a chance to be alone.

Rex didn't notice their departure, and when he finally lowered his head and opened his sad eyes, he was surprised by their absence. Lucy explained that the others had gone off in search of dinner.

"They can't do it alone," he exclaimed. "We should help them."

"It's alright. They've gone off so that we could be alone. I can see that you are very sad Rex, and it hurts me inside. You need to let the sad out and the happiness in."

"Don't you think I want to? I've tried. Oh, how I've tried." His voice was tight with emotion. "You don't have any idea of what I hold inside. You think you do, but you don't."

He stared into Lucy's brown eyes, which were at that moment filled with warmth and caring. With an expression of resignation, he suddenly nudged Lucy into a dark doorway belonging to a large building which was shut up securely for the night.

"I don't think you could possibly understand what I feel, but I'll try and explain if for no other reason than for you to let it rest, alright?"

Lucy nodded encouragingly back at him. Rex took a couple of deep breaths then began in a voice devoid of almost any emotion.

"One of my few memories of when I was young, was when I'd sleep with my brothers and sisters as my mother watched from her blanket. I remember feeling secure and incredibly happy. I remember watching as our door opened and humans entered our room. I saw a strange biped talking to the male that looked after us. The stranger got to his knees and began playing with each of us in turn. Mother was not happy about it and even began growling. Our human had to take her out of the room and shut her away.

The stranger finally got to me and petted me, tickled me, rolled me over, all things that I enjoyed, yet for some reason I didn't feel any warmth coming from him. It was as if he was simply going through some routine. Anyway, after a few minutes of this, the biped got to his feet and began talking to our human again and they left the room. I thought no more about it and resumed playing. A little while later, as we were all dozing after a rough game of tag, the bipeds came back. Our human reached down - I'll never forget this - and lifted me away from my brothers and sisters and handed me to the stranger. I didn't think anything was wrong until the biped placed me in a box with little holes in it and shut the lid. It was so dark. I can remember trying to peer out of the tiny holes and for a moment, could just see my family. Then, without warning, the box rose into the air and moved out of the room."

Rex had to stop for a moment to catch his breath and wipe away a tear.

"I never saw my family again," he sighed, trying to control the emotions that were rising within him.

"It's alright," Lucy said as she moved closer to him. "I'm here with you. Don't stop. Keep letting it out. I promise it will help."

Rex again looked into Lucy's gentle features and nodded, somehow knowing that she was right.

"It's not easy."

"I'm sure it's not, but try."

He again looked at the night sky before allowing the hurtful memories to surface. Lucy sat patiently next to him, knowing that Rex needed as much time as he felt necessary.

"After being taken from my family, I don't remember much until I was quite a bit older. My new human treated me reasonably well. I was fed regularly, exercised, and taught manners that humans thought appropriate, but in all my time as a puppy, he never played with me. I used to invent little games that I could play by myself, but somehow it just wasn't the same." Rex shook his head slowly at the memories. "Anyway, when I was in my early adult period, I was moved out of the big house and put into a kennel out back. There were ten other dogs, and at first I was overjoyed at the prospect of new friends and playmates, but that excitement didn't last long."

"Why?" Lucy asked in a surprised voice. She was staring intently at Rex, clearly riveted to his story.

"They were guard dogs," he continued, "They had no humour, no emotions; they were hard and brutal beasts. I remember wondering, what could turn a dog into such an uncaring shell of a canine? I found out though. I most certainly found out." Rex lowered his head and forced a thin smile for Lucy who nodded encouragingly.

"For the next... oh I don't know, six moon cycles maybe, I was taught to be a guard dog. My human found just about every possible way he could to break my spirit and turn me into as vicious an animal as possible. I learnt how to bite and incapacitate bipeds. How to knock a human to the ground in less than a second, how to... well you get the drift. Eventually, I presume he must have felt my training to be complete because he began using me just like the others. His business appeared to be the loaning out of dogs for specific guarding duties. We would be sent to protect everything from lavish homes with walled gardens, to nasty little junk yards filled with rusted metal and rats."

"How awful!" Lucy exclaimed.

"You know, I'd like to make light of it, but I can't. It was awful. I would never know where I'd be placed next. Whether it would be sheltered from the elements or be just an open-fenced enclosure where I'd have to keep moving all night long or freeze to death on the ground. After a while, all that became an accepted part of my life. What I could never accept, was the loneliness. Most of the time I could bury my feelings inside and carry on with life relatively well, but other times, I'd... I'd hurt inside. I'd hurt very badly. It was like a hot ball lodged in my chest - throbbing away, making it hard sometimes for me to even think. When you were all talking about your memories with your humans, I... I felt so..."

"That was very stupid of us," Lucy stated frankly as she shook her head. "We should have known better."

"No! You have every right to remember your good times. I should have become like the other dogs in the kennel and lost all my feelings, but Lucy, I never did. I tried so hard to become a cold and callous dog, but I couldn't. I never really learned to hate humans as I was supposed to. Every time I see a biped, I am supposed to feel hate towards them, but you know what? I don't. I can't. I want to play with them. I want to be taken for walks and be talked to, and have my stomach rubbed and my ears scratched and... Oh, Lucy!" Rex began to cry. At first, he fought back the tears, but as Lucy rested her head on his neck, he broke down completely and cried like he'd never cried before.

"I'm so sorry about this," he gasped, between sobs. "But you see what I mean. I'm not exactly your stereotypical attack dog, am I?"

"No, you're not, but there's nothing to apologise about. You're simply a sensitive dog who's had a tough life so far, but you know what? I have this feeling that all of that is behind you now."

"Do you really?" He asked hopefully, between sniffles.

"Yes, I do."

Rex gave her a huge, toothy smile in clear appreciation of her sentiments. Lucy was about to speak when the other three came trotting around the corner towards them.

"Find anything?" Rex inquired.

"We're not quite sure," Hans replied. "We've found an interesting scent, but we'd feel a little more comfortable if you were both with us when we check it out."

"Why?" Rex asked mildly puzzled.

"You'll see," Angel stated with a nervous grin."

Rex glanced at Lucy, who seemed as perplexed as he was, then with a brief shrug of his shoulders, followed the others to find out just what they'd come upon. Lucy trotted along behind the group, feeling quite proud of herself as she watched Rex, with his head raised high, reassume his position as leader of the team.

After no more than a couple of blocks, they reached the area in question. Lucy took one look at it and felt a shiver run the length of her spine.

The three explorers had found a place where part of the street branched off and ran down a steep incline under a large office complex. Above the sloping entry hung a bright yellow sign upon which was a large letter P.

Rex turned to Lester, "What's that mean?"

"I haven't the foggiest idea," he stated flatly.

"What about that over there?" Rex asked, gesturing to a large yellow placard fastened to one wall.

Lester moved over to it and began reading it as best he could.

"P ... Pa ... Park ..."

"There's a park down there?" Angel interrupted.

"Park ... parking! Not a park. Parking!" Lester announced.

"Great. So, what does that mean exactly?" Rex asked.

"I haven't a clue," Lester replied. "I know how to find out though."

"Why should we care what's down there?" Lucy pointed out. "I thought we agreed to stay above ground from now on."

"We did, Goldie," Angel said excitedly. "But stand over here and take a deep breath."

Lucy gave the Spaniel a look of mild scepticism then moved closer to the entrance as requested. She closed her eyes, raised her muzzle then took a long, deep breath.

"Chicken?" Lucy mumbled incredulously. "Roasted chicken?"

"That's what we smelled too," Angel announced. "Now do you see why we should go down and investigate."

"I don't know," Lucy replied with concern in her voice. "We're talking about being underground again."

"No!" Angel insisted. "We're talking about roast chicken!"

The five dogs all took a deep breath and reconfirmed their earlier analysis of the scent. All five again got a positive reading. Roast chicken it was!

"Well then," Rex said. "I think I should lead the way, don't you?"

The others all nodded emphatically. Rex smiled back at them then turned and, after a quick stretch to prepare his body, he stepped onto the sloping drive and led the group down into the dark and unknown territory below.

CHAPTER 26

The dog's nerves were on high alert, causing each animal to jump or yelp at the slightest sound or movement. It was a very odd place. The road-like surface descended for a while then flattened out for no purpose than any of them could see, except to allow biped vehicles to be stationed in neat diagonal rows. There had to be more to it than that, but the dogs couldn't seem to work out its true purpose.

They descended two more levels before they realised that the chicken odour was no longer present.

"Hans, Lester," Rex spoke with true leadership quality to his voice. "You two retrace our steps back up towards the entrance and see if you can find where we lost that scent. We'll continue on down and see if we can find out what this place really is."

The two nodded their understanding of the order and trotted back up the drive, sending the sounds of their nails on the road surface echoing off the heavy concrete walls.

Rex led the others further down into the depths of the place as the three searched eagerly for any clue as to its purpose. Every level appeared identical except that, as they went deeper, the biped vehicles became far scarcer and those that were to be found, seemed to somehow have an almost abandoned look.

Finally, they rounded one last corner and came to a dead end. There were only six vehicles on that level. On the higher levels, the walls had all been painted and posted with arrows and signs, but these walls were sorely neglected. Lucy approached one and noticed that it was covered with a fine sheen of greenish-grey moss. She smelled damp and decay and it made her extremely uncomfortable. It wasn't that the odours were foreign to her, after all, she had smelled them before on her walks with her human. In those instances, the odours had been outdoors and were coming from rocks and trees and were natural and appropriate. Down here, the odours had an almost evil quality to them as they clung to the abandoned and surfaces that bipeds had created, then forgot.

Lucy allowed a shiver to pass through her, then turned and saw that both Rex and Angel seemed to be having the same reaction. Without a word, the three turned from the dead end and began walking back up the sloping drive.

They had taken only a couple of steps when they heard Hans and Lester barking furiously from somewhere far up inside the structure. The three broke into a fast run as they sensed the urgency in their friend's voices. As they charged up the inclining drive another sound reached the three pairs of ears. It was a clanking, metallic sound, which for a split-second reminded Lucy of the terror she had felt in the rat tunnel earlier that day. This sound, however, did not have the weight or power of the tunnel beast. This was far lighter in tone. It was like the noise that chains rattling together would make added to the sound that Cook's metal mixing bowls made when they fell to the stone floor of the kitchen.

The two scout dogs sounded even more frantic as the three continued to climb closer to them. They seemed to be yelling something for the benefit of a biped, but Lucy couldn't quite make out the words because of the distance and the echo quality of the structure.

"We're almost there!" Rex yelled breathlessly as they rounded one last bend.

The three came to a sudden, frantic halt as they saw before them the reason for Han's and Lester's outburst.

The entrance, through which they'd so recently passed, was now entirely blocked by means of a very secure looking metal gate. It wasn't solid. It was made of metal links all joined together forming a tight fitting and impenetrable portal that covered every inch of the entrance. Because it was constructed from linked metal, the three could see beyond the barrier where the frantic figures of Hans and Lester were stationed as they howled forlornly into the night.

They were shut out.

Rex approached the barrier with great caution, keeping his eyes firmly fixed on it in case it decided to move again.

"What happened?" he asked through the links to the others.

"We were trying to find the chicken scent when this biped suddenly appeared out of nowhere and chased us out onto the street," Hans glanced quickly over his shoulder before continuing. "We didn't want to make a fuss so we let him have his way knowing we could sneak back in when he was gone."

"But he went to the wall over there," Lester said, taking over the story telling. "and pushed a button. Before we knew what was happening, this gate thing began coming down out of nowhere."

Hans carried on. "The biped stepped under it as it dropped and kept us away from it. The thing was fast. Before we could get around the human, it reached the ground and stopped. We've given it a good going over, and I've got to be honest, we can't make it budge."

Angel began to cry. At first gently and to herself, but then it grew with alarming speed to a full-on wailing, that was almost deafening within the confines of the concrete structure.

"Angel, what's the matter?" Lucy asked soothingly.

"What do you mean, what's the matter," she howled. "We're trapped. We're never going to get out. We're going to be here forever, and I'm scared and I'm cold and... and..."

"And what...? Come on tell us! We're your friends," Lucy coaxed.

And… and… we never found the roast chicken!" her pathetic voice cried out.

Rex and Lucy turned to each other both trying their hardest to not laugh at the poor Spaniel's outbreak.

"Oh, we found the chicken," Hans announced with peeve.

"Well, where is it, we're all famished?" Angel asked, her tears suddenly vanishing.

Hans and Lester both tilted their heads to the left of the gated entrance. Rex moved close to the barrier and looked to where they were gesturing.

"Oh, dear," he murmured.

Right next door was a small restaurant displaying the image of a white bearded human on a sign above white lettering. Rex couldn't read but knew the sign very well. Various night assignments had coupled him with bipeds that would dine from large cardboard buckets of chicken that held the same image. He had in fact, often wondered why an establishment that specialised in something as tasty as chicken would wish to display the image of an aged and bearded biped instead of a fine portrait of the culinary fare that they were offering.

"It's closed!" Angel announced as she tried to crane her neck against the barred entryway.

"It closed just as we got up here," Hans explained.

"But the scent came from in here," Lucy stated clearly, somewhat confused.

"It did seem to," Rex agreed. "It must have been carried in here by a draft or something."

"So, we got shut in here for nothing?" Angel sulked.

"Well," Lucy tried to find the right words. "Basically, yes!"

The dogs all stared blankly at one another until Rex suddenly started to laugh. His merry voice was so contagious that before long, the others had joined in. It was a good release for their emotions and as the laughter subsided, they all felt far better than before. They were still hungry but somehow the future didn't seem quite as dismal.

Just as the five settled down to discuss their next move, a human voice shattered the night air.

"Hey, you lot! Get out of there!"

Rex signalled for Lucy and Angel to back into the shadows afforded by their dark prison. Hans and Lester did not have that luxury and tried to squeeze themselves tightly against the gate hoping to go unseen by the approaching biped.

"Come on then!" the voice boomed." Get out of there, I said."

The towering form of the biped stepped directly in front of the gated entrance. Lucy could just make out that the biped was very untidy looking. His clothes were torn and filthy, his hair was matted and uncombed, and his face was covered with the hair that most bipeds preferred to scrape off with the aid of a sharp piece of metal. The human was holding a bottle in one hand and a filthy blanket in the other. In addition to his unkempt state, the biped also seemed to be having a great difficulty in standing up straight. He was constantly swaying from side to side. Lucy found that if she stared at him for too long, following his motion with her eyes, it made her quite queasy.

Hans and Lester tried to press themselves into the corner of the gate and wall hoping that that alone would satisfy the biped. Instead, he began mumbling unintelligibly at them and took a step forward.

Maybe it was because of the incline or maybe it was because he tried to kick at the dogs while still walking, but the biped suddenly cried out in astonishment as he toppled over and fell to the ground. Instead of trying to protect himself during the fall, his hands frantically sought out to protect the bottle. As his body reached the surface of the drive, the bottle slipped through his fingers and landed on the street, shattering into hundreds of bright shards of glass. Amber liquid flowed across the pavement and trickled into the gutter.

The human watched with wide eyes as the last of the fluid vanished from sight. He then lowered his head to his hands and began to cry with loud sobs that seemed to wrack his entire body.

Rex and the others eased themselves out of the shadows feeling that this biped was unlikely to do them any great harm. As they approached the gate they looked over to Hans and Lester who were also clearly now less afraid of the intruder.

"What should we do?" Angel whispered.

"I don't know," Rex replied. "Do you think he's alright? The fall seems to have hurt him."

"I don't think it was the fall," Lucy stated as she watched the sad biped weep uncontrollably. "I think it's his life that hurts him."

The others all looked from Lucy to the human then back to Lucy trying to understand her words. She simply smiled gently back at them knowing inside that she had just discovered a new side to her personality. She somehow was able to feel some of the pain that the poor wretch held inside himself. The others didn't seem to have that ability which, though puzzling to her, made Lucy suddenly feel rather special as if a barrier had been lifted between her and the human species. She somehow knew that from then on, her dealings and handling of bipeds would never be quite the same as before.

The dogs watched the man as he continued to sob into his dirt-streaked hands.

"He smells awful," Angel whispered to no one in particular.

"I don't think he means to," Lucy offered, in another demonstration of the new insight she felt towards humankind.

"Whether he means to or not, he does and it's foul. I'm going to go down another level," Angel said, flipping her ears back as she turned and strutted away.

Lucy was about to say something when she noticed Lester moving towards the human. She watched in rapt fascination as the Doberman stepped right up to the biped and positioned himself under his arm. Hans stood observing for a moment, and then, following Lester's lead, stepped towards the human.

At first, the biped seemed to be absorbed in his sobbing and didn't notice the two dogs, but then, he slowly raised his head and allowed his hands to descend into the back of each animal. Lucy stood riveted to her spot, fearful that Hans and Lester might be harmed, but instead, the biped's large and calloused hands began moving down each dog in gentle, petting caresses.

Hans and Lester both turned their heads slightly to offer the others a brief nod which clearly translated to, "We're fine, don't worry."

Lucy was touched deeply by the unselfishness of her friends' actions. There was quite clearly no great personal gain expected from their act. They had simply seen the need to give a little kindness and sensitivity and had given just that.

She felt her eyes misting slightly and turned away so as not to embarrass the others. As she looked back into the sloping structure her eyes caught those of Rex, who was clearly attempting to keep his emotions in check as well. His large, brown eyes were moist as he too looked away.

Realising that they had both been caught in their emotional reaction, they began smiling sheepishly at each other.

"Why don't we go down and join Angel?" Lucy suggested. "She's probably got herself into trouble by now anyway."

"Do you think they'll be alright?" Rex asked, glancing back at Hans and Lester as they snuggled close to the human.

"I think they'll be just fine," she said, smiling again at the gentleness of the scene.

The two dogs then turned away from the gated entrance and began descending in search of Angel.

They reached the next level down expecting to find her curled up asleep in some corner or other but found the area devoid of sleeping Spaniels.

That's odd," Lucy whispered.

"She probably went further down that's all."

They descended another level, but still found no trace of their friend.

"Angel?" Rex called out.

There was no response.

"Angel!" he tried again with more force causing his voice to echo back at them with a hollow flatness.

Rex and Lucy gave each other a puzzled look, then began walking down to the next level. They were moving much slower now, feeling that something was wrong.

They covered two more levels with no success. That only left the damp and seemingly abandoned one they had encountered earlier.

"Why would she go down there?" Rex whispered.

"Who knows," Lucy replied, shaking her head in mild frustration. The two dogs stared at each other for a moment, both preferring to not have to descend to the next level.

"We're being silly. You know that don't you?" Rex stated in as casual a manner as he could muster. "We've been down there once. It's just a little damp that's all. There's nothing really frightening. We're just being silly pups!"

"Do you mean that?" Lucy asked with a nervous smile.

Rex gave her a wink, which was enough to calm most of her fears. The two then began the descent to the bottom floor. They'd taken a couple of steps when Rex looked over at her and offered a reassuring smile.

Lucy was about to say how silly she felt at having been so scared of going any further, when all the lights in the place suddenly shut off, plummeting them into total darkness.

They stood there for what seemed like an eternity trying to accustom their eyes to the darkness. The problem was that it was simply too dark. Usually there was light of some description, even when one's surroundings seem devoid of all illumination. That was not the case where they were. Lucy blinked and blinked, hoping after each, to adapt her vision sufficiently to at least be able to see her own paws.

"This is ridiculous. I can't see a thing," Rex said.

"What do you think happened?" Lucy asked, trying to keep the fear from sounding in her voice.

"You sound scared, Goldie. There's no need. The lights were obviously on a timer. I've seen that a lot in my job."

"What's a timer?"

"That's when the human's want something to happen at a particular moment, while they're actually not even there to make it happen. Just like the lights; they wanted them to switch off by themselves at a certain time when they were nowhere near. It's quite clever really."

"I'm sure it is," Lucy said. "But... why would anyone want something to happen like the lights going off, if they weren't around to see it anyway?"

Rex was about to reply when he realised that he didn't have a good answer.

"That's odd, it always seemed to make good sense before, but you know, it does seem rather silly now that you mention it," he continued. "There was one job I remember at a country house when not only did the lights come on, but music came on as well, and you know what, the bipeds who lived there were away for a week. Every night though, as soon as it got dark, the windows would light up and music would start playing inside."

"That's very odd behaviour, even for them," Lucy said, amused.

"The important thing is that you shouldn't let this place scare you. The lights went off on purpose and, alright it is a bit dark, but we know where we are."

"Sort of," Lucy volunteered.

"We know there's nothing that can harm us down here, right?"

"Right!"

"So, let's keep moving and stay as calm as possible. In fact, why don't you take my tail in your mouth and I'll lead you down."

"I couldn't do that!" Lucy said, sounding quite embarrassed.

"Don't be silly, this is an emergency. Just hold it in your muzzle... gently please! And I'll guide you to the lower level."

"I'm not sure I feel comfortable with that. It's so... so... personal!"

"Really? You are so silly sometimes Goldie. After all we've been through together, you feel shy about holding my tail?"

"It's not decent. We don't know each other well enough for that!"

"Goldie, I'm not talking courtship here, though I should probably mention that sometime in the future, I just may; but for now, I'm concerned with getting both of us safely down to the bottom level and locating Angel."

"Do you mean that?"

"Of course, I do. We've got to focus on safety first. I wouldn't want to..."

"No, not that part," Lucy's voice held a gentle note of excitement to it. "I meant the part about courtship. Did you mean that part?"

There was a moment of complete silence as Lucy imagined she could hear her own heartbeat as she waited for Rex to respond.

"Yes Goldie, I did," his voice was warm and rich as he spoke the words.

Without another word being said, Lucy gently located his tail and closed her muzzle around it. She shut her eyes for a moment as a wave of total adoration swept over her, then Rex began to slowly lead her down the sloping drive.

CHAPTER 27

It wasn't easy. Even with his worlds of experience, Rex couldn't see where there was no light. They'd only gone a short distance when Lucy heard him bump into something metallic just in front of her.

"You alright?" she whispered.

"Yes, but I may have dented one of their vehicles," he responded in a pained voice.

She tried not to laugh or even smile, as he was certain to feel it through his tail. As they continued down the incline, even more slowly than before, the smell of the damp and decay began to reach them from the bottom level. Lucy tried to ignore it by recalling other, far more pleasant odours. She managed to retrieve a scent memory of Cook preparing a roast chicken in the oven. As she concentrated on the image, she began to not only smell the cooking bird with its seasoning of rosemary and garlic, but also those of the cottage itself. She could clearly smell the slightly lemony scent of the polish used on the wooden floors, of the flowers that bloomed directly outside the kitchen windows, even the tangy smell of the burned wood from the fireplace that seemed to hang on every molecule of air everywhere within the cottage.

Lucy was so transported by her recalled memories that she didn't notice when they had reached the bottom of the incline and the drive levelled out. She didn't even notice when Rex came to a halt, causing her to run right into his rump.

"Whoa! Steady on girl! Having a daydream, were you?" he asked.

"Actually, yes. I was about to tuck into a fine dinner of roast chicken. Couldn't you have kept going a little while longer?"

"Sorry Goldie, but we're at the bottom and ... ." his words suddenly ceased.

"Rex what is it?" Lucy asked, feeling the beginnings of icy fingers on her spine.

"Shh!" His voice was very tense. "Angel? Are you there?"

There was no reply.

"Angel, I know you're here. Come on, speak up." He tried to make his voice sound as casual as possible, but Lucy could clearly hear the tension within it.

They stood silently in the darkness, waiting for some sort of response. After what seemed like an eternity, Lucy was about to ask again what was wrong, when their missing friend finally replied.

"Yes, I'm here." Angel's voice was noticeably quiet and definitely that of a scared dog.

"Are you alright?" Rex tried to sound very calm.

"Yes, thank you."

"Where are you?" Rex inquired trying to sound almost disinterested.

"It doesn't matter," came the strained reply.

"Yes, it does. Tell me, where you are?" he insisted.

There was a long silence.

"You're not alone down here are you Angel?" Rex asked casually.

There was another long pause, during which, Lucy was convinced she heard quiet movement all around them.

"Angel," Rex tried again. "I asked if you were alone down here?"

They didn't have long to wait for an answer.

The bottom level suddenly lit up, blinding Rex and Lucy who were completely unprepared for the termination of the utter darkness.

"No, she's not alone," said a velvety voice that was filled with superiority.

It took Lucy a long time to be able to open her eyes to the bright lights. Finally, keeping her lids at half-mast, she was able to peer out and was stunned by the surreal and very bizarre vision that met her startled eyes.

Cats! Everywhere she looked there were cats. Some were staring with sparkling, yet expressionless eyes at her and Rex; others were slowly moving with eerie fluidity as their lithe, feline bodies twined and intertwined with that balance of passion and disinterest that cats find so easy to achieve. In the centre of the teaming mass of fur, was Angel.

She was clearly terrified. She was standing bolt upright, surrounded by purring and pushing felines who, though formidable, simply due to their number, did not seem in the least bit threatening. In fact, Angel didn't seem to be in any danger whatsoever, unless one could be damaged by overt affection. As each cat passed by her rigid body, he or she would press their head against Angel, and with sensual deliberation, would rub themselves across her, in a show of total abandon. While clearly pleasurable for the cats, Angel seemed to withdraw further into herself with each caress.

After recovering from the shock of this rather striking tableau, Lucy realised that there was light. Buckets of it! She looked away from the central mass of animals and immediately found the source of the illumination.

The few cars that were parked on the seemingly abandoned level had their headlights on, providing an astonishing amount of illumination in the damp confines of the lower level.

Lucy nudged Rex to point out the light source, but saw that his attention was firmly rooted elsewhere.

One cat was approaching them. Slowly, deliberately, and fearlessly, one cat had broken from the melee, and was now walking towards them with as much nonchalance as one would expect from a housecat approaching a saucer of milk.

While Rex and Lucy looked on cautiously, the animal circled the pair several times as his eyes passed over them with almost clinical interest. He was not a big cat, in fact as street cats go, he was quite small. His coat was a clear mirror to his obviously questionable lineage. His back was patterned randomly with black and white shapes that dissolved seamlessly into ginger grey stripes as they wrapped under his belly. His head was entirely black except for one ear which was stark white. His tail was almost the exact reverse, being entirely white but with a black tip. Three of his legs were black, while one was ginger-striped with a white sock. Though not a classically beautiful cat by any means, he was certainly a striking figure.

He finally finished his perusal of the dogs and stepped closer, focusing his eyes onto each animal, one at a time. Lucy almost gasped at the sheer beauty of the creature's eyes. They were green, but of a shade she'd only once encountered before. It was the colour of the ocean after a storm, as the first shaft of sunlight hits the water, which is still filled with sand and aeration following its tumultuous upheaval at the hands of the surface winds.

"So," the cat said calmly as it sat itself directly in front of them. "You're expecting our help?"

"No," Rex responded, slightly surprised by the question.

"Then why are you here?" the cat countered.

"It's a long story," Lucy replied.

"But you do want our help?" the cat interrupted.

"Actually . . . no," Lucy replied.

"You must have intended to ask us for something," the cat voiced. "or you wouldn't be here."

"To be quite honest," Rex joined in. "We're not entirely sure where here is, so you'll have to take our word for it that we didn't come here to ask for anything from you."

"You're joking?" the cat replied.

"Not in the least," said Lucy.

"No, we're not," added Rex.

"How frightfully odd," The now puzzled feline uttered as he began to frantically lick his left front paw. "So, if you don't know where you are, you therefore, presumably, haven't a clue who I am, or indeed who we all are?"

"Exactly," Lucy responded.

"Most odd. Most odd indeed." The cat began to clean its other paw. It seemed to find one particularly tough bit of soiled fur and had to use its teeth to nibble at the area between the claws. His eyes however never left the two dogs. He gave the matter some deep thought while continuing to chew between his pads, then suddenly lowered his paw and began to laugh.

At first, it was just a light-hearted little titter, but it grew rapidly into an out and out guffaw of incredible proportions. Lucy and Rex stared at the laughing creature in complete puzzlement, having not the slightest clue as to what prompted the outburst.

The cat turned to the other felines and announced. "They don't know who we are!"

Laughter then erupted in every corner of the lower level. It jumped from one group of cats to another, then back again. Angel had the good sense to use their mirth to slip out between the yowling animals and move closer to Rex and Lucy.

"What is going on down here?" Rex whispered to the Spaniel.

"You tell me? I was checking around a few levels further up when a couple of big tomcats grabbed me and led me down here."

The lead cat abruptly stopped laughing, and after wiping a tear away with one paw, his eyes again focused pointedly at the three dogs.

"You have, of course, heard of Los Gatos de la Noche?" he asked, expecting some clear signs of recognition.

Lucy and Angel shook their heads in unison. It wasn't until Lucy noticed that Rex seemed to not only have heard of Los Gatos de la Noche, but that he was suddenly quite pale and shaky. She realised that something very serious had just taken place.

"Perhaps you should take a moment to acquaint your friends with the Los Gatos," the cat said, smiling at Rex.

Rex turned to Lucy and Angel, and after a deep breath began. "The Gatos are famous. Legend has it that during the time of the black years in Spain a few cats got together and..."

"Sorry to interrupt," Angel interrupted. "But what were the black years.... .and where or what is Spain?"

They all turned and faced the Spaniel in amazement, even Lucy was stunned at this hole in her friend's knowledge, especially as she had come to believe that Angel was a very well-educated pup.

"Spain is a faraway country across a great expanse of water and the black years...," Rex explained patiently. "were the time, long ago, when the bipeds began to give up their houses and lands in favour of smaller dwellings called apartments. Humans who'd had numerous animal companions suddenly didn't have the space for them."

"So, they let them go free?" Angel asked hopefully.

"No, they didn't," Rex continued, his voice now low and serious. "They began an almost systematic, elimination of the cat population. Entire litters were drowned, older adults were taken away and given lethal injections, but the worse by far, was the neutering. Healthy adult felines, both male and female, were taken from their homes without warning and operated on so that they could never again have kittens.

"Oh, how awful," Angel cried, as she turned to the lead cat with an expression of great sympathy. "All this took place in Spain?"

"It took place all over," Rex responded. "But in Spain, something was done about it. A small group of cats banded together and vowed to avenge their fallen brethren. This group became known as, *Los Gatos de la Noche...or, The Cats of the Night*, as they are also known. They are no longer a small group. They exist in every country and have formed themselves into a formidable society."

Rex looked to the cat to see if he approved of his rendition of the tale. The grey-green eyes stared calmly back into his own without a trace of emotion. Rex began to feel uneasy and glanced over to Lucy for moral support.

"Close enough," the cat finally said. "Actually, we're not so much into the... how did you put it, avenging our fallen brethren thing, anymore. We're now more into... how can I describe it?... more refined pursuits!"

"Like what?" Angel asked innocently.

The cat took a step towards her and suddenly rubbed his head against her chin. "Such innocence. How refreshing! I'm talking about crime my long-eared friend. More specifically, crimes of the night."

"Oh," Angel murmured trying to back away from the still pushing feline. "Then this must be your... hide out?"

"Hide out! What a lovely term. It has a nice ring to it... hide out. Yes, you could I suppose, call this our... hide out. Wait!"

The cat suddenly jumped back, causing the three dogs to edge closer together in fear of what was to come.

"I haven't introduced myself, have I?" he said apologetically. "It's astonishing how one's manners seem to simply vanish when usually having to deal with the scum of the earth." He gestured to the other cats behind him.

As if in response to his remark, the other cats all ceased what they were doing and smiled over at their leader.

"Allow me to introduce myself. My name is Byxorician Ovintle Blyltrix."

"You're kidding?" Lucy spoke before she could stop herself. "I do apologise that was very rude of me. It's just that, that is a most unusual name."

"Do you really think so?" Byxorician Ovintle Blyltrix asked, with mild amusement.

"Don't you?" Lucy found herself replying.

"Actually, no, but if it makes it easier for you, everyone here calls me BOB," he stated with a huge grin.

"In that case... Bob, allow me to introduce myself and my friends. That's Rex, he's our leader."

"Charmed," Bob held out his paw, which Rex appropriately then licked.

"Angel, you of course know."

"Delighted." Again, the paw was offered. Angel was clearly slightly dubious about the whole thing but gave the offered limb a brief lick anyway.

"And I am Lucy."

"Simply enchanted," Bob purred as the paw was presented.

Once the introductions were complete, a silence fell over the group, as each tried to think of something to say.

"So," Bob said as he began to lick his own belly with long careful strokes. "Now that you know who we are, you must be bursting with questions. I will allow you one, as you are our guests."

"How did you get the lights to work on those cars?" Angel blurted out, without even conferring with the others.

Rex and Lucy both shot her a very disapproving glance, which she stoically ignored, keeping her eyes facing Bob.

"I offered you the answer to a question that could have uncovered any of the most cherished secrets held by the

Gatos, but instead you want to know how we control a simple human light! How simplistic. I like it. Well, my long-eared friend, it's very simple. The bipeds leave these vehicles here for varying lengths of time to be safely looked after and maintained. These ones on the lowest level have been here by far the longest. Though they are no longer cleaned very regularly, they do have their batteries charged once every lunar cycle. All we do is send one of our BHD Specialists into each car and turn the lights on. It's quite simple."

"BHD?" Lucy repeated questioningly.

"Oh yes! In our business, it's no longer possible to simply rely on feline instincts and abilities to carry out our work. We now use cats with specialised training in basic electronics, security systems, computers, you name it! They are our elite Biped Hand Dexterity unit."

"What exactly do you do that requires that sort of knowledge?" Lucy inquired, with keen interest.

"You'd really like to know?" Bob asked as he moved his grooming efforts to his tail section.

"Yes please," Lucy replied.

"What a shame then that your friend ... Angel isn't it, used up your one question. Oh well, life can be so hard sometimes."

"Please Bob, we'd love to know more." Lucy pleaded.

Bob stopped his washing and stood facing the three dogs. "Let me make one thing clear. The reason that Los Gatos has survived, is due to not simply our devotion to the cause and our talents, but because of our codes and rules. They were set down long ago, but even today, no cat ever breaks even one of them. Part of the code is that whatever we say we mean. It sounds mind-numbingly simple. But I believe that is one of the strongest attributes of our society and a key component to our survival. We always know exactly where we stand with anyone. It's what makes us so unified and efficient. That's the main reason human beings are always in such a mess. They always will be, as long as no biped can trust anything another one has to say. I personally would have thought that by now, they would have learned this, but I am obviously giving them far more credit than is truly due."

"But what's that got to..." Lucy began.

"What's that got to do with my only answering one of your questions?"

Lucy nodded.

"Very simple. I promised you the answer to one question. I meant one question. It's what I said, it's what I meant, and it's what I did. See how simple it is."

"But I didn't know," Angel mumbled sadly.

"You should always know the rules before entering someone else's domain. It's common sense," he replied matter-of-factly.

"Now look here Bob," Rex said, using his most serious tone. "We didn't know you were even down here. We were searching for chicken when we got shut in this place. Then Angel went missing and we had to come down here to find her, so you see, it's not as if we were unprepared for this encounter. We simply didn't know any of this would happen."

"Do you realise how silly that story makes you sound? You blindly stumble into a place you know nothing about purely because of a good smell! Then, you allow yourselves to be trapped with, if I'm not mistaken, half your team still up top, shut on the other side of the gate! Let me be blunt. Stop thinking with your noses. You have a brain. Use it. I watch dogs everyday sticking their noses in places I don't even wish to talk about. I mean really! I've seen you lot begin a romantic encounter after no more than a sniff at another dog's backside. Stop acting like such animals. You have eyes, and ears, and a brain. Use them. Think before you leap for a change.

The three dogs all hung their heads in embarrassed shame. Bob's words had evidently struck a nerve with each of them.

"There's no need to get down on yourselves," Bob added to try and cheer them up. "Most of it's in your genes and you can't help it. I know that. All I'm saying is give your brain a chance occasionally."

The three dogs nodded their heads. Lucy was the first to finally look up into the smiling feline features. It was clear that Bob was observing their every reaction.

"Enough of my lecturing. You lot haven't told me the details of your quest!"

"Our quest?" Angel looked confused.

"You obviously have a quest, otherwise you wouldn't all be together stuck here in the middle of the city, would you?"

"Well...," Angel began.

"In case you think that anyone's going to mistake you for a pack of street dogs, forget it," Bob stated with amusement. "I've never seen a bunch of hounds with so much human sense about them. It does show, you know."

"I didn't realise," Lucy replied with surprise. "What do you mean, it shows?"

"Simple. Your poise, your speech, your coats, and your figures. Everything about you points to lives that have been governed by humans."

Rex nodded slowly, as if accepting the cat's words without any argument.

Angel on the other hand seemed quite upset at Bob's observation. "I think that's very rude," she began. "Here we are, guests in your... your... whatever this place is, and you're calling us..."

"I'm not calling you anything," Bob interrupted gently. "There's nothing wrong with it at all, in fact, if anything, it's a plus."

"But you said...," Angel whined.

"I said, you don't look like street dogs. That's good. Street dogs usually look underfed, are battle scarred, nervous and very dirty. You're getting close in the dirt department, but apart from that, there's no comparison."

The three dogs took a moment to check each other out from their new perspective as non-street dogs.

"So, someone tell me about your quest!" Bob persisted.

"It's not a quest exactly," Rex said.

"It's more of a . . . ." Lucy tried to find the right words. "A . . . . ."

"Oh, for heaven's sake you two!" Angel interrupted. "It's perfectly simple. We were all dog-napped by the same gang of bipeds and imprisoned together in this horrible place near a river, which is where we met. We were in the process of trying to get out of London when one of our group got caught by the gang who is now holding him back at the same place they held us. Clear enough?"

"And you're going back to try and rescue him, are you?" Bob asked with keen interest.

"Of course," Rex replied.

"Do you have a plan?" Bob asked.

"Not really," Lucy said, slightly embarrassed.

"Well, where exactly is this place they're holding him?"

"We're not sure." Rex also looked a little subdued.

"So, let me see if I've got this straight," Bob said, shaking his head.

"You're on your way to rescue your friend, but you don't know where he is or what you'll do when you find him. Is that about it?"

"Not exactly," Lucy said, defensively. "We're actually on our way to meet St. Paul. He'll help us find Rodney. That's our friend's name by the way."

"Very nice," Bob said. "What's this about St. Paul and his helping you, nonsense?"

"It's not nonsense," Angel whined. "Everyone knows that saints are good humans and are always there to help bipeds or animals."

Bob looked to each face trying to keep his own from breaking into laughter. "You lot are too much, you really are! I don't know how you've stayed in one piece, but it's time you realised that it's not a game out there. The streets are tough and mean and are ready to swallow up a group of wide-eyed, pampered, innocents like yourselves, in the blink of an eye!"

Bob noticed Rex shaking his head slowly from side to side, clearly not accepting his words of warning.

"You think you're a tough one, do you?" Bob asked him with a coldness to his voice. "Been around have you?"

"Actually, yes," Rex answered forcefully. "I'm not a house dog. I'm a guard dog. I can take care of myself."

"Really!" Bob replied as he gestured to one of the tomcats standing back, observing the exchange.

"Yes, really," Rex countered as he watched the tom slowly approach him from the side. He tensed himself knowing that the large cat was there to obviously show him a thing or two about street smarts and toughness. He knew he was ready for any move the cat would try, as he shifted his weight onto his haunches, ready to spring up and out-manoeuvre his adversary.

The next thing he knew, something hit him from the other side. One moment he was readying himself for an attack from the approaching tom, the next he was on his back with legs splayed, as another tom that he hadn't even seen, held a paw full of razor-sharp nails against the pink flesh of his exposed belly. He dared not move as the cat clearly had the upper hand and could all too easily mortally wound him before he had a chance to shake him off his stomach.

"Thank you, Claxaloufidites," Bob said to Rex's attacker, who withdrew his claws and with a brief nod to Bob, turned and re-joined the other cats.

Rex got to his feet, and after a good shake to rid himself of the dirt and dust from the floor, turned to Bob with a growing smile on his muzzle.

"Point well taken," Rex said with complete sincerity.

Bob simply nodded his acceptance of the Doberman's words. He then turned to Lucy and Angel, who seemed totally stunned by the demonstration. Their eyes were as wide open as were their mouths. Bob could see that their breathing was fast and panting.

"Please accept my apologies ladies," Bob said. "But I felt that a demonstration was worth more than senseless words."

Rex stepped over to them and grinned broadly for their benefit.

"It's alright. I'm fine. He had a point to make and he certainly made it! He's right. We're obviously not particularly well suited for street life."

"But such violence!" Lucy said, her voice still trembling slightly.

"If I get Bob's subtlety, that was nothing compared with the violence we could expect to find outside," Rex stated.

"So," Bob said as if nothing had happened. "let's outline a couple of things which you may find helpful in your quest. By the way, yours is a quest. And a mighty noble one too!"

The three dogs felt a sudden moment of pride as they realised that the cat was indeed right.

"First," continued Bob. "St. Paul is not a human, at least not for a very long time. It's a Cathedral!"

"A what?" Lucy asked.

"A Cathedral," Angel replied, as she shook her head in self-recrimination. "I knew that! It's like a big church. Oh, how silly of me! Of course! St. Paul's Cathedral. Completed in the biped year 1711 by Christopher Wren as a symbol of..."

"Thank you, Angel," Lucy interrupted gently. "We get the point."

"I don't," said Rex. "How's this Cathedral thing supposed to help us?"

Bob laughed as he used his back leg to vigorously scratch under his chin.

"I don't think this is funny at all," Lucy said in a serious tone. "What do we do about Rodney now. Who's going to help us?"

There was a lengthy silence as one by one, the three dogs focused their attention on Bob.

"Oh no! Don't even think about it," he said, swishing his tail rapidly from side to side. "Los Gatos doesn't do mercenary work. I'll give you some advice, but that's it."

"This isn't mercenary," Lucy pleaded. "Rodney is an animal like you and I, who has been wrongly imprisoned by the same type of bipeds that forced the creation of your society in the first place."

"Maybe, but…" Bob tried to counter.

"Maybe nothing!" Lucy insisted. "What happened to all that stuff about Los Gatos fighting for their oppressed brethren? What about vengeance against tyrannical humans? What about…?"

"Stop! Enough!" Bob said, rising to his feet. "I told you, we don't do that anymore. We can't afford the luxury of soft-hearted ideals getting in the way of our primary interests."

"And those are…?" Lucy was beginning to sound peeved.

Bob stared long and hard at each canine face before replying. Finally, posing his body in a clear defensive stance he said.

"Profit!"

"Profit?" Lucy cried. "What happened to the…"

"Lucy!" Rex interrupted sternly. "This is none of our business."

"But…" she tried again.

"Lucy!" Rex again stopped her before she could say anything else. He then turned to Bob. "I'm sorry. Goldie here is extremely passionate about her views of right and wrong. Sometimes she insists on voicing them at inappropriate moments like this."

"There's no need to apologise. I only wish we could help," Bob responded politely, though still slightly defensive over his and Lucy's recent exchange.

"You could if you really wanted to!" Angel suddenly piped up.

Everyone turned and stared at her in amazement.

"Well, he could!" she stated.

Bob checked each face again while he began to carefully wash the underside of one paw. This went on for quite a while as the three dogs nervously looked on. Finally, the washing stopped.

"You three are very rude," Bob announced.

"What?" The three stammered in unison.

"Yes, very rude indeed. You come into my home, then, without so much as a by your leave, you start lecturing, not only to me but to the entire society of the Los Gatos, on how we should run our lives. That is what I call rude! I would like to ask that if you plan to remain here any longer…"

"Like we have a choice," Lucy mumbled, under her breath.

Bob continued, but now with a glaring eye towards Lucy. "That you will from this point on, begin acting like guests."

Lucy was about to respond, but Rex chose to bite her gently on the rump freezing her words.

With a furious look, she swallowed what she was about to say and stared angrily down at the ground. Rex looked to

Angel, who was also focusing on the floor. With a slight smile on his muzzle, he then dropped his eyes to join the others.

Finally, the three dogs slowly lifted their eyes and saw that Bob was in fact smiling quite genuinely at them.

"Would I be correct in assuming," he said with light amusement in his voice. "that a little supper would go down quite well about now?"

"Food?" Angel shrieked, forgetting all else as her tongue began lolling out the side of her mouth, giving her an imbecilic look.

"Yes, my dear, food. Sustenance, nourishment, feed...call it what you like! This is Wednesday and Andre usually prepares something quite exceptional on Wednesdays. Shall we see what he's put together this evening?"

The three canine heads nodded in unison as each dog began to fantasise on his or her own vision of what Andre's feast would contain. Bob stretched himself into a standing position then, with a flip of his tail, spun around and began walking away from them.

"I suggest you follow me," Bob stated without even looking back. "We don't deliver."

The dogs obediently got to their feet and followed the cat past the biped vehicles and through the sea of feline figures, which parted noiselessly to allow their leader to pass through.

Bob led the dogs to the farthest wall of the lowest level, and with great pride, and a sweep of one paw, gestured for them to behold the Wednesday night buffet. Against one wall and laid out on a flat protruding section of concrete, was the cat's big feast.

There could be little doubt for whom this meal was intended. Andre, it seemed, had done an outstanding job to cater to a feline's every whim.

At one end of the banquet *table*, the spread began with a selection of tiny sparrows, each artistically arranged on its own cabbage leaf. Next were what Lucy had first thought were raisins until, on closer examination, she saw that they were in fact flies, thousands of them. The display continued with delicacy upon delicacy until it culminated with Andre's 'piece de resistance'. At first the dogs couldn't even begin to guess what they were looking at. It appeared to be, and certainly smelled like, custard. Small round balls of it, each with a stick-like protuberance that stuck straight up out of each. It wasn't until they observed one cat bite into one that they realised they were custard-covered field mice!

"Help yourselves," Bob encouraged. "There's plenty. Andre always over does it."

The three dogs looked the length of the banquet, then forlornly back at Bob without saying a word.

"I thought you were hungry?"

The three shook their heads sadly. They were of course famished, but not enough so that they could bring themselves to eat any of the bizarre assortments that were currently spread out before them.

"It's not the food is it?" Bob asked with concern.

"No, of course not," Lucy answered politely.

"Good. Good. I'd hate to think you didn't approve of our little buffet."

The three dogs offered him their best smiles.

"You know, I just thought of something," Bob said, as if to himself.

He turned and trotted off towards one of the biped vehicles. He crawled under the front of it and could be heard scratching at something. They all then heard something drop to the ground. Bob reappeared, backing himself out from under the car, dragging a large, brown paper bag. He managed to pull the hefty bundle over to the three observing dogs then left it at their feet.

"I know you can't wait to dive into our fine feast, but just in case our meal might be a little too refined for your palettes," he said with a slight smile. "we arranged for a backup meal."

With that, he turned away and joined a couple of comrades already in line for the buffet. Lucy looked to Rex wondering what exactly was expected of them, when Angel acted on their behalf. She bent her muzzle to the brown bag and grabbed the bottom of it and lifted. The contents spilled out onto the ground, revealing piece after piece of still warm, succulently prepared, roast chicken. Even Angel looked stunned as she stood and stared at the dream meal that had been produced for their enjoyment.

Lucy looked up and sought Bob out among the myriad of feline banqueters. She spotted him almost immediately, standing in a group of tough-looking tomcats, clearly in the middle of telling them some sort of story. The toms hung on every word as they stared in rapt fascination at their noble leader. As if sensing her look, Bob glanced over towards her. She mouthed the words, "Thank you," to which she was rewarded with a clear, and amused wink from Bob, before he returned to his story telling.

The three dogs then settled to the ground and began their fine, and long overdue meal. At one point, Lucy suddenly remembered Hans and Lester shut out in the night, somewhere overhead. A passing Siamese assured her however, that they had been recently checked on and were fine. One of the Gatos had taken them some dinner earlier in the evening. They were now fast asleep, still nestled up against the unkempt biped.

Once fully sated, Lucy found it difficult to keep her own eyes open but knew it would be terribly rude to simply eat then nap when in someone else's abode. She turned to the others to try and begin some conversation but found that both were already fast asleep. Rex, in a dignified curl with his head resting on his own hindquarter, and Angel in a very unladylike pose, flat on her back with her legs splayed out to each compass point. Adding to the sight, was her tongue which was dangling out the side of her mouth and her small, but bulging, belly which protruded above her coat as it rose and settled rhythmically in sleep.

Lucy looked over to the cats and saw, to her astonishment, that they were gone. Not all of them, but certainly most. As she watched, she saw the few remaining felines as they cleaned up the last traces of their fine buffet. Then, one by one, they walked to a particularly dark corner of the level and seemed to simply vanish into the wall. As she continued to observe the parting felines, the lights of the biped vehicles suddenly clicked off, one at a time, halving the illumination with each disconnection. Finally, the last lights were extinguished, and Lucy was again faced with complete and utter darkness.

She felt her eyes growing heavier by the second as she heard the sounds of the last few cats depart their headquarters, presumably to begin their night's endeavours as decreed by the charter of, *Los Gatos de la Noche*.

Lucy closed her eyes and began immediately to feel the first fingers of sleep as they pulled her towards the dark and comfortable recesses of slumber.

Just then, she heard Bob's voice only inches from her ear.

"Don't stir my tired friend," his voice whispered almost dreamily. "Now you need to sleep. Tomorrow your adventure continues. I wish you and your friends every possible success. Remember, the Gatos will be with you always."

Lucy then felt the gentlest of licks against her muzzle. She wanted to look up and say something, but she knew that such a reaction was not appropriate.

Feeling a new sense of inner warmth and security, she allowed the sleep to finally take a firm hold and pull her down into its enveloping warmth.

CHAPTER 28

Lucy woke before the others, feeling surprisingly refreshed and invigorated. She lay where she was for a while, observing Rex as he continued to sleep. He appeared not to have altered his position even a fraction from the night before.

It took Lucy a few moments to realise that she was able to see. There was light. She raised her head and saw that the light was coming from above, from a series of long tubular devices that exuded not only light, but an annoying, high-pitched, buzz as well.

As she resumed gazing at Rex, she wondered what sort of dreams he would have. Could he, even after so hard a life, still dream moments of utter contentment as she did, or were his dreams built of darker material, colouring his fantasies with hurt and pain?

She continued to ponder this thought right up until something tapped her on her shoulder causing her to yelp and leap up in surprise. She spun around and involuntarily began to growl at whatever had touched her.

Lucy only saw the briefest glimpse of a very full and colourful tail as it slithered out of sight under one of the biped vehicles.

Lucy walked slowly over to it and cautiously bent her head to peer underneath.

Cowering in the darkness afforded by the metallic hulk, was a cat. An extremely nervous and frightened cat. Even in the gloom, Lucy could see that it was a very unusual looking animal. She had long hair (Lucy instinctually knew it was a she), giving her the immediate appearance of bulk, but on closer inspection, one could see that the animal under the heavy coat, was actually quite petite. Lucy couldn't make out much more because of the shadows, and for a good few moments, simply looked back into a pair of rapidly blinking, olive eyes that were nervously trained on her.

"I'm sorry if I startled you," Lucy said, whispering. "But you see, you actually gave me quite a start as well."

There was a long silence, then a tiny and timid voice wafted out from under the vehicle.

"I'm terribly sorry... I... I... didn't mean to frighten you... I simply wanted to introduce myself."

Lucy smiled back at the animal, waiting for the promised introduction. None came. In fact, the cat didn't utter another word. Finally, Lucy felt it necessary to break the silence.

"You mentioned something about introducing yourself," Lucy prodded softly.

"Oh yes...I... I did, didn't I? Thank you for reminding me."

Again, there was silence.

"Well?" Lucy tried to keep the impatience from her voice.

"I'm working on it," the cat replied nervously. "It's not that easy you know."

"Yes, it is. Look, I'll begin, shall I? My name is Lucy. What's yours?"

Again, no reply. Lucy waited and waited and was finally about to give up on the whole encounter when the timid voice responded.

"My name is Ryphoryl Ynextril Hydxmass."

Lucy shook her head in astonishment at the complexity of yet another cat name.

"I presume they call you Rye?" Lucy inquired hopefully.

"No," the cat replied.

"Well, what then?"

"I... I... told you. Ryphoryl Ynextril Hydxmass."

"Oh," Lucy said, somewhat embarrassed. "I'm afraid that your names are simply too much for me to cope with! I will call you Rye."

"If you must," Rye replied, almost dejectedly.

"And you'll have to come out from under this vehicle if you wish to carry on a conversation with me."

"Oh, alright," Rye sighed.

Lucy waited for the cat to appear, but after a while, realised that Rye hadn't budged.

"I'm waiting," Lucy announced.

"I'm... I'm... working on it," Rye replied nervously. "It's not easy you know!"

"Why do you keep saying that? It's perfectly easy. Now come out from there."

"I will." Rye sounded quite distressed. "Just give me a moment."

"I'm not going to hurt you, you know," Lucy said, comfortingly.

"Okay," came the unconvinced reply.

Lucy again waited for the animal to appear. Finally, much to her delight and by that time, surprise, Rye's head came into view.

"Well, hello!" Lucy said to the just visible face.

"I can't," Rye squealed and shot back under the vehicle. "I'm truly sorry. I thought I could, but I can't."

"What's wrong with you?" Lucy asked, feeling great pity for the obviously disturbed creature.

"I'm... I'm...," Rye tried to speak.

"You're... sick?" Lucy offered.

"N...No. I'm... I'm..."

"Shy?" Lucy tried again.

"N...No. I'm... I'm... a..."

"Oh, come on. Spit it out!" Lucy was again becoming impatient at the cat's reluctance to speak her thoughts.

"I'm a scaredy cat!" Rye blurted out.

"A what?"

"A scaredy cat. I can't help it. It's what I am."

"Well, there's nothing to be afraid of out here, so please come out from under that thing so I can at least see you."

"Why?"

"So, I can talk to you."

"You . . . You're talking now," the voice said.

"That's enough!" Lucy snapped, her good nature beginning to wear thin. "You come out here this minute, or I'll simply have to crawl under there after you!"

"You wouldn't," Rye responded with weak defiance.

"I most certainly would," Lucy stated firmly.

Lucy heard some movement under the vehicle then, with agonizing showiness, watched as Rye slid herself out from the shadows. With her eyes darting every which way in fear, Rye got to her feet and faced Lucy.

The first thing that struck Lucy was Rye's beauty. Her coat was simply gorgeous; long, full and resplendent as it gleamed under the harsh, buzzing lights. It was multi-coloured with patches of white, black and orange that covered not only her coat but her face as well.

The second thing that struck Lucy was that Rye couldn't seem to sit still. Not even for a fraction of a second. As Lucy tried to comfort the terrified cat with a glowing smile and happy pant, the poor feline seemed unable to control any part of her body. She would sit for a second, then suddenly begin licking a paw or limb with a frantic effort, only to stop with equal abruptness and begin scratching a completely different part of her anatomy. What made it worse was that one could tell from the pained look in her eyes, that her body's antics were not consciously carried out at all. They were more a side effect of her almost debilitating fear that seemed to consume her every action.

Lucy tried to ignore the twitching and ticking, but found that the longer she stared at the animal, the more she herself began to itch, as if catching the cat's own affliction.

Finally, Rye's nervous movements began to abate slightly, and Lucy felt she could converse without sending the cat into a frenzy of some sort.

"You know Rye, you have the most beautiful coat."

"Thank you," she replied with a tremble to her voice.

"I hope you don't mind my calling you Rye, but those names of yours really are very complicated."

"Do you think so?" Rye asked.

"Yes, I do. They're so long and so complicated."

"I think that's the whole point," Rye replied.

"The point of what?" Lucy inquired with real interest.

"The point of having a name!" Rye said with timid conviction. "With cats, every name is different. Just as every cat is different. I mean what's the point of being born a completely unique creature, then carrying a name that's been used hundreds or even thousands of times before. We feel that every single cat should always have their own name, fresh and new, for them to keep as their own. That's why they are a little long and complicated. It's not that easy to make up new names after hundreds of generations have gone before.

"I see," said Lucy with a mixture of surprise and interest.

A silence ensued as Lucy waited for Rye to speak further but no words materialised.

"Rye?" she asked casually.

"Y... Yes?"

"Did you want something?" Lucy inquired.

"No, why?" Rye replied nervously.

"Well, you did wake me up for some purpose, unless I'm quite mistaken."

"Oh... Oh... Yes. I forgot. I'm sorry. I get so scared sometimes; I can't think straight."

"That must be terrible," Lucy offered.

"It is... it is," Rye said, nodding her head emphatically.

Lucy waited for the reason for her wake-up visit. Again, no words were forthcoming. She finally cleared her throat noisily as a hint to the trembling cat. Rye simply stared back at her with a terrified and completely blank gaze.

"Oh yes," she suddenly cried remembering what she had to say. "I am your guide."

"My what?" Lucy asked, suspiciously.

"Your guide. I was chosen to stay behind and help lead you on your quest."

"Pardon my bluntness Rye, and please don't be offended because I'm sure you mean well, but aren't you just a tad fidgety to act as our guide?"

"No... n... not really. My frightened disposition has no effect on my tracking ability whatsoever."

"So, what have we here?" Rex boomed playfully as he suddenly appeared behind them.

Rye's beautiful coat instantly enlarged to double its size, a fraction of a second before she dived back under the biped vehicle with a shriek.

"What was that?" Rex asked, clearly startled by Rye's frantic departure.

"That was our guide," Lucy responded.

"I see," Rex said as he lowered his head to peer under the vehicle. "Sorry to have startled you... Uh..."

"Rye! We're calling her Rye. Her cat name is way too complex," Lucy stated.

"Rye... you can come out, it's quite safe," Rex coaxed.

It took quite a while, but eventually, after exhaustive patience, they managed to convince Rye that none of her nine lives were in jeopardy. Once out from under the vehicle, she gave herself a thorough wash with fast, darting motions that made Rex and Lucy feel just a bit on edge. They tried on a couple of occasions to interrupt the cleaning process to ask a question or two but were utterly ignored.

Rye finished with one last convulsive lick of her left shoulder, then, with a deep sigh, sat and faced the two dogs.

"So, where am I taking you exactly?" she asked shyly.

"I thought you were supposed to guide us?" Rex replied, haughtily. "I mean isn't that the point..."

"I think Rye needs some idea of where to guide us to?" Lucy interrupted gently. "Am I correct?"

Rye was staring intently down at the ground next to her feet. Lucy assumed the cat was deep in thought until she suddenly began pawing at something ridiculously small that was moving across the road-like surface. She managed to ensnare whatever it was on one paw, which she then raised to eye level for examination.

"Rye?" Lucy said, with gentle annoyance.

"Hmm?" Rye murmured to herself, her attention focused fully on her paw.

"Rye!" Lucy snapped angrily, causing both Rye and Rex to jump.

"What did you do that for?" Rye whimpered as tears began to form in her eyes. "You yelled at me!"

"If you're going to guide us, you are going to have to pay attention," Lucy scolded. "And besides, that was hardly a yell."

"I was only grooming!" Rye replied, with moist eyes downcast.

"Well, I'm sorry if I frightened you," Lucy said. "Are you alright?"

"Yes," came the pouty reply.

"And you won't go dashing off at the first thing that startles you?" Rex added.

"No." Rye raised her eyes to the two dogs. "I was chosen to guide you and that's what I'll do."

"Good," said Rex.

"Yes, good for you Rye!" Lucy praised. "Once we get going, I'm sure you'll be fine."

"Do you really think so?" Rye asked, hopefully.

"Absolutely," Lucy replied.

At that moment, Angel let out a loud howl in her sleep for no apparent reason. Rex and Lucy smiled over at their sleeping friend then turned back to Rye. She was gone. Well not completely gone; the tip of her multi-coloured tail was just visible as it flicked from side to side, back under the biped vehicle.

"As I said," Lucy grinned over at Rex. "once we get going!"

It took a while to coax Rye out from under the vehicle for the umpteenth time. Once out however, she seemed intent on trying to relax and help formulate some sort of a plan to find where Rodney was being held prisoner. The first phase was to join up with Lester and Hans, which turned out to be easy. Even as Rye volunteered (to everyone's surprise) to sneak up to the top level and check on the two dogs, they came striding down the sloping drive, both looking none the worse for wear.

Lucy introduced them to Rye and highlighted the previous night's encounter with Los Gatos. They were suitably impressed and eager to start off on what they all now termed to be their quest.

The dogs took turns describing to Rye, every single detail they could possibly recall about the place in which they'd all 'done time' at the hands of Squat Lady and the others.

Rye tried to connect their details to any area she knew, but without success. The problem was that the dogs' descriptions of the dilapidated buildings could quite easily fit almost all of the unimproved dockland territory.

"There must have been something unusual?" Rye urged.

"No there wasn't," Rex insisted. "There was simply row after row of old, brick buildings. There was nothing different about any of them."

"We're not thinking straight. There must have been something out of the ordinary," Lucy said, as she racked her brain trying to remember anything that would help. "We've just got to concentrate a little harder."

The dogs exerted themselves, trying to sort through the thin memories they all held of their escape.

"Wait," Angel suddenly squealed. "I know... the... the... oh, come on! What was it called... you know... the thing... the...?"

Her face began to turn red with exertion. The others looked on in silent hope, as she grew more and more crimson. "The anchor!" she finally blurted out joyously. "The big anchor, remember?"

The others all did.

"Very good Angel," Lucy cried. "The anchor, of course!"

"The anchor," sighed Lester.

"The big anchor! How silly of us," Hans said, shaking his head.

"That's a landmark alright," Rex stated.

The five dogs turned happily to face Rye.

"What's an anchor?" she asked timidly.

The dogs looked at one another with a mixture of disbelief and frustration.

"Sorry," Rye responded, with a double flick of the tail.

"Oh, come on you must know," Lester stated with conviction. "Bipeds use them to hold their water vehicles in place."

"Big hook like things," Angel added.

"On the end of lengths of chain," Lucy contributed.

The dogs all stopped their descriptions to see if anything was sinking in with Rye.

"Oh those," Rye remarked casually.

"So, you do know what we mean?" Rex asked.

"Of course. I may be scared but I'm not stupid."

"So, what do you call them?" Lester asked.

"What?" Rye replied.

"Anchors!" the dogs yelled in unison.

That only caused Rye to visibly shrink in front of them, and as she took a step back towards the vehicle, Lucy rushed to her side, full of apologies.

"We're awfully sorry. We forgot how sensitive you are. We only wanted to know what the cat word for anchor was."

"There isn't one."

"But there must be," Lester insisted.

"No, there mustn't," Rye countered. "Cats don't bother creating words simply for the sake of doing so. There's plenty enough to do without wasting our time needlessly."

"So, what do you call something if you need to discuss it and there's no word for it?" Angel asked, with confused interest.

"If there's no word for it, then it obviously isn't worth discussing, now is it?"

The dogs all glanced at one another and by some silent signal between them, decided to venture no further on the topic of cat logic.

"Alright," Rex said with as much calm as he could muster. "But have you even seen the giant anchor that we're referring to? It's a huge thing on a stone base."

"Yes," Rye answered.

"And you could take us there?"

"Of course," Rye answered. "I'm your guide."

"When can we leave?" Lucy asked.

At that moment, the animals all heard the distinct sounds of a biped approaching the lower lever. The human was whistling discordantly to himself and by the sound of it, was dragging a squeaky-wheeled object along with him.

"I would suggest right now," Rye said with clear urgency in her voice. Her earlier calmness began ebbing right in front of them. Her tail re-inflated and her twitching resumed its partial control of her body."

"Everyone ready?" she stammered.

They all nodded.

Rye took a deep breath and dashed to the darkest corner of the level. Just before she vanished in the shadows, she looked back to the dogs who hadn't so much as budged, even an inch.

"C… come… come on then… hurry!"

They all looked to Rex to see if he was willing to hand over their safety to the neurotic feline or stay and take a stand against the rapidly approaching biped.

With one formal nod of his head, the dogs dashed off after Rye's retreating tail. Rex and Lucy were the last to step into the dark corner and took a moment to look at each other before doing so. Rex gave her a warm-hearted push with his fine muzzle then followed her into the all-consuming blackness ahead.

CHAPTER 29

At first, the dogs could see nothing at all in the utter darkness that surrounded them. Rye had to move very slowly and provide continual verbal signals for the benefit of her followers. Without even having to ask, Lucy allowed Rex to provide his tail, which she clasped gently in her mouth as before.

Finally, after what seemed like an eternity in the darkness, they stepped down into a long and narrow cavern. Rye explained that it was a branch of the city's system canals that transported water that bipeds had already used. Rye pointed out, to the dog's relief, that the canals Los Gatos used only transported water run-off not actual . . . well you know.

The oddest thing of all was the light. The ancient slime-encrusted walls were clearly visible thanks to a dull, grey illumination that, on first inspection, seemed not to have an origin. Rye led the group to a break in the rounded ceiling where a cylindrical access plate with round holes in it led right up to the street itself. It was from those holes that what little light there was, found its way into the cavern.

As the dogs followed Rye along a narrow, raised walkway next to the fast-flowing water, they all took extra care with their footing, as a fall into the rushing torrent could only end in disaster.

Rye led them through one cavern after another as the canals branched and re-branched, forming a veritable arterial network far from the eyes of the bipeds above ground.

They finally reached, what the dogs all agreed, was one of the most staggering sights any of them had ever seen. The cavern they were in came to a sudden and very abrupt end. It simply stopped as its contents cascaded out into the open air and dropped to merge with the River Thames.

The dogs stood for the longest time, staring out from their gloomy surroundings through the circular opening that would have been the continuation of the cavern had it, in fact, continued. The bright light of day made their eyes sting at first glance, but as their vision adjusted, the discomfort slowly went away. The five dogs and one cat were then able to look out upon a bright, sunny and bustling day that awaited their pleasure. Despite the joy at seeing daylight, the dogs were still concerned about how they were going to find a way out of the cavern.

After a suitable pause, Rye pointed out a very narrow, stone stairway that was built into the cavern wall. At the top of the steps was a circular metal disk. She requested and received help from Hans (as he had by far, the largest head and neck) to push upwards with all his might to dislodge the obstruction.

It proved no match for Hans' strength, and he sent the metal disk rolling off along the surface street, much to the consternation of some passing pedestrians.

Rye stuck her head up through the hole and pronounced their escape route clear. The exit placed the dogs smack in the centre of a busy walkway which paralleled the river. Instructed by Rye, who was indeed proving herself to be a skilled guide after all, the animals dashed up and out into the bright sunlit day, then made directly for a large row of neatly manicured bushes only a few feet from the opening.

One by one, each animal made his or her move, and within minutes the entire group was reassembled deep within the bushes' protective perimeter. From their vantage point, the dogs could see that they were next to a very odd-looking structure that ran right up to a bridge which spanned the river. The bridge was nothing like the one they'd crossed only a few days earlier. Even with their limited memories of the crossing itself, they knew that this bridge was something completely different.

Firstly, on either side of its span were positioned, what appeared to be, tall, narrow houses at either end of the bridge. Each was very tall with overly decorative windows and painted blue rooves.

The second thing, which they found the strangest of all, was that the bridge, for that is what it must have been, didn't quite reach all the way across the river. It almost did, but in the centre, the roadway simply rose into the air at a ridiculous angle and left a good distance to traverse with nothing between the sides but air!

They looked on as a large river vehicle passed between the two raised roadway sections, hooting loudly as it went.

They finally shifted their attention when they heard Angel let out a single long-winded whine.

"What's the matter?" Lucy asked, with concern.

"That!" she said, pointing with her muzzle towards the large and ancient structure situated at the start of the bridge.

"What about it?" Rex asked.

"It's the...T... Tow... Tower... Tower of... L... Lon... London," Lester read from a large and decorative banner that hung from one of its walls.

"Exactly," Angel whispered. "The Tower of London. Do you know what used to go on in there?"

The dogs and cat all shook their heads in the negative.

Angel's voice was low and clearly filled with fear. "That's where the biped rulers used to chop off the heads of other bipeds. Sometimes even those of their mates."

"So, why are you so upset?" Rex asked bluntly.

"They cut off their heads!" Angel exclaimed.

"Did they ever cut off any dog's heads?" Rex asked, sounding very sure of himself.

"Well... no," Angel replied.

"Then I hardly think they'll start with us," Rex assured her. "Rye, what's the next move?"

"We have to cross that bridge," she answered.

"Hardly," Lucy mumbled more to herself than for anyone else's benefit.

"It's easy. I'll show you." Rye nodded.

The dogs all turned back to face the incomplete bridge and were utterly dumbstruck by what they saw.

The roadway was no longer separated in the centre with either end rising uselessly into the air. The bridge was fully intact. As they watched in amazement, biped vehicles were moving across it as if nothing had happened.

"But...," Rex tried to voice his confusion.

"That's Tower Bridge," Rye stated. "The bipeds built it quite cleverly. The middle bit rises and lets the bigger water vessels go under it. Then, when they're through, the middle bits go down again."

"It's called a drawbridge," Angel added. "In fact, Tower Bridge is one of the oldest examples of its kind. It was built in the eleventh century for the purpose of..."

"Thank you, Angel," Lucy interrupted gently. "But I think we should be going while the going's good, don't you?"

She turned to Rye for her opinion but found the spot where she'd been only seconds ago to be vacant.

"Oh, oh," Hans cried, pointing out of the bushes.

Rye was chasing a leaf. Not a big or particularly special one. Just a leaf. She was a good distance from the dogs, dashing after the object as she was consumed by her hunting instincts. She seemed oblivious to the passing bipeds who stopped and watched her antics with open amusement. The gentle breeze was strong enough to keep the leaf just ahead of Rye's pounces, and with each gust, the leaf and Rye moved farther away from the dogs and the bridge.

They tried to call after her but she either didn't hear or chose to ignore them. Rex took a deep breath, then without a word of warning dashed out from the safety of the bushes and ran at full gallop along the riverside walkway.

He covered the distance quickly and didn't even pause to alert Rye of his intentions. With as much care as he could muster, he grabbed the distracted feline by the scruff of the neck and hoisted her into the air. He made certain that he didn't pierce her skin with his sharp teeth, which wasn't easy, especially once she began to squirm and wriggle in his grasp.

Rex carried the furious cat all the way back to their temporary hideout, before putting her down on the ground. It took a moment before they could understand a word she was saying, as all she could seemingly do was spit and hiss. Finally, she began to calm down.

"How...how dare you?" she cried indignantly. "I was hunting. You never stop a cat when they're hunting!"

"You were chasing a leaf," Lucy said, sternly.

"Maybe to you it looked like a leaf, but to me, it was a dangerous and worthy adversary!"

"But how were we...," Lucy tried to continue.

"And I almost had him!" Rye shrieked with annoyance.

"I'm quite certain that we all feel equally rotten for interrupting your hunt," Lester said in a very sincere tone. "But you must remember that we are all counting on you to get us across that river and to the anchor place. Don't forget, one of our friends is in extreme danger and in need of our assistance."

Rye looked somewhat embarrassed as she stared down at her front paws. At first, the dogs thought she was still angry until they saw a tear run down her cheek and tumble to the soil below.

"I'm sorry," Rye said, in a trembling and quiet, little voice. "I can't help chasing things. I'm a cat. It's what we do. Haven't you lot ever suddenly felt some deeper emotion that compelled you to... I don't know... go chasing after birds or something? Even when you know it's not appropriate?"

The dogs all shared a guilty look between them.

"Now that you mention it," Lucy said with a growing smile. "We may have done just that."

There was a moment of silence before all of them suddenly burst out laughing. Even Rex, who tried to remain serious and leader-like, finally let it go and howled with the others.

Laughed out, teary eyed and exhausted by their own display of mirth, the group was near collapse and would undoubtedly have done just that had not Rye announced that it was time to cross the river. That statement alone seemed to rally the dogs back to their prior, determined frames of mind.

Rye checked outside the bushes to make sure their path was clear, then led the group at an extremely fast pace along the riverside path towards the bridge.

"The important thing," Rye explained while running. "is speed. When we reach the bridge, there'll be a lot of humans and a lot of vehicles. Just stay close to me and keep moving. Remember, whatever happens, keep moving."

The others panted back their understanding of the instructions. Even Rex seemed totally prepared to allow Rye to assume the responsibility of leading the dogs during this phase of the operation.

They ran past the formidable exterior of the Tower of London and marvelled at the condition of the structure, which even they could tell had to be very old indeed. They reached a flight of wide stone stairs that led to the approach road for the bridge. Rye led them down the steps, and then sharply turned to the right keeping them on a walkway which paralleled the busy road.

The group picked up the pace at Rye's signal, and veritably flew along the walkway, which, as promised, was crowded with bipeds. They were met with shrieks and yells of both amusement and anger as they forced the humans to jump out of their way.

After covering about a quarter of the bridge's span, a series of loud bells began to ring, followed by a very aggravating claxon sound that made the dog's ears hurt.

"Oh, oh," cried Rye from the front of the pack.

"What is it?" Rex called up to her.

"Nothing. Just run, that's all," came the reply.

Just ahead, a pair of ornate gates, began descending from either side of the roadway, blocking all the biped vehicles from moving along the bridge.

Lucy knew that something was clearly amiss, but followed Rye's lead with dogged trust, even as her stomach churned, alerting her to some as yet unseen danger.

They ran right under the gates and continued along the bridge, which was by then, empty of both bipeds and vehicles.

Suddenly, the road began to rise in front of them. At first, Lucy thought she was simply seeing things, perhaps because of the exertion, but she very quickly realised that the roadway was actually rising up in the air. Every instinct told her to stop and go back, but she remembered Rye's emphatic instructions to keep moving, no matter what.

The problem was that it was difficult to keep up the pace as the incline increased. Lucy could feel her heart pounding madly within her chest, as she used every ounce of strength to maintain her speed up the newly-canted road.

The good thing was that she could see the end of the raised road just up ahead. She presumed that it had to even out at that point. Lucy somehow found another bit of strength and hurled herself up the last few dog lengths.

Before she knew what was happening, she was in mid-air high above the rushing waters of the mighty Thames. She was about to let out a howl of fear, when she saw beneath her, the continuation of the roadway replace the lethal chasm that had been there only milliseconds before.

Lucy could see Rye and Lester, who had been in front of her before, as they tried to keep their balance on the downward slope of the road. She desperately wanted to turn her head, to ensure that the others made it across safely, but knew that such a manoeuvre could easily cause her to lose her footing and tumble the rest of the way to the flat part of the bridge, which was still some ways ahead and below.

As it happened, they all made the jump safely. Even Angel, who managed to somehow turn herself around in mid-air, then land on the other side, facing the wrong way.

Once on the flat part of the road, they dived under another set of gates and rushed through a group of bipeds who were madly applauding something. It wasn't until they reached the end of the bridge and veered off its approach road, that the group finally slowed down, and allowed themselves the luxury of getting their breathing and their heartbeats back to regular levels.

"What just happened back there?" Angel asked in a dazed almost trance-like voice.

"Look for yourselves," Rye said, shakily.

They all turned and saw that the bridge was back to appearing as it had before, broken in the centre with both halves pointing straight up to the sky. A large, water vehicle with smoke pouring from a raised cylinder in its centre, was slowly passing between the raised road sections as it moved under the bridge.

Lucy turned to Rye, fully intent on expressing her awe, fear, annoyance and general peeve over their recent brush with danger, but to her own chagrin, she felt herself simply mumble the word 'Wow!'

CHAPTER 30

Once the shock of the bridge experience began to wear off, it was replaced with anger. Anger at Rye for jeopardizing their safety, without even so much as a word of warning.

Surprisingly, Rye let each dog vent his or her fury without any show of emotion, she didn't even do her usual flinching or twitching that they'd come to expect. When they were finished with their verbal reprimanding, Rye looked each dog straight in the eye and began to smile.

"All better now?" she said, in a voice more suited to dealing with small puppies. "As your guide, my responsibility is to get you from point A to point B in one piece. Now, are any of you hurt?"

The dogs begrudgingly shook their heads.

"Did we get across the river?"

They nodded half-heartedly.

"Well then, stop acting like a bunch of spoiled little pups and be happy for the successes that occur, instead of for the failures that do not!"

The dogs turned to glance at each other after Rye's unusual and brave statement. Lucy, however, kept one eye on their feline guide. She watched Rye, who believing herself to be unobserved, slide behind a row of bins and out of sight.

Lucy waited until her friends were well into their conversation before she carefully backed herself away from the group and moved over to Rye's hiding place. She could hear the cat before she saw her. Rye was crying. As Lucy got closer, she could hear the distraught feline as she sobbed to herself behind the metal obstacles.

Lucy stood on the other side of the barrier, allowing Rye a few more moments of privacy. After what she considered was a suitable period, Lucy stepped around the end bin and saw Rye, huddled into a tight ball as she continued to sob almost uncontrollably.

"Are you alright?" Lucy asked gently.

"Go away," Rye answered, between intakes of breath.

"No, I don't think I will. At least not until I know what's upsetting you."

"Don't you know? Can't you guess?" Rye voiced with weepy surprise.

"Is it because the others got cross with you?"

"Hardly, though I would have preferred a slightly warmer show of gratitude."

"Well, what then?" Lucy asked with concern.

"Do you have any idea what it took for a scaredy-cat like me to lead you lot across a river like that?"

"Were you scared?"

"Yes!"

"Mind-numbingly terrified?"

"Yes, yes, yes!" she blurted out. "All of those and more. You have no idea what it's like."

Rye began crying again, this time quietly into her crossed front paws.

Lucy stood and watched her for a moment then said, "No I don't, you're right. But I'll tell you what I do know. It takes a very special creature to feel fear the way you do, and yet manage to overcome those feelings when it's time to ensure the safety of others. I think you are an incredibly special cat, Ryphoryl Ynextril Hydxmass, and I for one, am honoured that you chose to be our guide."

Lucy turned and left Rye to digest what she'd just said. Once she knew she was alone, Rye lifted her head from her damp paws and felt urgently for something tucked deep amid her paw pads.

Having re-joined the other dogs, Lucy entered their latest debate, which was a discussion as to which way each animal felt they should go to get them to the anchor. Lucy found it amusing that no dog shared the same directional judgment. She was about to add her two kibbles worth, when Rye interrupted the discussion. No one had even noticed her approach.

"I suggest we continue on," she said with calm assurance. "We've still got a long way to go."

"I don't suppose we could stop somewhere and find something to eat, could we?" Angel asked with a whine.

"Why?" Rye answered. "Didn't you eat yesterday?"

Rye glanced over at Lucy and gave her the briefest of winks. Lucy felt a moment of real joy at seeing the usually troubled feline appear, not only in control of her fears, but even displaying a touch of humour as well.

Rye took her place at the head of the group and led them off at a brisk pace. Angel was not satisfied with the cat's glib response to her serious question regarding food, and after walking only a short distance, came to an abrupt halt.

"I'm not taking another step until I hear something about when we're going to eat," Angel said.

Rye froze in her tracks and then turned very slowly to face the others. She eyed each dog, long and hard without a trace of any emotion showing on her face. She then focused on Angel and began to smile. Not a happy smile. Not even an amused smile. This smile was cold and soulless.

Angel took a deep swallow as she watched Rye slink towards her with slow, deliberate steps. The cat came to within inches of the Spaniel, holding her face directly in front of Angel's.

"So, you're hungry, are you?" she asked, flatly.

"Yes, I am," Angel replied, trying to sound unaffected by the cat's frigid stare.

"Well, you know what? So am I. And I'll wager Lucy is as well. And Rex and the others, but the strange thing is that I don't see them acting like a loud, spoiled, human child!"

"I am not..." Angel protested.

"Oh yes you are, and do you know what makes your whining all the more unbearable at this moment?"

Angel simply stared defiantly back at her.

"It's that you are willing to hold up the entire group which, may I remind you, is in the middle of a quest to rescue one of your own. A dog that I understand jeopardised his own safety to rescue you. And for what purpose do you wish to delay this expedition? Well...?"

"Never mind," Angel replied, as she cast her eyes down at her paws.

"That's better," Rye stated, as she strode back along the line and resumed her position at the head of the group. Lucy watched her with total astonishment, wondering from where this newfound bravado had materialised. She was about to let the subject drop when she noticed a rather odd scent waft over her as Rye stormed by.

She turned to Rex, who by his expression had clearly caught the same odour.

"What is that?" Lucy asked.

"I hope I'm wrong, but I think I know that smell," he said in a low and serious tone.

"Is everyone ready," Rye questioned authoritatively.

"Almost," Lucy replied, breaking ranks with Rex at her side. "Could we talk to you for a second."

"Make it snappy. We have a schedule to keep."

"It'll just take a moment," Rex said as he approached the now apprehensive cat.

"What will?" Rye asked suspiciously.

Rex walked right up to her and looked intently into her eyes. Rye tried to turn her head away, but Rex gently turned it back with one paw.

"Where is it?" Rex asked coldly.

"Where's what?"

"Don't play games with me," Rex voiced. "You're on Nip, aren't you?"

"What's that?" Lucy asked innocently.

"Aren't you?" Rex asked again, this time with more force.

The cat and Doberman stared at each other for what to Lucy appeared to be an eternity.

"Yes, I am," Rye finally responded. "But just a little. I needed it to…"

"Give it to me," Rex demanded.

"But…" Rye stammered.

"What is going on?" Lucy asked, with growing concern.

"Our guide here," he said flatly, without taking his eyes off Rye. "is on herbs. She's been using Nip."

"Nip?" Lucy asked, confused.

"Catnip!" Rex explained, "It's a natural herb that felines use to get high. Makes them feel euphoric and indestructible, isn't that right Rye?" Rex's voice was laced with anger and disapproval.

"Is this true Rye?" Lucy asked, incredulously.

The cat simply stared down guiltily at the ground.

"Rye?" Lucy tried again.

The cat slowly raised her face and looked sadly over at Lucy. Their eyes met and Lucy knew that Rex's accusations were undoubtedly true.

"Why, Rye?" Lucy asked gently.

"It makes me feel brave, and for a moment I don't have to be terrified of my own shadow. That's why."

"Where is it?" Lucy asked.

Rye held out her left front paw and turned it, pad-up, for Lucy to see. Tucked between the pads were two, tightly rolled leaves which Lucy gently removed with her teeth. She could taste the tangy, almost bitter essence of the herb as she deposited the leaves on the ground. Having unrolled them and seen the dried catnip within, Lucy shook her head in sadness.

"You don't need this Rye. Any cat that could lead us over that bridge had plenty of courage where it counts. Yours will come out naturally if you let it. This stuff is only masking your emotions. Believe me. You don't need it."

Lucy stared affectionately into the anxious eyes of the cat, who finally shook her head as she sighed loudly.

"Good," Lucy stated, then blew the dried herb, scattering it along the road where the wind joined in and dispersed it still further.

"You'll be fine," Rex said warmly as he gave her an encouraging nod.

"Thanks," Rye sighed. "Really, thank you."

Rex and Lucy re-joined the other dogs and allowed Rye to muster the group back into a line.

"Why do they do that to themselves?" Lucy asked Rex in a quiet tone, not wanting the others to overhear their conversation.

"I don't know, but it's a big problem among street cats. I've seen a lot of it in my day. It's a shame too. It can really mess up a cat's nine lives."

"Well let's hope we've helped one feline step away from it," Lucy offered.

"Yes, let's hope we did," he replied, smiling warmly back at the retriever, while marvelling at her seemingly endless capacity for compassion.

They marched on for most of the day with only a few brief stops for water or toilet needs. The sun finally sank out of sight behind a row of old, and time-ravaged, warehouses, causing the temperature to drop drastically.

Lucy felt a chill run through her and was having great difficulty in not thinking about food. She was very hungry but was determined to not be the one to raise the subject of eating. She also tried to ignore the aching in her muscles and blisters on the pads of her paws. Although she didn't want to admit it, she was becoming very concerned as to just how much further she could walk without the benefit of food or rest.

She glanced at the other dogs and saw that they were all in similar shape. Each animal had his or her head low to the ground with eyes focusing only a few paws ahead. They all were exhausted.

Rye gave the signal to stop, which they all did without complaint. They didn't even form into their usual circle just lay where they were in line.

"How long are we breaking for?" Rex asked their guide, in as casual a tone as he could muster under his exhaustion.

"What do you mean?" Rye asked him, clearly puzzled by the dog's question.

"I just want to get an idea how long this stop is going to last?" he tried to explain.

"As long as you like?" The cat replied, still confused by Rex's queries. "Unless you want to go somewhere else."

"Well of course we do," Lucy said, joining the conversation, wanting to make sure that Rye or the others didn't confuse Rex's questions with any notion that he didn't want to proceed. "We're all just a little tired and wanted to make sure we had time for a quick nap."

"Take as long as you like," Rye was starting to sound quite agitated by the dog's confusing line of questioning.

"But we have to reach the anchor by dark," Angel stated, flatly.

"I give up," Rye announced as she dashed through the exhausted dogs. She jumped up onto a large, stone block then began to climb up what looked at first, to be a large black tree..

Lucy watched the cat climb and felt a strange memory stirring deep inside her. She continued to watch Rye knowing that she was meant to recognise something in the cat's actions.

"You lot are too much," Rye yelled down at them from the top of the tree-like structure.

Lucy got painfully to her feet and walked to the other side of the thing. When she was alongside it and at a different angle, she began to laugh, quietly at first, then with all her remaining strength. Rye observed Lucy from her perch high above the ground and could only shake her head at the dog's actions.

"Well finally," she called down to her.

"What's wrong Goldie?" Rex asked, as he walked over to her.

She gestured through her laughter for the Doberman to examine what Rye was seated on with a little more care. He turned and passed his eyes over the thing then he too began to smile.

"Well, I'll be!" He exclaimed, joyously.

The two dogs stood side by side and admired the huge, black anchor for a good few moments before sharing the news with the others. Rye climbed gingerly down and approached the dogs with a definite sense of pride about her.

"Well done Rye," Lucy said, sincerely.

"Yes, very well done," Rex added.

"It was nothing," the cat replied smugly, as she began washing her tail.

"Now if we could just find something to eat, we'd have it made," Rex said, more to himself than to anyone else.

"That's easy," Rye stated simply. "All that's been taken care of."

With that, she jumped up and set off along the metal fencing that surrounded the anchor square. Without being asked, Rex and Lucy followed closely behind. The cat came to a halt by a gate that was located at what Lucy presumed was the entrance to the square.

Rye turned her back to it and began pacing away from it, while counting out loud.

"One . . . two . . . three . . . four," she counted.

When she got to eight, she stopped, then turned ninety degrees to her left, and paced nine more steps in that direction. Again, she stopped and made a course change, this time proceeding only six paces.

She had reached a pile of old and rusted metal piping, which had clearly been discarded a long time ago. She stepped into one of the larger ones and vanished from sight. After a few moments, Lucy felt the beginnings of concern stir inside her, but then saw Rye's rear end as it reappeared at the pipe's opening. She was dragging something heavy out from within the thing.

Lucy and Rex went over to give her a hand and almost immediately picked up the scent of food. Fresh food. Fresh meat food!

"Here let me," Rex offered, as he stepped in and picked up the large plastic bag by the handles.

"What is it?" Lucy asked excitedly. "It smells like meat!"

"You'll just have to wait and see won't you," Rye replied, with knowing smugness.

"But... but how did it... What...?" Lucy tried to form her frenzied thoughts into a question.

"Don't underestimate Los Gatos. We are very well organised," she stated proudly. "When you told Bob where you needed to get to, he not only assigned me as your guide, but sent out a team to arrange for some food to be waiting for you."

"Amazing," Rex mumbled with his mouth full of plastic bag straps.

"Not really. It's just how we operate."

"Well, I for one am greatly impressed," Lucy announced.

"Me too," Rex agreed.

As they approached the other dogs, Lucy noticed that they were all on their paws looking excitedly in their direction.

"Where have you been?" Angel shouted enthusiastically over at them. Her face then took on a sudden transformation as she spotted the bag hanging from Rex's muzzle.

"What's that?" she cried. "I smell... I smell... meat!!"

This got the others' attention as well.

Rex had to make them all step back as he emptied the bag to the ground. Angel's nose was as accurate as always. There in front of them were five of the largest, most perfect looking, sirloin steaks that any of them had ever seen.

They were all about to tuck in when Lucy spotted something.

"Rye, where's yours?"

"It's time I was off. My dinner's waiting back at the H.Q."

"But..." Lucy started to object.

"Shh! I've done what I was supposed to and that's all I'm permitted to do. Los Gatos code again. Anyway, you know your way from here."

"You'll remember everything I said?" Lucy asked.

"Yes ma'am. I certainly will," Rye stated.

"You did an excellent job," Lucy said, as she took a step towards the cat. She hung her head and whispered into one of her orange and black ears.

"And I don't think you're a scaredy cat at all."

Rye stepped away and brushed away a tear, which she pretended was merely a displaced whisker.

"Good luck, Lucy. Good luck to all of you. It has been an extreme pleasure."

Everyone bade her a fond farewell as she turned tail and ran off, vanishing almost immediately into the shadows.

Lucy immediately felt the loss of the little cat. She also felt the hunger, low down in her belly. She looked over to the others, who were waiting for some signal to start eating. She looked to Rex who as leader took the initiative and sunk his teeth into the tender red flesh.

The others did not need to be coaxed very hard to follow suit.

CHAPTER 31

Having devoured their steaks, the dogs nosed around the surrounding area and found an unlocked warehouse in which they sought shelter from the chilled night air.

They slept long and hard, well into the following day.

They spent a good deal of that morning talking over tactics as to how they would force their way into the prison building. They then fantasised about their own version of how each would deal with Squat Lady or Skull Face. They all agreed that it was a shame that Fat Man and Boxer, after succumbing to the metal beast in the tunnel, weren't around anymore. To have been able to battle and vanquish them all would really have been the perfect end to the quest.

As the morning stretched into early afternoon, the five were no closer to having formulated anything close to a formal plan. It started to become apparent to each of them that, not only didn't they know quite what to do, but if truth be told, they were a little hesitant about tackling the vicious humans in the first place.

During a particularly weak plan proposal offered by Hans, a scratching at the warehouse door interrupted the group.

Rex got to his paws and went to one of the many grease-streaked windows to see whom could possibly be trying to gain access to their current lair.

"What the...," he said in astonishment at the sight that confronted him. "Everyone come over here and look at this."

The others all joined him at the window and followed his gaze. They were equally as shocked.

Lined up outside the warehouse door, were dogs. Dozens of them. They stood in single file waiting patiently to be granted entrance into the building. Rex moved over to the doorway and pushed aside the piece of brick they'd used to wedge the warped wood in place.

As the door swung open on its rusty hinges, the five dogs looked out at the lengthy line of canines, wondering what they wanted. Thankfully, the dog nearest the door, presumably the one who had scratched for their attention, explained their presence.

"We're her to volunteer for the mission," the burly wolfhound stated.

"The what?" Rex exclaimed.

"The mission," the wolfhound reiterated. "The word's out that you lot are planning on going after the dog prison."

"Yes ... yes that's right. But ...," Rex stammered.

"Then you'll need volunteers, and by the looks of things," he cast his eyes along the ever-growing collection of hounds. "you're going to have quite a few of those!"

"But how...?" Lucy tried to ask.

"Anyway..." continued the wolfhound, ignoring her completely. "My name's O'Neil and my specialty is taking down the larger adversaries. I've done work in Croydon, Bromley and Lewisham. I'm fit and I'm ready!"

With that, O'Neil marched right past the five dogs and proceeded to the back of the warehouse. Rex gave the others a confused but cheerful shrug, then greeted the next applicant.

"My name's Curtis," said a thin, but fit looking Lab mix. "and I do walls. Natural balancer, I am!"

"Good," Rex voiced appreciatively. "Welcome!"

The Lab mix nodded his thanks then made his way into the warehouse.

The process took most of the afternoon, but by sundown they had amassed a truly impressive group of canine mercenaries. They were all tough, well-seasoned and ready to storm the target prison.

After formulating a very precise battle plan, the dogs went off in search of food. Rex offered any who wanted it, a place in the warehouse to sleep but they all preferred finding their own shelter. They agreed on a sunrise rendezvous prior to their big mission.

O'Neil was the last dog out the door and was about to wander off into the growing gloom of the approaching night, when Rex stepped up to him.

"You mentioned when you got here that word was out about our mission, but you never told us what that meant exactly? How did you hear about us?"

O'Neil gave the Doberman a crusty grin then lowered his huge head to Rex's ear. "Let's just say a little kitty told me." With that, he raised a paw to his nose in a gesture of 'say no more,' then trotted off into the night.

Just as he was about to vanish into the deepening shadows, he turned and called back across the deserted square. "Oh, and another thing...I was told to tell you that your supper will be in the same place as last night!" He then stepped into the darkness and vanished from sight.

"Did he say supper ... as in food?" Angel squealed joyously from somewhere within the warehouse.

Indeed, he did, and for the second night in a row, the dogs ate a hearty and very satisfying dinner. Instead of steaks Los Gatos had left them an astonishing quantity of incredibly tender and tasty lamb chops. For the first time in any of the dog's limited memory, they ate until they could eat no more. Even Angel with her seemingly bottomless belly, finally gave up with a couple of meaty chops still untouched in front of her.

Little was said among the animals that night as each delved into his or her own private thoughts. They knew that what lay before them at dawn the next morning was far more than a game or a chase. The next day was going to bring real danger, and though unspoken, each dog knew perfectly well that some of them might not even survive.

As Lucy stretched to relieve some of the pressure she felt from her overfilled stomach, she tried to imagine what death could be like. Her mother had told her that it was like a long sleep from which you never woke. That explanation had always satisfied her, but now, being faced with the possibility of real harm, she couldn't seem to equate the sleep part with death through injury. Did one simply fall asleep when hurt badly enough? Exactly how badly did one have to be hurt to fall into that kind of sleep? Could regular sleep become that sort of sleep? Who decided when a hurt became a sleep?

She managed to give herself a headache, allowing the torrent of unanswerable questions to tumble and flow all too freely within the confined area of her brain. She decided to ask Rex, who was certain to know more on the subject but found him to be fast asleep, flat on his back with paws twitching up into the air. Not a very dignified image, but he did seem content, at least in his dreams.

She lowered her muzzle to her front paws and let out a long sigh, which she hadn't even realised she'd been holding inside. She closed her eyes knowing that she had to get some sleep before the big battle in the morning.

As she began to drift away, she started dreaming about puppies. At first, she thought the adorable little dears belonged to someone else as she romped and played with them on a warm patch of lawn. Then it dawned on her that the five little brown and black pups were hers. They were her puppies! She stirred awake. How odd. She'd never had a dream like that before. Even after she'd watched them play and roll in her dream, she wondered what could have made her he come up with such a bizarre and unusual eventuality. Her having puppies!

Her conscious thoughts soon began to dissipate and swirl into a thin mist that then evaporated entirely, leaving Lucy to dream some more about her litter of five as they played on the sun-warmed lawn. As she looked on, a feeling of responsibility and pride filled her with such emotion that she suddenly began to cry in her sleep. The tears were not those of pain and fear, they were tears of pure, simple joy over emotions that had never before surfaced within her.

The mercenaries began filing into the warehouse before dawn. They looked rested and ready for battle. Some did morning stretches. Others practiced paw to paw techniques, while others played in one corner with a tennis ball that one of them had brought along. There was a sense of great tension in the air, which was both exhilarating and slightly frightening.

Lucy looked over the assembled crowd and wondered who among them would be hurt and who, if any, could even be . . . .

"Impressive isn't it?" Rex said excitedly as he trotted up alongside her.

"It most definitely is," Lucy agreed. "I almost feel sorry for those nasty bipeds. They're certainly going to be surprised when they see this lot!"

"Lucy?" Rex said in a mock serious tone. "You actually feel sorry for them?"

"I said almost," she replied with a wink.

The two stood for a moment longer watching as the final preparations for battle were completed. O'Neil then climbed onto an upturned crate and barked for some quiet.

The mercenaries settled down and all turned to face the wolfhound.

"Gentle dogs, we are here today, joined together as one fighting unit, for the task of freeing our captive canine friends. I would like to remind each of you that what you are about to do is dangerous. Some of you may be hurt, some may not even return at all, but the fact is that you, each of you, are about to not just free your imprisoned brothers, but will be striking a mighty blow against the tyrannical hand of bad bipeds everywhere. So, let's move out. And remember, keep your heads high and your teeth bared."

He looked down at the surging mass of eager dogs, then suddenly raised his head high into the air and let out a chilling howl. A dog in the crowd joined him, and then others did the same. Soon the entire assemblage had their heads in the air howling for all they were worth.

Even Lucy let out a brief howl then looked to the others with great embarrassment.

"Sorry," she said, blushing. "I got carried away."

"Lucy," Rex spoke in a serious voice. "There's something I've been wanting to say to you..."

"I know Rex... I feel the same," she said, interrupting.

"So, you'll stay?" he said, relieved.

"What!?"

"I wanted to ask you and Angel to stay back here at the warehouse where it's safe."

"I thought when you said that you had something to say...," Lucy tried to speak.

"Look, we've got plenty of animals for the attack. I just don't want you hurt."

"If you think for one moment that I've come this far to sit like a good little hound, waiting here for you while you go out and rescue Rodney, then you have another think coming!"

"But...," Rex shook his head.

"No buts! We're going with you. Right Angel." She turned to the Spaniel who was staring back at her with an expression of complete disbelief.

"Of course," she said sarcastically. "Why would anyone want to stay here where it's warm and safe, when we could be out there risking our coats? Thanks Lucy."

"I just thought that...," Lucy started to say.

"Hounds ho!" came the command as they all began filing out of the warehouse.

Lucy just had time to offer Angel a good luck nod before being swept up by the crowd and ushered outside in readiness for the attack. It was all she could do to stay close to Rex among the tide of canine mercenaries. Once they were all outdoors, the dogs broke into two groups. One was led by O'Neil, the other by a very rugged looking German Shepherd.

With hardly a word being spoken, the groups split up, exiting the anchor square from either end. Lucy, Rex, and Angel were in O'Neil's group and left the square by the river end. Hans and Lester were in the Shepherd's group. There was a strained silence that pervaded the ranks as the dogs marched towards their objective.

Lucy was surprised that the mercenary dogs seemed to know exactly where the prison was located. It seemed that the place had a reputation, not only among former inmates, but among most of the city's street animals as well. She managed to glean from a few snippets of conversation within the ranks that the place had been in operation for many years, and that it was about time someone rallied the dogs into closing the place down.

As the assault group moved along the shadows provided by a row of abandoned storefronts, Lucy began to recognise bits and pieces of the neighbourhood. It wasn't clear, and her memories were a little foggy, but certain things rang a bell for her. She could remember a doorway here, a cracked window there. She tried as hard as she could to put the memories into some semblance of order so she could gauge just how close they were to the prison. While she was still trying to sort out her memories, the group rounded a corner and there it was!

Lucy had no trouble recognising the horrid place. As soon as she spotted it, she felt an icy shiver run the length of her back. She heard a low growling from somewhere close by, then realised it was coming from her.

They were at the back of the prison, near the rear yard door through which they had escaped thanks to Rodney and his knowledge of doors. The team assembled directly across from the corner where they'd hidden when they had spotted Pru on that fateful day, so long ago.

O'Neil carefully checked all around them, then gave the sign for the fighting force to cross the street and meet up at 'Pru' corner. Rex gave Lucy and Angel a knowing smile, as it was clear that each of them was being inundated with memories of their escape day.

They kept their position until O'Neil saw the Shepherd and his group reach the far corner on the other side of the prison's main entrance.

The tension was thick. Lucy could hear her own stomach rumbling with nerves. She felt momentarily embarrassed by the sound until she noticed that she wasn't alone. The harder she listened, the more rumbling stomachs she could hear. She had to smile knowing that even these proud, and outwardly brave, fighting dogs suffered from the same internal fears and nerves that she did.

O'Neil checked the front entrance again, then signalled the Shepherd at the far corner.

The attack was beginning.

Both groups moved out from their cover and began edging along the wall in single file, with both columns converging on the entry door located halfway along the wall.

Lucy felt an almost uncontainable pride, deep within her as she watched her new mercenary friends in action. They were so professional, so brave, so utterly...

Both lines froze. The front spotters had seen something and given the warning tail wag.

Lucy tried to follow the other dog's line of sight but could only see a deserted building with cracked windows. Then she saw that something was moving on the wall. She had to squint to make out exactly what it was, but finally recognised it to be a squirrel.

She knew that couldn't be the reason for the entire squad to be frozen in place, but as she watched the slow, oblivious movement of the squirrel, she realised that every pair of canine mercenary eyes were riveted on the tiny little creature.

With one last spring across the space between two weathered brick walls, the squirrel vanished from sight. The dogs refocused their attentions on the prison entrance and again began to edge towards the front door.

They were only a few feet from their target when Lucy caught a flash of movement out of the corner of her eye. She looked around, just in time to see the squirrel reappear and leap from one of the old buildings onto the branch of an adjacent tree. She prayed that she alone had noticed the reappearance of the creature, and casually returned her gaze to the others.

Every single dog was staring wide-eyed and was panting at the squirrel.

Lucy couldn't believe what she was witnessing. What had happened to the training, the dedication, the...?

Her thoughts were rudely interrupted as the poor, witless squirrel trotted down the side of a tree then jumped onto the ground.

The mercenaries went crazy as many screamed, "Squirrel!" The dogs literally tripped over each other to break ranks and give chase to the now, fully aware, and very concerned, squirrel.

Lucy, Rex, Angel, Hans and Lester suddenly found themselves alone only a few feet from the prison entrance, watching as the last of the brave mercenaries rounded the far corner and vanished from sight in hot pursuit of one small, and to Lucy, inconsequential, rodent.

She turned to her friends, glad that they'd at least not given in to their hunting-lust emotions. She was astonished to see the three males shaking and drooling as they tried desperately to control their urge to dash off after the others.

"Rex, stop it!" she chided, in as quiet a voice as she could. After all, they were awfully close to the prison doors. "Hans? Lester?"

"We're trying," Rex managed to voice between firmly clenched teeth.

"Well, try harder. We're too close to fail now!"

"I know," came the strained reply.

Lucy looked over at her four comrades, three of whom were battling their primal urges to chase a squirrel and wondered what could possibly go wrong next.

She didn't have to wait very long to find out.

CHAPTER 32

Just as Lucy was about to suggest a calm retreat to regroup and re-plan, now that the assault force was down to just them, the prison door swung open and Squat Lady stepped from within.

"What's all the din out here?" she bellowed, causing far more noise than was ever present before her outburst.

Lucy looked to the others to see if they all were thinking along the same line as her. She felt a surge of satisfaction as each dog gave her a brief nod.

Rex was the first to move. He launched his muscular frame straight at the startled biped who tried to step back into the entrance. She might have made it too, if Angel, in a surprise show of bravery, hadn't dashed forward and sank her teeth into Squat Lady's bulging ankles.

The biped let out a blood-curdling scream and was about to reach down and grasp Angel when Rex hit her full on, knocking her backwards through the open doorway. Such was the force of Rex's assault that Angel was still in exactly the same position, except instead of an ankle clenched between her teeth, she was now clasping one of Squat Lady's black, lace-up boots.

Hans and Lester vaulted over the Spaniel, and by doing so, were the first within the prison proper. They both ran either side of the downed biped and found her to be groaning and dazed, and thereby of no immediate concern. Hans in a show of great caninity, even took a moment to give the hideous creature a lick of compassion. The two dogs then separated and went to either side of the entry hall, each covering one of the two doors that led from it.

With a reluctant sigh, Angel dropped the now well-chewed boot and together with Lucy, stepped into the building. Once inside, the five dogs were somewhat uncertain as to how to proceed. Their choice of action ended up being determined for them when Skull Face walked casually into the hall, completely unaware of the situation.

He took one look at the five, snarling dogs, then at the unconscious figure on the floor, and did the one thing that none of them was prepared for. He laughed. It wasn't a very pleasant laugh either. It was more of a cross between a horse's whinny and a squirrel's chatter. Such was the dog's amazement at the biped's reaction, they made the mistake of hesitating. Not for very long, but long enough for Skull Face to grab a club from a rack on the wall next to him.

He slammed the wooden weapon hard against the wall sending an ear-splitting crack echoing within the cramped space of the entry hall. It hurt everyone's ears and made the point that he was not only now armed, but also clearly very willing to use the weapon if necessary.

"So then, you scruffy mutts," he said in the reedy, nasal, voice they remembered from their earlier stay in the building. "What do you think you're doing here?"

He took a step towards the dogs with the club held at his side and ready for use.

"Wait a minute. I know you, don't I?" he said, pointing the club directly towards Angel.

"You too," he gestured at Lucy. "You're some of the lot that scarpered out of here the other day. Well, well, how nice to have you back."

He stepped towards the open entry door and kicked it shut. At least that was his plan. The door swung to within inches of its jam then stopped and slowly swung back open.

"What the...!" Skull Face exclaimed.

He kicked the door again but with the same results. He kept his eyes on the five dogs and stepped out through the doorway and onto the street to see why it wouldn't shut. He'd no sooner stepped through the doorway, when a fury of orange, black and white fur dropped onto his head and began yowling as it kicked, scratched, bit, and clawed the unsuspecting biped.

The dogs heard the familiar voice of Rye yell, "Shut the door! Now!"

Rex leapt forward and put all his weight against the heavy, wooden door and slammed it shut.

Lucy spotted an old-fashioned sliding bolt lock similar to the sort she was used to defeating in the cottage. She stepped over and gently, nudging Rex aside, used her nose to release the sliding bolt and manoeuvre it into place, bridging door and frame.

"Nice one, Goldie," Rex said, impressed.

She grinned smugly back at him just as one of the interior doors flew open. There, standing before them, was Fat Man. His face was bruised in a few places and appeared burned in others, but he was alive. Alive, and at that moment very angry.

As he stepped into the entry hall, Rex and Hans both dropped low to the ground and began growling with menacing intensity. Fat Man reached cautiously into his pocket and produced an odd-looking, black, cylindrical object. Suddenly, the object sprouted a thin metal blade that momentarily caught a shaft of light, causing it to glint in the biped's hand.

Lucy had no idea what made her do it, but she found herself suddenly in the air, having launched herself directly at the human. He raised his weapon to counter her move, but Lucy was not going for his body. She shot between his legs and through the open doorway. She heard the biped yell out with a mixture of fury and surprise then change to vicious obscenities aimed towards the others, who had clearly used Lucy's distraction as an opportunity to move a step or two nearer to their prey.

Lucy found herself in her old cellblock. The door through which she'd dived, led down a couple of worn, and sagging wooden steps to the smelly and cold passageway floor. She turned back to make certain she was not being pursued, only to see the heavy door swing hard on its squeaky hinges and slam shut separating her from the others.

She felt the icy tendrils of fear begin to creep along her body and fought to keep herself focused on the job at hand. She began walking slowly down the passageway, checking each enclosure as she came to it.

She didn't recognise any of the dogs. Many seemed to be newcomers. Lucy had a vivid flash of her first day in this cold and heartless place. She could clearly remember the fear and disorientation she'd felt, as well as the pain. She could still feel the hurt caused to her by Fat Man and his club.

With difficulty, she forced herself to shake off these memories as she continued along the gloomy passageway. She raised her head and saw the door to the exercise yard. It was closed, as she had expected it would be.

Some of the inmates were starting to take notice of her arrival and began barking excitedly. Others, especially the newcomers, greeted Lucy with mad enthusiasm, throwing themselves at the rusty mesh barriers as they asked all sorts of naive and hopeful questions.

Lucy managed to calm them down with guarantees of their impending rescue. The newcomers accepted her word with complete faith, whereas the others, those who had spent serious time in the place, gave her words little credence and remained calmly unimpressed.

It melted her heart to see one scared dog face after another, pressed up against the barriers, gazing back at her with desperate hope. She found time to give every single one an encouraging word or nod. She was beginning to feel very concerned about not having located Rodney. She'd never considered for even the briefest of moments that perhaps he wouldn't be here. That he'd been too seriously injured to justify the biped's returning him to the prison. What if he had been so badly hurt that they... they...?

"Lucy?" came a familiar, though weak voice. "Lucy is that you?"

Lucy looked anxiously down the passageway hoping to see the small terrier, but instead only saw cell after cell with each occupant pressed up against the wire mesh.

"Rodney, where are you?" Lucy called excitedly.

"I'm not exactly sure but you sound quite close." Lucy couldn't help but notice the weak quality of her friend's voice.

She picked up her pace and practically ran down the remaining length of the passageway. She reached the far door but still couldn't see him. She was about to retrace her steps, when Rodney's little voice came at her from only a few paws away.

Lucy turned and looked into the nearest enclosure. As before, she thought it empty, until to her surprise, she saw movement at the very back of the cell. There, blanketed in shadow was Rodney. He looked terribly small from her vantage point. Lucy felt a sudden almost overwhelming urge to hold and comfort her dear friend.

"Hello, Goldie," he said. "I'd get up and greet you properly but... well I'm not doing too well, actually. I'm a little weak."

"Don't you move! I'll come in," she replied, despite not having a clue as to how she would actually carry out that promise.

She took a step back and examined the metal-framed gate with a careful and critical eye. She was by no means an expert on the subject, but had, by instinct alone, managed to foil many door latches back at the cottage. Sadly, her limited memory couldn't recall the specifics of how she'd managed it in the past, only that she somehow had.

She tried a variety of pushes and nose lifts and even one hard head butt, all to no avail.

"Goldie if you...," Rodney tried to speak.

"You just stay quiet and rest," she ordered. "I'll work this out."

She continued with every door manoeuvre she could think of, but the thing just wouldn't budge.

"Goldie?" Rodney voiced, gently.

"Yes what?" she answered with growing frustration.

"I think you'll find you just need to pull it, not push it. It's not locked."

She closed her eyes for a moment in a gesture of annoyance, frustration and embarrassment, then took the rusted metal handle in her teeth and pulled it open. She approached Rodney with anxious concern, wanting desperately to know what was wrong with him.

As she stepped closer, she was finally able to see the Terrier through the gloom and was shocked by what she saw. His usually shiny coat was matted and dull and he had clearly lost weight. His eyes still had a small trace of their normal sparkle, but nothing like their usual radiance.

She leant her head down and gave him a couple of gentle licks hoping to reassure him of his soon to be restored safety and health.

"It's my leg, Goldie," he stated matter-of-factly. "I think I broke it when the vehicle tipped over."

"Haven't the biped's seen to it?" she asked with growing annoyance.

"No, they tossed me in here as soon as we got back and just left me".

"Do you mean they haven't even fed you or watered you?" she asked incredulously.

The tiny terrier shook his head as his eyes began to mist over with emotion.

"Oh Lucy," he suddenly cried. "I've been so scared. I never thought I'd see you again and I was certain I was going to die here."

"Well, that's just nonsense. I'm here now with the others, and you are leaving with us."

"You came back here for me?" he asked in amazement.

"No. I missed the fine food and company. Of course, it was for you silly! Now, I suggest we get you out of here and have that leg seen to."

"If you insist," he whispered, forcing a brave little smile. "But I can't walk."

"But I can," Lucy said as she gently took him by the scruff of the neck and easily lifted him into the air.

"Comfortable?" she asked, her full mouth.

"Fine thank you," he replied with slight hesitation.

Lucy was about to turn and leave the cell when a large shadow fell across them. Lucy felt pure terror for the first time in her life.

"So," said the all too familiar voice. "Isn't this a pretty picture!"

Lucy gently placed Rodney back onto the stone floor so as to free her jaws for what was coming. She had never used her teeth against a biped in any serious way, and the very thought of now having to do so filled her with dread.

The Squat Lady stepped into the cell and as Lucy turned to face her, she saw that the female was holding the everpresent club, not in a state of readiness, but in an almost casual manner at her side. This sight, instead of relaxing Lucy, made her feel even more uncomfortable knowing that it could only mean that the biped had something far worse in store for them.

Careful to not put any weight on his bad leg, Rodney got shakily to his feet. Unseen by Lucy, he took a tentative step forward and began growling in as menacing a fashion as his tiny, damaged frame could muster.

"You get behind me, Goldie," he said with great gallantry. "I'll protect you from this... this... monster!"

Lucy was touched by his show of concern and bravery and was about to gently dissuade him from continuing his efforts when the Squat Lady suddenly stepped aside. For a moment they couldn't see anything. Then Champ appeared, and as they looked on in dread, he stepped confidently into the cell and positioned himself next to the human.

"You!" Lucy exclaimed in shock. "But I thought you... you..."

"You thought I'd got what I deserved back in the tunnel?"

She nodded back at him in stunned silence. It was not just seeing him here, alive, that she found so amazing. It was his voice as well. It was the first time she could recall hearing it do more than utter threats or snap single word commands. She was utterly astonished to find it not to be the voice of a common canine criminal, rather to be rich in timbre, and unquestionably belonging to a dog of intelligence and breeding.

Her thoughts were interrupted as the Squat Lady grabbed hold of the gate and violently slammed it shut with herself and the three dogs inside. She lowered the metal horseshoe-shaped fastener into place then turned, and with a malicious sneer fixed to her already hideous features, glared at the trapped animals. She reached into her dirty, charcoal coloured sweater and retrieved a small box from which she shook out a white tubular object. She placed the thing between her puffy lips then, with the aid of another object she retrieved from her pocket, made fire, and set it alight.

Lucy could smell the odour of burning leaves and felt the smoke as it began to sting her eyes. She watched in fearful fascination as the biped inhaled a large cloud of the smoke then, after a moment's pause, blew it back out into the air.

Squat Lady continued to look down at Lucy and Rodney and began to smile in what can only be described as a truly grotesque display of yellowed teeth and unhealthy gums. She suddenly turned to the Boxer as her face took on a cold and lethal expression.

"Kill them," she commanded, "Kill them both!"

She pointed a pudgy finger directly at the pair to emphasise her point. Champ looked to her then to Lucy and Rodney but didn't move. In fact, he looked very perturbed by the entire situation.

"I said, kill them, you stupid beast. Now do it!" her voice was now raised and terribly angry.

As if to enforce her command she began to raise the club from her side.

"Kill them now, I say!" she shrieked, almost hysterically.

The Boxer took a step towards Lucy and Rodney and began to bare his teeth. As the two huddled closer together, they watched in horrified fascination as the dog prepared himself to strike. His muscles began to swell and ripple as he lowered his hindquarters, readying himself to spring into attack position.

"I'm not scared of you," Lucy cried defiantly at the Boxer.

"Neither am I," Rodney weakly concurred.

"I've noticed," Champ replied with a gleam in his eye.
He then sprang into the air.

CHAPTER 33

Lucy and Rodney had never seen anything like it before. Champ did indeed launch himself into the air, but only after he'd suddenly spun his muscular body around so that he was facing Squat Lady. She hardly had time to even scream before he struck her, full force in the chest. She fell backwards and hit her head with a loud crack against the brick wall. Her eyes rolled back into her head as she slid to the floor. The Boxer ran to her side ready to pursue the attack if needed, but after a quick inspection of her condition, announced, "She's out cold!"

The other two looked on in open-mouthed astonishment. Champ stepped over the prostrate figure of the Squat Lady and approached them with a warm and endearing smile.

"You stay back," Rodney said defiantly.

"Perhaps I should introduce myself," he responded with calm self-assurance. "My name's Sergeant Bonzo."

"Sergeant!" Lucy said with surprise. "Bonzo!?"

"Yes Ma'am. Scotland Yard Canine Squad. I'm a police dog."

"What!" Rodney exclaimed. "But you were... I saw you... we thought you were..."

"One of them?" Sergeant Bonzo offered.

"Well... actually... yes!" Rodney stated.

"That was the whole point. I was here undercover. We've had our eyes on this group for a while now. Nasty bunch."

"But you let them take me away," Rodney exclaimed angrily. "They could have used me like the others and... and..."

"Actually, they wouldn't have gotten very far," he replied calmly. "We were covering all the exits from the country and your description was well circulated before you'd been gone more than a couple of minutes. In fact, if you hadn't escaped from the posh couple, we would have nabbed the lot of them days ago."

"Well, perhaps you should have let us in on it?" Rodney said with mild annoyance. "We could have helped!"

"Maybe... maybe not," Bonzo explained. "The fact is, I wasn't the only one pretending to be someone else. You see..."

"Wait a minute," Lucy interrupted. "Are you saying that while you pretended to be working with the bipeds, there was another dog that was pretending to be something else?"

"Yes, only he wasn't a police dog; he really was a bad breed."

"Well, what happened to him? Where did he go?" Lucy asked anxiously.

"Didn't it ever surprise you how we were able to keep locating you no matter where you seemed to go?" Bonzo asked gently.

Lucy and Rodney glanced to each other then turned to Bonzo and nodded in unison.

"Come with me," he voiced gently.

Bonzo stepped to the gate then nosed the fastener up and pushed it open. He led Lucy and the limping Rodney down the passageway until they reached a particular enclosure. He gestured with a flick of his muzzle for them to look inside.

All they could see was a dog standing in the shadows facing away from them. Lucy turned to Bonzo with a puzzled look.

"That's him," Bonzo stated.

She peered through the mesh, but couldn't see who it was until the dog stepped into the light and turned to face her.

"I managed to trick him into the cell only a few minutes ago," Bonzo advised.

"Hans?" Lucy exclaimed. "Not you! There's been a mistake!"

She turned to Bonzo and was about to speak when Hans stepped to the barrier.

"Yes Goldie . . . me!" he said, coldly. "You bunch were so stupid. I tell you one story about a farm and a bunch of loving bipeds, and you fall for the whole thing. What a bunch of dim dogs."

"Why, you . . .," Rodney growled through the mesh.

"Watch what you say, you little . . ." Hans sneered back.

"Enough!" Bonzo snapped.

Lucy turned to Hans and shook her head slowly from side to side. "How could you? We were your friends."

"I don't have any friends. I don't need them. They only get in the way," he answered coldly. "I do what I do, for myself. I'm the only dog I trust and that's the way I like it, so why don't you take your happy, helpful, self out of here, and leave me alone."

Bonzo nudged Lucy away from the mesh barrier and led her from Hans' enclosure. She was clearly upset and shocked by the Rottweiler's words.

"Don't let him upset you. He's not worth it," Bonzo said.

Rodney followed slowly behind, growling to himself about what he wanted to do to the likes of Hans.

Angel, Rex, and Lester appeared at the end of the passageway and seeing the others, began to smile until they spotted the Boxer. They began to tense until Lucy trotted over to them and calmed them down with smiles and explanations.

After introductions were exchanged, Bonzo took the dogs to a window leading off the entry hall. It was jammed open and looked out over a back alley filled with discarded trash and junk.

"Is this how we're getting out?" Rex asked with concern.

"No, this is how I demonstrate the Canine Corp's communication grid." Bonzo replied proudly.

He stepped to the window and leaned his head out. He then let out a series of howls and barks for a few moments then stopped and listened.

Almost immediately, another dog could be heard somewhere in the distance repeating his signals. As the others listened on, yet another dog picked up the call and transmitted the signal still farther.

"The lads at the yard will get the word in just a few minutes," Bonzo stated.

"Then what?" Lester asked.

"Can we eat?" Angel inquired.

"Then they'll lead the biped squad out here and we'll close this case." he responded.

"We kind of messed things up for you, didn't we?" Lucy said, apologetically.

"Not really. We have enough on these monsters to lock them up for a long time." Bonzo gestured to the two unconscious figures of Fat Man and Skull Face.

"What will happen to us?" Lucy asked anxiously.

Bonzo turned and looked at her gentle features, then to those of the other dogs and smiled warmly. "I think you lot have had enough excitement to last you a lifetime or two. I think we need to get you back to your homes, don't you?"

Lucy felt tears of joy suddenly well up in her eyes as she realised that the nightmare was nearly over. She looked across at the dogs that, until a few days ago, had meant nothing to her, but now were her closest and most treasured friends. As her eyes rested on Rex, she could see the pain in his face, and she realised that he had no home to return to. He had only the hard and lonely existence that had become his world. He looked over at her and tried to mask his feelings with a smile, but she knew it was only for her benefit.

The dogs all went quiet as they heard the return message arrive from Scotland Yard. Bonzo smiled as he listened then turned to the others.

"They're on their way."

It wasn't long before the animals heard the distinctive sound of approaching sirens. By the time the policemen arrived, Sergeant Bonzo had cleaned up Lucy and the others and lined them up according to size. When the front door flew open, he gave the order and the five dogs stood to attention. First through the door were the biped policemen who scattered in various directions to secure the premises. Then, in walked Captain Salty.

He was clearly in charge. Tall, proud, and professional, the captain eyed the goings on with a careful eye as he evaluated the crime scene. He was older than the other dogs, though fitter than officers half his age. His grey hair simply added to his look of elegant, four-legged strength. The Airedale spotted Sergeant Bonzo and stepped over to him, pulling a biped on a leash after him.

"Sergeant!" he snapped. "What have we here?"

"Sir!" Bonzo saluted. "These are the dogs we've been tracking throughout London. They came back to rescue the others and helped us capture the bipeds."

Lucy sneaked a look over at Rex, who caught her glance and simply shrugged. As she faced forward again, Sergeant Bonzo gave her a brief wink and a grin which still didn't explain what he was up to.

"Well then...," The captain said. "it would appear that we have some true heroes amongst us, wouldn't it?"

"Yes sir," the Sergeant replied." It most certainly would. I think it's important that these dogs get special treatment, don't you? Also, the terrier's been injured in the line of duty. He'll need immediate care."

"Couldn't agree more. Well done, all of you," The captain said as he raised a paw in salute.

He then turned and joined the biped officers as they continued with their work.

"I'd better join them," Bonzo announced to the others.

"Thank you, Sergeant." Lucy leaned forward and gave his muzzle one, brief lick.

"Now steady on there, girl!" he blustered in complete embarrassment. "I'm on duty you know."

The others all laughed. Even Bonzo had to give in to the humour of the moment and suddenly began rolling on his back, laughing boisterously.

"Sergeant!" came the officious voice of the captain from somewhere in the building.

Bonzo leapt to his feet and cleaned himself off with great urgency.

"Yes sir!" he replied when he was suitably neatened.

"Come and give us the breakdown on this lot," the captain said from the other room.

"Yes sir!" Bonzo answered.

"What about us?" Rex enquired.

"Stay here. Some bipeds will be here shortly to take you away from this horrid place."

"What about going home?" Angel asked. "You said we could go home now."

"And you will," Bonzo answered. "But first we've got to get Rodney some medical care and you lot, somewhere safe when we can work out where you actually live?"

"That sounds a bit complicated," Lucy said, trying to hide the concern she was starting to feel.

"Actually, it's quite simple," he explained. "We've got all the reports of kidnapped dogs at the headquarters. All we have to do is notify your humans that you've been found, and you'll be home in time for supper!"

"Now you're talking," Angel stated as her tongue lolled out of her smiling mouth.

"Sergeant!" the captain's voice echoed through the premises.

"I'd best be off," the Boxer announced nervously.

"Well again... Thank you," Lucy nodded at him.

The others offered their thanks as he turned and disappeared through the door to the cellblock.

The dogs all looked to each other, expecting at least one of them to say something, but they all remained quiet as their thoughts took them back over the last few days and what they'd been through.

By the time, the white-coated bipeds arrived to take them away, they were all fast asleep.

CHAPTER 34

They were transported in large, white vehicles filled with individual, metal enclosures that smelled sour, and were slightly damp. Lucy remembered the smell from the cottage. Cook used to create the same smells when she would scrub the small, tiled room upstairs. She would pour amber liquid into the big, raised water bowl that the bipeds sat on to do their business, and the water would turn white and smell just the same way.

The journey lasted an awfully long time. Finally, the vehicle came to a stop and went quiet. The rear doors were opened, and bipeds were there to greet them.

"Oh my!" Lester suddenly shouted, "We're in for it now!"

"Why?" What's the matter," Rex and the others asked anxiously.

"Look!" Lester gestured to a large sign in front of the building they were being loaded into.

"What does it say?" Lucy asked urgently.

"Kennels. It says we're at the Camden Kennels!"

"His words sent such a wave of panic through the enclosures that it took the bipeds forever to unload the animals and get them into the building.

Finally, every dog was placed in their own enclosure, which weren't that much bigger than the ones back at the prison place. The bipeds where, however, were terribly nice and spent a great deal of time with each animal, calming and grooming them as best they could.

After they had left, the dogs were alone and began calling through their gates to locate their friends and find where each had been placed.

Lucy found that she was in a section filled with complete strangers. She had called down the line and been informed that the rest of her group were in an entirely different wing.

Even when a kind and smiling biped brought her a bowl of chopped beef, she couldn't help feeling almost unbearable pain at being separated from the others. She tried to eat a little, but couldn't even manage that, such was her anxiety.

She lay in her enclosure, trying to visualise each member of the group, hoping that by keeping their memory alive in her mind, she would feel some comfort inside. As she was thinking of Angel and her devious and glutinous ways, the smiling-faced biped returned to her enclosure and let herself in.

"Hello there, pretty girl," the biped cooed affectionately. "Sorry we had to put you in here, but the wing with the others was full until just a few minutes ago. Would you like to come and be with your friends?"

Lucy of course, didn't have a clue what exactly was being said, only that the words were kind and filled with caring. She looked up into the friendly eyes of the biped and gave her one polite bark.

"Good for you," the biped replied.

Lucy was then led from the enclosure and out of the wing. They walked through various holding areas then through one final door and into another section filled with dogs. Lucy couldn't grasp why she was being moved until she heard Angel's unmistakable voice cry out.

"Goldie! It's Goldie!"

At that point she heard the others, each in a different enclosure dotted along the passageway and each delighted to have her back.

The one voice that she'd missed the most, came from the far end of the row. Rex sounded not only happy, but highly relieved to have Lucy back, close at paw.

"You had me worried there Goldie," he said with feigned casualness.

Lucy was led halfway down the passageway and placed in an enclosure only two down from Lester.

"Where's Rodney?" she asked through the gate.

"We thought he was with you?" Lester replied.

"I hope he's alright," Lucy said, more to herself than to anyone else.

There was a moment of silence as each animal tried to find words to say.

Angel was the first to speak up. "What did you think about the beef!"

The others had to laugh.

The dogs spent the rest of the day introducing themselves to the other inhabitants of the wing. Each dog, one by one, introduced his or herself then gave a brief account of how they had been captured. The session went well into the night, and as the last dog gave his story, the rest began to settle down for sleep. When the story telling finally ended, the wing fell silent for a moment.

"Good night Angel," Lucy whispered.

"Good night Goldie," she answered.

"Good night Lester," she continued.

"Good night Goldie," he responded.

Lucy hesitated for a moment before continuing. She felt her heart beat faster just at the thought of him and knew then what she had been afraid to accept while they were still in danger.

"Good night Rex"

"Good night Goldie."

She closed her eyes and allowed a tear to roll down her muzzle as she accepted the joyous realisation that she was in love.

The entire wing was awakened at the crack of dawn as a young biped wheeled a food cart down the passageway and distributed one bowl to each resident. The biped was wearing round, black pads over his ears and singing loudly and discordantly at the top of his voice.

The bowl turned out to be filled with a dry, and very tasty, kibble mix that Lucy devoured without any show of manner or breeding whatsoever. She felt slightly embarrassed when she realised how greedy her display must have appeared to the others, but upon raising her head to check their reactions, found that all of them had seemingly done the same thing. They were all looking guiltily out of their enclosures expecting a reprimand from some quarter or another.

After a period of grooming, the passageway doors were opened on both ends and much to the dog's initial dismay and then total delight, bipeds began funnelling into the wing, each with an expression of urgent anxiety imprinted upon their features. Almost immediately, one group of humans, a male, a female, and a small child began squealing excitedly. They were joined in their revelry by one of the dogs. They were apparently his humans. The dog was released and left with the bipeds as they all fawned over each other with complete abandon and disregard for biped-hound protocol. It was not long before another family was reunited with as much, if not more exuberance.

One by one, each dog was claimed. At one point, Lucy distinctly heard Angel scream with delight as her mistress located her. She was only able to call out the briefest of farewells to the others before being whisked away.

It was that simple. All they'd been through, then in one brief second, she was gone. Lucy found it very disconcerting to realise that the Spaniel was on her way home and that she would almost certainly never see her again.

A short while later, Lester's human arrived. Their reunion was a little more formal than some of the others, but still as touching. There was none of the screaming and yelping, but as his gate was opened, Lester stepped out and walked soundlessly into his humans waiting arms. The two simply stayed holding each other for the longest time, then, again without a word, they separated and walked side by side out of the building.

By the end of the morning, there were very few dogs left in the wing. There was little talk as the tension rose with each passing minute. Lucy began to feel the beginning of concern about her situation. Where was her Man or Cook? Maybe they weren't coming for her. Maybe they didn't care that she'd gone? Maybe they'd found life easier without her. Maybe...

"Lucy? Lucy, where are you?" She suddenly heard her human calling from the far end of the passageway.

"Here! I'm here!" she called out breathlessly. She could hear him break into a run then suddenly, he was there, standing right in front of her, separated by the thin wire mesh of the gate. Her Man! He had come for her! He almost tore open the gate then stepped into the enclosure. Lucy tried to think of the proper greeting then suddenly found herself leaping into his arms. Oh, the joy she felt! She licked him, and nuzzled him, smelling and tasting him over and over again.

"My poor girl," he whispered. "What did they do to you? Cook called me in America and I flew right back. I've been so worried. Oh, my sweet girl."

He hugged her still closer.

Finally exhausted by their own display of emotions, they rose to their feet and Lucy allowed him to place her collar... (yes, her collar) around her neck then attach the lead. He walked her out of the enclosure and towards the exit.

They had only gone a few paws when Lucy remembered something. She stopped and turned back.

"What's the matter girl?" her man asked. "It's alright. I'm just going to take you home."

Lucy pulled at the lead, knowing that she was breaking all the rules. She had one more thing to do before returning to the cottage. She continued tugging her lead, pulling her Man until he gave up and followed her back along the passageway.

CHAPTER 35

Lucy slowly opened her eyes and watched as the mother duck escorted her young into the pond. She couldn't be certain, but the ducklings looked slightly larger than she remembered them. After the last one slid into the water, the mother took her position in front, and led the group in single file across the open water.

Lucy rolled effortlessly onto her back and glanced up at the billowy clouds as they sailed rapidly by overhead. A shaft of sunlight freed itself from the heavens and momentarily warmed her belly as it moved across her.

She stretched her legs to their fullest length, then rolled onto her paws and stood up. Lucy glanced over towards the Granger's property hoping to see the horses, but then remembered that they were in competition at that very moment up in the city.

She took a moment to glance about her and feel the warm comfort that comes from being home in a place you love.

She looked to the cottage and its sparkling white exterior then to the gentle rolling hills of the Downs.

She was home!

Lucy wandered over to the entrance and stepped inside the cottage. She took a moment to breathe in the tangy smoke smell that she so loved, then proceeded towards the kitchen. Before she'd gone more than a couple of paws, she heard a commotion coming from just around the next corner. She trotted over and cautiously peered in the direction of the disturbance.

"Why you mangy good for nothing...," Cook's words were playful as she scolded Rex as the two fought over a tea towel. Rex seemed to have the upper hand and was pulling Cook along the polished kitchen floor. Amazingly, Cook seemed to be thoroughly enjoying every minute of it. Without warning, she suddenly let go of her end and Rex went rolling backward, muzzle over paw!

Cook laughed herself into a veritable fit and had to hold herself steady with one hand on the countertop.

Lucy looked on with a pretence of distaste as she scowled at both of them. They pretended not to notice, but then both suddenly took off after her in an unexpected game of chase.

As the three tore through the sitting room her human called for their immediate attention. He had in his hand a paper bit with gold edging and fine squiggles on it.

"You're not going to believe this," he said excitedly to the others.

"What?" Cook squealed breathlessly.

Cook read the paper bit then looked to the dogs with open mouthed astonishment.

Lucy and Rex didn't know what was going on exactly, only that their Man and Cook both seemed very pleased about something.

Lucy hoped this might mean that Cook would let them have some of the bread she knew was being prepared at that very moment in the hot oven.

EPILOGUE

There wasn't a cloud in the sky or even the smallest hint of wind as they were led out onto the forecourt of Buckingham Palace. Lucy and Rex had recognised the place the moment they had arrived! At first, they'd been a little nervous, but everyone else seemed happy and relaxed so they decided that everything must be all right.

Lucy glanced over at the ornate fencing that enclosed the parade ground and for a moment, vividly recalled when they had sneaked through that very fence to evade the grey van. She was surprised to see that on this day, the area beyond the fencing was crowded with bipeds all pointing towards them.

As they reached the centre of the forecourt, Lucy spotted Angel and Lester. They were fully groomed and standing next to their formally dressed humans. After some brief catching up of what had happened to them all since their rescue, a murmur could be heard rising through the crowd. The dogs all turned and looked towards the portico through which they had escaped capture with the help of the two corgis. They saw to their utter delight that a small Yorkshire Terrier being carried towards them.

Rodney spotted the others then, wriggling like a maniac, had to be placed on the ground. He proceeded towards them with his head held proudly in the air and his left hind leg held securely in a white plaster cast.

When Rodney reached the others and greetings were exchanged, a silence fell across the entire area. As breaths were held, the main doorway to the palace opened and an elegantly attired biped made her way towards the group. Behind her were the two corgis, William, and Mary, and behind them, much to the delight of the dogs, were Captain Salty and Sergeant Bonzo. Needless to say, there were also numerous bipeds in attendance.

They moved to a spot directly in the centre of the forecourt facing the others. The elegant female stood in front of the group and began to speak into an odd metal thing that seemed to take her voice, and make it not only louder, but made it come from many different directions at once.

Lucy didn't know what she was saying, only that it appeared to be directed mainly at her and the other dogs. After a while, the female biped ceased talking and stepped back to be alongside the police dogs and their bipeds.

Captain Salty's biped then stepped forward and spoke a few words, at which point, Angel's human walked forward with her in tow. They stopped in front of the elegant female and were each given a small metal thing attached to a piece of colourful ribbon. The two bowed (as instructed in rehearsals), then walked back to re-join the others.

After another couple of words from the captain's biped, it was Rodney's turn. Lester was next. Then it was time for Lucy and Rex. She suddenly felt slightly nervous but could not for the life of her think why.

Her Man and Cook led the two dogs into position in front of the female. As Lucy looked at her face, she suddenly remembered her. She had been the one sitting and drinking from a dainty cup when the corgis had led them through the palace. In a flash Lucy's simple mind put the pieces together, and realised who the elegant biped in fact, was.

As the Queen of England placed the ribbon around her neck, Lucy felt her chest swell with almost immeasurable pride and joy. She gave the Queen a happy tail wag then gracefully stepped back with her man and re-joined the others.

The crowd surrounding the forecourt began to applaud and cheer. At first Lucy was puzzled as to what exactly they were cheering about, but then, as she looked down the line and saw Angel, Lester, Rodney and Rex, she understood that they were the ones being honoured that day.

She glanced over at the elaborate fencing and at the crowd beyond. Lucy noticed that among the throng of humans were many familiar faces from the animal world. She spotted a pair of cats as they dashed from shadow to shadow. They stopped for a moment and gave Lucy the unmistakable Los

Gatos salute, then just as she was about to wave back, Bob and Rye vanished into the crowd, completely unnoticed by almost anyone.

She then caught sight of Pru. She was beautifully groomed and attracting a fair amount of attention on her own.

"You should be in here with us," Lucy called to her.

"No, I shouldn't," Pru replied through the fencing.

Lucy knew that Pru meant just that. She didn't want the adventure or the ceremony. She was happy simply being beautiful. As she continued to scan the onlookers, she saw still more faces she recognised. She saw the kind biped from the underground train. She saw some of the policemen from the park. She even spotted Rumple, the kindly dog from the police kennel. He lifted a paw in a wave and Lucy noticed his entire coat begin gathering at his shoulder.

She was about to turn away from the fencing when she spotted someone else. At the far end of the forecourt, where the crowd was much thinner, she spotted an angry looking biped chastising his dog as they walked away. She could not be certain, but from a distance, the dog looked to be a Rottweiler. Somehow, she knew who it was. She silently wished that Hans would someday find happiness somewhere in his life.

As she turned back towards the gathered dignitaries, she realised just how much help so many strangers had given the dogs, without asking for anything in return. She knew that there was a lot of bad in the world. She had certainly seen some of it during her adventure, but she'd also found that there was also a lot of good out there as well.

She had to smile to herself as she again realised just what she'd been through and how much she had learnt. For one thing, the world was far bigger and more exciting than she'd ever imagined, and she'd only seen a fraction of it. She began wondering if she would ever get to see any more it when the crowd began murmuring and pointing excitedly to the sky above.

Lucy raised her head and immediately saw the reason for their interest.

Flying towards them at low altitude, was a squadron of geese. In perfect formation, the birds flew by in salute to their canine friends. In the lead position, Vol led his fellow aviators at roof level over the forecourt then tipped his wings and smiled down at the dogs as he led the others in a gentle banking turn back towards the park and their sheltered island.

Lucy looked at the faces of her friends once more and, as had become almost habit recently, found herself focusing on Rex with his hard, strong features. She felt her heart beat faster at the mere sight of him, but also at the joyful realisation that their life together was only just beginning. As if sensing her gaze, Rex turned and looked back into her eyes. His face broke into a huge and amiable grin as he nodded his fine head back at her, acknowledging and returning her own sentiments. She then let her eyes drop to her own belly, which had recently begun to swell. For some reason, just looking at her new bulge made her recall the dream she'd had of her playing with a litter of puppies.

"How odd!" she thought to herself as she felt a warm blanket of almost indescribable contentment envelope her.

Lucy couldn't have been happier.

THE END

Author's Note

L ucy is not a horror novel. If you are a fan of my darker books (Luck, The Lodge, Legacy, Lakebed) you should be warned that although there are a few scary moments in this book, it is not a horror story in any way. It is a gentle adventure story of self-discovery, initiative, and the power that can develop when strangers all pull together towards one common goal.

I wrote the original story of Lucy in 1995. The main character was called Amy at that time. The book was published in 2005 specifically for US school libraries under the title *Far From Burden Dell*. It got some rave reviews and hardly any sales! After some investigating, I found that the publisher did no real marketing other than placing the title in a couple of school-book catalogues. After some pushing on my part, she agreed to list the book on Amazon, but without an eBook version and any promotion, it soon settled into a quiet life of extreme obscurity. Soon after, the publisher was taken ill, and her business closed.

I always loved this book and did everything I could to get the rights back so that I could try my hand at promoting it. My requests fell on deaf ears. It wasn't until two years ago, when the publisher passed away, that I was able to speak with her family and have had the rights revert back to me.

Since that time, I have brought the story up to date, tweaked a few areas, renamed the lead character, and retitled it.

Lucy is the story of a pampered golden retriever who is snatched from her home in Sussex. Imprisoned in the slums of London, Lucy and a ragtag band of escaped hounds must navigate the terrors of the big city and try to find a way back to their respective homes.

When I wrote this book, I was years away from becoming active in animal rescue and adoption. This outpouring must have been an early indicator that our four-legged friends would end up playing a big part in my life.

I am a better man for it.

Author's Bio

Chris believes that stories should be able to transport the reader to different places, where they can experience events and dimensions that have never been considered. Chris is able to write  gentle fable-like adventures as well as opening the pages into dark and terrifying stories where dimensions co-exist with indescribable evil.

Chris Coppel was born in California and has since split his time between the USA and Europe, living in California, Spain, France, Switzerland and England.

Chris has held senior operations positions for both Warner Bros. and Universal Studios. Chris also held the position of Director of Operations for UCLA's Film School where he also taught advanced screen writing. Chris and his wife Clare spent many years helping animal rescue with Best Friends Animal Society in Utah. Before joining Best Friends, Chris was President and Managing Director of the Home Entertainment Division of Testronics in Los Angeles.

Following in his father's footsteps (Alec Coppel wrote Vertigo among many other successful movies) Chris has written numerous screenplays as well as several novels.

Chris is also an accomplished drummer and guitarist.

OTHER BOOKS BY CHRIS COPPEL

LUCK
THE LODGE
LEGACY
LAKEBED
LINER

COMING SOON
LINGERING
LIKENESS
LOGISTICS (A CHRISTMAS STORY)
LUNACY

Visit chriscoppel.com to see what's new.

Contents

CHAPTER 1 1

CHAPTER 2 16

CHAPTER 3 27

CHAPTER 4 36

CHAPTER 5 43

CHAPTER 6 57

CHAPTER 7 62

CHAPTER 8 73

CHAPTER 9 81

CHAPTER 10 94

CHAPTER 11..103

CHAPTER 12..115

CHAPTER 13..129

CHAPTER 14..136

CHAPTER 15..148

CHAPTER 16..158

CHAPTER 17..165

CHAPTER 18 174

CHAPTER 19 184

CHAPTER 20 195

CHAPTER 21..209

CHAPTER 22 213

CHAPTER 23 220
CHAPTER 24...234
CHAPTER 25 252
CHAPTER 26 270
CHAPTER 27...284
CHAPTER 28 310
CHAPTER 29 324
CHAPTER 30 335
CHAPTER 31 348
CHAPTER 32 361
CHAPTER 33 373
CHAPTER 34 382
CHAPTER 35 389
EPILOGUE..392

Author's Note 398

Author's Bio 400